THE
POTENTIAL

A NOVEL

DAVID A. DAVIES

BOOK PUBLISHERS NETWORK
Changing the World One Book at a Time

Copyright © Book Publishers Network
P.O. Box 2256
Bothell • WA • 98041
Ph • 425-483-3040
www.bookpublishersnetwork.com

10 9 8 7 6 5 4 3 2 1
Printed in the United States of America

LCCN 2014930789
ISBN 978-1-940598-21-5

For more information go to: www.thepotentialanovel.com

Editor: Julie Scandora
Cover Designer: Laura Zugzda
Typographer: Marsha Slomowitz

ACKNOWLEDGEMENTS

Many thanks go to Michelle Whitehead and Karalynn Ott for getting me started and pointed in the right direction. Special thanks to Sheryn Hara, Julie Scandora, Marcia Breece, Laura Zugzda, and Marsha Slomowitz at Book Publishers Network. Thank you also Matt Cail, and Erik Korhel for your contributions. Thank you to Jay Erickson for your insights, understanding, and friendship throughout the years. Last but by no means least, thank you to my biggest critic, my loudest cheerleader and my best friend, my wife Patty who without her love and support, this book would never have happened.

CHAPTER ONE

JULY 1995, BONN, GERMANY

THE THREE OCCUPANTS OF THE WHITE PANEL VAN REMAINED MUTE. Only the low rumble of the idling engine floated in the air. All three sat, sweated, and nervously twitched, but each stared at the driver's hand-held radio. Nearby a crane operator with the same radio sat idle in his cab as his load swung precariously in the wind high above the street.

Another driver in a flatbed truck on a different road stared blankly into the distance occasionally checking his rearview mirrors for any unusual activity. The hazard lights of his vehicle flashed incessantly as traffic navigated around his stationary vehicle as he also listened to his radio.

Minutes passed by, which seemed like hours to the waiting crew. In tight suspense, each member of the team played out his role in the operation and hoped everything would go to plan. Glancing at a watch, checking the scene ahead, all waited patiently for the mission to begin as the clock kept ticking.

All three radios squawked simultaneously—the American national anthem. The target was on his way.

The triangular shape of a folded Stars and Stripes flag lay on the lap of the United States ambassador to Germany, Winston Heymann, as he rode in the rear of his armored Cadillac in his two-car motorcade as it thread its way through the tight suburbs of Bad Godesberg. His left hand was placed firmly on the flag, and his right was supporting his chin as he gazed out the window contemplating life as an ambassador to one of Europe's most influential and vibrant countries.

The ambassador was heading to a cocktail party being held in his honor at the majestic Old Rathaus building in the center of Bonn following a hand-over ceremony of the old US embassy building to the German government. The event was short but significant in German-American relations post-Cold War, and Heymann, who had been an intelligence officer during the silent conflict, marveled at the changes in such a short space of time since the wall fell in 1989. As much as he would have liked to have been the ambassador to represent the United States in Germany during the first years of transition of West and East Germany, his role within the Department of State had prevented him from taking up an ambassadorship during the early years of reunification, but now, eight months into his new position as the number one American in the country, he was at last engaged in historical events.

The occasion was attended by the oberbuergermeister (mayor) of Bonn, the *buergermeister* of Bad Godesberg, a small delegation of local functionaries, some former US diplomats who worked at the Bonn mission, and an even smaller leftover skeleton crew of US Marines. As the Stars and Stripes was lowered for the last time over Diechmanns Aue No 9, a Marine bugler played "The Retreat." The flag, which now was securely in the possession of the ambassador, would be framed and mounted in the new, yet-to-be-constructed US embassy in the recently appointed capital of Germany, Berlin.

As Heymann played out the scene in his mind again of the lowering of the flag, he became oblivious of his surroundings and his overall profile in transit. As an endangered diplomat, the US ambassador was afforded a protective detail from the German police, who were with him every time he traveled outside the confines of the embassy grounds or his residence. It was therefore an almost farcical scene when the diplomat traveled by motorcade. In front was the official-looking polished, well-groomed, black-armored Cadillac Fleetwood Brougham, a shining example of US car manufacturing of the 1980s, and to the rear, the equally idolized, sleek, powerful and menacing, brand-new armored Mercedes Benz 560 of the German Police Diplomatic Protection Team.

In the past, the cities of Bonn and Bad Godesberg were difficult for security experts to protect and transition through. The German government formerly sat directly in Bonn itself; however, the world's representatives, embassies, and consulates were generally strung out into the Bad Godesberg environs, roughly five kilometers from the former German capital. As with most European cities, the streets were narrow, and the congestion was infuriating to even the most seasoned commuters. What linked Bonn and Bad Godesberg were the two well-worn parallel avenues of the Bundestrasse 9 and the elongated streets of Konstantinstrasse, Ubierstrasse, and Mittelstrasse.

Heymann's two-car motorcade on this day traveled the most-used Mittelstrasse route that led directly north from the former embassy towards downtown Bonn. For Ernst Kaufmann, a driver of US ambassadors for almost thirty-seven years, the traffic seemed light, and so his mind wandered back to the hectic but exciting days of past experiences as the number-one driver at the old US embassy.

Sitting to Kaufmann's right was the stern German police commissar, Juergen Weber. Weber was a twelve-year veteran of protective details, which is how he had landed this much sought-after and high-profile job. He'd already been on the American detail for almost five years; his professionalism and reputation for perfection were notorious in the ranks of the German Police Diplomatic Protection teams. Today however, his concerns were mainly with the newly assigned team of young officers traveling perilously close in the armored Mercedes behind. Weber could already see through his rearview mirror that the follow-car team of upstarts were all wearing the obligatory shades and trying to look as cool as movie stars. He tried to concentrate on the road ahead but was drawn from his thoughts, and a scowl came across his rather bulldoggish face when the routine, five-minute radio check came over his earpiece.

The protective detail had formed a habit of checking in with each other five minutes after departure and five minutes before arrival. Weber acknowledged the communication by double tapping on his radio switch, signaling *I'm okay*. Protocol denied Weber a voice reply, emergencies excepted of course, but what was frustrating, and in his mind unprofessional, was that he could hear the latest Madonna hit being played over the Mercedes car radio in the background. Kaufmann, who'd also picked up the transmission, broke into a wide grin. He'd been in the game long enough that he knew what kind of tongue-lashing the "kids" would get when they reached their destination and were out of earshot of others. Weber made a mental note and tried to maintain an impression of nonchalance. It wasn't working; he looked like a rabid dog snarling his teeth.

As the motorcade negotiated the everyday traffic, they approached the former site of the Israeli embassy, which was located almost halfway along the Bonn/Bad Godesberg corridor on the corner of Ubierstrasse and Simrok Allee. The Israeli mission, like its American counterpart although much smaller in design, was also built like a fortress. That building, long abandoned for Berlin, had already been torn down to make way for a new apartment block. Construction was underway, complete with a large crane looming over the worksite that was now hauling a large concrete slab upward towards the top floor of the new housing complex. Weber's frustrations were now put on the back burner as he watched the crane at work.

"Ah, bollocks!"

"What's the matter, Chris?"

"I didn't want to catch up with the ambassador so soon," Chris Morehouse replied.

Ted Holmes a junior administration officer for the CIA station in Berlin couldn't see what the problem was, so he pushed the driver for a little more information. "I don't see the problem. What's wrong with the ambassador?"

"I don't want to become part of the Caddy-Benz show. People still like to stop and stare at the ambassador or even throw some crap at him from time to time." Chris paused as he dropped his speed but continued his thought, "I know that nobody is on a routine journey here, but don't these people learn? I mean, look up ahead; there's the ambassador in his Caddy—diplomatic plates, stars-and-stripes flag on the front of the car— and following him is a big-ass Mercedes with a lollipop sticking out the roof. I mean, how unnatural does that look?"

"Lollipop? What are you talking about?" came the confused reply from Holmes.

"Yeah, it's the name the cops use for the temporary blue light they put on the car for motorcades. Because it's an armored car, you can't throw a magnetic dome up there so there's a little bracket that sticks out the roof of the car that is hard wired. On the bracket goes the blue light, like an ice cream on a stick."

"So what?" Holmes countered. "He's doing his diplomatic duty, and I guess that means flying the flag in an American car. I don't see the problem, but then again, you security people see things differently than us office pukes."

Chris gave Holmes a sideways glance and wasn't sure if that was a jab or just a statement and let it go for a second more. "It's just that I remember when we used to consider this route a little hot and we tried to avoid it, or we'd at least avoid being conspicuous as much as possible … just thinking out loud, that's all."

As they were talking, a little red Ford Fiesta pulled out in front of them, causing Morehouse to brake a bit harder than usual. He cursed inwardly for a second, *Wanker!*

Holmes noticed the frustration on the driver's face. "What's bothering you so much, Chris?" he asked. Chris Morehouse exuded a comfort factor to those around him, and thus his first name was the one most people, even professional peers and superiors, simply called him.

Chris hesitated before replying. "Well, driving in situations like this, you always have to play the what-if game."

"What's that? I don't understand."

"Well, for example, what if that little red Fiesta was part of an attack team? What if that flatbed truck in front of the Caddy was used as a blocking device? What if those two guys up on the scaffolding just halfway down the street—the ones who look like painters—are actually shooters?"

"Okay, I understand your train of thought, but where does that get us?" Holmes, impatient with the game, asked.

Chris tried not to sound condescending to the junior staffer but offered his opinion. "I don't think that the Ford is a threat. It looked like the driver was a male, mid-forties, of Arab descent, possibly Turkish; but they are notoriously bad drivers to begin with. His passenger was a woman, possibly the same age or thereabouts, wearing a black headscarf, probably indicating Arab or some kind of Muslim descent; and then there was also a child, a girl, possibly five to seven years of age, standing in the gap between the two front seats of the car, so no drama there. The car itself didn't look as if it was going to win any races soon, either. It actually looks as if he needs a couple more pounds of pressure in his rear right tire. The two guys up on the scaffolding look pretty German to me. They're not paying attention to their surroundings; they have their backs to the street. There's not much equipment lying around up there either, but you never know—that's why you play the game."

"Hmm, interesting I never thought about it that way. What about the truck you pointed out?"

"Not quite sure just yet—he's too far ahead for me to get a good look. I can't see his plates to see if he's from out of town or not. It seems like he's slowing the Caddy down a little, but then again, the ambassador's driver isn't the sharpest pencil in the box anymore, either."

"But doesn't he have the experience, some training?"

"To an extent yes, but the State Department still has problems in training foreign drivers to a decent standard." Chris knew from first-hand experience that the US Department of State's security training program in the 1990s rarely involved motor-pool embassy drivers from foreign countries, like Kaufmann. Instead, they focused their attention on US nationals, concentrating on teaching endangered diplomats who traveled overseas how to handle themselves while navigating through hotspots around the world. The puzzling thing about this practice, however, was that these diplomats rarely drove themselves on official business; they instead would rely on the untrained drivers of the motor pool to ferry them around. These drivers, who came from a variety of backgrounds, were generally referred to as foreign service nationals, or FSNs.

The typical FSN was a resident of the country he or she served in, hired from a community near the local US embassy. In addition to the motor pool drivers, a substantial proportion of each embassy's administrative/domestic staff was also FSN. Chris Morehouse, a former British soldier, was an FSN driver for the US motor pool in Berlin.

Although not exactly a member of the local community, Chris, an unemployed and out-of-luck foreigner in Germany, had simply responded, without any real forethought, to an advertisement for a driver in a newspaper he had picked up on a train in Cologne one day. He had been stationed in Germany with the British Army and decided not to return to the UK when his term of service was complete. As an independent-minded twenty-six-year-old, he thought he'd be happier managing his life the way that he wanted, away from the pub culture of moderate-income British society. He wasn't ready to go home to his family, either, although his mother and brother missed him. His mother had especially missed him—since Chris's father had passed away a few years before and she hoped that her eldest son would act as an authoritative figure to his wayward younger brother. But Chris had plans to see the world and make his mark in some fashion, in someplace of his choosing. He wanted to have a say in his own destiny—once he figured out what it was.

With a successful interview under his belt, Chris started work as a motor pool driver with the US embassy in Bonn; what happened shortly thereafter changed his life forever. Chris was soon recruited by the Mission Consulting Services (MCS), one of a myriad of internal departments that litter all US embassies around the world. At the time he didn't know what he had let himself in for by agreeing to work for this group. He soon was being used for all manner of trips and excursions and was constantly on call for quick runs to airports, restaurants, hotels, and the like. But it was only when a certain Mr. Nash began using Chris as a regular driver that he began to sense a difference in the people he was shuttling around. They were generally quiet people but exuded power—and they seemed to like Chris's unassuming yet careful manner. Before long, MCS formally requested Chris's full-time services from the motor pool, and after a few months, Chris began working for the department on a permanent basis. He was neither stupid, nor naïve, yet it still took Chris a few months to figure out he was working for the CIA—albeit indirectly.

"So what's still bugging you, Chris? If you've disqualified those possibilities, and quickly I might add, then why the concern?" Holmes asked.

"I don't know. I realize that we are on an unscheduled trip, and so is the ambassador ... of sorts. But whenever I see the Caddy traveling the same old routes, in the same style as it did just a few years ago, I get a slight chill up my back." Holmes looked blank-faced as Chris continued. "I know I shouldn't be so paranoid, but I guess I see things differently than others. And I know that Kaufmann won't even be considering half of what I've just said. I just play the game, and I suppose it keeps me sharp."

The hyper-vigilance of the what-if game was exactly what Chris's active mind needed. The endless hours of driving from point A to point B were kept interesting only by playing out such scenarios in his head. But this was a serious game to play; he was in effect playing with people's lives since the automatic follow-up to *what if* was *do what*? Go where? Where is the escape route? What are the options?

Chris rationalized his continual thought processes—unlike a number of professionals in the protection business—in a very simple manner: The easiest way to kill a VIP while in transit was to stop the car. What was the easiest way to stop a car with a VIP? Kill the driver! As such, Chris's self-preservation took priority in all matters of safety. If he was able to keep himself alive, keep himself out of danger, then those who traveled with him would also be safe. It was an oversimplification of the situation, but it worked, and those who hired him were quite satisfied at the precautions that he took. This positive mind-set was an important supplement to the practical skills he needed for keeping away from attack scenarios—and getting out of them when needed.

When he first started working for MCS, Chris attended the run-of-the-mill crash-and-bang training schools in the US and in other parts of Europe where he learned how to really drive a car. What followed shortly thereafter, however, were stricter regimes of expert one-on-one counter-terrorist training by the best instructors the CIA had to offer. He also learned personnel protection skills and counter-surveillance techniques that further enhanced his own self-preservation philosophy. He excelled so much at counter-surveillance that he was regularly spotting the German intelligence services assigned to protect and spy on the various government officials and visiting heads of state in and around Bonn and Berlin. Those at the Germany CIA station knew that Chris was no slouch, and definitely not just a driver. He clearly had potential, and they wanted to provide him with the skills to test it out.

Four cars to the rear of the Caddy-Benz show, Chris spotted the crane and the slab but told himself to relax a little while he could. It wasn't his business to worry about the ambassador; Berlin was a long drive, and it looked as if foul weather was about to close in. His mission to transport Ted Holmes to the fourth floor of the former embassy to check on the empty CIA station was complete, all he had left to do was get them both home. The last thing that he needed was to drive on the autobahn in the rain, sharing the road with idiots traveling at 160-plus kph who didn't know how to stop a speeding car in a hurry. He'd have to scan for escape routes in double time.

⸺◦∞◦⸺

Kaufmann was keeping to the posted 50 kph speed limit as he approached the junction of Ubier Strasse and Simrock Allee where a flatbed truck just in front of the Caddy came to an immediate and abrupt stop.

Weber's thoughts were quicker than his actions. He immediately thought back to his driver training and basic vehicle dynamics, the effects under braking and acceleration known as "squat and dip." The squat effect is most dramatic when rear-drive vehicles pull away sharply, causing the front end of the vehicle to rise up slightly and the rear end to squat downwards. It's a minimal effect, but more prominent in larger and heavier vehicles, like armored Cadillacs or flatbed trucks. Under heavy braking however, the effect is the opposite. The weight distribution of harsh braking forces a vehicle's front end to dip down and the rear end to rise slightly, causing less traction to the rear wheels. This was the deliberate intention of the truck driver in front of the car from Detroit.

Juergen Weber sat up sharply. He calculated that there was less than five meters of space for the Caddy to stop; they were not going to make it. He knew as well as Kaufmann that the combined weight of the armoring on the car and the lack of advanced braking systems would cause them to slide violently into the rear end of the truck. Another deadly combination came into play that Weber could not foresee: the slow reactions of Kaufmann and the inadequate steering capabilities of the large American car—which some compared to being as responsive as a tugboat.

Weber knew from his experiences as a former traffic cop that, in most vehicular accidents, drivers tend to focus automatically on the object that they are about to hit. This is a naturally occurring phenomenon that causes thousands of fatalities worldwide every year.

The unnatural action however, is to look away from the potential accident site and search for a natural gap, an escape route. If a hole can be found left or right of the blocking object to the front, then it is quite likely that the driver can concentrate on survival by steering towards the gap, almost without thinking about crashing into the object in front. This exercise is something that needs to be learned and, of course, practiced.

Kaufmann had never even heard of such a possibility, let alone thought of it; he was simply focused on the rear of the flatbed. The Cadillac rammed into the back of the truck as the flatbed's rear was coming down from the sudden dip forward. With a tremendous *thump* the Cadillac became wedged under the rear of the truck.

Both Weber and Kaufmann were jolted forward by the impact. Airbags were not an option on the aging Caddy, and if it were not for the seat belt that Weber was wearing, he would have hit the armored windshield at 50 kph. Ernst Kaufmann was not so lucky; his old habit of shunning a seat belt cost him his life. It is debatable, however, which incident caused his death first: his head hitting the bullet-resistant windshield or the steering wheel that crushed his ribs, causing his heart to stop.

Ambassador Heymann, also without a seatbelt, was luckier. Since there was a good deal of room in the rear of the limousine, the ambassador always liked to stretch out his legs. Thus at the point of impact, Heymann's entire body was not placed directly behind Weber but, rather, was positioned at an angle towards the center of the car. The violent jolt forward threw his torso into the cushioning of the front passenger seat and then downwards to the foot well, merely injuring his right shoulder and cutting his forehead as his reading glasses made contact with the seat.

Although the police follow car was never less than two meters away from the Caddy's rear bumper, the follow driver, with the aid of an advanced braking system and a more highly engineered car, managed to stop just inches away from the wreckage in front of him. It was then that the truck driver, recovering from the initial shunt of the collision, began to reverse—causing the Caddy to impact the Mercedes behind.

To those pedestrians and other drivers on the street, the commotion looked like a normal traffic accident, but to Juergen Weber and his team, the immediate thought was possible terror attack.

That instant, a faint explosion could be heard, and a small cloud of smoke appeared above the attack scene. The concrete slab once hanging from the construction-site crane began to plummet, accelerating downwards at a tremendous speed—coming to rest only when it had crushed the Mercedes that carried the flashy young guns of the German police. For all the expense and engineering that was invested in a Mercedes armored car, nothing could be constructed to withhold such an impact. The Cadillac was now sandwiched between the flatbed truck and the defeated Mercedes.

During the confusion, the small red Ford Fiesta, still traveling at 50 kph, careened into the rear of the Mercedes. The tiny Ford was neither fitted with the latest braking technology or airbags of any kind. As it hit the stationary Mercedes, six-year-old Gadwa, a Lebanese girl who was standing in the gap between the two front seats, was catapulted head first through the windshield and out onto the front hood, killing her instantly. The other two passengers, Akilah, Gadwa's aunt, and Samman, the driver, were both thrown violently forward but were saved by the seat belts that they were wearing. Other cars on the street plowed into the melee; an Opel smashed into the Fiesta, and a Renault crunched into the rear of the Opel.

Inside the Cadillac, Weber was in a state of confusion. Although badly shaken and suffering from what he surmised was crushed ribs, he quickly calculated his options while trying in vain to open his door. Standard operating procedures required that all doors be locked while in transit. It was solid policy normally—but now he was trapped; the mechanism had failed. So he clambered over his seat and into the back of the Caddy, falling on top of Ambassador Heymann, who gave a loud grunt. Weber's first priority was to protect his principal; his second, to work out an escape route. As he recovered his composure, he looked up in time to see a gunman and an accomplice approach the left rear door. He painfully drew his police issue SIG 228, knowing he could not use it in the confines of the Cadillac—lest causing a ricochet—but he aimed it at the door, ready. He was still trying to figure out what had happened when one of the assailants attached a box between the doorjamb and the roof of the Cadillac, a known weak spot on older armored cars. Weber saw his options quickly diminish as he realized that plastic explosives were being attached to blow the door open. He tried to cover his head as best he could and hoped that he had the ambassador well enough protected by shielding him with his own body.

The anticipated blast came within seconds. Weber half-expected to be blown into fifty thousand pieces, but the small charge only served to blow the door outwards while pushing a small section of the roof upwards, showering bits of debris both in and out of the car. Weber, cut on the head and arms by flying steel and plastic, looked up and thought, *Oh God, it's a kidnapping!* He drew his weapon again, expecting the gunman to return at any moment. As he waited for his probable death he became aware of his wounds. The weight of his arms suddenly seemed to drag his aim downwards, his vision was becoming impaired, and he knew he was losing consciousness. But he wasn't ready to give up—he had to keep fighting; the gunman was approaching. The next thing Weber saw was something totally unexpected: the flash of a black BMW hitting the gunman and sending him what must have been twenty-five meters down the road.

Chris, jolted back to the present, was able to take evasive action just as he saw a puff of smoke emanate from the crane above the motorcade a few cars ahead of him. He watched in horror as the concrete slab fell and his mind instantly went into overdrive; he managed to stop his car to the left of the traffic ahead of him where it sat at an angle, nearly into the oncoming traffic lane.

Curiously enough, no other traffic was coming in Chris's direction. His instincts then took over. *Is it an attack?* he thought. *Oh shit, they've blocked the attack site!* he realized with dread. Instead of letting his initial surprise and fear take over, his training took him out of panic mode. Chris hadn't decided his next course of action yet; he just knew that clearly the attack was not aimed at him—and he thought immediately of flight.

"What the fuck!" Holmes screamed as the dust rose from the concrete slab that had flattened the Mercedes. Chris then saw two dark-clad figures race towards the stranded Caddy, coming from his left and out of the adjoining but smaller street of Am Arndtplatz. He could make out that one person was carrying some type of machine gun and the other some kind of black box.

As Chris watched the events unfold in front of him, he knew instinctively that he had to do something. His mind raced at lightning speed, running through a shorthand of details: *Attack on ambo; that's got to be explosives he's carrying; potential kidnap scenario; dead Mercedes; no principal in my car; no risk.* Before he could analyze further, the black box was placed on the Caddy, and the explosives man retreated for cover. It took five seconds for it to explode. Chris immediately floored the accelerator of the agency BMW 525i and aimed it at the gunman, who was now moving towards the Cadillac.

"What the fuck are you doing? Back off, back off!" shouted a panicking Holmes.

"Shut up and hold on!" Chris yelled back as he hit the machine-gun-wielding attacker at almost 60 kph. He heard the crunch of bone and then watched as the gunman tumbled through the air and collided with a street bollard that crushed his skull in an instant. As Chris screeched to a halt he opened his side window—always a risk in these circumstances—but he needed to hear, smell, and sense the attack scene as it was unfolding. He knew there was more to come. The man who had placed the black box explosive on the Caddy had escaped being hit by the BMW.

Chris turned to Holmes and ordered, "Get the ambassador—go!" Holmes, a look of horror on his face, froze in place. Chris started to give him a shove, but at the same time, he caught movement out of his peripheral vision. As he looked in the direction from where it came. Chris could make out the shape of a shotgun as the explosives man, now armed as well, returned to the Caddy.

Chris already had his weak shooting hand, his left, on his SIG 226 pistol and raised his left hand out the window. He knew it was going to be a lousy shot out his window, but he had to try. As he raised his arm, he loosed off a round, which clipped the door frame. *Lucky the glass wasn't there*, he thought. The other five rounds flew in the general direction of the explosives man, and something must have connected because the man stopped in his tracks, dropped the shotgun, and collapsed to his knees.

Chris realized Holmes was still sitting next him. "This isn't up for discussion," he spat at the CIA officer. "Fucking go, or drive!" Chris knew that someone had to be behind the wheel if they were to escape. Holmes finally got out and made his way over to the wrecked Caddy.

Chris refocused his attention on his surroundings and the man he'd just shot. He cracked his door open slightly to get a better feel for the situation, but he didn't get out of the car. He spotted a hand movement from the now-prone explosives guy. Chris, engrossed fully in the moment, calmly put both hands on his SIG and fired two well-aimed shots into the top of the man's skull without batting an eyelid. Then his invisible antenna began searching for further movements, new targets, evaluating, planning, and getting ready for his next action.

He was getting frustrated, however. Holmes was taking too much time—but Chris knew he himself needed to be out on the street, in control of the situation, not crawling around in the back of the Caddy. He'd have to trust Holmes to take charge there. Further down the road, Chris soon saw the truck driver get out of his cab. The driver didn't look as if he was armed, and he wasn't advancing on the attack site. *No threat*, Chris surmised— but he nonetheless aimed his weapon in the general direction of the now stationary vehicle and fired a shot into the empty cab, a test. The driver got the message and took off quicker than Ben Johnson at the Seoul Olympics.

The attack has failed; they didn't plan for us to be here—and they're shit out of luck, Chris told himself. He reached back into the side panel of his car door and fished out a fresh magazine for his weapon, readying for whatever might come next. He expertly dropped his old magazine onto the floor and inserted the new one into his pistol, all while keeping his eyes on the street, scanning it for movement or new threats. Again he started to register details: *truck, inoperative; two bad guys down; third guy doing a runner; Mercedes and team, dead; Caddy, going nowhere fast; Kaufmann—shit he's had it; ambo, don't know; more bad guys? MOVEMENT LEFT!* He swung around just in time to see a figure get into a white Ford transit van parked on the side street, Am Arndtplatz. The van took off at lightning speed spinning its wheels, disappearing into the dense suburbs of Bad Godesberg.

The escape vehicle, it's all gone tits up for them! Chris thought as he tried to get a better look at the white van. Suddenly his head snapped around toward the Caddy as he heard two shots ring out from within. Chris, now up and out of his driver's seat, looked over just in time to see Holmes stagger backwards away from the Caddy, grasping his right shoulder. Weber was shooting at Holmes, not realizing he had come to his aid. Chris had to make a decision: leave the car, or hope that Holmes would evade further shots. He didn't contemplate for too long, though, as he realized that the attackers were now in disarray and some of the lead players were out of action. He had to get to the Caddy, but fast.

Chris got out of the BMW, weapon at the ready. He circled around the rear of his car and made his way to Holmes, who by now lay propped up against the rear wheel of the Caddy. He took a look at Holmes's wound and realized that, despite the blood, it was only superficial. "It looks as if it's gone straight through the top," Chris said. "You'll be okay. Can you make it back to the car?"

Feebly Holmes replied, "Yeah sure—can't drive though!"

"No worries; I just need your eyes," said Chris as he pulled Holmes off the ground. "Open all the doors on the car. Go!"

Chris, with his back to the wrecked Caddy, suddenly felt vulnerable; he was not in the command position he favored that enabled him to evaluate the entire scene. Instead, he had to focus on one thing: getting the ambassador out of the disabled vehicle and away from any further danger.

"Juergen, Juergen, it's Chris—don't shoot!" Chris shouted to the Caddy. He was well acquainted with Weber and the protective detail.

"He's passed out," came a muffled reply.

Chris poked his head around and into the inside of the embassy car, where he saw Ambassador Heymann struggling to get the unconscious police officer off him.

"What's going on? Who the hell are you?" a confused and bloodied Heymann blurted.

"Sir, my name's Chris Morehouse—I work for Richard Nash. We need to get out of here quickly, but I need your help with Juergen." With that Chris began pulling Weber towards the door. Heymann, feeling both relief from the weight of the police officer being lifted off him and relief in understanding that he was being helped, began pushing and shoving the German out of the car. Chris managed to flip Weber over, loop both his own arms under the German's armpits, and started dragging him out backwards and towards the BMW. Heymann got the idea and grabbed hold of Weber's legs. Chris started backpedalling as fast as he could. He made it to the BMW's open rear door and somehow squeezed himself in while still supporting Weber. With the help of the ambassador and plenty of pulling and pushing, they got the hefty German policeman in, and Heymann jumped in next to him. Chris ran out of room and fell back out of the agency car with a thump. He managed to roll far enough away, however, that he was able to kick the rear door shut. Holmes, for his part, closed all the other doors and now sat in the front passenger seat waiting, almost pleading to go.

Chris, back on this feet again, jumped back into the driver's seat where he belonged, depressed the clutch, selected reverse, and released the brake, but before he could hit the gas, a rear door opened and the ambassador got out. "What the fuck now?" Chris shouted. The ambassador was heading back to the Caddy, Chris slammed the gear shift into neutral and got out to see what Heymann was up to. As Chris was readying himself with his weapon he started to walk back to the Caddy when the ambassador headed back his way with a blood-soaked flag clutched firmly in his hands. Nothing more was said. Chris got back into his driver seat and again went through the motions of getting the vehicle moving.

Keeping his left hand on the steering wheel, Chris swiveled his body to look over his right shoulder and out through the rear window. As he began speeding backwards down Ubier Strasse, he couldn't help but notice an Arab woman standing next to the red Ford Fiesta screaming and throwing her arms into the air. *I have to keep going*, he told himself. *There're obviously people in need all around here, but now's not the time—there's no way to know if other incidents are brewing.*

As he made his way further back down the street, Chris noticed a man in a trench coat standing quite still, not 50 meters from the attack site. He didn't have time to analyze the man's presence, but he thought, *That's not right. There's blood and guts all over the street, and he's just standing there watching! What's wrong with this picture?* Chris kept on reversing the car until he came to the next junction where it was safe to turn around. *No need for any Hollywood style J-turns here, no unnecessary risks needed*, he reminded himself.

"Where are we going? Where we going?" Holmes started pestering.

"We've got to get to a hospital," Chris replied. "Give me the blue light under your seat." Then glancing in his rearview mirror at Heymann, he asked, "Sir, are you okay? You're bleeding!"

"Just a few scratches; I'll be okay," said the ambassador. "I'm more worried about Juergen—his blood is everywhere."

"Don't worry," Chris tried to play his best driver-in-charge-of-a-tense-situation. "We'll be at the hospital in less than ten minutes; just make sure he still has a pulse and is breathing."

Holmes by now had fished out the blue dome light from under his seat and passed it over to Chris, who realized that it, too, was covered in blood—probably from the suffering Holmes. He had forgotten that the man was probably in a lot of pain and in need of help too. "Hang in there, mate; we are almost there," Chris said to him.

The magnetic clamp stuck to the roof like glue and Chris flicked the switch on his built-in siren. Blue light flashing and siren wailing, they sped out of the suburbs and reached the Johanniter Krankenhaus within six minutes of leaving the attack site.

The howl of the siren attracted enough attention at the hospital that emergency personnel streamed out of the building. Chris screeched to a halt and jumped out of the car as quickly as he could. He threw open the rear door and began pulling Weber out when two male nurses hurried over to assist him. Holmes staggered out his car door only far enough to reach the front fender, where he collapsed to the ground in a heap, exhausted and spent. After helping the nurses place Weber on a gurney, Chris climbed back into the car to retrieve his pistol, which was lying on the passenger-side floor well. He could see that a doctor was now treating Holmes, so he focused his attention on Ambassador Heymann. A nurse was escorting the diplomat into the hospital, who was holding one hand to his head and the other had a death grip on the Stars and Stripes. Chris flicked off the siren and followed the crowd into the sanctuary of the emergency ward and, for the first time in the longest fifteen minutes of his life, breathed a deep sigh of relief.

CHAPTER TWO

DAY 1
JOHANNITER KRANKENHAUS, BONN

A PHYSICIAN APPROACHED CHRIS AS HE SCANNED THE EMERGENCY ROOM. Chris hadn't realized it, but he was covered in Juergen Weber's blood, and the doctor automatically thought that he needed attention. Instead, Chris asked that hospital security lock down the area and inform the local police immediately. He thought there was a slim chance that the attackers would still be seeking their intended target, so he wanted to be prepared.

As he was waiting for the security personnel to show up, he pulled out his cell phone and punched number eleven on his speed dial. After two rings, he heard the familiar voice of Carla Reeve.

"Hi Carla, it's Chris. I need to speak to the boss—it's an emergency."

Carla recognized the urgency in his normally jovial voice and didn't take time to respond, connecting him immediately.

"Nash here," came the familiar, even-keeled voice of his employer.

"Mr. Nash, it's Chris. I'm in Bonn, and we have a problem."

Chris began with a short version of the day's events and requested back-up as soon as possible—he was sure the ambassador was out of immediate danger, but he knew complacency could be deadly. Nash promised to sort things out from his end and that he would be on the next plane from Berlin. Chris just had to sit tight.

"Mr. Nash," Chris pressed, "I think we should get out of here. Hospital security just showed up, and I'm not impressed. Besides, this building is not secure; there's a dozen of ways in and out of this place."

"Okay, wait for your backup; then if the ambassador can be moved, do it. I'll let you make the decision, but keep in touch with me or Carla."

"Understood."

"Keep your head down. I'm on the way."

Two security guards appeared in front of the young driver, and Chris, in fluent German, quickly took charge—ordering one to move the BMW out of sight and the second to cover the room in which Ambassador Heymann was being treated. Chris briefly caught a glimpse of Heymann, who was being examined by a doctor. The ambassador gave him a quick smile and a single thumbs up. At least his injuries were one concern out of the way.

Pacing further down the hallway, Chris found the two rooms where Weber and Holmes were being treated. They were also in safe hands; his priorities were now becoming clearer. Wait for backup and then move with Heymann—no need to involve Weber or Holmes now. In the meantime, he needed to get a feeling for his surroundings. As he began a quick survey of the various corridors, rooms, and public areas, he began forming an improvised escape plan. He hoped that he wasn't going to need it but recalled his 7-P rule, which was drilled into him by his military instructors many years ago—*proper planning and preparation prevent piss-poor performance*—and he didn't want to screw up now.

Making his way back to Heymann, Chris noted that two police officers had also shown up. These guys were just first responders, though—not the professional protective detail that Chris had hoped for. Disappointed, he soon was overcome by a wave of doubts. *What the hell am I doing? I'm not supposed to take charge; I'm just a glorified taxi driver for Christ's sake! I have no authority here; shit, these people probably think I'm an American too, with all my giving out orders.*

He was shaken out of his thoughts by a police officer who informed him that a helicopter was inbound. Chris acknowledged the information but was unsure as to what it actually meant to him. He asked the officer to remain on guard at Heymann's door as he went in search of a bathroom. He needed to piss and needed a moment to clear his head.

As he was washing his hands of other men's blood, Chris looked at his own image in the mirror for a long while, noticing his tired and drawn look from the day's events. He stopped cleaning his hands mid-motion. *Holy shit, what the hell did I just do?* He stared deeply into his brown eyes searching for an answer. *I did my job,* he thought, gratified and relieved. *I did what I was trained for, and I fucking survived! Yes! That's what it's about, I survived!* He washed his face with a sense of confidence but soon realized there was still work to do.

As he exited the bathroom, he heard the unmistakable sound of helicopter rotor blades close by. He dove into a small cleaner's closet halfway down the hallway, took out his weapon, unloaded the magazine, and began counting his rounds. Satisfied that he had enough to get him through another small skirmish if need be, he reloaded and placed the SIG back in its holster.

He walked back towards the emergency room entrance with purpose and confidence. *Switch on, asshole, switch on—the day isn't over yet,* he told himself. He recognized the shape of a green SA 330 Puma helicopter on the hospital landing pad just meters away from the emergency room. On its side, emblazoned in white, was the word Bundesgrenzschutz (Federal Border Protection). Chris, grateful, realized that his backup had finally arrived. The rotor blades were kept turning as two well-armed, green-clad officers sprang out and sprinted towards the hospital. Both men were directed by the hospital security guards to Chris, who had by now taken up a position in front of the ambassador's room.

The taller of the two officers stretched out his hand and simply said in English, "Schmidt. How may we be of service?" Chris desperately wanted to say, *I'm just the driver. I don't need this shit. You take over!* But he shoved his negative thoughts back and said, "Thanks for coming so soon. Here's the story so far," and proceeded to give the officers a quick situation report.

Schmidt agreed that the hospital wasn't safe as there were way too many people coming and going and no way to control all the entry and exit points. "As soon as the ambassador can travel we'll take him back to our headquarters by helicopter," he suggested. It'll only be a fifteen-minute ride. There we have a safe area where he can be looked after by our staff. Then we can plan our next move. In the meantime, I can deploy my team around the hospital for further protection. Is that okay?"

Chris paused and thought for a millisecond. *Is that okay?* One of Germany's elite counterterrorist officers asking him if his plan was okay was *not* what Chris was used to in his role as a driver. *You're damn right it's okay!* He wanted to shout and jump for joy. But he needed to say composed. "Absolutely. I'll check on the ambassador."

Two minutes later a twelve-man team of elite GSG-9 (Bundesgrenzschutzgruppe 9) commandos of the German Federal Border Guard were deployed in and around the hospital complex.

Thirty minutes following that, Ambassador Heymann and Chris were airborne and heading northeast towards the outskirts of Bonn. After the promised brief ride, the Puma with its VIP cargo touched down at the home of the GSG9 in Hangelar, just in time for the heavens to open up and the rain to begin to pour. The party made a quick dash to a waiting bus, where they were met by two senior officers of the commando unit, and then they were ferried to the officer's mess just a short distance away.

At the mess, they were met by two officials of the Bundeskriminalamt—commonly known as the BKA, the German equivalent of the American FBI—who began, without introduction, a barrage of questions for the ambassador. As persistent as they were, the ambassador politely declined to comment on any event until US legal representation was present. So the two Germans, being deflected by the diplomat for the moment, focused their attention on Chris—who by this stage was looking rather disheveled and obviously a little vulnerable.

Chris held up his hand. "Just a second please," he said and then turned to Heymann. "Sir, with your permission, I would also like to wait for legal representation before I make any comments."

"I agree, Chris," the ambassador replied. "However, I think you and I should have a chat before we go any further. Gentlemen, if you'll excuse us." The Germans grudgingly withdrew to a respectable distance and left the two "Americans" to conduct their discussions out of earshot.

"Sir, Mr. Nash is on his way," Chris began, "but I do need to inform him of our whereabouts."

"Okay, but first, tell me what the hell happened out there today," Heymann asked. "My head is still spinning, and to me everything was such a blur. It still is, actually."

Chris took a few minutes to explain what he saw and did, recalling the attack in such precise detail to an awestruck Heymann, who could only shake his head and concentrate on a dark stain on the carpet in front of him. "I can't believe it, I really can't," he finally said. "And you think it was a kidnapping attempt?"

"Yes sir, sorry to be so blunt, but if they wanted you dead, it could have easily been achieved. That concrete slab was meant to take out the police."

Heymann, realizing how lucky he was, regained his composure. "Okay," he said, "get a hold of Nash; I'm going to call my office. I think we need to stay here a little longer than I anticipated." With that, the ambassador went in search of a phone, being trailed by the two BKA bloodhounds.

Chris dialed the office again. "Hi, Carla, it's Chris. Is the boss still in the office?"

"No I'm afraid not. He's just left for the airport. But he'll check in with me before he boards. Where are you?"

"I don't want to give you the exact location over the phone, but we're in a secure location, and I'm with the principal, and we're safe. If you look in your calendar, we visited this location about three months ago for a briefing. I think Mr. Nash was meeting with some guy called Baxter from the States. Not sure if I can, but I'll try to get someone from here to meet him at the airport and bring him in. Will he be alone?"

"No, John Bowman will be with him."

Chris scanned his memory for the name. *Bowman, Bowman ... embassy legal attaché, FBI? Okay, that's good*, he thought, having someone with a law enforcement background would help. "Listen, Carla," he began sheepishly, "sorry for being so short with you earlier. I'm under a little pressure right now." He wasn't used to being the guy in charge.

"Chris, it's okay. Nash explained everything to me. Just be safe, okay?"

"Thanks, Carla. I'll be in touch."

As Chris hung up his phone, a young and fit-looking GSG9 officer approached him. Chris recognized him as one of the pair from the helicopter.

"I think you will need a change of clothes and a place to get cleaned up," the officer suggested. "Have some rest maybe?"

"Yes, I think you're right, but the ambassador, where is he?"

"He's also taking a rest; we have a room for you next to his."

"That's great; I can't thank you guys enough for your help today. I don't know what I would have done without you turning up when you did."

"After some of the reports I have seen so far, I think you would have done well enough without us, sir."

Chris felt honored by the compliment and smiled for the first time in what felt like ages. "I don't think I introduced myself earlier," he said, stretching out his hand. "My name's Chris, Chris Morehouse, US Embassy Berlin."

"Captain Matthias Kettler, GSG9. Nice to meet you."

Chris chuckled, remembering the initial undercover name the man had given earlier that day and smiled, "Ah, yes, Herr Schmidt!"

—∞∞—

Richard Nash and John Bowman touched down at Cologne/Bonn airport at 2030h that evening. They were met by two Bundesgrenzschutz officers who spirited them away in an unmarked BMW.

As they rode silently along the autobahn towards the GSG9 headquarters, on another continent, a call was being made to Washington, DC, from a Virginian suburb by a sympathizer of the group that had carried out the attack on Heymann's motorcade.

"Hello?" a tired-sounding man answered.

"Good morning, sir. This is Jay calling from Jetaway Express. I have some information for you regarding an overseas shipment that you placed with us."

"Is there a problem?"

"Yes, there is. It seems that the package has gone missing."

"Did you just say 'missing'?"

"Yes sir, it seems that one of our foreign partners in Europe was unable to complete the transaction, and the package has been mislaid somewhere."

"Mislaid? What the hell are you talking about 'mislaid'? Those were not my instructions. Do you know how important this was to me? I can't believe that this has happened."

"I understand your predicament, sir."

"No, I don't think that you do!" the now wide-awake voice replied as he slammed down the phone receiver.

———— ∞∞∞ ————

Unbeknownst to Chris, John Bowman had been in the GSG9 officer's mess almost thirty minutes before he burst into Chris's room. Bowman had already spoken with Ambassador Heymann, the GSG9, and the two BKA officials—and he was now on the warpath. The FBI man found Chris and jabbed his finger firmly into the driver's chest. "What I want to know from you are three things," he began pompously. "One, why was an embassy driver carrying a weapon? Two, why did you put an American's life in danger? Three, why have you not cooperated with the BKA?"

Nice to meet you too asswipe, Chris thought as he stretched out his hand. "I'm sorry, we haven't formally met. My name is Chris …"

"Don't get cocky with me, son. I know who you are—you're in enough shit right now. Don't make matters worse for yourself by pissing me off!"

Chris needed to stick up for himself. There was no one else around to back him up. "With all due respect, Mr. Bowman, I deserve a little more courtesy than that. I had to make some tough decisions today, ones that drivers usually do not have to make, and I'm still on edge. I think we both need to calm down a little before we start talking about my actions—which in fact may have saved your American's life."

As the boisterous conversation carried into the hall, Richard Nash followed the din and intervened just in time to catch the hot-headed Bowman making a move towards Chris, hissing, "Who the fuck do you think—"

Just then a well-groomed head appeared around the corner of the door. "Chris, how's it going—are you okay?"

"Mr. Nash, nice to see you so soon," Chris said with relief. "Thanks for coming."

"I see you've met our FBI representative. Everything all right?"

"Fine, but could you sit in on our discussion? I think there are a few things that need to be explained."

"No problem. You look a little pale. Did you receive any injuries?" Nash seemed genuinely concerned with his driver.

Bowman felt he was being upstaged. "Mr. Nash, maybe we can have a word outside."

"If it involves Chris, no." Turning his attention back to his driver, he asked, "What's the status of Ted?"

"He was okay when I left the hospital," Chris replied. "Looks like a shattered collarbone. They'll keep him in there for a few days. I think he's going to be fine."

A perturbed Bowman interjected. "Hang on a second. I'm trying to conduct an investigation here. What's this guy doing carrying a weapon shooting up civilians on the streets like he didn't care who got hit?"

Chris started to get out of his chair, but Nash interjected. "John, there are a few things that need to be clarified here. You do not treat Chris like a criminal, and you will not talk down to him. He works for me directly and deserves the utmost respect for what he did today. Furthermore, Chris has been, how shall I put it … allowed certain privileges by working for my office and has been trained to carry and use a weapon as he deems fit."

Bowman seethed. "Why wasn't the FBI informed about this?"

"John sorry, but you simply did not need to know. Everything is legitimate, and the German authorities, including the ambassador I might add, approved the license many months ago. Chris has attended some of the best training courses that our office has to offer, and your suggestion that he acted like a cowboy is totally out of line. Now, I suggest we start from the beginning and hear Chris's report before we draw any other conclusions, don't you think?"

Bowman finally nodded in submission and looked warily at Chris. "We may as well get the BKA guys in here as well. They need to know how this thing went down." Bowman left the room in search of the Germans.

Chris tried to suppress a smile, but Nash could read his eyes perfectly. "Thanks Mr. Nash," the driver said, meaning it.

"Don't thank me yet. I've still got to answer to his boss," Nash responded glumly. The legendary tension between the CIA and the FBI was evident even here, out in the field, where cooperation mattered the most.

As all parties convened, made themselves comfortable, and switched on their various recording devices, Chris began his colorful recollection of events, leaving out not even the smallest of details. His audience, which had now expanded to include also Kettler and other GSG9 officers, were captivated as he reconstructed the attack site. Chris managed to sketch out in detail the various positions of all the players and vehicles. Yet when he tried to estimate the timings of the events, he was unable to pin down exactly at what time the first explosions occurred and when the last shots fell. Showing his fallibility, he apologized when the question was fielded. "Sorry, I guess I was too caught up in the moment to look at the time, but it must have taken only five to ten minutes at the most."

It was long past midnight when the last questions stopped, but Bowman, now somewhat placated, promised that over the next few days there would be further inquiries from all interested parties—and that Chris should keep himself available should the need occur. As everyone retired for the night, Chris, feeling protective, turned to Nash and asked, "What's going to happen to the ambassador?"

"He'll have his debriefing in the morning, and then he'll probably head back to Berlin. No need to worry about safeguarding him for the moment—the GSG9 will take care of him. He had some very good words to say about you, though. Whatever happens, you'll have an ally there. By the way, good job, Chris," he said with a wink. "Get some sleep. We'll fly back to Berlin in the morning."

DAY 1
WASHINGTON, DC

At 12:15 p.m. Eastern Standard Time, Senator Robert J. Corbin left his desk and announced to his staff that he was going out for lunch and would be back in an hour. The Senator left the Hart Senate Office building on foot and headed across to the Union Railway Station. From there he crossed a zigzag of paths that eventually landed him on the corner of First and K Streets. The Turkish deli at the intersection was not on the list of fine-cuisine eating establishments in downtown Washington, DC, but was, rather, a convenient and inexpensive alternative for many seeking a quick lunch on the go. However, Corbin was not interested in lunch. He sauntered casually into the deli and headed for the overfilled fridge near the cashier's register, where he retrieved a Diet Coke, placed two dollars on the counter, and then left without saying a word or even waiting for the change.

Mazzim, the deli owner seemed to pay little attention to Corbin; he took the cash gratefully and then quickly refocused his attention on a pretty little receptionist from a local law firm standing at the counter, who was becoming one of his regular and more pleasant customers.

Two hours later, Mazzim made a call to his Turkish wholesaler. "I'm sending you a fax with my latest order. How soon can you deliver? I'm in a rush, and I'm running out of everything." The wholesaler never received faxed orders from the fellow Turk; his customer usually picked up the goods himself to cut down on shipping costs. *This must be important,* he thought.

"How about tonight? I can make a special delivery for you. What time do you close?"

"Make sure you're here before ten. I'll be waiting for you."

"No problem—I can deliver on time. See you tonight."

The conversation ended with the wholesaler staring at the phone. In an instant, he pieced together the snippets of the call and tried to figure out what was going on. He'd already deciphered the semi-cryptic message: A meeting was obviously required, the runner was involved; and the meeting would take place the next day at 2200 hours at the prearranged site. But why? Against strict operational procedures, the wholesaler decided to make a few innocent calls for himself. Something was clearly wrong, and he needed to know before the meeting with the politician.

The next morning, Lufthansa flight LH355 from Frankfurt touched down at Washington Dulles Airport. Amongst the regular crowd of businessmen, tourists, and GIs returning from postings in Europe was a weary traveler carrying a briefcase in his right hand and a trench coat draped over his left arm. He made his way through the throng of arriving passengers to the carousel, where he waited patiently for his baggage.

After twenty minutes of being pushed and shoved in every direction by impatient travelers, the man found and retrieved his suitcase and then made his way to the bank of telephones outside the arrivals gate.

Senator Corbin was in his office, involved in a deep conversation with one of his staffers, who was briefing his boss on the latest topic of debate in the Capitol—energy consumption. Although no landline calls were to be put through during the meeting, Corbin's personal cell phone was close at hand. It suddenly rang, and the staffer halted abruptly in mid-sentence. Corbin without any excuses, flipped open the phone. "Hi, honey, what's up?" he said, using the term of endearment he had for his wife—although she did not have this cell phone number.

"I'm back," said a gruff voice.

With enthusiasm and a slight pause Corbin replied, "That's great, I should be finished around eight, so I'll pick you up then. Say hi to Margie for me. Bye." After he snapped the phone shut, he silently brushed off a piece of lint from his Armani suit and for a moment looked as if he was in deep thought. His steely blue eyes then gazed back up at his employee, and he quickly got back into briefing mode. "Please continue—you were just saying that SUV fuel consumption has doubled in the last two years, and …" The conversation drifted back to everyday senatorial matters, and Corbin, although on the outside appeared to be absorbed in the flow charts in front of him, was in fact on the inside consumed with his plans for the evening.

That evening, Corbin left his Cadillac at the parking lot of the Wolftrap Inn, a seventies style motel off Highway 123 in Vienna, Virginia. He walked through the complex as if he was heading to a room as a guest. Instead, he passed under the walkways and out to the rear of the building to another adjoining parking area, where he spotted Trenchcoat sitting behind the steering wheel of a grey Oldsmobile. Corbin got in the passenger seat and, without uttering a word, motioned for his driver to get moving. Heading north, neither spoke until they reached the Lee Jackson Memorial Highway ten minutes later.

It was Corbin who broke the silence. "You going to tell me what the fuck happened over there?"

"Sir, something went badly wrong," Trenchcoat acknowledged. "Nothing went to plan, and it seems our partners aren't playing by our rules. I think they attempted a kidnapping instead of carrying out the hit."

"Jesus Christ, what the hell have they done? This screws everything up. Are you sure?"

"Sir, I was there. I saw everything. That was definitely no attempt at assassination. They had a van on standby in an adjacent street ready to throw him into, and they had just enough explosives to blow open a door. We told them exactly where to place the stuff and how much they would need to blow the Caddy clean off the street."

"I told those assholes to get rid of him. What the hell are they playing at? Where's Heymann now?"

"I don't know, sir. The last I saw of him he was boarding a helicopter from the Bundesgrenzschutz at the hospital. He could be anywhere in Germany by now."

"Great, just great. Now we'll have a full-scale investigation into what happened. Can't trust those bastard Turks with anything. We're going to have to deal with Heymann later. For now, we've got to sort these assholes out—it's about time they realized who they're dealing with."

Trenchcoat continued to drive, explaining everything that had happened over the previous twenty-four hours. As the details became clearer, it was becoming obvious to Corbin that the Turks were trying to kidnap Heymann for a reason.

What Trenchcoat failed to do was to divulge in any detail the manner of Heymann's rescue. He was still astonished as to how it had all transpired and how quick the BMW driver was to react. He secretly admired the young man's capabilities and his ability to respond under extreme pressure.

As the story wound down, Trenchcoat headed back towards the meeting place. Less than two miles away, he stopped the car at the side of the road, got out, and headed out into the nearby woods. Corbin slid behind the wheel of the Oldsmobile and looked at his watch: 2100 hours. As frustrated as he was, he would have to be patient enough for his accomplice to get into position.

While he waited, the senator from Michigan contemplated how to move forward with his plans. Yes, there had been a kink in the road. Heymann needed to go—of that there was no doubt. He was sure there would be a second chance, somewhere, somehow. The Turks would just have to get it right the next time, or the deal would be off.

For Corbin, the product of a family of wealthy steel industrialists from Michigan, his plans were far more grandiose than those of Turkish idealists he was meeting tonight. As much as he coveted the cash, he was willing to go to any length to support his personal cause. Corbin's grand plan was simple, but years in the making. He wanted to become the president of the United States.

Although being the most powerful man in the world suited his ego to a T, Corbin's objective wasn't just about sitting in the Oval Office and having everyone acquiesce to his demands. It was about revenge—a long sought-after family revenge. During the Second World War, his father was brutally killed in the Philippines by the Japanese in the Bataan Death March in 1942. Corbin was only ten years old at the time, and he naïvely thought that one day he would find those responsible and bring them to justice. However, as he matured and became more attuned to worldly affairs, he realized that in order for proper punishment to be meted out, he had to have a smarter plan than merely exerting physical pressure on particular individuals. His goal, therefore, was to bleed the Japanese economy dry once he became president. He would avenge his father's death and that of all other soldiers killed in Bataan by restricting imports from Japan—especially from the newly thriving Japanese carmakers.

Corbin was passionate about his country, and he fervently believed in the sanctity of American manufacturing. More than once he had stood on the lines with the steel and autoworker unions to ensure that the home economy could flourish without Japanese influence and not close US plants as a result of their growth. He was often pictured surrounded by men in hardhats drinking beer and passing out cigars. It was an image he loved to portray, one of a fat cat who could just as well slum it with hardworking people.

As his presidential plans began picking up steam, he knew already that the vast majority of the blue-collar workforce in the country was in his back pocket. He loved them for their support, and they loved him for keeping their jobs and keeping their country "pure American."

Now only eighteen months away from declaring his candidacy, Corbin was finally putting together the last of the finances needed to drive his campaign. Although all his declared campaign funds were from legitimate sources, Corbin also held great private wealth. Most people naturally thought that the Corbin family estate was the chief financier for the entrepreneurial senator, which was true—to a certain extent. What most people were unaware of were the undisclosed bank accounts spread throughout the globe to be held for unforeseen circumstances, or should his presidential campaign begin to fail, to provide more kickback expenses for the rich and famous endorsements that he would certainly need. One of the sources for this shadow income was the Turks he was meeting tonight.

Corbin was shaken from his reverie by his cell phone, which chirped just one time. He started the car, pulled back onto the road, and headed to the prearranged meeting point. It took ten minutes for Corbin to make his way down a number of tracks and small roads to arrive at the abandoned trailer-park site in the woods. They were less than ten miles from the West Virginia state line, typical hunters' country. His two Turkish business partners were waiting for him in a dark-blue-panel van, backed up into some trees, facing the road. Having no need to acknowledge his arrival, Corbin drove past the van a short distance and stopped the car. He slowly got out and made his way in the moonlight to meet his co-conspirators, who had likewise exited their vehicle and made their way to meet Corbin.

Corbin decided that in order to assert his authority he needed to be direct. His former military background taught him that the best way to administer discipline was to get straight to the point.

"What the fuck are you doing?" he started. "I gave you a simple assignment, and you chose to ignore me. Do you realize that this puts our entire operation in jeopardy?"

It was Adem, the wholesaler, who answered. "My friend, my friend, please do not be angry with us …"

Corbin cut him off. "Don't call me your friend! What the hell is going on? I gave you specific instructions to kill that son of a bitch, and you didn't do it!"

Adem, offering his upturned hands in submission, shrugged his shoulders. "It is not my fault. My brothers in Germany took a different approach to the mission. I also expected the same as you. But for some reason, things did not go to plan."

"Not go to plan!?" Now Corbin was getting really agitated. "Your *brothers* didn't even *attempt* to kill him. What the hell were they playing at?"

"It seems that the commanders in our homeland had a different approach in mind. As you know, we have some brothers in captivity in German prisons."

Corbin felt his pulse quickening, as if he knew what was about to come next.

"It was felt that we could secure the release of our comrades if we were to capture the ambassador."

Corbin's eyes bulged wide with fury, and he clenched his fists. "I think you knew all along that was the plan, you son of a bitch!" he spat.

"No, my friend, no, please understand—we have no knowledge of such plans. Our organization is split up so that no cell has information of operations of other cells. That is the way we work; it keeps us secure. I received the information from my commanders earlier today to confirm the details. You have to believe me."

"I'm beginning to doubt every word that comes out of your mouth," growled Corbin. "You're just trying to screw me out of more money and make my life more difficult."

"Mr. Corbin, I do not wish to ruin our relationship. Our business transactions should not be affected by this setback."

"Setback? You stupid pricks don't realize what you have done. Don't you know that the FBI will be all over this? They won't stop. It may take them a while to get to the bottom of this, but they'll find out, I can guarantee it. I know how these things work. I'm on the Senate Intelligence Committee, for Christ's sake. I know how thorough these people can be, and they really don't care how long it will take. They will find out, you fucking idiot!"

Mazzim tried to placate the senator. "Relax, Yankee."

Corbin snapped. Nobody called him a Yankee. He took two steps towards the deli owner and slapped him full in the face.

That was the signal Trenchcoat was waiting for. He approached silently from the trees at the rear of the trailer park, not twenty meters away from the group. As Mazzim recovered from Corbin's slap, he began to lunge at the American but was stopped in his tracks by the cold steel of a gun barrel pressed firmly into the back of his neck.

"Stop right there. Everybody stay calm," Trenchcoat ordered. On your knees, asshole!"

Mazzim, with a look or horror on his face, complied and sank to the ground.

Adem screamed, "What is this? You come armed to our meetings? It is *you* who are betraying our friendship!"

Trenchcoat then swung his weapon at Adem. "On your knees, NOW!" he barked. Upon receiving an imprint of the 9mm barrel on his neck, Adem, too, complied despondently and dropped to the ground. Trenchcoat backed off a few feet to cover both Turks.

Corbin then took charge of the situation. "You two imbeciles had better listen, and listen well. You and your brothers have put our entire operation in danger. The latest shipment has already left Baltimore. However, I can stop it from reaching its destination if you don't do exactly as I say." He paused slightly for effect. "I want Heymann dead—do you understand? Dead! You will get a second chance. I'll get you the information you need to carry it out again, and this time there will be no fucking around for political prisoners. Do you *understand?*"

A shaken Adem replied tersely. "I don't have the power to make those decisions; I have to discuss this further with my commanders."

"I don't care what you say to your bosses," Corbin hissed, "but if you want your precious arms shipment, then you had better do as I say."

An eerie silence soon fell on the group as Corbin let the message sink in. Mazzim soon broke it, blurting, "Go do your dirty work yourself, Yankee!"

Corbin let out a long sigh and nodded to Trenchcoat and remarked, "It's about time you assholes learned a little respect for me."

Trenchcoat forced Mazzim to lie down to the ground in a prone position. He then placed the barrel of the Heckler & Koch MP5 SD sub-machine gun behind the right knee of the deli owner and pulled the trigger. The single 9mm bullet, which normally traveled at 3,000 feet per second, tore through his flesh and bone in a millisecond. Mazzim screamed at the top of his voice in pure agony. Now Trenchcoat and Corbin turned their attention back to Adem. "Tell your masters that Heymann must die," the senator said coldly, "or I'll stop your shipment. Is that clear?"

A shaken Adem feebly replied. "Yes, yes, please no more shooting. I'm but a messenger. I can't make those decisions, please understand."

Corbin still wondered if his message was really getting through and turned back to Mazzim, who was writhing in the dirt, clutching what was left of his knee in excruciating pain. He glanced again at Trenchcoat, gave him a brief smile, and nodded. This time Trenchcoat produced a knife and slashed it slightly across Adem's face.

Adem screamed like a girl and clutched his face. "You bastard!" he cried.

Corbin was feeling more relaxed now that both men were in pain. "Are we clear?" he asked the Turks.

"Yes, Mr. Corbin," replied a dejected Adem. "Heymann will die."

CHAPTER
THREE

DAY 2

ZEHLENDORF, BERLIN

CHRIS WAS LYING IN THE BATHTUB, TRYING TO RELAX AND NEARLY ASLEEP, when Astrid came bursting through the front door of their apartment. Chris had been living with the Lufthansa stewardess for almost eighteen months, and the relationship, with its fair share of ups and downs, was once again facing a possible conflict as their work schedules collided and expectations again failed to be satisfied.

"Chris, are you home?" came the shout from the hallway.

"Yeah I'm in the bath," he mumbled, jolted awake by her presence.

Chris could hear the bustle of returning suitcases and a set of keys being thrown onto a side table. The apartment, in a quiet and respectable area in Southwest Berlin, was spacious enough for two, but Chris, always conscious of every move, every sound, and every smell around his home, began picturing exactly how Astrid looked and exactly what she was doing. Although he had tried his best to put the memories of the last few days behind him, he nevertheless still felt anxious about his actions in Bonn. And Chris didn't want to admit it, but he was still on edge, especially when others were present.

He now suspected everyone and everything. Richard Nash even took notice and hinted that perhaps a vacation was in the making, something to help him ease back into his everyday life. However, try as he might, Chris could not back down—there were simply too many unanswered questions, too many faces, too much blood, too much mayhem. He needed to see the big picture. He wanted to know who had planned the attack and why. Chris was mature enough to know he needed to move on, put the incident down to experience, and simply accept the fact he had done the right thing—and there was nothing more to do.

He also knew there was still a job to do: he still had a duty to protect and serve his principal, Mr. Nash, and remain focused on that task. He therefore hoped that he could find some comfort and a little peace of mind at home. He'd been soaking in the bath almost an hour when his partner returned from her cross-Atlantic flight.

"How was your trip to Bonn, Chris?" she asked, flatly, from the hallway as she skimmed through some mail.

Chris hesitated. *Maybe she didn't hear about the attack.* "Fine," he replied. "How was New York?" The two partners were now almost shouting at each other through the walls.

"Oh, the usual, a little turbulence over Long Island, but otherwise okay."

Chris could hear the *click-clack* of Astrid's high heels on the wood floors approach the bathroom. Astrid came in and kissed Chris on the forehead. "You look tired," she observed, ruffling his light brown hair.

"Yeah, I had a few late nights this week; I guess it's catching up with me."

"Just give me a second. I'll get out of these clothes and join you," she said and headed for the bedroom.

As Astrid was changing, Chris closed his eyes and pondered telling her what had happened. He needed some kind of release, some way of just talking things out. He was happy that she had returned and realized, if nothing else, he could at least be distracted by her to forget for a while his chaotic situation and hopefully relax.

"Whose clothes are these?" The words broke his reverie.

Chris opened his eyes to see a confused-looking Astrid standing in the doorway clad only in her underwear, holding up the black sweater and blue jeans the GSG9 had given him to replace his own bloodied garments.

Chris, momentarily shaken, paused slightly before answering. "I had to borrow them from a mate of mine in Bonn; I had a bit of an accident."

"What are you talking about?"

Chris had to think fast now; he was usually quite careful in covering his tracks, but he'd forgotten about the borrowed clothes he'd tossed into the laundry basket. He hated lying to Astrid, but he'd been doing it long enough now, and he was getting good at it. "When we were packing up the rest of the stuff from the old office in Bonn, I found a couple of cans of paint. I went to move them out of the way, and one of the handles broke, and the top came off as I was lifting it." Chris began to smile and tried to put a light touch to the incident. "Yellow paint went everywhere—it was funny. I was with a guy from the office, and he got covered as well. We looked like Laurel and Hardy."

Astrid, not seeing the funny side pushed for more answers. "What about what you were wearing—where is it?"

"Shit, I had to get rid of it. I mean, there's no way I could have cleaned it off; it was totally ruined."

Astrid was now getting perturbed. "I hope that it wasn't the suit I bought you for your birthday."

"Sorry, honey, there's nothing I could have done; it was just a stupid accident."

"Accident! Why can't you be more careful?" She was raising her voice and getting angry; it was obvious that she needed to let off a little steam after a hectic flying schedule.

"But, Astrid ..."

"I don't understand why you're still doing that shitty little job anyway. The money isn't enough for what you do, always going here, going there, always taking calls and running off at all hours of the day. They treat you like dirt all the time, and you work way too many hours. Why don't you get yourself something a bit more respectable?"

"Like your job, I suppose?" he shot back, getting a little hot himself.

"What the hell is that supposed to mean?" She glared at him, her green eyes narrowing.

It began turning into a real argument. Chris sat up in the bath and Astrid, still in the doorway, stood with both hands on her hips, struggling to keep control.

"Well in your job, people treat you like dirt, you work long hours, and the pay is lousy, too," he said. "What's the difference?"

"Chris you are just a *driver*, don't you understand? You just drive people around and carry their bags for them. In my job I have responsibilities. I have to keep people happy all the time, and I am also responsible for the safety of hundreds of people. You just pick up the dry cleaning and keep the *verdammte* car clean!" Astrid yelled as she stormed out of the bathroom and headed back to the bedroom.

No TLC for Chris tonight, he thought. *I'm just a driver... just a damn driver.*

DAY 3
BEIRUT, LEBANON

The driver of the red Ford Fiesta was standing in the hallway of a small villa on the outskirts of Beirut. Only forty-eight hours had passed since the incident in Germany, and Samman, who had not been in his country of birth for a number of years, was confused as to why he was there at all. He was a simple Lebanese grocery store owner in Cologne; it was a prosperous business that he had been running for ten years with his wife and two sons. The only reason that Samman was drawn into the tragic set of events in Bonn was that he was, unbeknownst to many of his customers, a fervent supporter—albeit only financially—of the Lebanese struggle against Western influence in his home country. He was quite willing then to send a share of his profits on a regular basis to a cousin back home, whom he knew to be active in certain loyalist circles in and around the Beqaa Valley. Samman was not an educated man, but he was clever enough to stay away from the many shady Lebanese characters that peppered the Arab community in the Cologne area.

Samman was astonished when his cousin asked him to step out of anonymity and perform the task of picking up little Gadwa and her aunt at the airport and then taking them to an eye clinic in Bad Godesberg. It was a simple task, and he desperately wanted to get the task done right. He never knew what the aunt's name was, and he never asked, but he realized that only someone with influence and money in Lebanon could send a daughter overseas for expensive medical treatment. Everything was going fine until Samman got lost on the wrong side of town and pulled into traffic behind a Mercedes with a lollipop sticking out of its roof.

The grocer had been waiting in the hallway for 15 minutes before he was beckoned by a smiling man to follow him to the cellar. He told himself not to worry—that he had not done anything wrong—nevertheless, he still felt a little nervous. He followed his guide down a number of steps and eventually came to a well-lit corridor with several rooms. At the end of the corridor were more steps that led further down into the bowels of the villa. These steps led down to another smaller and less lit corridor, where the air was foul and it seemed that vermin nestled in every corner. A door was ajar at the far end of the hallway; he followed the smiling man to the room and was ushered in. As soon as he entered a bright light was shone in his face, immediately disorienting him. He was then grabbed from behind by two sets of very powerful hands and shoved into the center of the room, where he was forced to sit in a wooden chair.

Samman could not see a thing; the bright light was still in his face. What he could feel, however, were two leather straps being wrapped around his wrists and the armrests of the chair and then a blindfold being placed over his eyes. Panic set in, and he began to struggle, but he knew there was no point—he was trapped. And the worst thing about it was that he didn't know why.

After five minutes of silence, which seemed like an eternity, a voice from within the darkness finally said, "Now you know what it is like to be blind."

"Who are you? What am I doing here?" came the panicked response from Samman.

In reply, one of his captors struck the grocer firmly on the jaw. "You do not ask questions; speak only when you are spoken to!"

"But I have done nothing …." *Smack!* A second and even harder punch came at his face from the other side.

"If you have done nothing wrong, then you will only have to answer our questions."

Samman nodded and realized that these people were serious; he could feel blood trickling down his lower lip.

Silence ensued, and after a few minutes the voice came again. "Now you know what it is like to be blind … *and in pain.* My daughter was almost blind and in great pain. Now she feels nothing."

Samman began to sob.

"You will tell me everything about how my daughter died—every little detail. Do you understand?"

"Yes, yes, please don't hurt me—" Samman let out a wild scream as he felt the searing pain of a soldering iron burn through the skin on the back of his right hand.

"Speak when you are spoken to and answer truthfully," one of the captors shouted in his face. "Scream as much as you like—nobody can hear you here, and nobody would care."

"Budail—enough." It was Gadwa's father who again spoke. "I want our friend to cooperate, and I want him to see his family again." Gadwa's father was clever; he knew if you gave a prisoner a little hope of survival, then some cooperation would be forthcoming. This was not the first time he or his thugs had used this technique.

After two hours of harsh interrogation, a sweating and sobbing Samman asked, "What will happen now? When can I leave? I have given you all that I know. Please, please let me go!" His only answer was the sound of a toolbox being opened. He leaned his head in the direction of the sound.

"What are you doing? What's going on?" His blindfold was removed and his head was held in place by one of his captors. Samman blinked his eyes several times to regain focus on his surroundings. As his vision became clearer his heart almost stopped; he could make out the shape of a set of pliers just inches away from his left eye.

He recognized the sound of the voice as Gadwa's father, who was holding the tool and spoke in a calm non-affected voice. "My name is Abdul Al Haafiz," he said, "and I am, as my name implies, the Protector. Allah himself has blessed me and given me a mission to rid our great land of the foreign invaders. As a reward for carrying out this great task, the great Prophet gave me a gift, and her name was Gadwa."

Samman began breathing heavily; sweat was now streaming from every pore in his body and a small pool of urine formed between his legs.

"You have taken away my treasure; you were responsible for her death."

"No, no, please it was not my fault," Samman began, looking for excuses. Then he added, "There is something else, something I remember." The Protector lowered the pliers and motioned for him to continue. "One of the dead gunmen, I saw his face as he was being taken away. I have seen it before ... I am not sure —maybe at the Turkish market near my home. I don't know. Please, please have mercy. I too have children, and they need their father."

The Protector seemed to be lost in thought as he contemplated this last piece of information. After a short while, he turned to Budail and said, "Release him." Samman was overcome with joy, and as soon as he was released from the straps, he leapt out of the chair and fell to his knees to kiss the hand of the Protector.

"Thank you for sparing my life, thank you. Praise be to Allah!"

"Enough," the Protector said with contempt. "Go, leave this place. If you ever speak of me or what happened this day, I will remove not only your eyes but also those of your children. You have provided me with valuable information, and I will call on your services again. Go in peace, my friend."

Samman didn't need a second invitation; he remained silent and bolted for the door. As he entered into the corridor, he was overcome by the stench that greeted him when he had first arrived on the lower level of the villa. He stood momentarily to place the smell, and as he scanned the floor his face turned to shock as he could make out the decomposing body of Gadwa's aunt lying in a corner. Her eyes had been removed. The next thing he felt was the cold steel of a pistol being placed at the back of his neck. He froze in place. He never heard the shot, and he was dead before he hit the ground.

The Protector bent down to retrieve the spent cartridge from the blood-stained floor. "That was for you, my little Gadwa, but there will be more. This I promise; I promise with my life."

He turned to one of his two subordinates and asked, "Budail, are the Turks still in the valley?"

"Yes, the transactions are complete. They will leave tomorrow."

"No, they will never leave this country," the Protector stated. "Kill them all."

"We can't do that, we need their busin—"

The Protector moved with lightning speed, grabbing Budail by the collar with his left hand and violently shoving the pistol he was holding in his right hand into Budail's face, screaming, "You do not question my orders! Do you understand?" Budail stared in disbelief at his commander's outburst and simply nodded silently his submission. The Protector backed off and regained his composure. "Budail, my friend, you are my most trusted lieutenant. We have fought many battles and killed many of the enemy together. Have I ever failed you? How can you begin to doubt my judgment now, when we are making so much progress in our glorious struggle?"

Budail and the Protector had indeed been together for many years and fought many a battle, but Budail had a special skill: he knew when to keep silent. He had seen his comrade and leader like this once before years ago, when the man's mother and father were killed in an Israeli air raid on his hometown of Bint Jubayl, near the Israeli/Lebanese border. The air attack had come as a reprisal for a Hezbollah rocket attack into Israel that killed twelve children in a schoolyard near the border. Abdul Al Haafiz, the name he still used back then, was a junior commander with Hezbollah at the time, and when he heard of the attack, he found the captain in charge of the rocket battery and ripped out his tongue with a bayonet. Reprimanded by his superiors, he was ordered to leave the militant organization, never to return.

The Protector, however, would not be dismissed so easily. A former civil servant with the Lebanese Ministry of Agriculture, he did not want to give up the struggle and formed his own small group that became known as the Lebanese Revolutionary Forces, or LRF. The group was staffed with like-minded individuals, who thought the true threats of a free and prosperous Lebanon were not women and children but those who invaded his country and those who supported them.

A few minutes passed, and a now calmer and more rational Protector added, "Budail, please trust me and carry out my orders. We will speak to our South African friends about our business. I am sure there are enough—how shall I put it?—crack heads in Cape Town who are interested in some of Lebanon's finest produce."

DAY 3
ZEHLENDORF, BERLIN

Chris rappelled slowly down the side of the five-story building. He was wearing a black Nomex suit and a standard British Army S6 respirator. On his right thigh was strapped a 9mm Browning Hi-Power pistol with thirteen rounds; slung on his chest, a fully loaded Heckler & Koch MP5 SD. He gingerly inched his way down the side of the structure, coming within inches of his entry point. He froze in place, not daring to move a muscle, lest he compromise his position. He moved his head slowly left and right to see if the other team members were in place, but there was nobody else. He waited a few precious seconds, knowing that timing was crucial. He eventually, though reluctantly, broke radio silence, clicking his switch to confirm the mission, whispering into his microphone, "Zero, this is two sitrep, over." No reply. Again he tried: "Zero, this is two sitrep, over." Still nothing. He looked upwards in desperation, only to see two members of the SAS team give the dreaded wave-off-abort signal.

Chris began running through his options. As he did so, he felt a firm tugging on the rope; the team was trying to haul him back to the roof. Chris tried to avoid hitting the wall; a sharp jerk would cause a sound. As he was slowly being raised, his mind was racing. *Why had things gone wrong?*

Suddenly the rope gave way, and he felt himself falling downward, towards the window that was supposed to be his entry point. He came to an abrupt halt directly outside the large pane and stared in disbelief. The mission was definitely compromised. One of the terrorists was inside looking directly at Chris, the anti-terror commando dangling on the rope not five feet away.

In an instant, the cry went out, and terrorists from all sides came running. One, who Chris knew to be the group's leader, ran closest to the window, drew his pistol, and shot twice. Luckily Chris was wearing a bulletproof vest, which saved his life, but the hits stunned him nonetheless. Chris contemplated shooting back, but he was in a no-win situation; he now had five terrorists pointing weapons at him. He anticipated the others opening fire on him but was curiously relieved to find that they did not. Instead, the leader disappeared into the nearby room where the hostages were being held and then returned, dragging a screaming twelve year-old girl by her long blond hair. The leader made her kneel down in front of the window and held his pistol to her head.

"NOOOOO!" Chris began to scream, but the sounds wouldn't come out. "Take me, you bastard, take me!" he mouthed in desperation. To his horror, the terrorist simply smiled and then pulled the trigger. The girl slumped to the floor like a rag doll. Chris closed his eyes to block out the image, but when he opened them, the terrorists were still there, laughing at him. He tried in vain to kick in the window where the bullet holes had ruptured it—he frantically wanted to take the terrorists on; he'd gladly sacrifice himself—but the glass would not break. He drew his weapon to shoot, but as he did so, the rope finally gave way, and he felt himself falling once again.

Chris woke with a start, immediately sitting up rigidly in bed. He thought he'd screamed out, but as he looked over at Astrid, she was still in a deep sleep. He was sweating profusely and trembling as if he was in the middle of an LA earthquake.

He looked at the clock; it read 5:12 a.m. He got out of bed and made a move for the bathroom. Walking into the corridor's cool air made him tremble more, and he began to feel nauseous—he thought he might throw up. He made it to the sink in time and ran a cold tap, letting the basin fill up and then dousing himself in the cold, relieving water. Leaning over the sink, he kept his eyes closed for a few minutes and began to take stock. He remembered having nightmares as a kid, but this was something new to him as an adult.

He left the bathroom and headed towards the living room, glancing in on Astrid as he passed the bedroom—she had still not stirred. He lay down on the couch in the dark and closed his eyes but could not put his mind to rest as the bad dream replayed in his head and he wondered, *Why was it so vivid, and what the hell did it mean?* He hoped to drop off back to sleep, but no such luck. Now wide awake, he realized that he had to do something to take his mind off things. Chris resorted to one of his favored problem-solving methods: he decided to go for a run.

He left the apartment at 5:45a.m. and began a slow warm-up jog through the deserted Berlin suburbs. As he reached the start point for his usual mile-and-a-half, timed run, he slowed to a walk, flicked the timer on his wristwatch, and then began to run in earnest. To anyone else on the streets that morning, Chris would have looked like a man running as if his life depended on it.

During his years in the military, Chris prided himself on keeping his conditioning to the highest of standards. He was jokingly known in his unit as a fitness nut, but he ignored the jibes that his comrades so willingly dished out towards anything even slightly beyond the norm. He had the stoutness and stamina of a Welsh pony but was also very nimble on his feet. He loved to run, and he usually ran hard. He was difficult to beat.

Chris had a fair head of steam going on this run. His breathing was measured, but his pace was lightning quick. The mile and a half was his favorite short distance, and his personal best time was 7:45 minutes, wearing military boots. There were few in his unit that could have surpassed that. This run was going to be a good one; he could feel it. Anything between 8 and 8:15 was his target. Less than eight minutes these days was just a dream, even with the Reeboks he now wore.

As he concentrated on his route, he felt as if a huge knot of pressure had just been released from within him, and he was able to give himself an extra boost as he passed the halfway mark. He dared not look down at his watch but kept pushing himself to keep going. He began breathing harder, his lungs warming up; the sweat came back, and his entire body was working like a well-oiled machine. Chris ran like a man possessed, oblivious to his surroundings and focused only on finishing his goal.

As he came around the final bend, he could make out the shape of someone ahead, pushing something. *I don't need this crap—get out of my way*, he thought to himself. As he neared the figure, he recognized that the shape was a bum pushing a shopping cart steadily up the road to who knows where. The transient heard the thumping footsteps and turned around to see who was approaching. As he was doing so, he turned his shopping cart directly into Chris's path.

Chris collided with the trash-filled cart just as he was coming to the last sprint of his race, and his momentum threw his body into the cart, turning the whole thing on its side. A split-second reaction prevented him from falling flat on his face; instead he was able to roll over on his shoulders. Many months of practice falling in his martial arts classes finally paid off as his response was exactly as he had learned; what was not expected, however, was his next reaction. As Chris came out of his roll, he came into a crouching position, and as he was doing so, his hands reached around to his back to pull out his SIG pistol. He swung it out expertly and trained it on the target in front of him, the homeless man.

The man silently put up his hands, breaking Chris out of his adrenaline-fueled offensive posture. Chris dropped his own arms and slowly put the gun back into its holster. Horrified at what might have happened had the situation escalated, he profusely apologized and quickly turned for home.

The walk back to the apartment took much longer than anticipated. He could have taken a much more direct route, but his mind was racing with a myriad of images of events past, present, and future. Although he rationalized his actions in Bonn—he killed two bad guys and saved at least three good ones—he could not put matters to rest. And clearly it was affecting his actions here and now.

As he racked his brain, he scanned the street ahead, taking in his surroundings and seeing that Berlin was slowly coming to life. It began to rain; lights were going on in houses along the street; he could hear an alarm clock somewhere nearby pleading to be silenced. He witnessed the first of the blue-collar workers diligently leaving their homes—the ones that always left at the same time every morning, carrying the same lunch box, walking to the same newsstands, and waiting for the same trains. He noted a young man running to a parked car, still dressed in his nightclub clothes and turning back to grin at a girl in a window he probably picked up the night before.

He also noticed a man walking his dog wearing a trenchcoat. *Trenchcoat!* Chris's little open window on life closed shut in an instant. His reaction was based in an old habit of his; if he didn't know someone's name, he'd always immediately assign some kind of label to them, usually based on a visual image. His mind raced back to the scene in Bonn and the image of man who stood to the side, so still, watching it all unfold, doing nothing. Since the only thing Chris had to go by at the time was what the man was wearing, the name stuck: Trenchcoat.

Chris stopped walking and stared at the man now coming towards him with a reluctant rain-soaked golden retriever in tow. *Trenchcoat—what the hell was that about?* Chris thought, once again returning to the puzzle of that day. *The man in Bonn, who was he? What the hell was he doing there? Did he have something to do with the attack? Why was he so composed?*

Chris didn't realize that he was still staring at the man and his dog as they stood before him.

"*Ist alles in ordnung?*" asked the stranger.

"Yes, I'm fine, sorry," came Chris's confused reply, and he began his trek back home with a bit more determination in his stride. He knew what he had to do; he had to find out who Trenchcoat was and figure out if he was really part of the play or just another member of the audience.

DAY 3
BEQAA VALLEY, LEBANON

The Protector had been walking through the foothills of the Beqaa Valley for many hours, taking a circuitous route to his final destination; he was still contemplating his interrogation of the grocer earlier in the day. He was closely followed by Budail and another of his trusted lieutenants, Faris, who had also been with the Protector since the beginnings of the LRF in the early 1980s. The leader of the group took his own security very seriously as he made his way to the weapons cache high up on the plains above the low-lying villages and towns of northern Lebanon. He knew that, because of his notoriety, he was being watched by the Israelis, the Syrians, and the Americans; he therefore took no chances and always took the long, safe way to get to his hideout.

The Protector knew the hills well. He had first wandered into this remote region years before the wars of the seventies and eighties in his role as a junior agricultural official inspecting irrigation projects throughout the valley. For the most part, he enjoyed the work for he could see the results of his efforts firsthand. He became friendly with the farmers and peasants who toiled on the land in some of the bleakest landscapes the Middle East had to offer.

The only problem was that the Protector became disillusioned with the people he was working for and their corrupt and subservient ways. He hated that Lebanon had been the slave of the larger and more powerful Syria since it was occupied in1976, hated the neighboring Jewish domination and power, and most of all, hated the American arrogance, decadence, and stupidity for fanning the flames of the inferno that was the Middle East. He was frustrated, angry, and grieved by the failure of his government's inaction against these protagonists, and laughed at the ineptitude of the Palestinians for even trying to stand up to the occupation of the holy lands.

The Protector rationalized that if the Palestinians were to be effective, then they should have been active in 1948 and pushed the Jews back into the sea as they were still trying to organize. To wait until the mid-1960s was in his eyes an utter failure. As the struggle in the Levant spiraled out of control in the 1980s and Lebanon became a playground for generals, spies, politicians, and terrorists, the Protector—a devout Muslim—did not wait long to heed the call to defend his land, as if it was a call from the Prophet himself.

He joined the Hezbollah, which was born in the back alleys and slums of Beirut. He soon became a local commander of a small unit whose members were fighting house to house with the myriad other fractious groups struggling to keep the city's demarcating Green Line intact. He earned a reputation as a good commander who would take responsibility for his and his men's actions and who was able to take calculable risks.

As the Lebanese civil war came to an end, the fight against Israel in the south continued. The Protector retained his status within the Hezbollah ranks and subsequently earned the respect of his commanders for a string of successful operations. It was only when his parents were killed that Al-Haafiz truly changed. After becoming more vociferous and belligerent, the Protector lost the faith and confidence of the infamous terrorist group, and he planned his own way to carry on the fight. He collected a following of twenty-five disenchanted soldiers who were also looking for better ways to combat the enemy. Yet, though the will to fight was there, the arms and finance were not. So the Protector went back to the Beqaa Valley to find those funds.

During one of his early tours for the Ministry of Agriculture, he came upon a remote region with acres of unharvested poppy fields. He kept the secret to himself for many years until he knew that he could use the knowledge to his advantage when the time was right. When the time came, he employed a small staff of locals, who were only too willing to harvest the crops for a reasonable fee. The Protector financed the whole operation with the sale of his own home in Beirut and the profitable textile business his parents once owned there. He made his camp in the valley and intended to live off the profits of heroin while also using them to finance his terrorist campaign against the common enemy.

As his camp grew, so did his following. He soon realized that having close to 150 well-armed soldiers in one location was becoming too conspicuous. The Protector, therefore, decided to change his group's guerrilla-like structure and establish within the surrounding towns and villages a terrorist-cell format. Thus was the LRF formed. The base camp in the mountains became a narcotics farm and a training facility. It was hidden well enough that very few outside the group knew it was there; nevertheless, the Protector regularly packed up camp and moved deeper into the mountains, often straying across the less-marshalled Syrian border.

The farms soon multiplied, and his workforce grew. At first, Hezbollah leaders were aware only of the LRF's training facilities, and they soon began working with the Protector to train "foreign interests" who were also struggling for revolt or freedom in various parts of the world. Again, the Protector sensed opportunity, especially with the Europeans, and he soon began selling heroin through contacts provided by his terrorist cousins. His heroin-for-arms business soon became very lucrative, and his power base grew immense. Eventually Hezbollah were subcontracting terrorist operations to the LRF outside Middle Eastern borders.

As the Protector's small group now approached the cache in the hills, the leader spotted four of his comrades coming from the opposite direction. These soldiers were the mules that he would use from time to time to carry all manner of contraband, and they were now returning from being tasked to retrieve the goods from the aborted Turkish transaction that he had ordered, based on the information gathered from Samman, the grocer. The Turks involved, whose corpses now lay strewn across a trash dump in the outskirts of Beirut, were each missing an eye; these were now handed to the Protector. Identification from the four bodies was removed a day earlier and sent to a contact in the Turkish terrorist organization, the PKK, who were the supposed recipients of the illicit goods.

The message was clear: Lebanon was now closed to Turkey for the Lebanese heroin trade. The Protector did not realize it, and he probably didn't care, but with these actions, he had just sparked a minor crisis in Lebanese/Turkish underground relations.

DAY 3
GRUNEWALD, BERLIN

Richard Nash sat in the rear of his chauffeured BMW, pretending to read the newspaper he held in one hand while expertly swinging an oversize cup of coffee to the motion of the car with his other. The chief of the CIA's station in Germany had just left his home and was on his usual Wednesday morning ride to the office. The idea of the swinging motion was to keep as much coffee in his cup until he and Chris were out and away from the bumpy road that led up to his residence in the posh Berlin suburb of Grunewald. It was only when Chris had managed to get into regular commuter traffic that Nash could relax a little and actually begin to read his newspaper and enjoy his beverage. Chris was still on high alert, however, tuned into his surroundings, his antenna up scanning for possible what-if scenarios.

Although the typical morning pleasantries between driver and principal had been exchanged at the house, not a word was spoken again until the car was humming along the highway. Nash finally broke the silence. "How are you doing, Chris?" he inquired.

Chris briefly looked into his rearview mirror and could see that the newspaper was down. He knew his boss wanted to talk. "I'm fine, Mr. Nash. Thanks for asking."

"I guess things are settling down a bit for you now after the Bonn episode?"

"Yes, I suppose so, although I think that Mr. Bowman still wants to talk to me."

"Yes he probably will need to at some stage; investigations like this could go on for a while yet. I'll give him a call and see what I can find out."

Chris let the statement hang, deciding not to reply and instead just to concentrate on his work.

"I'm going to be out of town next week," Nash continued. "Why don't you take a bit of time off as well? You must still have quite a bit of vacation coming to you."

"I do, sir, but there is still work to do. I mean I still need to run decoys and such. Just because you're away, it doesn't mean that people need to *know* you're away."

Nash smiled; he had to admire the young man's commitment to his work. Yet he thought it was more important that Morehouse take some time to regroup. He didn't want to see so much potential destroyed over an incident his driver hadn't yet been fully prepared for. "I think we can let that one go for a while, Chris," he said. "Go ahead, make some plans, get out of Berlin, and go get some sun or something."

Chris glanced back to his mirror. The paper was back up; the conversation was over. "Okay," he acceded. "I'll see what's available. I'll get your itinerary from Carla and work around your schedule."

But Chris still had things on his mind. "Mr. Nash," he began, "sorry to disturb you, but there is something else."

Nash lowered the paper again and looked deeply into the eyes of his driver, reflected in the rear-view mirror. "What's wrong Chris?"

"It's about the attack. I remember, I mean, I have a feeling about something—something that wasn't right."

Nash hesitated for a moment and stared out of his side window. "All right, Chris. Why don't you stop by later on? I'll get Bowman to come up, and we'll talk it through. Give Carla a call for a time frame—probably in a few hours or so, okay?"

Chris removed a sweaty palm from the steering wheel and rubbed his trouser leg. "Okay. Thanks, Mr. Nash." He looked back into the mirror, and the paper was back up.

DAY 4
US EMBASSY, MITTE, BERLIN

Ambassador Heymann's presence was requested in Washington. The US State Department, in its infinitive wisdom, had decided it was time to discuss the Bonn incident with him face to face. Heymann still had a few days left before his departure, and even though he remained under police protection, he still maintained a busy schedule of dinners with his foreign counterparts, receptions at the various German ministries, and some high-level discussions with large industry investors, one of which was the German car manufacturer BMW.

Headquartered in Munich in southern Germany, the Bavarian automotive giant was expanding its market in various regions throughout the world, including the United States. For a number of years, BMW had a manufacturing plant in Spartanburg, South Carolina, for the specific intention of a high-stakes rollout of the BMW Z3 sports car. The two-seater roadster was initially designed with mainly the American driver in mind, but sales were booming in the United States, and demand elsewhere around the world made BMW's prospects for the little sports car seem very bright indeed.

As such, Heymann was invited to attend a formal reception whereby official notification would be given to the press of the well-known fact that the South Carolina plant would move into phase two of its operations and hire an extra five hundred workers from the local community to meet the high demand of the Z3. The real purpose of inviting Heymann to BMW headquarters before the press conference was for the CEO to say, essentially, *How about that tax break, Uncle Sam?*

The ambassador's flight left the private side of Berlin Tegel Airport exactly on time at 0800 on a grey drizzly Thursday morning. Heymann planned to stay in Munich for the day visiting BMW, and he also intended to stop by the US Consulate in Munich as a courtesy to his friend and colleague, the US consulate general. His plan was to return to Berlin that evening, spend Friday finishing up at the embassy, and then depart early for Washington on Saturday morning.

In light of the recent attack on Heymann, BMW sent their private Learjet for the VIP. Heymann and his small entourage boarded without much fuss; the ambassador was keen to get the morning's activities behind him. As he settled back for the hour-and-a-half flight to Franz-Josef-Strauss Airport north of Munich, the ambassador's German police protective detail were frantically skirmishing with their colleagues, each group vying to be the main guard on the ground to meet him. Ambassador Heymann was to be met by the Bavarian State Police, who had jurisdiction for the area he was visiting and, therefore in their eyes, were in charge of his protective duties. The State Police of Brandenburg, where the US embassy in Berlin resided, had other ideas: Heymann was *their* charge, and they therefore sent their own protection team to Munich via car to act as the lead protection unit. The double protection, however, created a mismatch of communications.

Since the attack in Bonn, the BKA had not been sleeping. They were investigating a number of leads in the same methodical fashion that had netted them a number of high-profile captures within the notorious German Red Army Faction (RAF) in the seventies and eighties. As the investigation on the Bonn attack widened to include a number of German states, snippets of information were fed to the General Kommissar of Polizei in Berlin, the US State Department, and the FBI. From the Kommissar, information was passed to the Brandenburg polizei, who analyzed the information but did not disseminate the data to the rival state police departments—especially not the Bavarians. In the minds of the low-level police bureaucrats, that was a job for the BKA.

This type of rivalry—or as some in the executive protection business would say, childishness—began as far back as 1977 when the RAF successfully kidnapped the German industrialist Hans-Martyn Schleyer. In that case, the Bavarian police were tasked with protecting one of their own native sons, who also happened to be high on the list of potential capitalist targets for the left-wing RAF terrorist group. Schleyer, who usually traveled the country extensively, was working in Cologne for an extended period of time, and the Bavarian polizei, while working hundreds of miles from home, refused to cooperate with their local counterparts since their methods differed greatly and the Bavarians were convinced their way was the correct way to protect a fellow Bayerische mensch.

As fate would have it, on the day Schleyer was kidnapped by the RAF, his stubborn but proud Bavarian protective detail were all killed when they could not radio for help, as they were not even on the same frequency as the local police department. The reputation of Bavarian ineptitude and arrogance stuck, and few people wanted much to do with them for decades thereafter.

From Heymann's perspective, both the Bavarians and the Brandenburg polizei had people on the ground and were making their final preparations for his visit; the ambassador was just along for the ride until he had to don his diplomatic hat and wave the Stars and Stripes.

CHAPTER
FOUR

DAY 4

BAVARIA, GERMANY

A WHITE TRANSIT VAN, SIMILAR TO THE ONE USED IN THE BONN ATTACK, was identified by the BKA as a potential transport vehicle for a suspect group of Turkish militants based in the Düsseldorf area—a group they had been observing for some time. The license plate number of that van, however, was the crucial piece of information that was never filtered down to the Bavarian Police.

The suspect van now sat in the parking lot of the Gasthof Neuwirt, a boarding house approximately five kilometers from the Munich airport. At 0905, the driver of a brown Mercedes dropped off two young Arab-looking men outside the abode. The twosome quickly found the locked vehicle at the back of the gravel parking lot and, with keys already provided, got in and drove through the village of Halbergmoos, heading north toward the airport. Within eight minutes, they had driven past their objective and were heading for their holding position at a parking area in the village of Altmoching. Only two minutes from the holding position was Tor 15 (Gate 15) of the Munich Airport.

Tor 15 was one of many "crash gates" that surrounded the airport that was constructed for emergency services, which needed quick access to the outer areas of the airport. What was so special about this particular gate was that it was also built near an observation mound for amateur plane-spotters that was higher in the center than the three-meter-high fence line. To the left of the mound was a set of bushes, which provided enough cover for a large vehicle and a man to stand alongside without being seen by the distant airport authorities.

At 0920, the white van left its holding position and arrived at Tor 15 exactly two minutes later. Hassan, the driver, parked the van off the side of the road behind the bushes. His colleague, Ali, pulled out a set of binoculars from his backpack and, without a word, headed for the observation mound. To the casual observer, Ali looked to be just another plane-spotter going about his hobby. As he scanned the air for his target, however, Hassan was busy unloading a US-made surface-to-air Stinger missile from the back of the van.

The Learjet, readying to land, came into view as predicted. Now timing was everything. The Stinger was already unpacked, charged, and ready for its victim. Although they had practiced time and time again, Ali and Hassan had not considered the heavy rain that had poured down on Munich the night before. As Hassan came out of hiding with the Stinger on his shoulder, he ran to the mound but slipped on the still-wet grass. He fell hard, and the nose end of the firing tube dug into the nearby soft grass.

Ali, who was still focusing with the binoculars and counting down the range to target, was expecting Hassan already to be at his side and in the firing position. As Hassan fell, he spewed out a dozen curses that distracted Ali from his task. Ali, realizing what was happening, grabbed Hassan by the scruff of the neck and dragged him the rest of the way up the mound. During the ruckus, Ali dropped his binoculars into the mud at his feet. Hassan finally regained his composure and reached his firing position, awaiting orders from his observer. This time it was Ali's turn to curse as he set about the task of cleaning mud from the lenses of the binoculars. The plan was in danger of falling apart when Hassan, who could now see the jet clearly with his bare eyes, aimed the Stinger in its general direction— although he thought it was too late as the Learjet was almost touching down. What was worse, the jet was landing on a strip much further away than the one that was planned. Both men began to mentally question the intelligence that they had been given. It did not matter, as Hassan heard the familiar warbling tone that the Stinger sang as it acquired a target, and as he was trained to do when he heard that sound, he pulled the trigger.

The missile left the tube at supersonic speed just as Ambassador Heymann was touching down at Furstenfeldbruck Military Air Base on the Western outskirts of Munich. The BKA's suspicions had been substantial enough that they had quickly made the necessary changes to the ambassador's planned flight. Back at Franz-Josef-Strauss Airport to the North of Munich, the Stinger had just destroyed a Learjet, which, if Ali had had clean binoculars, could have identified as a jet without the tell-tale BMW logo on its tail fin. Instead, a Russian oil tycoon of dubious character, his mistress, two bodyguards, and his flight crew all lost their lives. The BKA never intended for the Russian to be killed; however, it was convenient that blame for the flight's loss could easily be laid at the hands of organized Russian crime and not terrorists who had slipped through federal surveillance.

DAY 7
LARNACA, CYPRUS

Four days later after his conversation with Nash, Chris found himself waking suddenly as the German LTU jet touched down at Larnaca Airport in Cyprus. The flight from Berlin was only four and a half hours long, but as soon as he boarded the plane and strapped himself in, he fell asleep. Chris always managed to sleep on planes; he realized that this was the only time that he could really switch off—no phones, no emails, no paperwork, no work. For Chris there was no point in worrying about turbulence or midair crashes; everything up there was out of his control. And in keeping up with another old army tradition, he subscribed to the idea that if you're not busy doing something useful, you should sleep— because you never know when you'll get a chance again.

For the moment, he was traveling alone. He had planned to meet up with Astrid for a four-day extended weekend getaway. However, to do so, she had to switch Lufthansa flights with a colleague and work a flight to Paris first. So Chris basically had twenty-four hours on the Mediterranean island to himself. His plan was simple: get a few beers at the hotel bar and crash out early.

During the buildup to the holiday, he had contemplated once again coming clean with Astrid. Up until this point, he had never told her of his work. She thought he was just another embassy driver, and he thought that she wouldn't believe him or take him seriously. But after Bonn, he realized he needed his partner to understand the risks and the importance of his commitment to what he was doing. Yet the last thing that he needed was her spouting off to her Lufthansa colleagues during a flight that her boyfriend worked for the CIA. The strain of the rocky relationship was coming to a head again, and in his mind, to improve things, he needed to step up a gear and get closer to his partner. Maybe during their time together away from Berlin, away from their jobs, he could loosen up and tell her the truth—and perhaps earn a bit more respect and understanding from her in the process.

As he left the plane, Chris automatically went into high-observation mode; it was second nature to him now, whether he liked it or not. Often times, though, it could be fun, a game. He laughed inwardly as he noted all manner of small security flaws around the airport and managed to identify immediately the official police officers and security teams and also what Chris deemed as the undercover cops.

As he surveyed his surroundings, he had a brief Homer Simpson *doh!* moment and was forced to snap out of his routine as he realized that the game was also being directed at him. Chris's offensive attitude and bearing made others like him aware that he was observant. The negative side to this was that the friendly forces on the ground did not know if Chris was a colleague or an adversary. As he waited for his baggage at the carousel he noticed that more than one pair of eyes were on him. Cyprus, after all, was a convenient hop, skip, and jump away from the turbulent Middle East, and both the bad guys and the good guys knew it was a hot hub for all types of illegal and dangerous activity and accompanying policing. Chris needed to shake the image he was presenting and get the eyes off his back.

When his luggage eventually came around the conveyer belt, he made a show of bumping into people to get to it. As he retrieved his one and only suitcase, he pretended to check the label, but in actuality, he loosened its catches. When he attempted to walk away with the case in hand, it split open, splaying all its contents across the floor. This obviously drew more attention to him, but on the other hand it made the local security think, *What an idiot!* Not satisfied with performing Bozo the Clown for a small audience, Chris deliberately left a pair of shorts behind as he was repacking the case. The result was effective, as other travelers began laughing and shouting at him to retrieve his belongings. Chris gingerly picked up the shorts, outwardly smiling sheepishly but inwardly feeling quite gratified at his performance.

After finally passing through Customs—where he was not checked but waived through—he wandered the airport for another twenty minutes, as if lost. His attempt to make himself look like a loser was successful: The locals were now concentrating not on him but on a loud group of drunken Dutch tourists who were getting slightly out of hand at the Customs desk. Only when Chris was in the back of a taxi on the way to his hotel did he allow a satisfied smile to spread across his face while he thought seriously to himself, *Lesson learned, dumbass. If you're on vacation, act as if you're on vacation.*

———— ∞ ————

Three hours later, a report of Chris's airport antics was sitting in front of Richard Nash. As he perused the details, he allowed himself a big grin, and his decision, although made much earlier, was finalized as he prepared a cable to Washington.

———— ∞ ————

Chris's plans just to enjoy a few beers in the poolside bar of the hotel did not go well. He had indeed started off slow, but soon a few more Brit tourists appeared, and the talk turned to an upcoming cup final football game of Liverpool versus Manchester United. Of course, a heavy drinking session ensued.

He woke the next morning with a sore head and a slightly guilty conscience. He remembered that during his drunken state the night before, he had almost picked up the poolside barmaid. Whether she had played too hard to get or he was too drunk for her to bother, he did not know; the only thing that he was aware of was that he luckily woke up alone. It was approaching midday when he finally dragged himself out of bed. He had about three hours before he was to meet Astrid.

He felt crusty and lightheaded. But instead of jumping immediately into the shower, he put on his exercise gear and headed for the hotel sports club. From experience he knew that the best way to kill a hangover was to sweat it out and then have a cold shower. He got on the treadmill and began pumping out the miles. The only problem with this theory was that his stomach on these occasions often out-ruled his will to flush the alcohol out via sweat. Within fifteen minutes he was throwing up in the gym bathroom. It wasn't anything unusual—this was also part of an old, tried-and-many-times-tested hangover remedy.

After spending close to ten minutes making best friends with the toilet bowl, Chris got to grips and made his way back up to his room for a well-deserved cold shower. Forty-five minutes later after he had shit, showered, and shaved, he was back on track. He headed down to the hotel bar once again, hoping that the young girl from the night before would not be there to embarrass him. He sighed with relief that she was not.

After reading a copy of the trashy UK tabloid *The Sun* back to back and having consumed a fair-sized pot of tea, Chris decided to surprise Astrid at the airport. He began making his way out there in a rental car that was delivered to the hotel for him that morning. Although he'd be early by about thirty minutes, he decided that perhaps that was good; he was definitely going to switch off and play tourist for a change.

After parking the car, he wandered over to arrivals, where he found a good vantage point to camp out and wait for Astrid, a few local tourist brochures in hand to keep him occupied. As he was waiting, he took in his surroundings. He watched a grand melee of mothers, fathers, brothers, sisters, and grandparents, all eagerly waiting for a loved one to return from overseas trips. Chris could never get excited on these occasions, as he had seen it time and time again at airports: mothers pushing their luck by trying to get into the inner restricted areas; kids running wild, not sure what to expect; and fathers pacing nervously as they'd parked their cars illegally just outside the arrivals door.

Chris finally spotted Astrid, her leggy form struggling to get her pull-along baggage through a scrum of families tied up in a knot at the arrivals gate. He made a move forward to greet her but paused for a second longer as his instincts told him something was wrong.

He was right. Astrid was not alone. In tow was a tall, dark-haired man that he recognized as one of Astrid's crew. It was not strange for crewmembers to work together on numerous flights, but the problem was that neither of them was wearing their Lufthansa uniforms, and there was something about their body language that did not seem right. They were both moving in unison, as if connected by a short string, and they were moving way too close together to be just colleagues.

Chris's heart dropped like a stone. He tried to move, but his legs froze in place. Then instead of willing himself forward, he took a step backwards, out of sight and further away from the arrivals gate, behind a pillar. Perhaps it was innocent enough; perhaps he misread the situation—after all the battle with the hangover was not completely won, and his judgment was probably still a little cloudy. Something was off, though, and he needed to find out what the hell was going on. As he regained control of his emotions, he started to move back around the pillar and towards Astrid.

As he did so, he collided with someone. "Sorry," Chris automatically said, but the man with the square neck and short haircut did not look back and did not apologize himself. Chris was a little perturbed by this—

it took two to tango—however, he had other things on his mind, and he began to take a few steps away when he froze again as he realized exactly who he had bumped into: Trenchcoat.

Chris's world was now turning upside down as a myriad of thoughts and emotions exploded inside of him. He was faced with two choices: He either had to challenge his girlfriend or follow the man that he thought he recognized as Trenchcoat. He first scanned the concourse to find Astrid; he spotted her standing near one of the exit doors in what seemed like an in-depth conversation with her colleague. She was pointing at her watch, and the man she was with looked as if he was leaning in to kiss her.

Chris spun around quickly to look for Trenchcoat and spotted him heading for the rental car services. He tried his best to memorize the man's description: roughly six feet tall, slim build, around 180 pounds, blue eyes that could have pierced armor plate, blond close-cropped hair, a deep tan, and Beach Boy smile; a typical aging early forties surfer dude. Chris took one more look back at Astrid and saw that she was hugging her co-worker and then said to himself, *Fuck this news*—and made a move after Trenchcoat.

Chris maintained a safe distance from his new target. His quarry, on the other hand, was not practicing any kind of field tactics that Chris had played around with only the day before. The simple reason for this was that Trenchcoat was not alone. It looked to Chris as if a minder had appeared not more than five feet away from Trenchcoat, and there was another player circulating the hallways, doing a pretty bad impression of being nonchalant, trying to blend in. Before the player could identify Chris, he dived into an open elevator in an attempt to make it back to his car. It was obvious that Trenchcoat was there to pick up a rental, so why bother waiting around?

Chris walked at a brisk pace back to the parking lot. He found his car and retrieved his camera from a bag in the trunk. Timing was of the essence. From his previous observations, he knew where the rental agencies parked their cars, and he headed on foot in that direction. There were only three rental agencies to choose from anyway—Avis, Hertz, and Budget—so the odds were in favor of him spotting Trenchcoat and his team.

Unfortunately when he got there, there was no one in sight. He had circled the underground parking area a couple of times, and he knew it was just a matter of time before he'd be noticed and questioned by a rental car employee—or worse, a security guard. Chris was beginning to think that his luck had run out, and as he was pacing through the garage he started to question his actions again. *This is bullshit—what am I doing? This is definitely not my job. What am I going to do if I see him?* Nevertheless, he held his camera in his right hand down by his side. He was no expert photographer, nor was he trained in taking surveillance pictures, but he knew he at least had to try. His need for answers from Bonn was overriding his better judgment in Cyprus.

As he continued to walk through the parking lot, he heard a car approach and glanced over his shoulder. He saw a silver Mercedes with three people inside, slowly approaching him. He spotted a man in the passenger seat with a blond buzz cut.

Chris wasn't sure if this was what he was looking for, but without raising his camera, he began taking pictures with his right hand down by his side. At the same time he covered his face with his left hand, as if he was sneezing. He must have gotten five or six shots off by the time the car had passed; he felt certain he had gotten the license plate, but he was not sure what else he had captured. Now the question was what should he do with the information? After Chris had aired his thoughts in Bonn before the trip, he realized that Nash wasn't wholly convinced that the Trenchcoat lead was valid. Bowman thought the driver was just trying to get more recognition and blew him off completely.

As Chris headed back to his car, his mind raced. *What the hell's going on? Why is Trenchcoat here? Who is he? I've got to get to the phone. I need to call the boss. But what if I'm wrong? I'll really look like a dickhead. Shit! What the hell am I doing?*

Uncertainty aside, he quickened his pace and tried in vain to memorize every little detail from the last thirty minutes. The problem was that the images of Astrid being at the airport with another man confused his thought processes. He tried to put those behind him and focus on the problem at hand but knew he would have to deal with Astrid somehow and sometime very soon.

The search for his rental car was taking too long, and he realized that he was on the wrong floor of the parking garage. Time was ticking away. Chris made his way to the stairs to get back up a level. As he entered the stairwell, he again began to think about what he saw. *Why is a guy like that chaperoned by two players like that? Why is he here? Who is this guy?"*

Again his lack of experience plagued him, and he felt a sense of apprehension as he kept hearing Astrid's words, *"Chris you are just a driver.*

Don't you understand? You just drive people around and carry their bags for them ..." He tried to wipe them from his mind and quickened his pace, taking the steps two at a time. A plan was forming in his mind: *Get the car; get to a phone. Should I get to the embassy? Maybe I should just leave this alone ..."*

BOOM! The door at the top of the stairs flew open, straight into his face. Chris was knocked totally off balance and fell backwards down the stairs. For him, it seemed as if someone had suddenly turned out all the lights in Cyprus.

Chris was brought back to his senses when he heard the cries of a baby. He struggled to open his eyes and focus on his surroundings as the cries grew louder and the agitated voice of a young mother blabbered in what sounded like incoherent Greek. As he tried to get up, he realized that he was at the bottom of the stairs facing the wrong way with one shoe missing and his shirt halfway up his back. As he managed to get into a sitting position, the woman was still yammering at a hundred miles an hour at the top of the stairs. He looked at her and said in a semi-confident tone, "It's okay, luv. I'm all right. I just fell down the stairs." She obviously didn't understand a word because she kept going on, and the baby on her arm kept crying.

The mother eventually produced a pack of tissue and, while almost losing her own footing on the stairs, made her way next to Chris and began dabbing at his nose, only for him to realize that he was bleeding and now feeling pretty nauseous again. The mother, finally fed up with the cries of her child, threw the pack of tissues to Chris, said something unintelligible, and walked back up the stairs. Before she opened the door to the parking lot, she hesitated and took one last look at Chris at the bottom of the stairs. "Drunken Engleesh pig!" she shouted, and stormed away. Chris perked up to that one.

"Drunk? What the hell are you talking about, woman?" he shouted back, but she was gone.

He sat there for a few minutes more, his head tilted back, trying to stem the flow of blood from his nose. His senses slowly started returning as he felt his body beginning to ache in a number of places. His head throbbed, and he felt a large bump forming at the back; luckily he wasn't bleeding there. Both his elbows were scuffed up, and his back felt like ten cats had stretched their claws all over his skin. He gave himself a minute more, but then felt a cold, wet sensation all the way up the left side of his leg to his hip. He reached back to figure out what it was when he saw a broken bottle of whiskey at the foot of the stair, next to his missing shoe. He took one whiff of his hand and realized that the drunken pig reference must have seemed quite accurate. "Great, just great—I hate whiskey," he said to nobody in particular.

Chris finally got back on his feet, dusted himself off, and retrieved his shoe. He had to steady himself on the handrail, and he climbed back up the stairs to go again in search of his car. He wasn't sure if he was going to make it without throwing up or passing out. "This is a great way to start a holiday!" he blurted out loud. As he made his way out of the stairwell and across the parking deck, he drew a few glances from other travelers and thought, *Well at least I'm keeping up the appearance of a typical Brit on holiday—I must look like shit.*" He tried feebly to quicken his pace before other caring mothers decided to throw some obscenities his way.

He finally made it to his car and immediately took a look in the mirror to assess the damage. His nose was turning purple, and a black mark was forming under his right eye. The eye itself was swollen. Dried blood was evident all over his chin and down past his Adam's apple; he did indeed look and felt like shit. Chris then pulled out his wallet from the front pocket of his jeans to look for his parking ticket and some cash. Finding both, he turned on the ignition, put it in reverse, then suddenly stopped and said out loud, "Where's my fucking camera?"

Chris's camera was being expertly dismantled by one of four people riding in a silver Mercedes heading out and away from the Larnaca International Airport. Kostas Kidis, a local customs official, was driving the car that had picked up Trenchcoat and his team as planned at the Avis counter. Chris's assumption about the group picking up a rental car was incorrect. It was a good theory; however, his own experience at being followed and watched didn't mean that he was an expert at actually following and watching others.

Trenchcoat had spotted Chris as he had exited from another gate at the arrivals terminal; however, he needed to be sure that the man standing less than thirty feet away from him was in fact the same person he had seen driving Heymann away from the attack scene in Bonn. His quickly formulated plan was to bump Chris and wait to see what reaction he got. One of Trenchcoat's men, call sign Preacher, later confirmed that the subject looked surprised as he stared back at Trenchcoat after the contact.

Trenchcoat decided to act and sent Preacher to circle around behind Chris and observe his actions. It was only through Preacher's initiative and split-second decision making that he retrieved the camera, which he was now holding in his hands.

Not many words were spoken in the car, but Trenchcoat was worried, wondering to himself, *Are we under surveillance? Was it just a coincidence?* His instincts told him no, the driver was a novice; there was no way he could have followed and tracked Trenchcoat and his team to Cyprus. He had covered his tracks well, even meeting his team members Preacher and Danny in Amsterdam shortly after the botched Munich operation. He rationalized that it must have been simply fortuitous, but he decided he also needed to take more precautions and utilize Preacher and Danny to the best of their abilities. He knew that he had two reliable men whom he could count on: The two former Green Berets were professional, loyal, discreet, and took orders without question; furthermore, he paid them well.

Money was not the motivating factor for Preacher, who now contemplated his actions from a short while before. Being thoroughly the professional that he considered himself to be, he analyzed the way he took his target down and how quickly he retrieved the camera. He could see room for improvement, especially when he thought a mother and baby had spotted him coming out of the garage stairwell, but it was an on-the-fly plan, and it had worked. Although he had been doing this kind of work for some time, he still, nevertheless, enjoyed it and gave himself a quick mental pat on the back.

This was why he worked for his former commander; this was the work that Preacher relished—having the chance to work on unorthodox projects and special missions. There were no hard and fast rules; you had to think on your feet or get hurt. Always on the edge—that's what he lived for.

Virgil McCain, known as call sign Preacher, had been a Green Beret for six years when his wife of two years urged him to give up the long spells away from home, the secretiveness of his work, and the resulting heavy drinking binges. Begrudgingly, he gave into his wife's demands and left the only family he had known. After a couple of years of drifting between meaningless jobs outside the military, he landed a relatively good security job protecting oil-rich Arabs living in the United States. By that time, his wife had left him anyway because he could still not become the stable, responsible family man that she needed, and his only friends were his army buddies—who were still living the life that he wanted.

McCain realized that—screw the wife—he never should have left the military. He was a soldier, and nothing else mattered—that was his life, that was what he was cut out for, and that was what he would die for. One night while he was on duty at a large suburban villa his Arab clients had rented in Scottsdale, Arizona, repeated calls for him over the radio went unanswered. He was eventually found behind a garage, in a fit of depression, holding a Smith and Wesson revolver in his mouth.

It was only a former Marine, also on duty that night at the villa that talked him out of killing himself. He pointed McCain in the direction of the Veterans Administration for help; the Marine had been there too.

What was not known to men who had left the military but who still craved the life, like McCain, was that in preparation for covert paramilitary operations around the world, ex-Special Forces like the Green Berets—who had specialized skills and aptitude—were kept on secret short-lists held by agencies like the CIA, NSA, and Department of Defense. It was easy enough for government agencies to call on active-duty personnel for legitimate operations, but when things were needed in a hurry and off the record, ex-military types were often called upon to serve as contractors, to be dropped into hot zones before the men in green showed up.

As soon as McCain entered himself into a program of counseling, however, his name was taken off the secret government list, and his fate was sealed; he would never serve his government again.

After the incident in Scottsdale, McCain let everything go. He joined a biker gang, performed some petty crimes, gained weight and sported a droopy Hulk Hogan mustache, began covering himself with tattoos and all around lived life rough. He was always one step ahead of the law but was pretty close to choosing a full-time life of crime. Although he was no longer suicidal, he still didn't care about life as he knew it.

One of the few people who had access to the government's ex-Special Forces list was one of McCain's former commanders, who paid him a visit one night at a local biker bar. The commander suggested that McCain could be employed in the line of work he relished but outside the US government. It was the lifeline that Virgil needed; finally again, someone wanted him for his skills, his military expertise. Once more, it was his chance to prove himself.

The commander was Colonel James R. Whittaker, US Army, known to Chris only as Trenchcoat, and was part of a small private enterprise, Venture Concepts, Inc., which had the explicit purpose of penetrating security and identify weaknesses at US military bases around the world on behalf of the US government. The company had been in business for years with contracts coming in quicker than they had the manpower to cover the assignments. The company, however, was legitimate enough to stay under the radar of government watchdogs, which was quite simple with the assistance of a certain member of the Senate from Michigan who had founded the company.

As soon as Preacher joined Whittaker's team, he established a close working and social relationship with another ex-military man, call sign "Kodiak." His story was similar to Preacher's, so their bond was tight. But Kodiak's loosening grasp on reality had hit him less than two months after leaving the army.

An Alaskan native, Danny "Kodiak" Robson was honorably discharged from Fort Lewis, Washington, after agreeing that recurring back problems would prevent him from keeping his jump wings—which would there- fore force him to lose his Special Forces status. Nine and a half years of jumping out of aircraft and kicking in doors on counter-terrorist opera- tions had finally taken its toll with the highly accredited staff sergeant. He was offered a number of positions to keep him "in green," but being a regular ground-pounder or army staffer was of no interest to him, and he soon left his beloved profession.

His resulting depression surfaced when he woke to a trashed apartment one morning in the small picturesque town of Fort Steilacoom, which overlooked the sprawling Puget Sound in Washington State. As he stum- bled out of bed, he tripped over an empty bottle of Jack Daniels, which he realized he could not remember starting—it could have been twelve hours before or even two days before. He was drunk, and he had been for quite some time. He tried to get himself squared away and start tidying up the mess in the apartment, littered with empty pizza boxes and even more empty beer cans. He did not realize for some time that a strong, cold breeze was blasting its way through the living room, but when he did, he made his way over to the window that overlooked the Sound. He stopped in his tracks when he saw his old .308-sniper rifle, propped up by an old kit bag, pointing out the window.

With his heart in his mouth he took position behind the weapon and, without adjusting the alignment, took a look into the rifle's scope. It was aimed directly at the entrance to the Steilacoom passenger and car ferry, which runs to the smaller islands throughout the Sound. As he was looking down the scope, a ferry had docked and a number of foot passengers were disembarking. He could see quite plainly the faces of individuals walking up the ramp to waiting cars and buses. He turned his head away in horror and disgust and, without looking, removed the live round out of the chamber of the gun. That was the day he stopped drinking.

Throughout its inception and development, Venture Concepts' CEO, US Army Colonel James Whittaker, was continually testing his group to see who the loyal and adept members were. His smaller and less complex contracts involved his team jumping a fence at an air force base and having his guys take close-up photos of jets, helicopters, supply yards, and so on—all with the innocent but valuable intent of highlighting inadequacies in base security. They actually left messages behind in sensitive areas that read: "Hey GI, VC was here."

Under the direction of Senator Corbin, Whittaker eventually escalated the break-ins to stealing vehicles and small arms found at the bases. Whittaker told his Blue and Green teams—his less-trusted employees—that the weapons would be returned, and no harm was done. However, he had also put together a secret Red Team, comprised of his most-trusted men. This team focused on military storage facilities and stole weapons and vehicles with no return to sender intended. Thus his Blue and Green Teams continued the legitimate side of the business while his Red Team pushed the envelope.

Soon pallets of ammunition were being taken out of the ammunition bunkers and warehouse facilities with the stolen trucks and Humvees they found. The arms were then transported to a central warehouse in Michigan where a company called Dunbar Haulage would store, package, and eventually deliver them to Baltimore Harbor for shipment overseas to a number of terrorist groups and organized crime gangs on behalf of the "US Military." The only person from Dunbar who knew of the stolen hardware was Chuck Dunbar, the owner and operator of the company. Being a half-brother to Senator Robert Corbin did have its perks, after all.

The road from the Cyprus airport back to the hotel was as rough as Chris felt. It didn't take long, but his head was still throbbing and the blood inside his nose had dried up, making it difficult to breathe. Once again his thoughts ran wild as he tried to find reasons or logic for the most recent events. Chris felt that this time, however, unlike in Bonn, he was not in control—someone had controlled him, he had ended up being a target, and he didn't like it. He initially thought he had been mugged but soon dismissed the thought as his wallet, complete with all its contents, was still in his possession. He soon concluded that he had been targeted and the camera was stolen for a reason. Somehow, Trenchcoat's players had spotted him and were able to take immediate action—but then again, what the hell did he know? He was so far out of his league it wasn't even funny. He had no idea who he was dealing with, how many there were, and what they were up to. Chris's counter-surveillance mindset and positive get-out-of-jail attitude did not make him a savvy offensive player; he knew this. Chris often thought that he was very much a follower and not a leader in this game. He wondered glumly if he should just cash in his chips and get out and find something else to do.

Despite his misgivings, Chris at least knew the first steps he needed to make now: he had to get to a phone, call Nash, and explain the story, as nonsensical as it sounded; then he had to get cleaned up.

Suddenly a moment of dread surfaced: Astrid. Even with the problem of his physical state, the obvious difficulty of explaining to Nash the attack and the potential of another confrontation with Bowman, what he feared most was the inevitable encounter with his girlfriend.

He made it back to the hotel in one piece, which was more than what could be said about his rental car. As he was parking in the hotel lot, he reversed over a high curb too quickly and crumpled the underside of the rear bumper. *Some driver I am,* he thought. *Good thing Mr. Nash wasn't with me.* He didn't have time to dwell on it, however; he just had to count his losses and move on.

Walking through the hotel lobby, he couldn't help notice Astrid sitting at the bar, drinking a coffee. She also noticed him, and a look of disgust crossed her face. As Chris approached, her face turned to concern as the red blood stains on his blue shirt were as apparent as if he was carrying a neon sign that said, *I'm in trouble.* She got up from her stool at the bar and immediately put a caring hand to his face, asking, "Chris, what happened to you?"

He paused, not sure what to say. He had tried to come up with a script for this moment while he was parking (and crunching) the car, but now he was speechless.

"Chris, *was ist mit dir los?*"

Chris hesitantly replied, "I took a bit of a fall, that's all. I'm okay."

Taking a step back and looking him over, she replied with another question. "You fell over, are you sure?" Tears started to puddle in her eyes. "Chris, you promised me. You said you wouldn't drink so much again—" she began.

"Astrid, I haven't been drinking. Last night I had a few, but like I said, I just fell—"

"Don't lie to me," she shot back with a look of pure anger. "I met some of your friends while I was waiting for you. You were drunk in the bar last night, and you are drunk now. You still stink of booze. You said that you wanted to stop drinking so much. Why are you doing this—why are you doing this *to us?*" she pleaded.

"Astrid, I can explain," he said apologetically, but it was too late; tears were streaming down her face.

"Yes I had some beers last night, but it wasn't a heavy session," he lied. "And earlier at the airport—"

"Airport!" Astrid almost screamed. "You weren't at the airport—you were probably with that bar slut you picked up last night, you bastard," and she slapped Chris across the face drawing a sliver of blood from his nose. The impact sounded and felt like a boxer's bell being sounded for the last round. "What happened, Chris? Did her boyfriend show up and show you what a loser you really are?"

Chris stood silent again. The words could not, or would not, come out.

"Well, say something, dammit!" she pushed. "What happened to your face? Did you get beaten up?"

"No, Astrid. There's a lot you don't know about me," he finally responded sternly. "But we're both hiding something, aren't we?"

A perplexed-looking Astrid questioned his response. "What are you talking about?"

"I was at the airport. I saw you with your friend from Lufthansa. I actually thought most airline stewards were gay, but I guess not that one." Chris was getting his confidence back, and he knew that more was to be said. "How long have you been sleeping with him?"

Astrid remained silent for a change, and her tears dried up enough to show genuine surprise. She was usually the argumentative one, but now she was totally taken aback.

Chris pushed further. "Well, what's going on?"

"Chris, I'm sorry. I wanted to tell you, but I was not sure how or when."

His heart almost stopped for a second time in a day. He had called her bluff and was right. But this time, that didn't make him happy.

Chris took Astrid's hand and looked deeply into her eyes. "You know, I've always cared for you, always loved you, but I'm not sure if I can get through this. Why is this happening?" It was his turn to feel emotional, and although he was doing a good job of holding back his tears, he was dying inside. He kept looking into her to find an answer, but her attention was focused over his shoulder. Astrid's companion was standing less than ten feet behind him.

Chris felt the presence of someone staring at his back and turned around to see the flight attendant—with his perfect tan, perfect hair, and perfect smile. Chris was taken aback. "Mate, do us a favor and give us a few minutes, will ya?" he asked and then turned his attention back to Astrid. "Can we talk about this?" he implored.

"No, Chris, I think it's too late," she replied, although the tears were back.

"But there's still much to talk about …," he pressed.

"Excuse me, MATE," came the arrogant Germanic voice from behind him. "I don't think she wants to speak with you right now," he said as he placed a hand on Chris's right shoulder.

Without turning to face him, Chris said firmly, "Listen, Fritz or Hans or whatever, I asked you nicely to back off. If you'd give us some room … please, I'll say pretty please if you like." And then turning to his soon-to-be-former-girlfriend, he said simply, "Astrid, look, we need to talk."

"*Dirk, bitte nicht,*" she pleaded with her new companion, who still had his hand on Chris.

Dirk paid no mind. "Look, *Chris,*" he said snidely, "she does not want anything to do with you. Why don't you go and get yourself cleaned up—you're starting to stink up the place." Dirk strengthened his hold on Chris's shoulder and tried to motion him away from Astrid.

Chris dropped his head and sighed … he really didn't want to fight, but he saw where this was headed. He quickly lifted his left hand to Dirk's right hand and grabbed the other man's wrist with force. He then spun his own body towards the right and at the same time slapped the steward in the stomach with the back of his hand.

Momentarily winded by Chris's quick move, Dirk couldn't believe what was happening. Chris tightened his grip on his rival's wrist and followed through his spin by ducking under Dirk's arm and ending up behind his attacker. He then twisted the wrist around so that he had Dirk's fingers pointed upward and his arm pulled out straight. Chris increased the level of pain by pushing the fingers down hard and, with his right hand on Dirk's elbow, began pushing him down to the floor. Chris bent his right leg slightly, dropped his grip from the elbow, and pushed his left leg back as if ready for a kick.

"Chris, no, please, no!" came the screams from Astrid.

Chris held Dirk in this position and contemplated his next move. Yes, he had thought about a kick to the face or ribs, but he held back.

He held his adversary long enough to realize that the man wasn't going to be much more trouble, but every time that Dirk tried to get out of the hold, Chris would increase the pressure. Without taking his eyes off the steward, he coolly said, "Astrid, it doesn't need to end like this. If we can get a few moments alone, then I can explain."

Astrid was in shock; she had never seen Chris so composed or quick to react in a violent situation. His tone was eerily calm, too, as if he was talking about the weather or which wine to choose for dinner. She looked into his eyes, and it seemed as if he was enjoying himself. She started to move towards him. "Chris, I don't know you; I thought I did, but I obviously don't. Whatever we had is gone—it's over—let him go, please." As she was pleading she began to move forward as if to intervene. Chris countered by maneuvering Dirk as a shield between them. This caused a little more pain to Dirk, but Chris didn't care about the man. As Dirk's groans became louder, Astrid tried to help him by raising him up, which ironically caused more pain than relief.

That was when Chris realized that it was of no use. He shifted his body weight one more time, releasing his right foot to unleash a forceful kick, but he stopped short of making contact with the steward's chin, instead holding his foot in place. "Listen, MATE," he began, "I think we can stop playing now. I'm going to let you go, and let's just leave it there, okay? I'm not in the mood for pissing around like this."

He then turned his attention to Astrid but still held his foot and grip on Dirk. "I just need to get cleaned up, and I'll check out," he said to her. "Where're your things? Are they up in our room?"

She couldn't believe it—Chris was like a rock. He was still in control of Dirk, and he was talking to her as if nothing was happening. She answered sheepishly, "No, my bags are in the car outside."

"Okay, well you know where to find me if you need me," Chris replied. "I'm going to stick around here for a while. Give me a call when you're ready to talk and please don't ever forget, *Ich leibe dich.*"

He removed his right foot and released his grip. It was over. Dirk was in no shape to retaliate, enough words were spoken, and silence ensued. Chris turned and walked away but could not help but look over his shoulder one last time. Astrid was kneeling over her new boyfriend offering comfort, and neither was paying attention to him. *Maybe I did hurt the little prick after all,* he thought. *Now, what other surprises can I expect today?*

CHAPTER
FIVE

DAY 8

PORT OF LARNACA, CYPRUS

"When you get the chance, and I mean today—tonight—get rid of Kodiak."

Preacher stared back in surprise at Whittaker as his boss's words sunk in. He was about to protest, but his superior was quicker to respond.

"He's becoming too inquisitive, asking way too many questions—and we don't need him developing a conscience. Make it look like an accident." Whittaker paused for effect. "Do you have a problem with that?"

Preacher obviously did. Danny—Kodiak—was his friend as well as his comrade, but he didn't want to push his luck. He remained silent but could not look Whittaker in the eye.

"He will not leave Cyprus, Virgil. Do you understand?" Whittaker insisted. There was still no response. "Good."

Whittaker didn't want to let Preacher dwell too long on the task, so he moved on to planning. "Let's get going. The Turks should be here shortly. If I see an opportunity, I will distract Kidis or whoever else is in the area, understood?"

Preacher reluctantly nodded his reply as he repeated his adaption of Tennyson's lines to himself, *Ours is not the reason why; ours is to do or die.*

DAY 8

BEIRUT, LEBANON

Budail had been right; killing the Turks was a bad move and short-sighted on the part of his leader. Part of the tradeoff with dealing in drugs was payment in kind with the weapons they needed for the LRF. Neither Budail nor Abdul Haafiz was sure where the weapons were coming from, nor did they care. They were happy that the minimal cost of supplying the naturally grown heroin crop to junkies in Europe and elsewhere provided them with a strong arsenal to maintain the struggle against the common enemies of Lebanon.

But Budail was worried, being number two in the LRF; he was responsible for logistics and managed the transactions of drugs for weapons like a professional trader. Lebanon was known for its skilled marketing and trading capabilities, and Budail, having inherited skills from his forefathers, was equally adept at the task. Unknown to his leader, Budail had established a good working relationship with his Turkish trading partners, and heroin and weapons were not the only things that were exchanged on this part of the black market.

Everything was being bought and sold at cutthroat prices—from Nike sneakers to Mercedes limousines. For Budail, it was a fringe benefit of working in the underworld in which he readily profited. But now, one of his main supply lines was cut. Everyone knew an arms shipment from Turkey was due, and Budail had hoped to get to his Turkish partners before the LRF operations team carried out their deadly work.

It was not to be. The Turkish suppliers were dead, with their throats slit and their eyes cut out.

But Budail was not to be outdone. Yes, he would carry out his leader's wishes and establish links with the South Africans. The potential of good quality of arms was there; however, he was more interested in his own gain, his own greed. Although he was an idealist and a fanatical nationalist, he was also an entrepreneur. He was thinking about his long-term future. He knew that peace would come to the Levant one day soon and men like Abdul Al Haafiz would be searching for work and in need of an existence. Budail, on the other hand, was planning for his future and retirement now.

He therefore took it on himself to go into Turkey and re-establish ties with his contacts to ensure that his black market trade would not be endangered due to the recent killings. He also wanted to investigate the possibility of getting the arms shipment moving again or, at least, at some point in the future. He was banking on the South Africans' participation, but if he could get the Turks back in the game, he would be a rich man. He knew he was taking a risk, but he crossed into Syria and headed for Turkey with nothing but a few overnight things, a forged Turkish passport, and a lot of cash. He knew whom to contact but was not sure of the reception he was going to get; after all, he wasn't dealing with saints or angels—these were out and out thugs, and they did not hide their emotions well.

DAY 9
MUNICH INTERNATIONAL AIRPORT, GERMANY

Special Agent Nick Seymour of the FBI was searching Terminal 2 of Franz Josef Strauss Airport in Munich for his colleague John Bowman. Seymour, who was officially the assistant to Bowman at the US embassy in Berlin, was taking a vacation in the Munich area when the order came through that both Bowman and Seymour were to reach Cyprus by the fastest possible means.

It was no surprise that Bowman was frustrated over the fact that he of all people needed to rush to the Mediterranean on the whim of a driver. During his second interview with Chris in Bonn, Bowman's temper flared up, and harsh words were exchanged again—so much so that Nash considered escalating the incident to FBI headquarters in DC. Nevertheless, it was plain to everyone that there was a distinct dislike on the part of Bowman towards Morehouse.

Neither Nash nor Morehouse understood why this hatred and animosity existed. Chris took it all on board and accepted the fact that the aggression and open hostility was the norm, so he would simply have to put up with the nonsense. Besides, he had survived many a working over in his army survival-training sessions. If a barrage of abuse was what was dished out by the real feds, then he would have to suck it up and cooperate. The ironic thing, however, was that Chris was the one that had instigated the whole Trenchcoat lead. It was he coming to the investigation to *help*—he was not hindering anything.

Bowman saw things differently. Over a week had gone by since the Bonn attack, and the pressure for answers was on. It was one thing to explain away the inadequacies of the German law enforcement or the lack of co-operation from various parties—but John Bowman, veteran FBI agent, was getting absolutely nowhere, and people both near and far began to notice.

Agent Seymour finally caught up with Bowman near one of the check-in desks. The older agent had his head stuck in a public phone booth. Seymour saw that his counterpart was deeply engrossed in conversation with his hand over his mouth to avoid others reading his lips. Seymour approached but held back as Bowman noticed his partner and gave him the two-minute finger drill. Seymour thought nothing of it and backed away, planting himself at a nearby bench where he waited patiently.

Nick Seymour was the exact opposite of his seasoned partner. Bowman was the typical, strong, Irish cop with an attitude to match; Seymour was the soft-spoken, well-liked, intelligent Yale graduate. Having only been with the bureau for four years the rookie was on his first overseas assignment. To win a Germany posting was a prize worth its weight in gold to Nick and his peers.

Nick was a rising star in the ranks of the FBI. He adapted well to the internal politics and policies of the agency, which most—including his current partner—could not begin to make sense of. The young agent's rise to fame began with a string of money-laundering arrests, which made him a hot prospect for senior management, as the bureau's interest in white-collar crime was extremely popular. It was during this time that a number of federal agencies were re-evaluating their financial existence, as the end of the Cold War dissolved the war chests on which they happily survived. Nobody was chasing the KGB in Washington, DC, anymore; what the bureau needed now in a time of economic and political change were bright people who could both count beans and make arrests. The one thing Nick lacked, however, was overseas field experience; hence the plum Germany posting.

After waiting a few minutes more for his partner, Seymour could tell that it was going to be a while and sauntered off to find some reading material for the journey. He knew that very few words about the mission would be exchanged on the plane; mum would be the word until they arrived in the safe confines of the US Consulate in Cyprus. Although Seymour needed to be brought up to speed on the hasty travel request to get to the island resort, his professional attitude to operational security would prevent him from pushing Bowman for information. That is, unless the senior agent instigated a conversation, which, Seymour rationalized, would be highly unlikely since his boss was a stickler for being tight-lipped even in the best of times.

As it turned out, Seymour was correct. A few pleasantries were exchanged when Bowman got off the phone, but nothing was mentioned about the job at hand. The younger man realized that Bowman was in a foul mood, a little worse than usual even, and therefore he decided to kick back on the plane, catch up with his daily newspaper reading, and simply wait for further instructions.

The flight took off without incident, and the tough old Irishman fell asleep almost immediately. Nick concentrated on the financial section of the *New York Times*, and his mind began to play with the figures in front of him.

Three and a half hours into the flight, the plane reached the edge of the Mediterranean Sea. Unbeknownst to the FBI agents flying thirty-four thousand feet above the blue water, directly below their position was the freighter *SS Juno*, formerly known as the *SS Claudia*, registered out of Liberia, which was steaming its way through relatively calm seas to the very same island destination. The freighter, battered and bruised from years at sea, was on its final leg from Baltimore and the Canary Islands with a deadly cargo generously supplied by the "US Military."

———

The *Juno*, which actually began its career as a gun runner many years prior, was the perfect vessel to ship illicit cargoes. When it was known as the *Claudia*, in 1987 the freighter made the headlines when it was intercepted by the Irish Navy off the coast of the Emerald Isle, with weapons destined for the IRA. Unlike Senator Corbin, the supplier of the cargo back then was already the highest power in his land and sought no further political gain other than to assist in bringing down the West by whichever means necessary. By losing his cargo with the *Claudia*, however, Muammar Gaddafi, merely shrugged off the incident, played innocent for a while, and redirected his anti-Western actions to other interests in the Middle East.

Initially impounded by the Irish Navy and after a thorough investigation, the *Claudia* was simply sold at auction to the highest bidder and picked up by a consortium of presumably legitimate German businessmen, whose interest in the vessel was merely for haulage around the rough seas of the Baltic. Unbeknownst to the Irish authorities at the time, the "German businessmen" were a group of East German State secret service agents (the Stasi) whose intentions through its front company was haulage—but it also transported cargoes of the harmful kind.

This was not the first time the *Claudia* had been in the hands of the Stasi. Before Gaddafi loaded his stock on the vessel, the ship was owned by a Hamburg businessman, Max Kohler, who was known as an underground arms supplier and someone who acted as a go-between for criminal gangs, terrorist organizations, and corrupt or rogue states. Most of Kohler's weaponry was of Soviet make, and his suppliers were the Stasi, who simply traded on behalf of the KGB.

During the Cold War, Directorate V of the KGB ran schools, which the West thought were gulags in northern Russia. These camps were actually specialized terrorist training schools with one mission in mind—to use terrorist cells and nationals from other countries to fight on behalf of the Soviet Union when the time came. Until the inevitable war with the capitalist West began, the KGB left the terror groups to conduct a campaign of mayhem in the Middle East and elsewhere around the globe.

Thus the loop was closed: the terror groups had a cause and needed training and weapons; the KGB needed subversives to disrupt and distract Western forces; the Stasi from East Germany traded through the West with people like Kohler; and ships like the *Claudia* were used to supply the demand. The wheel of fortune broke only when a junior East German bureaucrat misspoke during a press conference in Berlin and announced mistakenly that the East German people were free to come and go to the West through the wall as often as they wished.

The fall of the Berlin Wall began that day in 1989, and the chain of events that transpired thereafter ended the Cold War, the Communist Empire, and the Soviet state-sponsored terrorism against the West. Nevertheless, disgruntled Stasi officers still wanted action; they still believed in the glory of the Communist Party and hated the capitalist machine with a vengeance. Though wise enough to realize that overt actions could not breed success, especially since most of them were now marked men, an outlet was needed.

After Max Kohler was released from his ownership with the capture of the *Claudia*, he made his way to Berlin to reacquaint himself with his former arms suppliers. During that time, the Stasi questioned Kohler's other exploits and the procurement of weaponry other than that from the Soviet arsenal. As it turned out, there was a slow trickle of arms coming from the United States—albeit in low quantity but with very high price margins. The source of those weapons was a former staff sergeant at a US Army armory in Kentucky, who upon being investigated for his activities committed suicide by blowing himself up in his car with some stolen munitions. Part of the investigative team into the debacle was a certain Captain Whittaker, who had full access to the case materials on the suspect. Conveniently, before Kohler could be implicated again in an international arms smuggling ring, the names of Kohler and Whittaker were never seen together on a piece of paper or brought up together in any conversations—or so Whittaker thought.

As the Stasi was crumbling along with the wall in 1989, Western intelligence agencies lined up en masse at the gates of the Stasi headquarters on Normannenstrasse in the Lichtenberg district of East Berlin. The wall was being hammered into thousands of pieces around the city; at the same time, Stasi agents worked around the clock shredding and burning as much confidential material as possible. When it became apparent that their efforts were fruitless—the shredders broke down, and the burning was taking too long—they began to tear up documents by hand. But it was still not enough.

The CIA, MI6, and the French DGSE were some of the first to pour through the gates at the massive fortress-like structure, which was surrounded by a mob of disgruntled and recently made, new Germans. Although the horde of civilians mostly burst through the gates to salvage personal information, the newly arrived intelligence officers were tipped off on where to look first for the files that were vital to their respective countries.

The success of those raids uncovered a whole host of information on individuals involved in espionage around the world, as well as agents in East and West Germany who were either in the employ of the Stasi or their masters, the KGB. The files and the subsequent gold mine of information from the material found within became known as the Rosewood files. The volumes of information in the files provided valuable insights into the way that the KGB and Stasi played mother and daughter in the murky world of international spy networks—and it also showed the depth to which the Stasi had permeated East and West German society with undercover Cold War agents. It was no wonder, therefore, that amongst the crowd that day at Normannenstrasse were people who thought that they were under suspicion of the Stasi, those who actually were and had something to hide, and then those who had relatives or friends incarcerated by the state police.

In 1989, Esther Reichert was one of those disaffected few who suffered under the totalitarian machine as her grandfather was serving time in the infamous Bautzen prison in Saxony, East Germany, for aiding and abetting defectors to the West. As a result of her grandfather's exploits, Esther's career as a journalist in East Germany came to an abrupt halt; her role model had been taken away and thrown into the deep dungeons of the communist regime. She bore no ill will towards her relative, as she knew deep down that he was right and that communism was just an inconvenience, rather than an ideology. What she wanted more now than anything was to free her grandfather and clear his name as a political activist.

Esther was one of the first Germans through the gates of the Stasi when they opened and the teeming mass of people streamed through. She had been standing in the freezing rain for hours, waiting to get into the compound, not knowing that she was brushing elbows with intelligence agents from a number of countries who were by this stage eyeing each other up with both loathe and admiration on the historic occasion. After searching in vain for three hours, sifting through mounds of paper for anything with her grandfather's name, Esther realized that it was going to be a mammoth task. She had been pulling open unending numbers of file cabinets and drawers, finding only information that was relevant to people other than her.

Looking for information on Bautzen was impossible. There were files full of numbers, code words, pictures of places, people from a thousand different places and times—and she could not make any sense of any of it.

Feeling exhausted and despondent, she began milling around the corridors without any real purpose in mind. As she walked the maze of hallways almost ankle deep in paper, she noted groups of people kneeling in the debris trying feverishly to decipher it—some happy, some sad, some getting out of control. It was a surreal experience, digging through the dregs of a complete intelligence organization, trying to figure things out as a layperson.

As she approached another area, she realized that the search there was being done more systematically by a group of serious but silent men. They were also overloaded with the jewels of the finds, and now and again, sheets of paper would catch in the wind and fall to the floor as they whisked the files away out of the building. On a whim, Esther gathered up some of the fallen treasure and stashed it away in her bag without paying attention to what exactly she had. She hung around until one in the groups of silent men noticed her and gave her a long cold stare, which was warning enough for her to get out of the way.

She aimlessly wandered a while longer, picking up titbits of information as she went but finding little of value. There was nothing concrete that she could lay her hands on, and the information that she found satisfied her curiosity only for the short term. She completely forgot about the sheaf of papers in her bag as she decided to trudge home in the rain.

Three weeks later, Esther's grandfather was released from Bautzen. Once reunited, she told him about her adventures at the Stasi building, and he cried in admiration when he heard the news. Esther also showed him what she did get, but explained that she could not identify its contents or value. They meant nothing to Markus Reichert either. He could not read between the lines of the puzzle, as there was too much missing; however, he realized he needed to get rid of the documents to avoid any further repercussions. He had spent too many years behind bars to start trusting people, politics, and new "better" regimes now. So he turned to his younger sister, Anna, for advice.

Anna Reichert met with her brother two months after he was freed from prison, which was the first time they had actually seen each other in the twenty-two years since her defection. Anna was the first person that Markus had smuggled out of East Germany within the very first days of the wall being built. He had gotten her out at one of the now-defunct border crossings near Hildesheim in West Germany. Markus did not know it, but due to his sister's influence, he was released much sooner than others from Bautzen. Since all contact was broken between the siblings on that day at the border, Markus had no way of knowing that his sister had become a successful lawyer in the United States and had also married a man of some influence.

When Anna had crossed the border more than two decades earlier with her brother's help, she was picked up by a patrol of the US Military Police, who took her in for questioning. She was held in a detention center with other defectors for some time and interrogated by a number of officials. This was the spark she needed to start her career as a lawyer since she found the whole process to be unjust and totally inappropriate. She was a defector—not a criminal or spy. During one of her questioning sessions, however, a young captain from the US Intelligence Corps caught her eye. As time went by and things took their own natural course, the two became lovers and eventually lifelong partners.

After receiving those Stasi papers from her brother all those years later, Anna herself could not understand what was implied in the documents, but she realized that it was significant enough to share the find with her husband. He could at least take a look; after all, if anyone would know if the information was important—and what to do with it—that person would be the US ambassador to Germany, Winston Heymann.

Senator Corbin got wind of the same information as soon as the Rosewood files came to light in the United States. Being on the Select Committee on Intelligence, he was privy to any knowledge that would impact the national security of the United States. Although the Rosewood files were no longer a threat to the United States since the CIA, NSA, DIA, and FBI had combed through them after digging them out of the Stasi compound, Corbin still had the capability to call in any case he wished. When he heard of Rosewood and the potential links the names were purported to have with the KGB, he jumped at the chance to delve into the papers himself.

At first Corbin thought the information was damning only to the Soviet Empire and the KGB, and as such, there was no need to worry. It was only later when the initial excitement died down that tiny bits of data trickled through, information which piqued everyone's interest again. One of those snippets caused Corbin some grave concern and a few sleepless nights. The name of a US Army captain was found on Stasi correspondence, and it was implied there was a link to illegal arms shipments. No names were mentioned in the halls of Congress, however, as even some classified information was held back by the chorus of intelligence agencies. Nevertheless, Corbin could easily read between the lines and suspected the worst. By making a few innocent calls, he established that the new pieces of information were coming from someone in Germany, but no names were mentioned.

At once Corbin feared for his safety. He knew he needed to act fast and get rid of the German information source. As he dug further into the material and studied the method that was used to gather the intel, it came to light that the link between East Germany and the US military during the Cold War was a very tenuous one. In the Rosewood files, there were too many acronyms and code words for the layperson and most politicians to understand; the only worrying parts were the mentioning of a certain staff sergeant from Kentucky who peddled arms and of his subsequent demise and then the mention of a mid-level US Army officer who took up the investigation—and the trade—a few months later. Corbin rightly surmised that he was close to being compromised. What was more worrying, however, was that it was rumored Ambassador Heymann, being a former intelligence officer, had figured out who the officer was.

Winston Heymann was a smarter man than most people realized. He was one of the best junior officers the US Intelligence Corps ever had; he was a natural linguist with a gifted memory for small details. Many thought this rising star could fit easily into the clandestine ranks of the CIA and quite comfortably excel at foreign intelligence; but that was not to be. He decided to pursue openings with the State Department instead, focusing on the political whole, rather than portions of the intelligence pie. As Heymann gathered speed at State, however, he did from time to time step on people's toes—especially those from the Senate.

Heymann had chalked up some prestigious titles, which earned him much respect, but when he held the position of chairman of the Foreign Appropriations Committee for a number of years, where he oversaw the export of US trade around the globe, he became a despised man. He and his staff controlled what big businesses in the United States did and what big business wanted to do overseas. He was the trade link with every US ambassador and embassy in the world.

When the decline of the US auto industry in the seventies and eighties hurt hundreds of companies in the United States, both large and small, Heymann was tasked with ramping up campaigns for the export of US-made materials, such as coal, wheat, and corn. One of the lobbyists for exporting steel overseas at the time was the Republican representative from Michigan, Robert J. Corbin. Corbin and his cronies rallied and badgered Heymann for a chance to sell more steel on the open international trade market, but he would not budge. Heymann argued that there was a shortage of steel in the United States and that America would need a stock to bounce back with when the time came. Besides, he argued, steel from Japan and Germany was easier to produce and sell in Europe and Asia; customers there would buy that steel before they'd spend money on inferior-rated products from the United States.

Calling US products inferior was bad enough, but it was Heymann's mention of Japanese steel that infuriated Corbin. Corbin's long-range plans had been coming together nicely before the diplomat stuck his nose in. As a result of Heymann's comments, political warfare and a mud-slinging match ensued. Corbin crossed the line when he accused Heymann of favoring Germany because of his wife's nationality.

Heymann had many friends in high places, and while he did not rise to challenge Corbin publicly, he made his thoughts known to those that controlled Corbin. Corbin took a hit in the popularity polls after a public wrist-slapping from the leader of the Republican Party and was ordered to back down on his attacks on Heymann. Corbin seethed with rage, which alienated him from his allies. But he swore in public that he would re-cover— and swore in private that he would get his revenge over Heymann.

Bowman woke with a sharp jolt. The seatbelt sign was on as the plane bounced around on its final approach into Larnaca airport. He was tired, grumpy, and his shoulder was killing him, but he stared straight ahead and thought of the reason why he was here in the first place. *I don't believe I'm wasting valuable FBI resources on a two-bit driver who doesn't know his elbow from his arse,* he thought to himself. *This shit is getting out of hand.*

CHAPTER SIX

DAY 9

ISKENDERUN, TURKEY

BUDAIL WAS BANKING ON HIS ABILITY TO CONVERSE IN TURKISH as he made his way through a number of small villages, keeping to the safer routes along the costal roads of southern Turkey. On reaching the bustling port of Iskenderun, he camped out in a coffee shop for the best part of the day, watching the comings and goings of the local populous. He fitted in quite well and engaged with some of the locals, chatting about the daily grind of living in this part of the world—oblivious to the fact that he was a known entity and had been under a crude but effective form of surveillance since he had first sat down in the café earlier in the day.

───≪≫───

At dusk they made their move. Budail was sitting outside the coffee shop, close to the curbside, which made things a lot simpler for a pick-up, which they did as swiftly as if they were picking up a delivery of fish for the local market. The blue Citroen van did not come to a screeching halt but rather, casually came to a gentle stop. No one batted an eyelid when two men nonchalantly got out, grabbed Budail by the arms, and loaded him unceremoniously into the open doors of the van. Those that did notice were given a few stern looks—which spoke volumes. Nothing seen, nothing heard, that's the way it was in this part of the world. Nobody wanted to cross the local Mafia.

Strong hands pushed Budail face first to the floor of the Citroen. He didn't struggle, as he wasn't expecting some kind of reception party. He had no choice but to go along; he knew he was going to play with some hard men. What he did not expect, however, was the plastic cuffs around his wrists and the hood that was placed over his head. He began a muffled protestation but all he got in return was a firm thump to his face. He soon got the message and submitted to his captors' directions. *If this was the way to get rich and play with the big boys,* he thought, *then so be it.* He figured they had too much to lose by killing him, so he didn't feel too threatened, at least for the moment.

DAY 9
LARNACA, CYPRUS

The Lufthansa Airbus carrying the two US FBI agents touched down in Larnaca International Airport as expected, exactly on time. Since the airline giant was one of the biggest customers at the island resort, it was directed straight to the main terminal, which was more than could be said of the smaller charter companies, which were forced to disgorge their passengers onto the boiling-hot tarmac.

Bowman and Seymour retrieved their baggage and headed out through Customs without being questioned, as they both held their diplomatic passports in plain view. Standing at the arrivals gate of the main terminal was a consular driver holding a placard of a stars-and-stripes flag, waiting to pick up the two Americans. The driver approached the older of the two men. "Mr. Bowman, Mr. Seymour? I am Nahmi from the consulate, and I am here to take you to the office, but first, this is for you."

Bowman accepted a the sealed envelope and walked away, leaving Seymour and the driver in limbo, to read the brief message that was presented on US State Department letterhead and was signed by the US consulate general:

> *Special Agent Bowman, please report to the Larnaca General Hospital and contact Investigator Kostas Kidis of the Larnaca Customs Bureau, who is waiting for you. The body of an American citizen has been found in the harbor.*

DAY 9
US CONSULATE, LARNACA, CYPRUS

Chris sat in the lobby opposite Marine Post One inside the US Consulate in Larnaca and contemplated once again what was happening to him. After reporting the events from the Cyprus airport to Nash from a secure phone in the consulate building earlier that day, he was told to get back to his hotel and wait for further instructions.

Nothing could have been worse. He needed to be busy; his head was throbbing, and his mind was working overtime. He realized that he was speculating way too much about things, but if Nash bought in on Chris's hunches, then there must be something worth analyzing further. Still, he was given orders, so he left the consulate and returned to his empty hotel room.

He had slept for a number of hours when the phone woke him out of his slumber. Chris had an uncanny knack of being immediately alert, coherent, and ready to roll after being awoken; this instance was no exception. Dying for something to do, he was like a five-year-old kid with a new present, just waiting to peel off the wrapper.

However, when little kids open their presents, wide eyes and smiles are the usually first things that happen—but for Chris, on hearing the news that he was to get back to the consulate to meet with FBI agents from Germany, his face looked as if he had just received a pair of plaid woolen socks from his great-grandmother for his birthday.

After waiting for almost two hours outside Post One, Chris was introduced to Nick Seymour by the aid to the consulate general. Nick explained, to Chris's dismay that Chris would have to wait to talk to Special Agent Bowman about the events at the airport. Since the consulate did not have an FBI presence in Cyprus, Bowman had been requested at the last minute to assist with the recent death of an American in Larnaca. Seymour further explained that this type of response is commonplace throughout the world when the local authorities report the death of a foreign national.

What Seymour did not divulge, however, was the fact that the difference in this case was that this American was found in a shipyard that normally had strict access controls and, hence, the local law enforcement involvement with the US Consulate.

With not much else to do other than wait for Bowman to return, Seymour and Chris camped out in the small break area where the Armed Forces Network was showing a taped football game. As time went by, Seymour ended up explaining to Chris the complex rules of the American version of football, and the personalities of the circus that comprised the National Football League.

Chris, not knowing where his boundaries lay with Nick, tested the ground. "All that's missing is popcorn and a couple of beers, right?"

"That and a pissed-off Irishman," replied the young agent.

"In that case, then, it should be Tylenol, whiskey, and a rope," countered the Brit with a large smile on his face.

"I saw some brandy and Twinkies in the back if that will help," suggested the American.

Nick then had to explain what Twinkies were, and the banter continued for a while longer. It was obvious that the two were going to get on well.

The pissed-off Irishman at that point was standing over the corpse of the American that had been fished out of Larnaca harbor. Joined by Bowman in the mortuary were the city mortician, the local coroner, and the shady-looking character, Inspector Kostas Kidis of the Cyprus Customs Bureau. It was Kidis who had called in the incident when he was on a routine inspection of a freighter in the harbor. He could not explain how this American came to be inside a restricted area only that witnesses stated that the man was standing too close to the dockside when a forklift spilled its load, knocking him into the gap between a freighter and the seawall. The stevedores working the dock could do nothing to help the man as the swell of the sea and the docked freighter crushed his body up against the dock time and time again.

The freighter had to be moved, and divers were sent down to retrieve the body. The last thing that was recovered from the belongings on the body was the sopping-wet US passport of one Danny Robson, which Bowman now held in his hand. But Bowman wasn't too worried about the passport itself; he was more intrigued by the equally wet English/Turkish pocket dictionary found in one of Danny's pockets.

A disgruntled and tired-looking Bowman returned back to the consulate with Kidis in tow. As the two entered the break area, they found Seymour and Chris having a good time watching the football game. Nick and Chris both stood up quickly, however, eager for instructions. As Chris was raising himself out of his lounge chair, he came face to face with Kidis, who gave him an extraordinary stare. Chris did not think too much about it, but thought that he recognized the man from somewhere. Since no introductions were made, he thought no more about it. Bowman simply barked a few orders: Chris was to sit tight, and Nick was to go with him. *Fine, whatever*, Chris thought. *Shouldn't have come here in the first place.* He sat back down to continue deciphering the game.

An hour later, when Kidis was being escorted out of the building, he asked one of his FBI escorts who the young man was in the canteen, and wishing to remain respectful and cordial, the FBI agent told Kidis exactly who Chris was and what he was doing in the consulate. By that time, Chris had decided to switch off for a while and dropped off to sleep in one of the lounge chairs in front of the TV, oblivious to the comings and goings of the consulate staff.

He was later rudely awoken by Bowman, who kicked the back of his chair.

"Okay, Limey, let's go; time for our chat."

"I love you too, honey," came the flippant but quiet reply from Chris.

"What did you just say, asshole?"

With a smile on his face, Chris just said, "You're too funny."

"What the hell is that supposed to mean?"

"Nothing. Nobody uses 'Limey' any more. How old are you anyway?" Chris was on a roll; he sensed Bowman's mood and decided to play with it for a while.

Bowman got up in his face but kept his temper in check. "You're really starting to piss me off, you know that? If you don't stop being such a smartass soon, I'm going to really come down on you. Don't forget that inside this building, you're subject to US law, and around here that means me. You don't mean shit to me or to the US government—and I can have you canned in a heartbeat."

The one thing that had stinted Chris's promotional prospects in the British Army was his knack for not knowing when to shut up. If he was dealing with a professional who showed him some respect, then he was a great soldier and always kept his opinions to himself. But when someone disrespected him when there was no need, he could never stop from spurting out stupid comments, like "Yeah, yeah, you're the sheriff, I'm the bad guy, get out of town by sunup tomorrow. Heard it all before." This is the comment he now delivered to Bowman.

As old and decrepit as Bowman looked, he could still manage a hard takedown when necessary. He surprised Chris and moved quickly and expertly, taking the younger man to the floor and squashing his face into the canteen linoleum. Keeping Chris in a stiff-arm lock, Bowman bent down to shout in his ear, "Keep it up, asshole, keep it up—and I'll not only hurt you, but I'll find the darkest, dingiest cell in Cyprus to dump you in and forget about you for a long, long time. Are we clear?"

Chris nodded in submission, just before a Marine guard and Nick Seymour arrived and separated the two antagonists.

Seymour tried to get things back on track. "I'm not sure what's with you two," he said, "but we came here for a reason. I think we need to focus on the problem at hand and get to work. John, I think you need a break for a while. Why not take a breather?"

Bowman stood there massaging his left shoulder and winced a few times when he hit a certain spot. "Don't tell me what to do, you little shit! I'll decide how we're going to proceed. We're going to leave for Berlin in the morning, but right now we're all going to go upstairs to the office, and if it makes you happy, we can all play family for a while so we can get to the bottom of this useless lead that Wonder Boy here has put us on to, okay?"

With nods all around, the procession moved to a spare office on the next floor to conduct the interview, hoping to understand Chris's encounters over the last twenty-four hours.

It seemed like the air had been cleared between Bowman and Chris for a while, but it was still plain to Seymour that they would not be sending each other season's greetings this Christmas. On a positive note, the ensuing discussions weren't too argumentative, and at one point, Bowman actually praised Chris for his level of detail in recounting certain parts of his story. Saying that, however, it was getting late, and it seemed that they had exhausted as much out of Chris as was possible, so Seymour found the consulate duty driver, who was crashed out in his car and got him ready for the trip to the hotel.

They were all in the car and ready to leave when Bowman remembered that he had to make a call and went back inside the consulate. It took about ten more minutes before Bowman reappeared and got into the car again without making any apologies. The twenty-minute drive was spent in total silence, as nobody knew what should be said. They arrived at the hotel without realizing that they were not the only Americans on the road that night.

———⊗———

Colonel Whittaker was directing the Customs guy every step of the way from the back seat of the Mercedes, all the while imagining what needed to happen next. Preacher was up front in the passenger seat with a 9mm Glock sitting on his lap, ready to jump if and when necessary. Whittaker kept his underling on a short chain; he had his reasons for not taking out the threesome in the consulate car ahead of them as they negotiated traffic through the busy streets. He had other ideas of how things should transpire, which he was not about to share just yet.

On arriving at the hotel, Chris left the two agents at check-in and headed for the dining room to see if he could find a table out of the way for himself. He considered asking Nick to join him but decided against it since he didn't want to piss Bowman off by not asking him, too, so he ate alone.

It was close to 8 p.m. and already dark when Chris started heading back to his room. He was tired and needed some sleep. It been a hectic day—and who knew what tomorrow would bring. There was no sign of the two FBI agents as he navigated his way through the maze of corridors, and for once, the hotel was actually quiet in comparison to the evening that Chris had spent at the bar the night before. He thought about that night and now felt a little frustrated with himself for not pursuing the lead with the barmaid just a little further after Astrid left; he didn't feel like being on his own.

It was eerily quiet in his part of the hotel as Chris inserted his key into the lock of his room. The only sound that could be heard was the creaking of the hotel room door that led to his temporary abode.

Preacher locked on immediately to the silhouette standing in the doorframe, the backlight of the corridor shedding his target in total darkness. But it didn't matter; the intelligence was good—this was definitely the mark. All he had to do was point and shoot.

As Chris struggled to find the light switch in the entryway of his room, he heard footsteps approaching in the hallway and looked back to see a hotel waiter carrying what looked like the remnants of room service from somewhere down the corridor. Chris kept his eye on him for a short while, established that the man was no threat, and then turned his attention back into the room. As his eyes were trying to focus on the dark surroundings, he shut the door, but his eye caught a glimpse of a red beam off one of the wardrobe mirrors. He immediately hit the deck as three shots rang out in quick succession.

The shots were powerful enough to pass through the lightweight door and come to an abrupt halt inside the head of the waiter who was innocently passing by. The noise of the shots and the clatter of the catering tray on the corridor's hardwood floor would have been enough to wake up the dead. Chris scrambled around on the floor looking for cover, as the beam of infrared passed through his room, scanning for its prey. As he made a few quick moves towards the bed, shots rang out again, and this time screams could be heard from the corridor. Obviously other patrons had heard the din and found the carnage in the hallway. Chris, by this time, was on his back almost under his bed, watching the red beam criss-cross its way through the room. As he was trying to figure out his options, someone opened his door only to be greeted with a few more bullets.

Chris wasn't sure what was going on, but he did know a few things: He could not hear the empty cases of the rounds hitting the floor, he felt a cold breeze in the room, he could not smell the acrid smoke that usually followed automatic fire, and he could not sense any movement from his attacker. *He's not in the room,* he thought. *He's outside, and the fucking window is open. What the fuck is going on out there, and who the fuck is outside my door?*

"Chris, Chris, are you okay?" It was Seymour. He was out in the corridor and trying to peer inside Chris's room.

In an almost a whispered response Chris replied, "I'm okay. Shut up a minute. There's a guy outside the window." This was followed immediately by five rounds of rapid fire. The gunman must have heard the conversation and began spraying the room from left to right in a wild arc from the ceiling to the floor, the last shot coming to rest just inches from Chris's head.

Nick began again. "Chris—"

"Shut the fuck up, will ya!" his newfound friend spat. More shots were fired. "Are you trying to get me killed, or what?"

"Where are you?" Seymour started again.

Where do you think I am, dumbass? thought Chris, but he did not reply. This time two shots were aimed at the door. *That should shut him up,* he thought.

The situation was grim. Chris was on his back, looking at the peppered walls and watching a red beam cross the room. There was a dead waiter in the corridor, and an inexperienced FBI agent was hindering—not help-ing- –the situation out near the door. On reflection, Chris thought, *At least he's trying. Where's Bowman?*

Then just like that, the beam was gone, and there was silence. Chris lay there a few minutes more and then decided to make a move. He reached up to the bed, pulled a pillow down, and threw it to the other side of the room. Nothing, no reaction—and no more shots. He turned onto his stomach and crawled to the edge of the bed. He did not peer in the direction of the window; instead, he gauged the distance to the corridor from his bed.

As he was contemplating a sprint to the door, Seymour burst in and started pinging rounds out the open window from his service revolver. The shots were going in no particular direction, but that was all Chris needed. He was up and out of there without a second invitation. As Seymour emptied his gun, he also began backtracking out the door. Again, no shots were fired in reply.

Both Chris and Seymour were running down the hallway and towards the hotel lobby when they spotted Bowman running towards them, gun in hand, from the opposite direction. As they all congregated near the reception desk, Chris couldn't help notice that Bowman was sweating profusely, and he also seemed quite out of breath. If Nick noticed, he didn't let on. Instead, he began with a barrage of questions and statements to both Chris and Bowman.

"Does someone want to explain to me what the hell is going on?" the young agent burst out. "I almost got my ass kicked back there!"

Chris remained silent but perplexed and thought to himself, *Who was the target again?*

"We need to get out of here," Seymour continued. "They may be coming back for more, we—"

"We sit tight, we wait until the cops show up, and then we'll formulate a plan," interjected Bowman, who was still having difficulty trying to recover from his jog up the corridor.

"Tell me what happened, Nick, and slow down. We'll be okay here. If something else was going to happen, they would have come through the main door by now."

Chris noticed an air of confidence returning to the older agent. *Does he know something that we don't?* he thought.

"Give me your report, Nick!" the voice of authority was returning. Bowman was taking charge of the situation.

Chris sat down as Nick spouted off in accelerated English the events as he saw it. It was obvious his adrenaline was still coursing through his system as the inexperienced agent repeated himself more than a few times. Chris, strangely enough, was totally composed. After the initial shock of the attack, his heart rate was excited but not overly pumped up. In retrospect, the attack in Bonn was more heart-racing than being shot at in his hotel room.

Or was it the fact that Chris was soaking this up? He was actually beginning to enjoy himself in a weird kind of way. He had almost lost his life, but he felt as if this was the type of thing that he could really do—be in the middle of the action and be a part of the intrigue, the mystery, and the unanswered questions. He was neither a fool nor naïve; he knew he had to be careful. He still didn't have any answers, or more important, he still didn't have any authority to do something in return. At the base of it, he was still just a driver. *But one day,* he thought, *one day things will change.* At least he hoped so.

"Chris ... Chris, are you okay?" It was Bowman, and he almost sounded sincere. "Tell me your version of what happened. Laughing boy here needs a drink before I can get much more sense out of him."

The conversation trailed off with another detailed account from Chris, during which half the police force of Larnaca had turned up in the hotel lobby, also searching for answers. Bowman gave instructions for Nick and Chris to sit tight in the manager's office while he went and flashed his badge to the local powers-that-be. Not overly concerned with what Bowman was going to do, Chris only wanted to crash somewhere out of the way. He felt desperately tired, and then suddenly it hit him: *Shit, what would have happened if Astrid had been in the room? Maybe she is better off without me.*

Chris made his way back to the reception desk to see if she was still in the hotel; she was not. She hadn't even checked in after the embarrassing incident in the bar that afternoon. As Chris turned to go rejoin Nick, he spotted Bowman in deep conversation with someone who had his back turned to him. Bowman saw the young driver and stopped in midsentence, gazing in his direction. Chris saw that the back belonged to Kostas Kidis, who followed Bowman's stare and then turned to look at Chris, who was standing just twenty feet away. Kidis gave him a long, hard, dirty look, which Chris interpreted as him not being needed and that he should go away. Chris recognized the man from the consulate, but he could still not figure out where he had seen him before that. He didn't want to waste any more time on it, so he took off to find Seymour, who he thought was probably in the bar consoling himself.

Chris did find Nick in the bar—with a drink in one hand and a telephone handset in the other; he was about to make a call. Chris couldn't pinpoint it, but it looked as if Nick had changed. He seemed much more composed, back in control, and ready for action, or at least pretending to be.

"You wanna drink, buddy?"

Chris was embarrassed for the rookie agent. "No, I'm okay," he said. "Thanks."

"Don't mind if I do, actually," Nick said as he reached over and retrieved a bottle from behind the bar.

Seymour poured himself a large one and took a quick swig and then looked back at Chris.

"You're so fucking cool," he started. You know that? ... Doesn't anything faze you?" The comment came across as a little arrogant, and Chris also recognized a tint of jealousy, so he remained silent. "I know who you work for, and I realize that you have had some form of specialized training, but look at you ... Shit, look at me. I'm supposed to be the professional, and I've got to go and change my panties soon. But you're standing there cooler than a cucumber. Doesn't this shit bother you?"

Chris remained neutral and showed no emotion. Yes, the shit *did* bother him, but he didn't show it, at least not outwardly. He had taken the self-pity route years before and had also hit the bottle, and hit it hard. But this was not the first time he had been under fire, and neither had been Bonn. Two tours of Northern Ireland had seen to that.

"Listen, Nick," he said, "maybe you need to cut back on the booze. Bowman will be back in a minute, and he'll be pissed off if he sees you with a glass in your hand. Let's go find out what's happening."

"NO, I want to talk to you first," the agent insisted. "What makes you so special? How the hell did you get involved in this mess in the first place?"

Chris hesitated but decided to proceed slowly and tactfully, trying to keep things in perspective. It wasn't as if he would become close friends with Nick, but it would be quite possible that Chris would have to drive him to an airport one day or wait at a restaurant for him to finish his meeting or carry his luggage. It just wasn't socially acceptable for a driver to be chums with the management, even in this day and age.

"There's nothing special about me," he replied. "I'm just a guy in the wrong place at the wrong time ... I have no idea what's going on, and the truth of the matter is, yes, I was shitting myself. Don't forget, Nick, I'm just the driver; I didn't ask for this crap. The small print on my contract definitely did not say, 'Please get shot at while on vacation.' And by the way, I forgot to say thanks for being there; I'm not sure what you were shooting at, but it must have taken some balls to come charging in as you did." He held out his right hand as a gesture. It did the trick, as Nick was forced to put his glass on the bar and take Chris's hand.

Chris then employed a trick that he had learned many years earlier from a German dentist who had treated him regularly. He kept hold of Nick's hand and began pulling him away from the bar, without the agent knowing what was happening. It is an occupational hazard for those in the medical industry that, if you give people the opportunity to talk, they'll not shut up; they will go on and on and on. Therefore, you have to keep smiling. Let them chat a little but keep them in physical contact, dragging their sorry ass to the door at the same time. Most people are usually out and paying their bills before they realize that they were kicked out instead of ushered out.

Chris had managed exactly that. He let Nick spout off a little more about how scared he was, all the time smiling, nodding, and keeping contact. Nick stopped only when he realized that he was back in the lobby with an angry-looking Bowman headed directly for them.

"We're leaving," came the blanket statement—and that was that. The same tired consulate driver was standing in the hotel lobby waiting to take the party back to the confines and safety of the US Consulate. It was getting late, and it was obvious the driver was not a happy camper. Chris sympathized but juvenilely quipped at Bowman, "Oh goody, can we sit together?" Bowman shot him a look. Chris received the message and kept his mouth shut, following the FBI man out to the car.

⚬⚭⚬

Whittaker and Preacher were on the move. The botched attempt on Chris was enough to get them out of Larnaca, and they needed to get out of there in a hurry. Kidis had paved the way for them before the attack by supplying one of his official vehicles and a driver who was on standby to take the two "guests" to the airport at a moment's notice. Minutes after they fled the hotel, and within an hour of being picked up, they were standing in line waiting to board a charter flight to Adana, Turkey.

It was a risk that Whittaker was willing to take, leaving by a very obvious route. Since he had a number of associates slowing the Cypriot investigation down to a crawl, he felt he had justified his own actions. Besides, two Canadian tourists were not going to be suspects, and nobody at the airport was even concerned with incidents that had taken place in the city, not just yet.

Chris Morehouse was becoming a real liability now that they had missed their chance to take him out. Whatever speculation had taken place beforehand was now turning into real facts. It was clear to Whittaker that someone was listening to the driver's statements, that it would only be a matter of time before the investigation would get more intense, and that the net would eventually close—but not if he had anything to do with it. Whittaker also had formidable survival skills, and he knew he had to look out for himself, even if Corbin had promised him the world after he gained the presidency. There would be another opportunity to take out the driver; Whittaker just needed the time and place to be right. But today he had to retreat.

Whittaker also needed to regroup after the painful loss of Danny. He was not emotionally attached to the former Green Beret, and as far as he was concerned Danny was a casualty of war. What bothered him, nonetheless, were two things: one, he had lost his only Turkish speaker in the organization; and two, the Turks did not show for the handover at the port. Cyprus was the neutral ground that they were all content with—but that was now compromised with the events over the last twelve hours.

His worst fears were that all the events taking place were connected, that somehow the driver had alerted someone that took a serious interest in and prevented the Turks from getting to Cyprus. But his intel was saying different. He was told by his insider that Chris was a nobody and there was no link or law enforcement plan in place to prevent the shipments. It was all too confusing, and Whittaker needed to get out of Cyprus to create some breathing room. He needed to head to Turkey to find out where his contacts were and why there was a no-show and no contact.

—∞∞∞—

Normally Kidis would receive a confirmation call from the Turks to let him know they were on the way for the meet. They always used Larnaca as the neutral meeting point, but the captain of the *Juno* knew of the final destination only once the Turks were actually on board his ship. The Turks usually took their security seriously, and for operational purposes, the meeting call was only one-way; Kidis had no number to call back. Flying to Turkey and reestablishing contact with the Turks was the type of contingency that Whittaker had planned for but hoped not to have to implement. The whole purpose for Whittaker and his team being in Cyprus was to ensure that the cargo could be picked up without a hitch, but now he would have to change his plans, and he hoped it wasn't because of a dumbass driver.

In the meantime, the freighter *Juno* headed back out to international waters. There were enough supplies on board to last for a couple of weeks if needed, but neither the ship's captain nor Whittaker were keen on leaving tons of munitions circle the Mediterranean Sea indefinitely until the ship found a home.

DAY 10
BERLIN TEGEL INTERNATIONAL AIRPORT

The Lufthansa Airbus A320 had just touched down at Berlin Tegel Airport from its four-and-a-half-hour flight out of Cyprus with Bowman, Seymour, and Chris on board. Only twelve hours had passed since the Cyprus hotel attack on Chris. It was an uncomfortable experience for him and the two FBI agents, who all spent the entire time before their flight at the US Consulate, which was not designed to house overnight guests. But nowhere else was as secure.

It was usually a short taxi from touchdown on the runway to the terminal at Tegel. However, this time the plane veered away from the main building and out to a holding area at the north end of the airport complex. All the other passengers on board were oblivious to the redirection until the pilot announced that due to a police incident at the airport, all flights were to hold on the apron until further instructions were given by air traffic control. By the time the plane finally came to a halt, Bowman, being his usual impatient self, immediately demanded to speak to the captain by flashing his badge to every flight attendant who crossed his path.

"He must be desperate for his beer," Chris commented.

Nick just shrugged and returned to his copy of the *Financial Times*.

After about twenty minutes, Bowman returned, looking a little flustered by something, but he wasn't letting on what he had discovered. As he got himself resituated, the pilot announced that the airport had been locked down by the police and all passengers were to remain seated until shuttle buses could be organized to ferry everyone to a nearby hangar. Now Chris understood why he saw a number of other aircraft also seemingly in limbo, just sitting on the tarmac. It took more than an hour before buses showed up to ferry the passengers off the plane.

As the mobile staircase was attached to the outer skin of the plane, the cabin crew announced that everyone was to remain seated, which Bowman took as a sign to get up and gather his things. "Let's go, Nick," he ordered. "You too, Limey."

With a chorus of moans and groans, the remaining passengers watched in frustration as the small group were the first to leave the plane. At the foot of the stairs, an airport car was waiting for the threesome, which then proceeded to the terminal. Bowman killed the silence. "There's been some kind of shooting at the terminal; apparently there's a bunch of bodies, so they went to lockdown. They're not sure yet if there are any US citizens involved, but they've asked for our assistance since we were in the area, just in case."

"What's that got to do with me?" Chris chimed in, although in reality he didn't want to be left out of the action now.

"I'm not letting you out of my sight just yet," Bowman replied. "You're just along for the ride, buddy. Don't ask anything, don't touch anything, and just do as I say, and we'll get along fine, okay?"

"Yeah sure, no worries," Chris said. *No need to be a smartass right now*, he thought.

It was more than a random shooting; it was a bloodbath. Chris counted at least six bodies lying on the floor at one of the arrival gates. There must have been more deaths, he thought, observing the number of body parts strewn around the area. He recognized it for what it was—an explosion. Glass was shattered everywhere; black and grey streaks lined the walls, ceiling, and floor; blood intermingled with body parts; congealing blood pooled on the marble floor. It was the full violent-death package.

As Bowman gingerly made his way through the massacre, he couldn't help but notice that Chris wasn't fazed by the scene; in fact it seemed to him that Chris was taking it all in, analyzing and digesting—while Seymour, on the other hand, was holding a handkerchief in front of his face and was now looking a lot paler than a short while ago. Chris didn't realize it, but his coolness came shining through again as he crouched on his haunches, taking in the horror that lay before him. It did disturb him to witness such human waste, but he had seen death before on a similar scale.

—⚙—

During his first tour of Northern Ireland, Chris was part of an army vehicular patrol in an area which known by the Brits as "Bandit Country" in County Tyrone, when the lead Landrover of his small convoy hit a landmine, instantly killing five of the six occupants aboard. On exiting his vehicle, Chris's section came under sustained machine-gun fire, which took the lives of two more of his platoon.

Realizing that the commander and two senior NCOs were out of action, Chris, who had earned only his corporal stripes just six months before his deployment to the province, took charge of the situation and rallied the remaining troops for a counterattack. Due to Chris's actions, there was no further loss of British life that day—which was more than could be said for the three Irishmen lying face down in a ditch, courtesy of his marksmanship. But the small victory was bittersweet for him; he took the loss of life of his fallen comrades hard. He volunteered to pull his best friend's dismembered body from a tree twenty feet from the blast site, and though he didn't show any emotion while doing so, later he cried himself to sleep.

The remainder of that tour went off relatively well without any further loss of life or serious injuries to Chris's unit. But it was on his second tour, which he had volunteered for, where things got hot. He'd been shot at again in an ambush while on a foot patrol in Newry, had petrol and acid bombs thrown at him during riots on the Falls Road in Belfast, took shrapnel from a mortar attack on his barracks in Londonderry, and suffered constant abuse from men, women, and children who did not want him to be in Northern Ireland. All this was not known to Bowman, or for that matter anyone else, including his family or close friends—or so he thought.

In hiring Chris, the CIA had called in a few favors from its British counterpart, MI6, to establish the young driver's credentials. From the information given, Richard Nash and others in the agency were highly impressed. Nash knew that Chris was not going to be just a driver for much longer—at least if he had anything to do with it.

A familiar face greeted Chris as he was still scanning the attack scene at the airport. Matthias Kettler was in plain clothes but obviously on duty and working the crime scene with his local counterparts. Chris was surprised to see the GSG9 officer at the airport.

"We keep meeting under the strangest of circumstances, Chris," Kettler began and offered a handshake.

With a sad look on his face, Chris replied, "Yeah, but I got here after the fact this time." It was as if he felt somehow responsible for the mess in front of him. Bowman and Seymour were out of earshot so he pursued his need for information. "What the hell happened anyway?"

"Well, it's still a bit of a mess right now," Kettler replied, "but we think that it began as a shootout between two rival groups, which then turned into the grenade attack right here. Further down the concourse, there are more bodies with bullet wounds, and there are reports that there may be more corpses in one of the parking lots outside. We're still trying to piece everything together; I've only been here a short while so I am still not fully up-to-date."

"Holy shit, this is nasty. Any idea of who the gangs were?"

"Not gangs, Chris, rival terrorist groups … Turkish and Lebanese. That's why I was called in. What about you—what are you doing here?"

"I'm on vacation," remarked Chris. "Can't you tell?"

DAY 10
SOUTHEASTERN TURKEY

Whittaker decided that since he and his men put their lives on the line every day, it was worth the risk to drive on the treacherous Turkish roads. Thus he and Preacher rented a car and headed east out of Adana along the E90 towards Dokuztekne, where they would pick up the E91 and head south to the port of Iskenderun.

Preacher was, for the second time in his adult life, struggling in the deep pit of depression. He had killed his friend by stabbing him in the kidneys and then shoving him in-between the dock and a ship. To add to his dark mood, his marksmanship, a point of pride, had been called into question by Whittaker for failing to kill the driver, Chris Morehouse, at the hotel in Cyprus. He tried his best not to dwell on both incidents, and he was lucky the roads and the weather now demanded his full attention. He just needed to get back in the saddle and move on.

Whittaker, for his part, wasn't depressed at all—he was just in a foul mood. He put the Kodiak incident down to proactive operational security, although he later realized that he may have been too eager by getting rid of him in Larnaca. On reflection, he surmised that having Preacher take his friend out had put the ex-Green Beret in the wrong frame of mind, and therefore, he was more apt to make mistakes.

The first three shots should have been all that was needed to take out the driver, but Preacher's shots were all over the place. Whittaker thought that perhaps he should have done it himself—he was the expert—and in his mind, he was the more professional killer. His thoughts led him to consider bringing someone else into the operation. If Preacher was indeed burnt out, Whittaker would have to find a replacement.

As he contemplated the situation, he ran his tongue over the top row of his teeth. He reached up and snatched the rearview mirror away from Preacher's field of view to check his pearly whites and his killer smile—a smile that bedded his wife on the first date, a smile that took Preacher's wife when Whittaker went in search of the man who fell into a bottle.

It's no wonder they call him the Gucci Colonel, Preacher thought as Whittaker studied himself in the mirror. *The guy is so vain he would put a supermodel to shame—he can't walk past a hallway mirror without checking himself out.*

Whittaker picked at his teeth for a short while and then checked his hair before reluctantly putting the mirror back in its rightful place. As much as he disliked his own wife these days, he was grateful to her for getting his teeth into pristine condition.

The journey that should have lasted two hours took almost three as a huge rainstorm battered the roads and the wind forced cars to drive snake-like, slowly slithering forward making slow but gradual progress. On finally reaching Iskenderun, Whittaker directed Preacher to a café, where they could make a call and wait for their contacts to show up.

They took the opportunity to fill their bellies—which was timely, since while dining Whittaker caught a familiar Turkish face as a man walked into the café to use the bathroom. Whittaker quickly paid the bill, and he and Preacher headed outside in time to be met by the Turk.

"Follow, please," he said as he brushed by the pair. Preacher and Whittaker stayed five steps behind the man as he traipsed through the busy marketplace and town center. They eventually made it to an empty taxi where the Turk produced a set of keys and got in. The Americans didn't need further prompting; they climbed in with him.

After fifteen minutes of hectic driving through the congested streets, the party arrived at an old abandoned fish-processing plant. The Turkish driver parked the car out of eyeshot from the main road and headed by foot into the decrepit structure. As soon as they entered through a door in the largest warehouse, Whittaker's gut instinct told him something was wrong. He stopped in his tracks, but it was too late. He was about to take a step back when he felt the cold barrel of a shotgun at the back of his neck. He didn't struggle; he only glanced sideways to see Preacher in the same situation.

Four men appeared from the shadows, each carrying a submachine gun pointed directly at the Americans.

"Whoa, hey, what's going on here? There's no need for this!" Whittaker protested.

"James, normally I would say it is nice to see you, but under the circumstances, it is not." The voice was that of code name Fezman, who had walked over to the group from an old office nearby.

"What are you talking about, what circumstances?" Whittaker was confused.

"My sons, James, my sons."

Whittaker stared blankly at the rotund, balding Turk. "What the hell do you mean? I don't know your sons."

"They are dead, James. They were on the way to meet you in Cyprus from Beirut … and now they are dead."

"That has nothing to do with me!" Whittaker shouted.

"But I think you lie, James. I think you lie. I will get the truth out of you—and that my friend, is a guarantee."

Fezman gave a quick nod to his men, who reacted quickly, outfitting their detainees with zip ties and hoods. Preacher began to struggle, but Whittaker calmed him down. "Cool it, man; let it play out," he said in the most even tone he could muster.

Elsewhere in the plant, Budail was having a terrible time. His captors also suspected him of killing two of their gang, which he tried in vain to explain that he had nothing to do with; it was his boss that had issued the order. He was now sitting on a cold concrete floor with a hood over his head and his wrists tied very tightly behind his back.

Ever since he was a child, he had had problems controlling his bladder; and due to his relative poor upbringing in the slums of Beirut, the chance of preventative medicine eluded him and his family. As a result, he now sat in a pool of his own urine. He was scared not only because he didn't know what was going to happen next, but also because he knew it would only be a matter of time before the solid part of his digestive system would also fail—and the thought of sitting in his own feces made him shake and sweat profusely.

He was alone in the room and it was deathly silent. Time dragged interminably. The seconds, which he was initially counting, turned into minutes; the minutes turned just as easily to hours. This was so far removed from the perfectly arranged retirement plan he had imagined; he hated his life right now.

His head began to spin as he desperately concentrated on controlling himself. Such was his pain that he began to pray. He was so engrossed with reciting verses of the Koran that he didn't hear the muffled and distant shouting outside the room. He began to sway as he went through his prayers, as if he was in a trance, a state of second being outside of his body.

He still didn't hear the shouting, which was now the screams of a handful of men in the corridor just outside his room. Budail was only drawn out of his stupor when a body landed on top of him, and he was forced to snap back to reality. There were now several men in the room—perhaps as many as five or six. It sounded if his captors were struggling with another prisoner, another to share an unsure fate like Budail. His hopes were raised; perhaps it was another brother from the Levant.

It didn't take long for the scuffling to stop and the punching and kicking to begin. Budail's head snapped around when he heard the first voice: "Mother fuckers, you pieces of shit!" a man spouted. Then a more commanding and direct voice responded, "Shut the fuck up and take it—take it for Christ's sake!" But the beatings continued, and the two voices went silent. Budail was confused. *Americans here,* he thought. *What is going on? What have I got myself into?*

Sitting in urine and feces was one thing, but to be a prisoner in the same room with Americans was another. He wasn't sure which was worse. All his life, Budail was conditioned to hate and fight the Israelis and the Americans. It would have promoted him to a position of respect and authority if he could have killed some of these sworn enemies, but now he was in an impossible situation. His dreams of getting in touch with the Turks to reignite the business partnership were fading as he surmised that he was in way over his head. If the people that took him captive were capable of kidnapping two Americans, then they were a far more serious force than he had anticipated. He now thought that he may have been picked up by the wrong group, not the people he had been dealing with all these years. *That stupid bastard,* he thought, blaming the Protector. *We should have never have killed the Turks.* Budail's frustrations were now aimed at his commander as he cursed the lack of forethought and his leader's short, fiery temper.

Desire for revenge brought him back to the situation at hand. He now tried his best to concentrate and establish a point of reference, which he got when he heard the sound of something moving on the floor in front of him across the room and what seemed like something scraping up against a wall. Then silence. He strained to listen for more, almost not daring to breathe, thinking his jailers might still be in the room, waiting for him or the other captives to make a move.

Minutes passed, and he heard another sound from the same direction; but he heard no more voices, no more scuffling of feet—just heavy breathing and the sound of someone moving along the floor. After a short while, Budail fell back into his previous state; his nausea and the pain from his bowels were back. The adrenalin from the action in the room had served only as an injection of fluids into his system, and he desperately needed to relieve himself. He involuntarily let out a low groan.

Preacher's head spun around the instant he realized that the groan came from the other side of the room. He thought he knew where Whittaker was since they were thrown into the room together. He was worried that if he moved or made another sound, one of Fezman's henchmen would strike another painful blow, and he was in enough pain as it was. Yet the other presence in the room did not appear to be that of a captor. He was infinitely curious to know who the presence was, but his instincts told him to remain silent. And so there they sat, as if in a duel, two contestants waiting for the other to make the first move. But what of Whittaker?

Whittaker was unconscious. His orders to Preacher to take things easy had earned him a swift blow to the back of his head from a rifle butt, which knocked him out. Preacher didn't know it, but he was lying only three feet away from Whittaker.

For an hour he and Whittaker sat almost staring at each other through their hoods without knowing it. When Preacher started scraping his head against the wall in an attempt to remove the hood he found that it wasn't tied down, so he actually made progress. In a short while, he managed to get the sack cloth to the top of his head; it was enough for him to peer out from underneath and take in his surroundings.

It was only then that the stench hit him. He spied the shape of a man across the room that looked as if he had soiled his clothes—and it was not Whittaker. As he slowly scanned the room, he saw the prone body of the colonel lying not too far away from him. At first he thought the officer was dead, but with relief, he could see the rise and fall of his commander's chest.

Just as Preacher was sizing up the situation, Whittaker let out a loud "Jesus Christ, my head hurts!"

"We're not alone," Preacher quickly replied.

"What?"

"We are not alone," he repeated. "There's another person in the room."

Whittaker said no more and struggled to get himself into a sitting position, grunting and groaning as he did so.

"Lean over towards me," Preacher whispered. "I can get your hood off."

Across the room, Budail remained perplexed. He understood a little English from the various US Army field manuals that he'd seen over the years, but he could not now see or understand what was happening, so he remained silent.

Both Americans were now looking across the room, staring at Budail. In a way they felt sorry for him, as he looked like a non-combatant, clearly one who could not control his bodily functions too well. On the other hand, he was there for a reason. Since they themselves were there for illicit intentions, Whittaker rationally surmised that the other man in the room must also be a player caught out unawares.

CHAPTER SEVEN

ISKENDERUN, TURKEY

AFTER SOME TIME, AN IMAGINARY BOND SEEMED TO FORM between Whittaker, Preacher, and Budail. The Americans actually sympathized with their fellow captive, thinking that the man in the cell, in his dilapidated state, had just been caught up in some messy business deal with their Turk captors. They had absolutely no idea that the arms they themselves had been peddling had been destined to go indirectly to the man sitting on the floor in the opposite corner of the room.

The guards had not been back since the Americans had been deposited in the cell-like room. Hours had passed, and Preacher used the time to think of escape routes or ways to talk himself out of the situation. Finally, two of the guards did return, and at first they approached the now unhooded Americans. But as soon as they saw the state that Budail was in, they broke into laughter and pelted the Arab with a barrage of abuse. To cause further embarrassment to their prisoner, they removed the sack cloth to reveal his face.

Now with the guards' backs to the Americans, Preacher saw his chance. He made eye contact with his boss and intimated that he wanted to take action. Whittaker nodded his approval; he didn't want to be stuck in this hole any longer either.

Preacher didn't need any further commands. Still lying on the floor, he turned himself on his side and swiftly kicked the back legs of the guard nearest to him, who immediately fell to his knees with a shriek. The second guard spun around and reached for his weapon just as Budail, in a burst of self-preservation, used both his feet to kick the man from behind. As the second guard fell Whittaker tried to stop the man from falling on top of him; he held his feet up in defense—and not a second too soon. His right foot caught the guard directly in his Adam's apple, incapacitating him.

By this time, the first guard had recovered but was still on his knees, reaching for his dropped weapon. Preacher kicked the man in the face, but it only served to stun the man for a second.

A second was all Budail needed. He jumped up to his feet and dropped his full weight, almost 220 pounds, on top of the guard. Preacher moved in closer and wrapped his legs around the now prone Turk that Budail had dropped on.

Whittaker, not wanting to be left out of the action, also jumped on top of the pile, adding his weight in order to keep the guard down. Preacher by this time was using all his leg strength to squeeze the neck of the Turk. It seemed as if it took forever as Preacher looked into the bulging eyes of the man he was trying to kill. The man was strong, and he tried to struggle, but the weight of two men on his back and the legs wrapped like a vise around his neck were just too much. Preacher watched as the life's blood drained from the guard's face, his breathing was coming in short, sharp bursts, but the Turk would not give up. Preacher, getting tired, would not let up either, and he squeezed again.

Whittaker could sense that the kill was taking too long and he untangled himself from the pile. He got to his feet and with his best impression of a professional wrestler, he dropped on top of the Turk and Budail with a full body slam. That did the trick. The Turk went limp.

As they began extricating themselves from the dead guard, Preacher looked over to the first Turk they had taken down. He was lying face up, grasping his throat with two hands. His breathing was making a disturbing cackling sound. The man's larynx had been shattered. It wasn't terminal and a tracheotomy would suffice until he could get professional medical care. Preacher knew this, but he was not a professional caregiver—he was a professional killer.

Preacher stood up and surveyed the scene; Budail had somehow managed to free himself of his bonds and was assisting Whittaker with his. Preacher didn't wait for any prompts from the colonel this time; he raised his right foot directly above the incapacitated man and drove it down with all his might—directly onto the injured man's throat, crushing his larynx completely. For good measure Preacher dug in with his heel and twisted his foot until he could hear the shattering of even more bone and gristle. It did not take long for the man to pass.

Preacher, his foot still in its place, then stared back at Whittaker. It was as if he was asking for vindication, acknowledgement that he was back in the colonel's good graces.

Whittaker gave a slim smile and nodded. *Good man,* he thought. *Good man.*

The whole event took less than five minutes, and during that time not a single word was uttered between the prisoners. Now all three captives stood and looked at each other, not knowing what to say. Whittaker motioned for all to remain silent and then hinted to Budail to take one of the dead guards clothes so that he could get out of the soiled clothes that he was wearing.

During the time that it took the Arab to change, the two Americans huddled in a whispered conference.

"What's next, boss?" Preacher began. "Does he come with us?"

"Why not?" Whittaker responded. "It's obvious that he helped out. I don't know what he has done to deserve being here, but it must be for a good reason. So let's keep a close eye on him. But if he's a local, maybe he can get us out of here."

Preacher nodded in silent agreement, and they both turned to Budail, who was now dressed and checking the action of a pistol. Both Americans were taken by surprise and took a step back.

"Shit …," Preacher blurted out.

Whittaker laid a reassuring hand on Preacher's wrist. "It's okay."

Budail realized his mistake and made an attempt at an apology, whispering, "Sorry, sorry," and placing the gun in his waistband. The two Americans remained in place, not knowing where they stood with their newfound friend. Budail brushed passed them, retrieved an Uzi submachine gun lying in the corner, and handed it to Whittaker. "Sorry, sorry," he repeated.

Whittaker looked deep into Budail's eyes and thought, *This seeming bungling idiot is not all we thought him to be. He knows his weapons, and he knows that we all need to be together if we're to get out of here alive. He needs us—and we probably need him.*

Once comfortable with each other, Whittaker looked at Budail and motioned with his fingers the symbol for walking out, then put his fingers to his lips, urging him to remain quiet. Budail got the message, but when he approached the door they all froze in place. Shots were ringing out somewhere else in the facility.

Whittaker motioned everyone down. He was anticipating more company and decided that the cell would be their defensive position until things quieted down outside. As they patiently waited, a firefight erupted with shots and small explosions being heard throughout the complex. Minutes went by, and soon all they could hear was a single shot or two at random intervals. Whittaker calculated that it was time to move.

Budail headed for the door, and Preacher, looking for guidance, found it when Whittaker followed. All three proceeded down an unlit corridor of what looked like some disused and rundown office space. As they moved from area to area, they checked for other signs of life, but saw none. When they finally came to a large warehouse and open space, Budail got the shock of his life. There must have been ten well-armed men standing waiting for them, weapons drawn. In the center of the mass stood the Protector. Budail's heart missed a beat as he dropped his weapon and fell to his knees, calling "Allahu Akbar, Allahu Akbar."

Whittaker saw the futility of raising his gun against the mass that stood before him. He thought his day could not get any worse.

—❦—

Budail was shocked at the sight of his commander standing in the flesh before him. Although he was aware that Abdul Al Haafiz knew some of Budail's own contacts and the locations where they operated, he did not think that the Protector would ever have the audacity to move out of his relatively comfortable surroundings in Beirut and be out and about in the middle of the black market.

The Protector, however, had not been idle. Soon after dishing out orders to kill the Turkish dealers, he instructed his intelligence section to investigate a lead that he had received from Samman, the Lebanese grocer. Haafiz would not be satisfied with killing a few soldiers who were merely transporters; his conviction for revenge ran much deeper. His purpose was to scare people into knowing that he was looking for retribution for the death of his daughter and that he would not rest in peace until those who carried out the attack were brought to justice—his justice.

The grocer had been correct: the lifeless face of the Turk that he had seen after the attack in Bonn had been a relatively well-known figure in the Turkish community of Cologne, and word had soon spread throughout the city that the man died in the kidnap attempt on the US ambassador. Again the Protector was not satisfied with killing or the death of cannon fodder; he needed to know *why* this had happened in the first place. He needed to know who had given such orders, so that he could be punished in the same way as the captain who ordered the rocket attack that resulted in the death of the Protector's parents. It would not be pretty. To Haafiz the lust for revenge was now his sole reason for being. First his parents and now his beloved Gadwa—all lost to the bloody hands of others. It needed to stop; it needed to end his way. If he had to, he would pay the ultimate price for what he thought was right.

But if he was to die, then it would be by his own design and not before he revenged the death of his loved ones. The only problem was that the Protector was making a grave mistake.

He moved around the warehouse like the possessed soul that Budail had witnessed days earlier when the barrel of a warm gun was stuffed into his face. The Protector came seeking information, and he was not concerned on how he obtained it. He started with the youngest of the Turkish gang, who happened to be the nephew of Fezman. The young man pleaded for mercy as he had no information to give about the Bonn kidnapping. By the sixth dead body, the Protector had moved on to Fezman himself realizing that the fat Turkish commander was telling the truth, and so he ended his life with the same lack of remorse as with the others, with a 9mm bullet shot through the eye.

After the slaughter, the Protector found himself a comfortable office chair, which he had placed near the butchered men. The smell of blood was everywhere, but it did not faze him in the least. He sat quietly and began to relax as if it was just another day at the office with nothing to worry about. He took a long deep breath and then sighed as he contemplated his next move. His men all looked around at each other anxiously, concerned about what would happen. One of his lieutenants began to utter a request. The Protector simply waved his right index finger as if to say *silence*, and the warehouse became as silent as a tomb.

The mistake he was making was not as apparent to him as he first realized. Again, his temper got the better of his judgment, and he flew into a rage that could only be appeased by exerting pain and suffering on someone, anyone. His drive was the thought of his little Gadwa and the pain that she had suffered throughout her short life. He still mourned the death of his parents, and he cursed the world when his wife attempted to take her own life as she grieved the loss of their daughter.

After Gadwa's death, Haafiz cried himself to sleep and ate little for days, so traumatized was he. He could not and would not function for days at a time. Gadwa was his gift from the Prophet. Her life was his life; her pain was his. She could not be replaced, but she could be revenged.

As with all business decisions, a new strategy or tack in day-to-day operations needs to be discussed with a board of directors. Cutting off supplies to the Turks was a business decision made by the Protector alone when he was in a fit of rage. Budail, the voice of reason and his executive officer, was slammed for opening his mouth. Others from his organization pleaded with him for reason and understanding—but it was not to be. The CEO of the company had spoken, and death was the order of the day, and he had decided that he would lead by example. However, by killing the head of the Turkish dealers, Haafiz had inadvertently cut off his own supply of quality American weapons. The bigger problem, though, was that he cut the supply lines of two other large illegitimate corporations—Hezbollah and the nefarious Turkish terrorist organization, the PKK.

The Iskenderun fish-processing factory had been abandoned for more than thirty years. It was never a solid building, as it was built in the early 1900s without much thought to longevity. As with many structures in this part of the world, it was constructed with much haste and not a lot of money or oversight. What money was spent lined the pockets of local building inspectors, who were only too willing to turn a blind eye to shoddy craftsmanship for the right price. Nevertheless, since 1902, it had stood the test of time—but all the locals knew that one good gust of wind would surely collapse the entire building.

As the Protector contemplated his next move, he became aware of a light odor emanating from the factory. Even after decades of inactivity, the bowels of the processing plant still regurgitated the remnants of dead fish. Rumor had it that the last owners of the complex, who went out of business, simply walked out with all the employees one day, leaving everything in its place. They managed to turn off all the processing and canning equipment but left the fish to rot. It took the local city council another three years to do anything about the place, but by then the damage was done. Just like the paper mills of the Pacific Northwest and the infamous aroma of Tacoma, there would always be the smell of something foul in the air in Iskenderun.

The Protector felt as if he had to get out of there and get moving again. He was becoming more and more frustrated, even as he tortured and killed off the members of the Turkish gang. If he'd only known that standing before him was the man who had orchestrated the attack on Heymann, his worries would have been over. As he sat on an old office chair in the cavernous warehouse, he drew himself into deeper thought, but his deliberations were disturbed as the wind picked up and the building began to shake. Rain had been battering the facility for hours, and the ill-maintained roof let in torrents of water, which formed great pools on the factory floor. In some areas, the sound gave off the mysterious feeling of being in a cavern behind a waterfall.

To confuse the issues swirling around his head, the Protector now had two Americans in front of him—and he had no idea why they were here. He contemplated "questioning" his new captives, but he also needed to talk with Budail.

As he was mulling over his approach, the decision process was taken out of his hands. The wind and rain had picked up enough to start the building swaying, while the stronger gusts lashed the decrepit old factory. The wind finally ripped off a section of the roof, which caused the rusty old structure to start to buckle. A steel crossbeam loosed itself from the interior structure at one end of the building, and the domino effect was enough to get the supporting walls and infrastructure to collapse with it. Sheets of metal and old timbers began raining down at one end of the building, and the disintegration made its way towards the group, who were by now staring in disbelief at nature's destruction.

Whittaker was the first to react, grabbing Preacher by the collar and yanking him in the direction from which they had come. They ran towards a shipping dock that had a three-foot pit where trucks had been backed in for shipments. They both managed to cover themselves as best as possible by crouching against the concrete structure of the pit. Preacher risked one last look at the destruction and caught a glimpse of gunmen being crushed by a storm of falling masonry and old steel. He never looked back again as a sheet of corrugated metal fell within inches of his head just as he was peering over their cover.

———— ∞∞∞ ————

Preacher and Whittaker must have crouched in the same position for fifteen minutes as the last of the debris from the fish factory fell. The sheet of metal that had narrowly missed Preacher's head was now lying on top of both Americans and had actually acted as a shield from other falling materials. They felt somewhat safe, even while the wind and rain continued to beat what was left of the old building into mercy. Whittaker was aware that the threat of further damage to the structure and themselves was a distinct possibility. They needed to get out of there soon.

Whittaker was still feeling a little out of sorts from his encounter with his captors in the makeshift cell. That hit to the head, combined with a piece of flying ceiling tile landing on his head during the storm, meant he needed more than a little help to get on his feet. Preacher got things moving and began to shift wreckage around so they could get out. Managing to extricate themselves from the pile of rubble, dust, and remains of the old factory, Preacher and Whittaker took in their surroundings. The rain was still falling heavily and what remained of the structure was likely to fall down at any moment. Time was not on their side, but they could not leave, as somebody inside had their passports, which had been taken earlier by Fezman's men.

They started searching dead bodies and soon came to realize that it could all be in vain. There was simply just too much debris to contend with, they had no tools or machinery to move the steel and masonry, and there was no way that they would find everyone in the mess. They found Budail's head ten feet away from the rest of his body, decapitated by sheet metal.

They had no money, no credit cards, no passports; they were really up shit creek without a paddle. As they dug in desperation to find their documentation, they heard a faint cry from underneath a pile of wood.

"Americans, Americans, over here!" Preacher was first to respond. He dug frantically, searching for the voice. Whittaker, exhausted, reluctantly joined in the dig and found a hand, then a wrist, to grab a hold of. After much exertion, the man was freed from the tomb, and he dusted off what looked like an inch of masonry dust.

The man was elated about being rescued but held off giving Whittaker a hug of thanks. Instead, he pulled out of a pocket two American passports and two wallets. "Thank you, thank you," he said and shook hands with both the men. "I need go to Germany. You help me … I have money. You help me?"

Whittaker and Preacher exchanged looks and smiled for the first time in what seemed like ages. It was Whittaker who answered and grabbed at the documents. "Yes, absolutely," he said and gave the Protector a gentle but kind slap on the back.

—⊶⊷—

The storm that had collapsed the old fish factory was still raging, but another in the warehouse had also not perished there: one of the youngest of the Turkish gang was alive but trapped in the rubble. He considered trying to free himself but held his place for the time being in fear of being discovered by the mad Arab and suffering the same fate as the rest of his colleagues. From his hidden position, he could see everything happening around him, but he couldn't understand a word that was spoken. Yet he was intelligent enough to figure out—or so it seemed—that the Arab and the Americans were friends.

Power went out throughout the port city as trees and power lines collapsed under the heavy weather. Hours earlier, the captain of *Juno* reluctantly sought the shelter of the harbor to spare his ship a battering by the high seas and gale-force winds out in the Mediterranean. His cargo had become unstable enough that his crew was in danger of being hurt or killed by the volatile goods aboard.

The weather did play into the captain's hands for a short time, however, as the storm kept most people indoors. So nobody checked the freighter as she pitched and rolled through the breakwater to the dock. The harbormaster was busy taking care of his family at home; he couldn't have cared less who came or went on a day like this.

As the *Juno* found a berth in the crowded dock, the captain realized there weren't even any stevedores to assist in tying the ship up, so he ordered a few of his younger crew to leap onto the quayside to take in the lines. As the last of them were secured, lights around the harbor began to flicker on and off, trying to compensate for the lack of natural light. Lightning streaked across the nearby sky, and anything that wasn't securely tied down dockside made its way into the harbor's turbulent waters. The captain of the *Juno* peered out from the bridge. He had been at sea long enough to gauge the progress of a storm. The black sky in daylight, the thunder, and the close lightning told him it would get worse before it got better.

With this type of cargo, he decided his crew would be safer on land than on the ship. He was about to issue the order for all ashore when a bolt of lightning hit a nearby power transformer mounted on a pole. The captain looked on in horror as the pole and its power lines toppled towards his ship. The pole, with sparks flying like a child's Fourth of July sparkler, hit the foredeck of the *Juno*.

At once, one hundred thousand volts snapped their way down the live wires and onto the deck of the ship. It didn't matter that the cargo hold was covered or the crates of guns and ammunition below were crated and lashed down—what mattered was that the oil and gasoline drums had spilt on the deck during the storm. One of the crew struggled to get away from the live wires, but he slipped on the greasy surface—allowing more of the fuel to make its way to the hungry electrical force squirming its way on the deck.

The explosion could be seen, felt, and heard for miles around. It was so deafening that the sound of thunder almost became a dull afterthought rather than an imposing display of nature's fury.

Whittaker and the Protector's faces were lit up like Halloween pumpkins as they stared in awe at the massive fireball coming from the port. They were heading out of town in a stolen car. Preacher, who was driving, exchanged glances with Whittaker. They knew what type of explosion it likely was, especially with the *Juno* so close by. The Protector remained in awe of the sight, not offering any comment except a quiet, "Drive. It's best we drive, yes?" And with that, Preacher put his foot down and headed out in search of an airport that could take them out of the country.

Mehmet, the only survivor of the Turkish gang at the warehouse also recoiled at the sight and sound of the huge fireball permeating the storm-darkened sky. He did not know what it was or what it meant; he just knew he had to get away from the canning factory as quickly as possible. The Americans and their Arab friend had gone; it was safe to attempt his escape.

Of the fifteen people who had entered the old factory that day, only four made it out alive. As Mehmet extricated himself from the rubble, he searched in vain for others of his gang. All he found were the remnants of dismembered corpses and blood, mixed in with the dust and debris of the fallen masonry and old steel. Amazingly, he only had a superficial wound to his head, which, although it stopped bleeding, had left a long trail of blood down his face and onto his clothes. He knew he wouldn't stand out too much when he staggered through the storm-beaten streets;

he could pass his injury off on the flying wreckage, which still filled the tempestuous skies.

After a half-hour of walking, the young Turk finally made it back to his gang's local café. There were a few patrons inside, mostly those that hung out there on a regular basis and sipped tea, smoked, and played cards all day, every day. Many of the regulars were a bunch of "old boys" who were no strangers to local criminal activities, and more than a few had spent some time locked away for their past indiscretions.

When Mehmet entered, some of the old crew rallied around him, offering him aid and helping clean him up. They knew there was a story to match his head wound, and all were eager for a bit of action. He knew that he was in trusted company; what was spoken openly in the café was held confidential—unless a stranger was present, which in most cases was never. Everyone knew everyone in this part of the town.

The local brigade commander for the PKK was amongst those who sipped age-old tea and chain-smoked their way through the day at the café. On hearing the boy's news, he flew into a small rage and swore to himself that vengeance would come. He never liked or trusted Americans, and now it seemed that two agents, probably CIA, were in his area—disrupting his operations. Although he wanted to be the one to find and punish the saboteurs, he knew he needed to push this information up the chain of command to divisional headquarters, which would in turn request action from the PKK general command in Istanbul.

It didn't take long for the PKK command authority to come to a decision. They reached into their bucket of special projects—some of which were operations that just needed the requisite support and logistics before being put into action. As with most terrorist organizations, the PKK had a number of pending operations on their books—some of which would never see the light of day, others that were low-level attacks, and others that if carried out would have serious political and military implications. There were five operations ready for implementation in the next few days, following the administrative process. Two were considered top priorities: one in Berlin and the other in Washington, DC.

CHAPTER
EIGHT

MITTE, BERLIN

THE CONVERSATION STOPPED MID-SENTENCE as one of the passengers pointed at Chris.

"It's okay. Chris is on board; he works for me," Nash said, easing the passengers' doubts about the sensitivity of the conversation and the discretion of the driver at the wheel. There were in fact three passengers in the car that Chris was driving—his boss, Nash, a senior diplomat from the Department of Defense, and a three-star general in uniform who was riding shotgun with the Brit. Chris paid attention only when he heard his name mentioned and gave a quick glance in his rearview mirror to look at his boss. "Steven," Nash explained further, "Chris has been vetted. He's been with me for some time now. Anything said in this car remains in the car."

The DOD official carried on his conversation about the conflict in Yugoslavia, aware that if the CIA chief of station said the driver could be trusted, then on his head it be, although he did change his tack by prolonging the topic, but in a much vaguer fashion.

Chris didn't care about what was being said. He was concentrating on the road ahead and playing out potential attack scenarios over in his mind; that was his job.

The CIA car was returning from a trip to a meeting with the representatives of German Military Intelligence and the Bundesnachritchtendienst in Berlin. The meeting overran its scheduled two-hour time slot, and Chris was trying to make up time on the road. They were less than a mile from the embassy when Chris noticed a black Mercedes at the traffic light directly in front of him. Although the light was green, the car remained in position at the stoplight. As Chris proceeded slowly ahead, the light changed to red, and the Mercedes still sat in its position. The conversation in the car stopped cold when a passenger, who was wearing what looked like a cheap suit, got out from the stationary car and proceeded in the direction of the armored BMW.

Chris's mind went into overdrive with real-time what-if scenarios. He checked his rearview mirror only to see a rather large truck coming up quickly behind him. He looked forward again to analyze the situation as it was unfolding before him. Alarm bells went off in his head when Chris could not see the suspect's right hand; it was obscured by an unfolded map the man was carrying.

The three-star sitting next to Chris began sweating profusely and reached for the already locked door handle.

Chris went through his options as the seconds flew by and the man still approached his car. He could not back up, as the truck was now so close behind him that he could only use his side mirrors to view what was going on behind him.

Although he was in a tense situation, he was still at an advantage since he had spotted the potential trouble early enough ahead of time. He was not surprised; he was alert and ready to take action. Almost two car-lengths away from the blocking vehicle in front, he gave himself two options: going around the stationary Mercedes either to the left or right. But the man was still approaching, and coming on quickly. As the gap between Chris and the man began to narrow, Chris began to turn the wheel towards the approaching suspect while still keeping the vehicle moving at a very slow crawl.

Chris knew what he was going to do next—he was primed and ready to move; all he needed was one more threat indicator for him to spring into action. There was absolutely no doubt now in his mind about what he was going to do next. This is what he trained for. There was no element of surprise. He was in the zone and ready to go. If the man revealed a weapon from behind the map, then Chris would gun the engine and run over his sorry ass. He was so focused on the target in front of him and the surrounding pieces that he felt totally alone; it was as if his passengers did not exist for a moment, as they all sat there in an imaginary competition to see who could hold their breath the longest. The only sound from the car was the low but menacing grumbling sound of the powerful V6 BMW 525i engine, waiting to spring into action.

But Chris didn't feel right; there was something wrong. He took a breath and reconsidered his options: one, run the bastard over; two, put his foot down and pass the stationary car on the left; three, jump the curb on the right, ride down the sidewalk and take the next right, turning at the corner; or four, do nothing.

One of the valuable lessons that was taught by his instructors during these types of scenarios was not to do what terrorists expect you to do. If there is an obvious means of escape, such as passing a stationary car on its left into no oncoming traffic, then that's what the terrorists planned. Who knew what was in the car in front or what was down the street further? Was the ambush further down the road, and the Mercedes was a rear-blocking vehicle when you got into their favored kill zone? Was the best option to jump the curb, take out a few trashcans, and drive through some bushes at the side of the road? What if there was a bomb planted exactly at the junction? What was around the corner to the right? Does the suspect want Chris to go around either way and not back up?

All these things were flashing through Chris's mind. He knew his passengers were willing him to do *something*, but he stayed focused on what the man in front was about to do next. The others in the car didn't realize it, but Chris needed one more piece to the puzzle before he would to act. He needed to see that weapon; he needed to see the man's right hand. He needed someone outside the car to do something first.

By this point, the man was almost even with his car, and Chris looked quickly over to his right as he noticed the three-star become more and more uncomfortable with the situation. Chris gunned the engine one time and which made the car jerk forward. The approaching man hesitated a second and, with a look of fear on his face, stepped away from the vehicle. Chris then made his decision ... he would do nothing.

The traffic light changed back to green, and the driver of the Mercedes sounded his horn, waving for his passenger to come back to the car, which the man in the suit dutifully did. The man got back in the car, and both driver and passenger drove away. Chris trundled precariously forward and, as soon as the light changed to red, hit the gas and shot through the intersection knowing how illegal that was. Nothing happened—no bombs, no shots, no terrorists in the bushes, nothing. Whatever it was, it was over. The only sounds that could be heard then were those of a racing engine and of three men in the car relaxing in their seats.

It took Chris another three minutes to get to the embassy, and no further words were spoken as he dropped his passengers at the main entry to the building.

The only time that Chris would open a door for someone was if that someone was a lady. If he was with his boss and any of his male guests, then they would open the doors for themselves. This time was no exception. After all, who would drive the car away in an emergency if the shit hit the fan? There would be no time to draw a weapon and take bad guys down. Chris's mission was to get off the X and get away from the attack site—hopefully with his boss in the car. And so from the comfort of the vehicle, he watched the train of VIPs enter the building while he scanned the surrounding area for possible problems. All doors were closed to the car, and all bodies were inside the safety of the building, but Chris waited a few minutes more before driving away, just in case a new mission was requested.

As he was still scanning the area, Nash reappeared and opened the front passenger door. "I thought you were going to run him over," he said with a wink, "but I'm glad you didn't."

Chris gave just a hint of a smile. "I just did my job, Mr. Nash."

"Well you're doing a fine job, and even the general realizes that. We'll talk more later. Go relax awhile, and we'll see you later, okay?"

"Okay, Mr. Nash, no worries. See you later," Chris replied and then waited another full minute before eventually pulling away and heading for the embassy motor pool, where he generally hung out while waiting for his next assignment.

Since he worked for the CIA indirectly, only a select few knew exactly who Chris drove for. None of the other German and foreign nationals at the motor pool had a clue whose chauffeur he was , much less an idea of what exactly he was trained to do. To the other drivers, Chris was part of the pool but had been assigned VIP duties because of his bilingual skills. Some of the crew who had been at the embassy much longer were a little jealous of Chris's quick promotion from general driver to VIP chauffeur but weren't envious of his long periods away, nor did they covet the strange hours that he worked.

Chris parked his car amongst the other official vehicles outside the dispatch office and headed towards the drivers down-room. On entering, he said hello to everyone, who for the most part were playing cards, and he planted himself in front of the blaring TV. As he began to unwind, he had to check himself from smiling too much in case someone noticed and began asking questions. Instead, he scrolled through his thoughts, trying to assess and justify his actions from the non-incident earlier. *Why didn't I run the sorry-ass over?* he thought. *Why didn't I jump the curb? What made me do nothing but earn praise from my boss?*

The simple reason was that the CIA went to considerable lengths to train Chris the way that they wanted him trained. The evaluation and tough decision making were part of the one-on-one training that he received. Although he was trained to handle a vehicle by former NASCAR drivers who showed him how to drive fast but safe, his real education and conditioning came from people who dissected vehicular terrorist attacks, which had occurred all over the world.

His main mentor was one of the first Americans on the scene of the Martyn Schleyer attack in Cologne decades before. He vehemently argued that with better mental preparation, Schleyer's driver would be alive today to tell people how he had averted a terrorist kidnapping. The Germans didn't listen, but the CIA did.

Unfortunately the skilled professionals, the ones like Chris, who can read an incident like an NFL touchdown play and take action when needed, owe their lives to the men and women who have given the ultimate sacrifice in the everlasting fight against terrorism.

Although the general in the car may have thought otherwise at the time, everything that Chris did, or did not do, was taught and calculated. He correctly rationalized that although he was approaching a choke point, an area where a vehicle or person must enter to get to a destination, he was not on a scheduled trip; therefore the risk of an incident was far lower than usual. He recognized that the black Mercedes was not from Berlin; it had license plates from Frankfurt. The man who approached the car was black and wearing a suit, an unusual sight in Germany, but not in an area that was permeated with foreign embassies from all over the world, including Africa. The man was also carrying a map of Berlin. In the few seconds that Chris had to make his decision of no-action, he correctly assumed that a black man wearing a suit in a hired car from Frankfurt, who was carrying a map, was likely lost and simply looking for directions. But how painful it was for the general, who did not know that but, instead, sweated bullets.

—⚬⚭⚬—

Chris and Nash arrived at the CIA officer's residence at 7:05 p.m. on Friday evening. Chris was able to vary his route well enough that it was hard for an adversary to track the routine. But it was only when the gates of the residence were closed and the engine turned off that Nash opened up the conversation. "Chris, why don't you step inside for a few minutes," he invited. "I just need a quick chat. You can wait in the library if you want."

"Sure, Mr. Nash," Chris said, "I'll just turn the car around, and I'll be right in."

A few moments later, Chris was patiently standing in the library when he was startled by the low menacing growl of Wilhelm, the Nash's rather large German shepherd. Although Chris and Wilhelm had met on numerous occasions before, the dog still liked to announce his authority to friend or foe. After realizing who Chris was, however, Wilhelm trotted off across the hardwood floors to find something more interesting than just the guy who always took his parents away. Chris began to relax a little and tried to take in his surroundings. He had been in the Nash library before, but it was just as interesting each time.

There were pictures of Nash and US presidents, Nash and foreign dignitaries, Nash in foreign places, commendations from various governments and agencies—it was all there. There were books of fiction; dictionaries in German, French, Russian, and Chinese; signed copies of biographies from former presidents or famous politicians; books on politics, history, science, military affairs; and even the classics of Shakespeare, Hemmingway, and Dickens. The list went on and on.

Chris had also on more than one occasion browsed through the volumes of photo albums that lay around the room, often wondering how much Nash had seen and experienced and what it would be like to be in a similar role, not just being a spy, but actually being a *chief of spies*, making life-or-death decisions, making decisions that could turn into international scandals, running agents …

"Chris, how's it going?" Nash popped into the library, breaking his driver's reverie. "Please, sit down a minute. I won't keep you long." Nash placed himself in a comfortable high-back leather chair. "I have to head out to DC on Saturday. I realize this is short notice, but I've got to attend some meetings and such. Can you drop me at the airport?"

"Yes, sure, Mr. Nash. What time shall I pick you up?"

"Probably around 0700, but I'll know more tomorrow afternoon … I also need for you to go to Washington as well. Carla is still trying to get your ticket squared away, and she'll let you know when you should leave."

Chris was taken aback. He had never been to the United States with his boss and immediately thought he was in the shit for something.

Nash picked up on the body language. "Don't worry, Chris. You haven't done anything wrong," he assured. "Some people at the office would like to chat with you. Besides, I think you're coming close to your bi-annual training week, aren't you?"

"Yes, but I think there's quite a bit to sort out for that kind of trip," Chris replied, worried that he might not be ready in time.

"It's okay, Chris. Carla is working on it with the head office. I expect that you'll be away for about two weeks. Can you handle that?"

"Sure, Mr. Nash. I'm flexible enough. My grab bag is already packed for a short trip, but I can repack that pretty quickly."

"Good, but what about Astrid? Is she going to be all right with you taking off?"

Chris hesitated before he answered. *Was Nash just playing a game that he already had the answers to?* There was more to his reply than a simple yes or no. The government, especially its clandestine services, promoted stability in relationships. The theory was that if an employee in a high-stress environment was able to relax with his partner, then the risk of doing something illicit was minimized, unless the partner was also complicit in illegal activities such as was the case with Aldrich Ames. Conversely single men or women posted overseas by their governments were at risk to honey traps or entrapment by other governments, or tended to engage in other stupid pastimes, such as drugs or gambling. Although Chris was not a direct employee of a government, he was still expected to maintain an appearance of a well-balanced individual with good personal security and high ethical standards; nevertheless, it did not bode well to lie to the chief of station CIA Germany.

"Mr. Nash, Astrid and I are no longer together."

The poker-faced Texan replied with sincerity in his voice. "That's too bad, Chris. I'm sorry to hear that."

"We had a difference of opinion, and we decided to go our separate ways," Chris said and shrugged, not knowing what to say next.

Nash could tell it was hurtful for Chris to talk about it, and he didn't let him dwell on it for too long. "Well, maybe this is a chance for a change, get out of here for a while, get some of that kick-ass training you've been telling me about. Go bash some cars up and shoot some guns and get it out of your system. Get your focus back on track."

That last statement stung. Chris thought that he *was* focused. Again he thought, *He already knew. He's just playing, the clever bastard,* and with a smile replied, "There's nothing like crashing perfectly good cars to boost the morale, Mr. Nash. I'd be more than happy to go."

"Great, see you tomorrow. Have a good night."

"Thanks, Mr. Nash. You, too."

DAY 11

COLOGNE, GERMANY

The Cologne airport authorities had struggled with their airport and its lack of sufficient space for many, many years. While the German government still resided in Bonn, the regional hub at nearby Cologne grew only slightly to accept international flights. However, these were still only European international flights and not any from further afield. The runways were capable of accommodating larger international aircraft, such as Boeing 747s, but the gateways around the terminal were not. So the majority of flights that landed at Cologne were from Lufthansa, Air Italia, Air France, Turkish Airlines, and other short-haul carriers.

The capacity crunch was exacerbated by the growing attractiveness of Turkey as a favored vacation spot for German tourists and the ever-growing interest of Turkish nationals wanting to find work and visit families in Germany. In 1995, the Turkish guest-worker population there grew to two million, and the trend seemed to indicate the number could double in five to ten years.

German government officials who still traveled back and forth between the new capital and the old were tired of dealing with the throngs of travelers who caused traffic chaos and safety issues each weekend at the airport. The situation worsened when members of the German parliament—who thought themselves better than tourists—and the Turks made pact with the German Federal Aviation Office.

As such, all Cologne-based flights to and from Turkey with Turkish nationals aboard were shifted to Sunday and Wednesday evenings only. This resulted in virtual Turkish national air convoys on those evenings. The other half of the deal was to send all other tourists to the larger and more accommodating Dusseldorf airport, just an hour's drive north of Cologne.

For the most part, the madness at Cologne airport subsided, at least for a while. But Sunday nights at the airport resembled a never-ending melee at a Turkish bazaar.

The German police eventually got involved in trying to control the mayhem, even running a recruiting campaign directed at hiring third-generation German Turks who were fluent in both languages and able to deal with the Turks in their own cultural way. Still, each time the convoy of aircraft would disgorge new travelers, the baggage area turned into a mosh pit of Turks duking it out for luggage that all looked alike.

When the Protector saw the craziness of it all after arriving from Adana, he gave up his search for what little baggage he had and simply walked away.

Although the German authorities thought they were making a wise decision to combat the airport madness by focusing all their efforts in dealing with the traveling Turkish guest workers, what they inadvertently did, however, was to take away valuable security resources for other important operations.

When government VIPs were forced to use a commercial airport for travel, protection details were heavily involved in the transportation of their executives. Only a select few of the residing German cabinet were allowed to use the nearby Cologne-Wahn military base for official travel, as on numerous past occasions bureaucrats thought themselves above the rules and used military transportation for personal use.

Therefore, the number of VIP travelers traveling via the Cologne airport grew, and the need for a saturated security presence there was high. A number of federal agencies were involved to maintain order and protect officials.

The German FBI was the lead organization for that effort, with members of the GSG9 on permanent standby in nearby Bonn-Hangelar. Other uniformed members of the border police, the Bundesgrenschutz, were also permanently on duty—and their numbers always doubled when VIP traffic was high.

To all outsiders, the Cologne airport looked like a high-security environment with surveillance specialists and covert teams deployed around every choke point around the airport.

But the Sunday that the Protector arrived from Turkey, the only security protection in sight was the clique of German/Turkish police who were busy breaking up fights and impounding illegally parked cars—an unenviable task, which was just as bad as herding cats. VIP protection or covert surveillance was not even a second thought for the overtasked street cops.

So nobody gave the Arab a second glance as he passed through baggage and into the Customs control area with nothing to declare. The video cameras were pointed towards baggage claim, to catch those starting fights or stealing bags. If the cameras had been facing the exiting travelers, as designed by the security consultants, then the face of the Protector might have been captured and used for later analysis. The image might have triggered an alert to Interpol that one of their persons of interest had just arrived in Germany with the much-needed time-and-date stamp affixed to the video image. It was not.

If the Protector thought the Customs and baggage area inside was chaotic, what waited for him outside the restricted area was worse. On first appearances, it looked like a crowd at a football match waiting in tense anticipation for their team to score a goal as the sliding doors opened to allow travelers out. As soon as the doors moved an inch, everyone outside stood on tiptoes, waiting for some action, only to slump back down disappointedly as the faces before the crowd did not match any members of the team. Two young cops tried in vain to hold the crowds back and allow the travelers to leave, but the mob only pushed back as a foaming-at-the-mouth German shepherd police dog tried to bark order into the chaos. The Protector finally made his way to the busy taxi stand and hopped in for a ride to downtown Cologne.

DAY 14

VIENNA, VIRGINIA

"Where's Whittaker?" the senator asked. Corbin and his inside agent were sitting in Corbin's car in the parking lot of the Wolftrap Inn in Vienna.

"How should I know? I haven't been in contact with him since he left Cyprus," came the reply.

Perturbed, the senator shot back, "So where's the *Juno*?"

"Last time I checked, she was headed for the Turkish coast," the agent said. "But Whittaker gave me that info, so who knows where it is now."

"Jesus Christ, what *do* you know?"

"Hang on a second. You told me to keep a low profile. You need me on the inside—not on the outside playing soldiers."

"Yes, but I didn't tell you to keep yourself out of the information loop. We're blind right now without Whittaker; we need to re-establish contact with him ASAP. Start digging around in that agency of yours. You must be able to find something out. Don't you know some guys over in Turkey? What about that guy you used in Cyprus?"

"Don't tell me my job, Senator; I know what I have to do. I'll track him down soon enough. What about Heymann?" The agent knew he'd hit a sore spot.

Corbin's demeanor changed dramatically. "Yes, that's the other thing I need to talk to you about. I need you to go and talk to the Turks."

DAY 15

FREDERICK, MARYLAND

A carrot was definitely being dangled this time. Agency employees back at the US embassy in Berlin had chatted with Chris from time to time about coming on board as a full-time CIA employee, but Chris put this down to morale boosting or team building, and he never took the conversations seriously. Besides, how would it be possible for a British national to become a member of the world's leading intelligence agency? He had no real education, no affiliation with the United States other than his current job, and on paper, he was just a driver. What could he possibly have to offer to an agency that only picked the cream of the crop from the best educational and military institutions in America?

But this time it really was different. Nash picked Chris up at his hotel in McLean, Virginia, and the older man actually did the driving, taking him to a safe house on the outskirts of Frederick, Maryland. Needless to say, Chris felt extremely uncomfortable being in the passenger seat.

At the house, Chris was met and left alone with a CIA recruiter for almost four hours of discussions. This was not an interview for a specific job; they never are with the CIA. This was a psychological evaluation, and this time he was really being considered for employment with the "office."

Afterward, Chris was exhausted; he had never been through that type of questioning before. The CIA recruiter went through Chris's entire past—his school years, his relationships, his military days, his likes and dislikes, his taste in women or whether he was interested in men, if he had taken drugs, if he knew anybody who took drugs or peddled drugs, if he had a problem with drink, if he knew people who drank excessively, if he gambled, if he had a pornography collection, if he survived on lentils and oatmeal or steak and eggs. The questions ran from general to obscure and were endless.

Chris was sharp enough not to get trapped, as many of the questions, although never repetitive, had similar answers to questions already answered. He maintained his focus throughout the ordeal, and he knew he was being prepped for real-time processing. He knew that, since he had not submitted any paperwork or an application of any kind, they were not at the employment-offer stage. They were just digging into his past and present to establish his state of mind and see if he could withstand the scrutiny.

Chris's bona fides had been checked out many months ago without his knowledge while he was working at the embassy. The face-to-face meeting was to let Chris know people were interested in him and they were going to ask some very personal questions from here on in—if he was interested in continuing, that is.

Nash dropped him back at his hotel around lunchtime and told him to kick back for a while, as he was not needed the next day. During the drive back from Frederick, Chris had discussed with Nash what was worth seeing in the area. Since Nash was passionate about the Civil War, he suggested Chris head out to Gettysburg, about an hour and a half away, for a day trip. It would be a welcome break. Chris wasn't quite over his jet lag from the Europe-US flight the day before, and the virtual interrogation by the recruiter left him a little more than drained. A drive up to Pennsylvania seemed a great way to switch off and enjoy history for a change, instead of being part of it.

DAY 15
COLOGNE, GERMANY

The very essence of guerilla warfare is based on the fact that, in order to achieve its goals, the insurgent group relies solely on the community for which they are fighting for everyday support—this includes a denial of resources to the invaders or occupying forces in a particular area.

If the will of the people is stronger than the invading armies, then success is likely guaranteed over time, however daunting the task. Freedom fighters or nationalists have exploited those basic tenets throughout the ages and all over the world in order to achieve prolonged and costly campaigns by foreign invaders. As such, groups of collective resources, which are actively denied to opposing forces, are always readily available to those fighters who push the cause.

Napoleon was besieged by guerillas in the 1700–1800s in Spain. The Vietnamese also overcame multiple aggressors by using the same guerilla tactics in the 1960s and '70s, and many modern terrorist groups began their campaigns by utilizing guerilla doctrines.

In modern day warfare, guerilla tactics are limited in their successes, as powerful armies have mastered logistics and are able to sustain themselves for longer periods than in the days of Napoleon. Nevertheless, the tradition of communities supporting causes against opposing militaries or political upheaval still remains.

During the early days of the Northern Ireland Troubles, the IRA had huge support and resources from local communities. These tactics of fighting for the populace while also relying on them for support were not lost on well-organized terror groups, such as Hezbollah, whose modern-day reach for support from any means far exceeds its campaign boundaries. This extension of reach provides invaluable infrastructure and strength to communities who have no support or care from governing agencies.

Hezbollah relies heavily on outside finance to support its community activities. It is so well organized that it gathers funds from charities that seem legitimate and harmless, but through complex banking schemes and black-money transfer agencies, these charitable organizations are able to funnel funds to enrich Hezbollah's vast war chests. In addition to the funds that the charities gladly supply, a steady string of martyrs are also recruited to beef up the ranks of Hezbollah's soldiers.

However, there are those in the Arab community that cannot or will not undertake military action, and therefore, they provide other services, such as the provision of safe houses, cars, planes, boats, money, food—and even weapons. In a number of countries, these support networks are controlled by a local imam and mosque, which has a staff of sympathizers willing to engage with the home struggle from afar.

The Protector knew all this, and he knew where to go in Germany to find the specific assistance he needed. He had already turned to the network for help when he sent his daughter for her eye treatment and was offered a number of contacts in Cologne who would be able to look after his family as long as was needed.

The Protector found the mosque that he'd been looking for shortly after he arrived in the city. Realizing that he could not wake the imam at such a late hour, he checked into a nearby hotel that catered to Arab guests with no questions asked and for cash only. If you didn't have enough for your stay, then Allah would help. Another Hezbollah front.

The next morning, the Protector went to the mosque and requested time with the imam to pray for guidance, solace, and direction. He explained that he had come to Germany to visit to the place where his daughter was killed so he could understand what had happened and be at peace with her passing.

The imam sympathized wholeheartedly with the man before him and provided a list of names and numbers of those who could be called upon to offer assistance and, of course, be discreet. But the imam had a feeling his guest was unusual. He seemed educated and influential, and although he seemed pious enough, the imam knew he was not dealing with just another soldier from the homeland, but someone of authority and cunningness. He therefore provided his visitor with one of the mosque's unseen and unheard of security force members to act as driver and liaison for navigating the German/Arab community. The Protector was honored and promised that the gesture would not go unnoticed by those in the homeland.

Tariq, the mosque security guard, drove the Protector the forty-five minutes from Cologne to Bonn, to the spot where Gadwa lost her life. The Protector knew that, after seeing the location where she died, he would not be himself for some time thereafter. He therefore took the opportunity on the ride down to quiz Tariq about those who were of influence in the Arab community of this part of Germany. He wanted to know what groups were active, who was involved in criminal activities, who were the influencers, the quiet partners, who was dealing in drugs. He also wanted to know more about the Turks—how strong they were and how the current struggle was progressing. But most important of all, he needed to know who he could rely on in the area and if Tariq could be of assistance if things became strained with his private investigations. Tariq was all over it. He and a few of his cousins were eager to get in on some action—as up until now all their efforts centered on protecting a mosque that everyone knew was never going to be attacked.

Berlin was still in turmoil. Cologne had initially started off with some violence between the Lebanese and Turkish communities, but the strength and resolve of the German police in the state was strong enough to prevent things from escalating out of hand. As such, all was quiet in the city with the cathedral along the River Rhine.

The Protector dismissed Tariq when they found the spot where his daughter had perished. He needed time alone to grieve, to cry, to pray. He sat on a low wall where the crash occurred, staring off into space and reliving the moments he had with her before she left for her eye treatment. His tears would not dry up, and he cried so hard while there that he gave himself a serious headache.

On regaining his composure, he began to take a closer look at his surroundings. He noticed the traffic patterns and the way that people used the space around him. As he became more aware, his mind shifted to the attack itself. He had been able to gain quite a bit of intelligence on the attack from open-source media and from others who were more familiar with the event, those from whom he had managed to coerce information. His educated mind took over, and he tried to play out the scene in his mind as best he could. He came to the same conclusion as others at the attack site that day: it was not an assassination attempt; it was a kidnapping. Now he knew how it had happened. Next he needed to know who had organized this and why.

He got up from his perch at the wall and went to find Tariq. He wanted to find some Turkish fellows to interview.

DAY 15
FBI HEADQUARTERS, WASHINGTON, DC

The afternoon after spending time with the CIA recruiter in the morning wasn't so much fun for Chris. It was back to work with his least favorite topic: the FBI. He was told by Nash that the FBI wanted to have a briefing with him on the Bonn incident, and now the Cyprus attacks. Nash also informed him that Bowman and Seymour would be there to offer their reports too. However, Nash did mention off the record that he thought the two agents were in town to get their wrists slapped for not making any progress on either of the investigations.

It was a cloaked warning for Chris to be careful. As such, the agency provided an escort for Chris—a man named John Cox, from the CIA's Office of Security. His job was to oversee proceedings and make sure the FBI didn't take any liberties with Nash's protégé. Nash himself couldn't stick around as he had some other pressing meetings to attend to.

As Chris expected during the discussions, Bowman was his usual un-cordial self and reverted back to name calling, further criticizing Chris's actions in Bonn, and even more so of Cyprus. Nick Seymour was also there, but he remained in the background. And although he offered no direct support to Chris, he did roll his eyes from time to time when Bowman went off on a tangent.

Other FBI special agents in charge came and went and wanted to get in on the action, but Bowman held his ground and maintained that he was leading the investigation. Chris got the impression that Bowman had been reined in by a superior or two because when he was not ranting and raving, some of his questions were structured and well thought out. Chris at first wondered if it had to do with his CIA chaperone being in the room, but then it actually seemed that the FBI were pursuing some form of lead as several questions were aimed at the Trenchcoat information. Throughout the session, Chris remained calm. His answers were also well thought out, which engendered praise from some of Bowman's visiting colleagues, much to Bowman's irritation. Cox took notes; Seymour smiled.

The day ended on a high note as Nick Seymour gave Chris an insider's tour of the Hoover Building, the FBI's home turf. The driver was fascinated by the sheer volume of it all as he came to realize that the history of American law enforcement was all here in this one building. The enormity of the responsibility of the FBI really hit home for Chris when Seymour explained how things were done with investigations, forensics, and so on. Chris felt a new level of respect for the bureau and wondered why the CIA and FBI were so infamously antagonistic.

He'd also wondered if he would get the same tour of the CIA headquarters at Langley, but a shadow of doubt came over him again after seeing the internal workings of the FBI first-hand. Certainly the CIA was too big, too secretive, and too vaunted to give tours to mere drivers. He started to think that he didn't deserve to be there for an interview after all. He felt in spirit that maybe he didn't belong there. Christ, he wasn't even an American. He was torn between plying his trade for an elite professional organization where he could actually make a difference and stepping back and becoming just another expat Brit in Germany, just trying to earn a crumb and keep out of trouble.

The only problem was that Chris loved being in the thick of things, and Bonn and Cyprus, while scary and exhausting, just fed that need. He didn't know it, but his past excursions in Northern Ireland had just been appetizers.

DAY 16
GETTYSBURG, PENNSYLVANIA

It seemed to Chris that prominence followed him everywhere he went. Coincidentally on the day he decided to visit one of the world's best-kept battlefields, he stumbled into a crowd of people listening to the US Army Chief of Staff Colin Powell giving a rendition of Lincoln's Gettysburg Address. Although the event was open to the public, Chris felt uneasy about being there, as he was not invited, so he backed off. He managed to extricate himself from the crowd and get to the parking lot, where a pack of VIP vehicles were waiting. He could feel scrutinizing eyes on him from both the uniformed and non-uniformed protection teams that roamed the area. He began scanning for an exit, then remembered his Cyprus adventure, and switched immediately back into tourist mode, holding up his map in one hand and his new camera in the other, keeping his head down and walking away. It paid off; nobody paid him any further attention.

It was only later when he was back in his rental car and heading back to DC that he analyzed what he had seen: Powell, giving his speech, surrounded by at least five agents; two or three more possible agents in the crowd; one security driver per unmarked VIP car; local and State Police; and finally, one K-9 team.

Although Chris was in the parking lot for only a few seconds, he recognized what the lead VIP car looked like—its color, license plate, model, the amount of antenna on its roof and trunk. He knew that it was armored and most likely had a very adept driver for the task of protecting the VIP in transit. Chris also recognized which cars were the lead and follow cars, which were the "strap-hangers," or entourage vehicles, and then the dreaded press-corps vehicles. He noted which way they all parked, which way the VIP would get to his car. He identified the exit route that they would take, and he noted the possible backup routes and exits that were blocked from the public.

He'd noticed all this in the space of a short walk through a crowd and a parking lot. Now he realized why the CIA wanted him: He was an immensely skilled observer.

Chris's counter-surveillance skills were phenomenal when he was in the zone. His situational awareness in Bonn had saved lives; his skill at handling the black man in the suit at the stoplight showed that he was a cool calculated player. He saw things that others didn't.

Even during his driver-training sessions, comments were made about how well he noted details and how he soaked up everything in his surroundings. He did not have a photographic memory, but he noted things that mattered. You couldn't ask Chris to work out the formula for Pythagoras or even make basic algebra equations; however, he stored information that could be translated later, vital pieces that were part of larger puzzles. Information was the key. Information is what intelligence agencies live for, breathe for, die for, and Chris was highly skilled at gathering information, at least in his own way. He laughed to himself as he recalled his interview at Frederick, and a random thought came to mind: *Maybe that recruiter should get his wife to sew on his right sleeve button. It's going to fall off soon.* Details. Chris saw the details.

DAY 16
COLOGNE, GERMANY

"American?" the Protector asked as he stopped pacing. He turned to the man strapped to the chair and moved quickly to him. Blood was still dripping onto the floor from the socket of what was once the thumb of a right hand. He jabbed the captive in the chest with a screwdriver to get his attention. "What American?" the Protector shouted.

The prisoner screamed again as the screwdriver slowly bored into his chest, but he began to splutter his answer between moans and sobs. The Turkish man went on to explain how he was met by one of his cousins from Washington, DC, in Cologne. With him was an American who was only known as Fred.

Fred wanted to assassinate the US ambassador in Bonn, and the American gave the intelligence and finances needed to plan and carry out the attack. When the American left Cologne, his cousin remained behind to explain and clarify who Fred was and who he worked for. The Turks agreed amongst themselves that a kidnapping of an ambassador would bring more attention and more leverage when securing the release of their Turkish brethren locked up in German prisons.

The Protector paced again in silence but then returned to the prisoner to kick him in the shins. "Again, dog, tell me again!" To which the prisoner complied.

On hearing the story the second time, the Protector contemplated his next actions. "Again, tell me again," he repeated, this time in a more passive voice. The silence dragged on after the final rendition. The Protector was smartly comparing the first story to the second and the third. When they matched, he knew the man was not lying, and he decided to take a break from the interrogation. He motioned to his newfound soldiers to go outside with him. "Get him a bandage for his hand," he said. "Clean him up; we may need him."

Four hours later, the Protector returned and paid another visit to the prisoner. He pulled up a chair next to the man, lit a cigarette, and leaned over to him. "Tell me the story again," he said, "every detail, my friend. Please do not leave anything out." Which the Turk obediently did.

When the man had finished, the Protector calmly asked him a barrage of questions: When did the meeting occur? Where? Who was there? How much money was paid? Who handled the logistics? How much information did the American give? How did they practice the attack? How many people were involved? The Turk gave it all up, but blurted out towards the end of his dialogue that another American named Barney had showed up at the meeting to explain explosives and the armoring of the US embassy Cadillac and what its limitations were.

On hearing this last piece of information, the Protector exploded and punched the man in the jaw three times. "What other information are you holding from me? I told you to tell me everything, you piece of shit!" And he pounded the man more.

The Protector finally stood back and motioned to one of his men to take a small finger. The man did as he was told but only managed to break the bone and not remove the finger, which was left hanging by ligament and skin. Fifteen minutes after the screaming had stopped, the Protector motioned again to remove another finger. This time the soldier was more successful and removed the finger completely. Screams, then sobbing, then silence filled the room. The man was about to pass out from the pain. The Protector whispered into the man's ear for what seemed like the thirtieth time, "Tell me the story again."

After another two fingers were removed, and another two hours of hard interrogation, the Protector decided he had heard enough. But instead of feeling relieved by having all the information, he fell into a deep depression.

He now knew the identity of the men who had ordered the attack, he had the names of the two operatives, Fred and Barney, and he had before him the man who had completed the mission. He removed himself from the room to pray, not for forgiveness, but to pray for Gadwa.

As he left in search of his prayer mat, he stopped in his tracks and thought to himself, *Surely not, surely not the men I found in Turkey. But the descriptions … It could not be.* His mind bounced in all directions; he was so unsure. It mattered not. If they were the operatives who had orchestrated the attack, then so be it. But he had the name of the man who had ordered the attack—Corbin—and he thought he must be the devil himself.

CHAPTER
NINE

RONALD REAGAN WASHINGTON NATIONAL AIRPORT

A FEW DAYS LATER, CHRIS WAS SCHEDULED TO TAKE AN EARLY FLIGHT to Birmingham from Washington, DC. Part of the plan with his visit to the United States was that he would get his bi-annual training completed while he was in-country, so Nash had arranged for Chris to head to Fort McClellan, Alabama, for a weeklong crash-and-bang driving and shooting course. Although Fort McClellan was known as the home of the US Military Police training school, it also housed a Special Operations Wing, in which the art of executive protection was taught by the military for the military. The MPs that were assigned to protect the US Army chief of staff that Chris had spotted at Gettysburg probably had received their training from the same instructors in the same facilities. This would not be the first time Chris had visited the camp, and it probably wouldn't be the last. In fact, he was looking forward to meeting up with some of the instructors he was familiar with and sharing some war stories over a few beers.

Chris had already checked in at the Delta Airlines counter at Reagan National Airport when he caught a glimpse of someone he thought he knew. The airport was so crowded, though, so it was difficult to get a good view of the person. When he eventually came to an open space, Chris spotted the person again. *Ambassador Heymann,* he said to himself.

The diplomat was heading in the same direction as Chris, who automatically went into protective mode. It was not something that was intentional; it was as if someone had flicked a switch, and instantly Chris became Heymann's shadow bodyguard. Chris still had a guarding instinct for the endangered diplomat.

Heymann was flanked by a woman around his age and a much younger man. The companions, whom Chris did not know, were in fact Heymann's wife and his nephew, who often traveled with his uncle and sometimes acted as aide on business trips. The nephew, a varsity basketball player, dwarfed his relatives—and whether it was intentional or not, people automatically assumed that the young, fit-looking man was the ambassador's bodyguard. But when stateside, State Department officials, even if they're actively serving as overseas ambassadors, don't rate protective details. In fact, most of them don't even rate a reserved parking space at the State Department's headquarters in Foggy Bottom.

Heymann's small party halted amongst the droves of other busy travelers, pausing directly in the center of the departures concourse. They conferred with one another for a moment when they realized they were heading in the wrong direction. The group did a complete about-face and nearly came face to face with Chris, who had been tailing them, keeping an eye on the ambassador. Heymann recognized the young Brit.

"Chris, this is a nice surprise," the ambassador said cheerfully. "How are you, young man?" Heymann outstretched a warm hand.

"Fine, sir, thank you," Chris replied, feeling a little uncomfortable and probably blushing. He had been trying to be inconspicuous.

"This is my wife, Anna, and my nephew, Charles," continued the ambassador.

"Nice meet you, Mrs. Heymann," Chris said. He nodded a greeting to the tall athlete as well. Anna Heymann beamed a warm and genuinely infectious smile.

"Chris, my husband has told me so much about you. I'm really glad to have this opportunity to meet you and thank you for what you did in Bonn. Thank you for saving my husband's life," she said, after which she leant across and pecked Chris on the cheek. Chris began to melt. Anna Heymann was an extremely attractive and sensual woman, and her warmth was felt by everyone around her, him now included. Chris had to concur with many others who thought that Winston and Anna made the perfect couple.

Chris was embarrassed. Being the typical Brit he was a little standoffish when it came to public displays of affection, and this time it was no different. He blushed as they touched, but the ambassador broke the tension.

"So what brings you to these parts, Chris? Where are you headed?"

"I'm headed to Alabama, sir. I have a weeklong training course to attend there."

"More training, eh? I guess that you should be training a few of them, based on your recent experiences. I heard about the Cyprus adventure, by the way. It's an exciting life you lead young man—but be careful, won't you?"

"Yes, sir, I'll try," was all Chris could mutter. He blushed again; he was not good at this.

"Well, we're all headed up to Nantucket for the week for a little R&R, as they used to say—but it seems we can't find our way around this blessed place; it looks like our gate is the other way." Heymann looked a little bemused. "So, when do you get back from Alabama, Chris? Are you going to have time to join us for dinner sometime when you get back to DC?"

Chris felt exactly like the general who sweated bullets. He was way out of his comfort zone now, and he hesitated. "Sir, I'd be honored, but I'm not sure if that is appropriate."

"Nonsense," Anna Heymann butted in. "You must. I would like to hear more about you, Chris. It's the least we could do while you're in town."

Chris began to protest, "But I'm not so sure …"

"Okay, so it's settled then," she persisted. "Shall we say a week from now?" They all began to exchange contact details and then, with flights to catch, said their goodbyes.

Chris finally breathed a sigh of relief as he watched the small party leave. *I suppose I'd better tell the boss about this one,* he thought. He turned and walked away. After about ten paces he heard a loud scream. It was Anna Heymann.

Chris dropped his carry-on bag and broke into a run. A circle of people had gathered around the screaming woman, and more shrieks came from others surrounding them. Chris pushed his way through the crowd to see Heymann's nephew holding his uncle's limp body; the young man was white as a sheet. Chris bent over to see what had happened to the older man and feel for a pulse. There was none.

The young man, still holding his uncle, turned the body to Chris, who saw a stiletto knife sticking into the medulla of Ambassador Heymann's skull. There was little blood. It would have been a fatal and instant death. He probably felt nothing of the pain, and it would have been over before he hit the ground. As Chris realized that there was nothing he could do for the ambassador, he searched the crowd for Anna; she was not there. He pushed his way back out of the crowd and saw her running down the concourse as if she was on a mission.

Chris sprinted to catch up with her. As he got closer he could hear her shouting, "Stop that man, stop him!"

"Which one, Mrs. Heymann? Which one?" Chris blurted. It took Anna a second before she realized who was talking to her. "Chris, oh thank God! The tall one," she pointed ahead, "with the leather jacket and blue jeans."

Chris tried to find the man in the sea of people, but it was difficult. There were just too many in the crowd.

Chris suddenly shouted at the top of his voice, "STOP THAT MAN!" and then focused on the only person who did not stop and stare. It worked—he spotted his target not more than fifty feet away.

"STOP THAT MAN!" he screamed again at the top of his voice, and the crowds around him fell almost completely silent. The assassin made the mistake of turning around just for a second to identify who was chasing him, and it was enough for Chris to win some valuable ground. The assassin broke into a dead run, barging his way through the crowds of people amassed in the departure hall.

Chris was gaining ground, but he still wasn't close enough. He needed to slow the man down. He scanned the area for possible weapons to use and spotted a cylindrical trash can propped up against a pillar. He raced over and stuck his hand into the open face container, immediately covering his hand with sticky garbage that he hoped wasn't the last remains of a diaper. "OUT OF THE WAY! OUT OF THE WAY!" he screamed as he hobbled unbalanced under the weight of his improvised weapon. The assassin stupidly tripped on some baggage as he was looking back to see how close his hunter was. He could not have picked a worse set of bags to trip over.

The Canadian International Youth Ice Hockey Team was on the final leg of a three-week tour of the United States. They had just played their last game in DC and were at the airport about to head to New York as part of some well-deserved vacation. The whole team was looking forward to the down time and a little relief from the uncharacteristically disastrous tour. Of the six games they played, they had won only one. They had also lost one of their star players in a bust-up on the ice in the last match; he was still in hospital with a concussion. Team morale was low, and it was plain to see that one or two of the team were still in aggressive moods. The last thing that they needed was some idiot busting through their ranks and messing up their gear as they were trying to check in.

"Way to go, prick," and "Asshole!" came the shouts from the young men as two of them lurched forward to confront the man who fell to the ground, knocking over their formidable stack of duffels and sticks. The assassin landed face down on the floor, and soon felt the nearing presence of someone after his blood. As he tried to regain his posture, he reached inside his jacket and retrieved a pistol from its holster. He managed to turn around on the floor just as the first hand grabbed at his shoulder. He let off a series of rounds into his attacker and then realized to his horror that he had just shot a young boy in the chest at point blank range.

The usual airport hustle and bustle came to a screeching halt. Screams could be heard throughout the area and people were racing for cover like cockroaches behind a refrigerator. The gunman regained his composure, moved the limp body of the boy out of his way, and scrambled to get off the ground. As the man began to regain his footing, Chris took the opportunity to hurl the trash can twenty or so feet along the marble floor like a bowling ball, catching the man directly behind his knees and causing him to crash to the ground with a sickening thump.

Chris first thought that he had made the man tumble so hard that he cracked his head on the hard floor and wasn't going to get up, so he held off for a second and slowed to a jog to catch his breath. As he neared, he noticed that the man was still on the ground but beginning to move. He was about to jump on the assassin but held off, wary of the gun used just seconds before. He hesitated a second too long. Five young Canadians violently pushed Chris aside and pounced on the man who had killed their teammate. They began to lay into him like barbarians. Their combined strength was enormous; the man on the ground was helpless.

Chris recovered quickly and gauged what was happening. He dove into the melee, hauling the youngsters off the gunman. He understood only too well their desire for revenge, but he rationalized quickly that he needed this man alive in order to answer questions; he was a vital link in the obviously well-planned hit on Heymann. Maybe the only link.

As he began pulling the boys off, Chris took punches and kicks himself. It was becoming a real soccer hooligan scrap as fists and feet were flying in all directions. He managed to get to the bottom of the scrum and position his body between the killer and the rampaging Canadians, holding onto the man as best as he could. He couldn't afford to lose him now. Then suddenly it all stopped as quickly as it started. Chris could hear calmer voices issuing commands and restoring order. The airport police turned up just in time, before Chris was about to lose the fight. As he was dragged off the assassin, Chris looked back at the body that lay before him. A police officer checked for a pulse but shook his head; there was none. The man's face was pulp; there was blood everywhere. Chris's link to Heymann's assassination was gone.

DAY 17
LANGLEY, VIRGINIA

"Filtered distribution—what does that mean, Richard?" The head of the West European desk at CIA headquarters posed the question.

"Basically, we filter what we have to distribute to the various committees on intelligence. We would not be breaking any laws; we would still pass on relevant information to interested parties. However, I would say that since we're still developing these leads we pass on just enough information to keep them in the loop."

Nash let the thought hang for a moment and then added, "There's no need to inform them right now that we suspect one of their own, and neither do we want the FBI to get in on this. I say that we inform Congress and the president that we continue to find valuable information in the Rosewood files that needs further analysis and investigation."

"I agree with Richard," said the chief of station for Turkey. "If Heymann does want to approach us with something that's worthwhile, let's give State, the Hill, and POTUS just enough to say we're looking into some serious leads resulting from recent events in Europe."

The meeting had been in session for a number of hours already. It was called by the heads of those divisions that were most affected: Western and Southern Europe and the Middle East. Also around the table in Langley were the chiefs of station for Germany, the United Kingdom, France, Turkey, Lebanon, and Israel. Quietly sitting at the head of the long conference table was Quentin Cartwright, the deputy director of operations for the CIA who, although he let his subordinates brainstorm the session, headed the meeting.

"The question is, Richard," said the Israeli chief who joined in the conversation, "is this an undertaking that needs operational support, or are we still talking intelligence gathering, and therefore, should it be considered a project just for your team?"

The deputy director for intelligence was not present at the meeting. Cartwright was the senior person in the room and had been brought in only due to the potential ramifications of an investigation against a member of the US Senate and the need for potential liaisons with other intelligence agencies outside the United States.

Richard Nash pondered for a second but then replied confidently, "I think there is enough information right now to go to a full-blown operation, although it's not serious enough that we're at code-word status yet. On the other hand, I think we do have enough information to establish a joint ops and intel team. The reports from the Pentagon are disturbing enough with the amount of weapons and material that has gone missing already, but since the FBI and ATF are already involved, it's unlikely that we're getting all the information we need. I actually think that the FBI is already practicing my filtered distribution concept with us—so why don't we pursue things along the same lines? But, let's be cautious—if we go to code word right now, we'll definitely stir things up. So let's just kick things into a higher gear and be careful about telling people what we're trying to achieve."

It was time for Cartwright to intervene. "It seems we have a bit of a dilemma on our hands. We know that an undertaking of sorts needs to take place. Yet to leave this just as an intelligence-gathering and analysis exercise is not enough, and a code-word operation would be too much. Therefore we have to create *something* if the information from Heymann is valid enough to ensure that we catch this thing before getting out of control. And I think, gentlemen, that *control* is the key word here."

He turned to Nash. "Filtered distribution is slightly implicit in this case, Richard. However, I think your train of thought is interesting. Let's call this fact-finding mission 'Fallen Robin,'—we can get a computer generated code word later if we need to take things to the next level. You're the closest one to this, Richard; run with it and use whatever assets you need. Keep everyone around this table informed, and let's see where it takes us … and let's not forget the bureau. If they have an inkling that arms are being smuggled out of the country, then we need to know what they've got and where they're going. Who's meeting with Heymann and State?"

"That will be Richard and me," Mike Reynolds, the division head of Western Europe answered. "Heymann is currently taking a few days off to head up to New England, but after that, we'll have some time with him to hear what he has to say."

"Okay," Cartwright replied. "If there's nothing else, let's leave it there. Thanks everyone. Let's stay in touch on this one. Richard, stay behind a second, would you …"

The meeting was adjourned, but Reynolds leant over to Nash as he was getting up to leave. "Let's go to lunch when you're done," he said. Nash nodded and waited patiently for the room to clear.

After a few more minutes of discussing Fallen Robin, Cartwright changed gears, "How is your young Brit shaping up? I hear that the psyche guys tried to rough him up a little the other day."

"He's doing fine, Quentin," Nash said, certain that Chris had done well. "I think that he's a sharp kid. I'm not sure yet how we're going to get him on board, but as you know, I think that he'll be a valuable asset to us one day—or should I say, already is."

"Yes, I saw those reports of yours from Bonn. He's got some balls, I'll give him that. Is he ready to come over, though?"

"I think we're still a little early. I mean we need to grab him and show our interest. He wants to get his education completed, international relations from what I understand, and there is also the issue of the green card, but I know that he wants to get involved with us. It's not just juvenile thoughts—he's quite mature."

The conversation was interrupted by Nash's pager, which he thought he had silenced. Instinctively he picked it up and smiled. "Speak of the devil, and he shall appear. It's Chris … oh my God!" Nash sat upright, and his face turned ashen. He read and reread the message: *Heymann has been killed. I'm being held by National Airport Police. Please help.*

The precise reason Nash gave out his pager number to Chris was in case of emergencies, but this was not what he was expecting. "Quentin, I think we've just gone to code-word on Fallen Robin," he said gravely. "Winston Heymann has just been killed."

DAY 17
RONALD REAGAN WASHINGTON NATIONAL AIRPORT

"Okay, let's start with the basics. Name?"

"Chris Morehouse."

"Address?"

"Dahlemer Weg 50, 15319 Berlin, Germany."

"Huh?" The police detective looked up from his notepad. "Are you German?"

"No, I'm British."

"Okay, so you're a Brit living in Germany. What are you doing in the US?"

This was the moment Chris was dreading. He knew he had to tell the truth, but his was not an easy story to explain. The cop didn't know that Heymann's death was an assassination, not just a random homicide.

"I'm heading to Alabama to see some friends," Chris replied, which was in effect partially true.

"Who was the guy that you were with?"

"I don't know. I wasn't with him."

"But you were trying to protect him."

"Yes."

"But you didn't know him?"

"Correct."

"Did you know the other person that was killed?"

"Yes."

"If you give me one more yes or no answer without an explanation, I'm going to smack you in the mouth!"

Chris went into full panic mode; he didn't know what to say. *Fuck, I'm going to regret this,* he thought, *but I can't get the boss involved yet. I don't know who else can help me.* Then he blurted out, "I need to contact the FBI."

"Aw shit, and I thought that this was going to be easy," the cop said as he turned to the one-way mirror. "Guys, call the men in the white coats. We've got ourselves a mental patient here!"

He turned back around to face Chris, with a very serious look on his face. "J. Edgar Hoover is not going to come and rescue you. You've had your one phone call, and I hope you didn't waste it by ordering pizza because we don't take deliveries."

"No, I ordered donuts, you fat bastard," Chris let slip. He couldn't help himself.

The cop fell silent for a moment and smiled. "Now that was funny. Perhaps you do belong in a padded cell. But you're not going anywhere until you start answering my questions."

"I need to talk to John Bowman or Nick Seymour of the FBI before I say anything else."

"Yeah, yeah, dream on buddy ... Why did you kill Winston Heymann?"

"What? I didn't kill anyone, you prick—I was trying to protect the guy who did!"

"Oh, I get it. Let's ask the dead guy who did it."

Chris almost smiled; he thought that he was the *smartarse*. "I need to talk to the FBI," he repeated.

"So who was the guy shooting up the Canadians, if you killed Heymann?"

"I-DON'T-KNOW. I need to speak to the FBI."

"Why? What makes you so special that you need to talk to them?"

"I work for the US embassy in Berlin."

"So let me get this straight. You're a Brit living in Germany, heading to Alabama to see some friends, and you just happen to be at the airport where there are now two dead bodies, and you want to talk to the FBI. Who do you work for at the embassy, the CIA? Hah!"

Chris realized that he had said too much, and he felt cornered. "I need to talk to the British embassy. I'm entitled to legal representation."

"You only need a lawyer when you have done something wrong. Have you done something wrong, Chris, like kill two people? Who is chasing you, Chris, the NSA? Are the aliens trying to get you? Did you take some medication today that you weren't supposed to?"

Chris began to sweat, and the cop recognized it. He seized what he thought was an opportunity. "Why did you kill the guy with the gun, Chris?"

"Jesus Christ, give me a break. I haven't killed anyone!" Chris shouted, getting tired of the game. "And, I need to talk to the FBI."

There was a welcome tap on the door, and the fat cop got up to answer. Without needing to turn around, Chris heard the cop's footsteps exit and the door slam behind him.

Chris was alone in the interview room. He had been at the airport police department almost two hours before his ordeal even began with the police detective. He had been able to get his message out to Nash before questioning began, and he had hoped he would have been bailed out before he got himself into the exact situation that he was in now—pleading to speak to the FBI and nobody taking him seriously. He contemplated coming clean with the local cops, but he rightly surmised that they would not believe him. His only hope had been having Nash show up before being questioned and, failing that, dropping Bowman's name.

Chris sat there for a lonely fifteen minutes before the door suddenly opened again. "Okay, Chris, let's go." It was Nash.

The two rode in silence. An agency driver was at the wheel, and Nash had already explained to Chris before getting into the car that they would debrief at the safe house they had used a few days before.

Arriving at the farm in Frederick, Nash ushered Chris into the lounge where the Brit had had his initial psychological evaluation. Waiting for him were the psychologist and the fat cop.

Chris took a step back, not knowing what was going on. "It's okay, Chris," Nash began. "Let me introduce Gene Brooks. He's one of our instructors at the Farm. Sit down; let me explain." Chris's head began to swirl; he couldn't make sense of it all.

With everyone comfortable, Nash opened the session up. "I'm afraid we set you up, Chris," he said. "We can go over the Heymann incident later; we've already pieced things together from the CCTV footage from the airport police. I'm sure that the FBI will need to speak to you soon enough, but we decided to take your arrest as an opportunity to test you, and, unfortunately, you failed."

Nash let the words sink in for a few seconds. "Gene was pretty good at pushing your buttons, and I realize you were trying to be truthful, but you walked straight into a trap. If you're considering a career with us, then you need to stay focused in situations like that. One of the final tests at the Farm is an interrogation. We put candidates in similar positions as what you just went through and push them hard to find out where their breaking points are. You need to learn from that experience and consider your options before opening your mouth. Do you understand?"

Chris, thoroughly embarrassed, sheepishly replied, "Yes, Mr. Nash."

"Okay, now let's get back to Heymann. What exactly happened, Chris?"

Before Chris replied he noticed that the psychologist had his button repaired on his jacket. *At least I have that skill,* Chris thought to himself.

DAY 19
WOODBRIDGE, VIRGINIA

Cindy Whittaker sat in the food court of the Potomac Mills shopping mall waiting impatiently for her appointment. She was tense, jumpy, and on her fourth cup of coffee. She had made the trip to the mall a dozen times before to get herself some new clothes or shoes, but this time it was different. Heading south out of DC, she missed her exit not once, but twice, and the typical forty-minute drive in calm traffic ended up taking more than an hour. It didn't matter. She was still early. Cindy was in total disarray. She was entering into a world that was totally foreign to her, and she still was unsure of her pending actions, but she knew she had to do something.

Now sitting in the very center of the crowded food court, she sweated and squirmed the time away as she justified her actions to herself. Although she tried to remain calm, she could not help but think about what to say and how she would put it. She went over her own story in her mind and began woefully to reminisce how she had gotten into this situation in the first place.

—❦—

Cindy Whittaker was a bitter woman. She held the US military in total contempt and blamed the army for all her problems. She knew it was always going to be a difficult life being a military wife—not knowing when her husband was going away or coming back, what he was doing and if he was safe—or if he was in real danger. He had told her from the beginning that Special Forces was like that: He couldn't talk about his work, and she would have to accept that fact. But it was the unknown and the loneliness of a newlywed in a foreign country with no apparent personal or moral support that fueled her animosity and loathe for the military machine.

The relationship between James Whittaker and Cindy Parks began after Whittaker graduated from West Point. They met while both were vacationing in the Caribbean shortly before his first assignment to Germany. He was the young, fit, fresh-looking second lieutenant from Pennsylvania; she, the cute, demure dental assistant from Montana.

After knowing each other for only eight months, they were engaged and expecting a child. The attraction between them at first was purely physical. On paper, they didn't have much in common—she knew little of the military, and he knew about dentistry only from his desire to keep his naturally gorgeous set of teeth healthy.

What he promised to Cindy, though, was a life away from the logging and mining towns of Montana, a chance to see the world and be part of it—not just become another barefoot and pregnant welfare recipient from Loserville. All he wanted was someone pleasant to come home to and a companion to be socially acceptable with.

His stories of bravado and adventure captured her attention and thus drove her ambition to get away from the dilapidated, booze-infested home that was truly fit only for raccoons, where men took center stage and women were just an afterthought.

It didn't take Cindy long to jump on the Jimmy Whittaker bandwagon, and she decided to join him any place he went. It didn't matter where—she would be by his side. Unlike anyone she knew growing up, he was strong, brave, resourceful, and intelligent—and above all he loved her. Or so she thought.

While the long stretches when Jimmy was gone were hard, Cindy did enjoy exploring Germany with their son, Jonathan. Jonathan was a gorgeous little boy, and the locals doted on him. He learned to speak a few words of German when only a few years old, and everyone certainly thought he was destined for great things.

Jonathan was only nine years old when a drunken enlisted soldier stole a Humvee from the base motor pool in Stuttgart . The soldier, in his drunken stupor, decided to take a ride to the married quarters to challenge the father of a girl who was refused to him because she was an officer's daughter. As the young specialist drove, tears streamed from his eyes and spilt Bourbon ran down his chin. His blurred vision did not allow him to focus on his speed or the lines on the road. The only thing that caught his eye was the sight of a small child falling off a bicycle on the sidewalk, at which he laughed hysterically. He kept his eye on the child and completely missed the basketball rolling onto the road in front of him and, following in hot pursuit, Jonathan Whittaker.

Cindy had to identify the body, and she went into complete shock: her only son, dead in the base morgue—and his father nowhere to be found. When Jimmy left, he said it was only a regular field exercise and he would be back in two weeks. But none of the base staff was aware of his whereabouts; there were no field exercises taking place that involved his unit right then. They simply did not know where he was. Such was the way of the Special Forces, they said.

For five days, Cindy sat in solitude—waiting by the phone, sitting by the door, weeping for the loss of her child, and praying for the return of her husband while shutting everyone else out. The base chaplain tried his best to console her, and even neighbors took turns staying with her, but she didn't want them there, and as soon as she got a chance, she would lock herself in her apartment to grieve alone.

When Whittaker did come home, he didn't recognize her. She was totally incoherent, and prescription drugs and empty booze bottles littered the apartment. It looked as if she hadn't washed for days. Pools of vomit and urine stains were in evidence everywhere; she clearly would evacuate any bodily fluid whenever she needed to, wherever she was situated. Her eyes were shallow, black, and empty. Crusts of vomit stained her chin and neck. He thought that she was probably lucky to be alive. He didn't pay attention to the fact that there was no child in the apartment to welcome him home, and it was only when a neighbor, seeing the open door to the residence, told Whittaker the tragic news.

That was more than five years ago. Now, with Whittaker gone to who knows where again, Cindy was alone in Washington, DC. It was the anniversary of Jonathan's death, and she was depressed. She hated her husband; she hated the army for keeping him away; she hated her life. She blamed him for always being gone; he blamed her and beat her for not looking after their son. Their fights often turned violent, and after one especially severe beating, she had a miscarriage, which turned out to be the only opportunity for a new family that they would get.

In another incident, Whittaker flew off the handle when he came home to Cindy's badgering again after a two-week assignment.

"Where have you been this time?" she asked.

"You don't need to know," was the curt reply.

"Well, I am not the only one who needs to know!" she shouted.

They were in the bedroom, and Whittaker stopped unpacking his things. "What?" he asked, curious.

"I talked to your CO last week," she said, "and I asked him where you were, and he didn't know."

"You stupid bitch!" he hissed.

Whittaker had been with Corbin in Turkey setting up new shipment routes. He was worried that this type of thing would come back to haunt him one day. It was true that his CO didn't know where Whittaker was, and neither did anyone else in his unit. All they knew was that he was permanently seconded to work for Senator Corbin as a military aid, so no one would ask where he was or what he was doing. The problem that Whittaker had was one of perception. If people thought he wasn't telling even his wife where he was or when he would be back, then something was off.

Neither Whittaker, nor Corbin anticipated Cindy Whittaker stirring the pot. He had to regain control.

He threw a punch and hit her on the side of the head. Then he threw a second, then a third. He continued the onslaught, and in-between blows, he ordered her, "Don't ever …" *thump,* "**ever** ask anyone …" *thump, thump,* "where I am!" *thump, thump.* By the end, she was curled up in the fetal position on the floor. He grabbed her curly blond hair. "I swear to God," he threatened, "if you do that again, I will kill you. Am I clear? Or do you want some more?" There was no reply.

Cindy knew that she was in a desperate situation. She needed to get out of the hole that she was in and retake control of her life. But she had nowhere to go. She was miles from family or close friends, trapped with no way out. Even if she wanted to go back to Montana, she couldn't—she had no money. Restricting cash flow was Whittaker's way to control her all the more, even while he was amassing considerable sums from Corbin. Whittaker didn't let Cindy know they were financially well off; if she knew, then she might spend too much money, which would have aroused questions by the army—another headache that Whittaker did not need. Thus she was a virtual prisoner in her own home and had been for years. She always had to wait for his return before she could buy groceries or even pay bills.

It took her almost two months to save up enough change to buy herself a bottle of booze and enough sleeping pills to knock down an elephant. She was a quarter of the way through the bottle on the night she decided to end her misery for good. She picked herself up off the floor and made her way to the bathroom to retrieve the pills. The hardwood floor in the apartment always creaked and groaned everywhere but more so just directly below the bathroom medicine cabinet. She stood there for a second, rocking back and forth on the floorboards as she contemplated her fate. The boards sang out as if in pain. "I told that bastard to fix this fucking floor ten times!" she fumed. "Ten times, ten … Jonathan was almost ten, you bastard!" she sobbed, and she fell to the floor, pounding it with her fists, the image of James Whittaker in her head. "Bastard, bastard, bastard!" she yelled.

Oblivious to the cuts that had formed on her hands and the blood that dripped on the floor, she got up and ran to the kitchen. She returned with the largest frying pan that she could find and began beating the floor again with a maniacal passion. She pounded and pounded at it until she broke through—and heard the clang of metal on metal. At first she thought she had hit a water pipe, and she stopped to take a breath. Her chest was heaving, her eyes were swollen and full of tears, and her hands were red and raw—but she did not feel the pain. As she began to regain a semblance of control she noticed that she had not hit a water pipe but, rather, a large metal box lodged under the floor.

An hour later, she made herself coffee, tended her wounds, and took a long hot shower. She'd found the way to get her revenge. It was her husband's insurance policy, but it was not the type that money can buy.

It took Cindy almost a full day to read everything inside the treasure chest from under the floorboards. A lot of the information was the usual military paraphernalia, commendations, ribbons and medals and the like, but there were some interesting pictures of her husband in what looked like some Middle Eastern countries with people that she didn't recognize. But when she came across inventories for weapons, billing information for Dunbar Haulage, transportation schedules, and details of Venture Concepts, Inc., she realized that she could put her husband away for a long, long time.

But that wasn't all she found. It was as if her husband was storing this information as some sort of "get out of jail free" card. There were numerous references to shipping schedules, which all began with "As instructed by Runner …" Digging further, she found a small black book with a list of names and beside it other words, which slowed her comprehension of the information. She didn't understand if Virgil McCain was really a Preacher, or why Danny Robson had the annotation of Kodiak Red1. There were other strange names on the list: Fezman, Customer, Clear View, Gatekeeper, Primal Ocean, Indian, Wrap Up—the list went on and on. For the most part, she ignored the twenty or so names that were associated with the list, but she did come to a halt when she realized who Runner was: the Republican senator to the United States Senate for Michigan, Robert J. Corbin.

It took Cindy a couple more days to figure out what she was going to do. When she did, it was as if she had found a new lease on life. She even allowed herself to smile and start caring about her appearance again— something that had been missing in her life for many, many years.

———&———

As a general rule, bored housewives typically watch everything and anything on TV to keep themselves occupied while waiting diligently for their spouses to return from a hard day's labor. For most, midday soaps generated enough interest to keep them going for months at a time. Cindy, however, was not into the *Young and the Restless*, *Oprah*, or home shopping—she was a news junkie.

It started when she was working in Germany as an administrative assistant to a group of military journalists who provided content to the US military's daily newspaper, the *Stars and Stripes*. As a result of her work, she took a mild interest in army life and also politics. She never would have thought in her wildest dreams that a girl from a small hick town in Montana would become so enamored by international and domestic politics. But she became fascinated with the military twist of goings-on back home and other parts of the world, and she became an avid reader of other publications, including the *International Herald Tribune*, to gain a different, albeit conservative, perspective.

Thus the names Corbin and Heymann were not strange to her. She was acutely aware of the public spats between the antagonists, and Cindy actually once saw the sympathetic ambassador at the Weisbaden Military Hospital when she was part of the welcoming committee for a released American hostage from Lebanon. She was covering the story with one of the journalists from the paper and relished the thought that she could be part of such a historic event; she was totally mesmerized by the ambassador's words. In the speech that Heymann gave, she found him to be compassionate, warm, and conscientious of the former hostage's feelings; the man had spent the last few years being held prisoner somewhere in a dark cell in Beirut.

It was a good time in Cindy's life; she actually felt happy and was considering a potential new career as a journalist—that was until she lost Jonathan.

As much as the loss of his son affected his wife, James Whittaker's actions after the boy's death stopped his military career in its tracks. With pending manslaughter charges, the young GI was confined to barracks until his trial began. Just a week before the military court date, the young specialist was found by his colleagues, strangled to death in his room.

Everyone from the base commander to the military police suspected Whittaker of the act, but nothing was ever proven. Nevertheless, much to the dismay of Whittaker, the investigation and lingering suspicion turned into a large black mark on his records—so much so that the colonel would never reach the senior rank of general or progress far enough to have any real responsibilities.

It mattered not; his fate had been already largely sealed when he had thrown his lot in with Corbin years before. The two had met when Corbin was a congressman who, along with others, was sent on a fact-finding mission to Lebanon. Although security was provided by the host country, America wasn't taking any chances with its representatives, and a team of Green Berets, led by Whittaker, were assigned to protect the delegation while in the country. The weeklong trip was well choreographed and proceeded without a hitch. At the end of the mission, however, Corbin surprised everyone and announced that he would be staying a few extra days to visit other parts of the country. Whittaker and two other soldiers were assigned to stay behind to look after the congressman.

If Whittaker was alarmed when Corbin presented a .44 Magnum revolver to a Lebanese friend at a private dinner one night in Beirut, he did not show it. Whittaker's expression remained neutral, and he looked away; it wasn't his position to question what was happening. Later when Corbin and Whittaker were alone in the hotel bar, the Michigan man started the discussion. "You never saw that, Lieutenant."

"Yes, sir."

"If you did, who would you go to?" Corbin tested.

"Since I haven't seen anything, sir, I can't answer that question." There was a pause in the conversation, and Corbin took a moment to puff on his cigar and sip some whiskey while Whittaker sat silently anticipating the next question.

Whittaker broke the silence after the stare down waned. "I don't understand politics, sir. It's not my job to. If the United States is considering arming someone in this country to assist in the people's struggle ... Sorry, sir, it's not my opinion you are looking for."

"But it is, James. Talk to me."

"If the US wants to provide these camel jockeys with arms, then let them have it. If we let them shoot the shit out of each other, and it stops our boys from getting killed like in 83, then I am all for it." Whittaker was referring to the Beirut bombing of the US Marine barracks in which 241 servicemen were killed by a truck bomb.

Corbin nodded; he liked what he had heard. "I am going to take you into my confidence here, but understand this ..." He leaned forward in his chair, coming within inches of Whittaker's face—a threatening move. "If anyone else hears of this conversation, you will be counting crab boats and weighing bear shit in the Aleutian Isles for the rest of your military career. Understand?"

"Yes, sir."

"Good."

Corbin moved back into his seat and continued in a more casual tone. "What I need is information on what types of weapons these guys need. I need someone to be here to dig into this, find out how these guys operate, and so forth."

Whittaker was confused. "I'm not sure what you are talking about, sir," he said, truthfully.

Corbin answered straightaway. "I am offering you the chance to make a difference, to stop US servicemen from being killed in shitholes like this."

And that was how the relationship truly began.

———⊶⊷———

And so Cindy waited at the food court in the shopping mall, nervously playing with her coffee cup, looking nonstop at her watch, searching in all directions for a familiar face and hoping not to see one—all the while clutching a large brown envelope, waiting for her appointment.

Crushed by the news of Heymann's death, Cindy decided this was the right time to push things along, to get her story out, to make her husband pay for her pain, but also to identify Corbin as the instigator of the diplomat's demise.

But this was not the first time Cindy had been down this road. When she first found the evidence weeks before, she had sent an anonymous letter to the law offices of Lauren, Rees, Heymann and Associates, in Washington, DC, containing what she thought was enough information to garner some interest in Corbin. It was of course circumstantial information, but she was clever enough to sort through the material and pass along just a sample of what was to come—with the hope of gaining a financial reward. She was not asking for much, just fifty thousand dollars to provide the real damning evidence of a major political scandal.

———⊶⊷———

On receiving the first batch of documents, Anna Heymann initially dismissed it as bogus—but, nevertheless, she was intrigued. On further investigation, the information from the unnamed source plus the earlier documents from her brother started Anna's mind racing with conspiracy theories. She wanted to know more.

———ᕼᖇᕼ———

Chris did not like these types of assignments. It was a quick on-the-fly job that he wished he could turn down, but the request—and it was a request—came from Nash, and Chris did not like to disappoint his boss. Especially after his disastrous failure with Gene Brooks's interview.

———ᕼᖇᕼ———

It was only a few days before Winston Heymann's funeral, and Anna was back at work; it helped her to keep busy. When Chris arrived at her offices, he could tell that, although she looked busy, her mind was not on her work. She explained that due to the ongoing investigation into her husband's death, the Washington, DC, police department had assigned her close protection, which she strongly rejected. She felt that she was in no need of constant supervision and did not want any restrictions on her life; she simply wanted to be left alone. If they insisted, then they could place a police car outside her home.

It was during this time that Anna made a call to Richard Nash, requesting Chris's services for a short while or, at least, while she was in town. Although Nash thought this strange, he nevertheless relented. Nash already suspected that Anna Heymann had something to share about Fallen Robin and surmised that he could use Chris to put a few pieces of the puzzle together for him.

———ᕼᖇᕼ———

Chris hated this type of work simply because it was too unpredictable. He was unarmed and did not know the lay of the land nearly as well as he would have liked. He was out of his element, had no back up, and with no situational intelligence, he had only his instincts to rely on. This was not the art of executive protection that he loved so much; it was an on-the- fly exercise in adapting, improvising, and overcoming. If something happened, he'd just have to make do.

Walking side by side with Mrs. Heymann through the mall, he rationalized that he could only tone things down and take a covert bodyguard approach, acting as a companion rather than a protection agent. Although he tried to act casual, he still felt uncomfortable; he didn't know his principal that well, and he hadn't even been informed of where they were going or why. There was zero preparation for this trip. Yes, he had been there once before, but that was on a shopping trip on one of his layovers for training, so he was relatively unsure of the ground.

As they entered the complex, he was glad that Mrs. Heymann stopped to look at the mall directory, which also gave him a sneak peek at the layout. He quickly scanned for the possible exits, but as he was looking for the mall security office, she took off. It was obvious to Chris at that point she was not here to pick up some new shoes. Chris was half a step behind and cursing to himself.

As they approached the food court, Chris scanned for possible targets. His eyes quickly locked eyes on a woman sitting by herself who was staring directly at Anna. Anna was unaware of this fact, however. At first Chris thought about closing into protect his principal, but he held off a second longer, scanning the area further—and still the woman sat and stared.

Chris designated her as Tango 1, first target. He checked her eyes for signs of danger. Next, her hands: one hand was on the table, one underneath. *Shit*, he thought to himself, almost out loud. Then he looked at her feet: firmly under the table, not pointing away—and she was wearing high heels. *Good for now*, he thought. *Still Tango 1.*

Next he scanned for a Tango 2. *Did she have backup? If she was an assassin, what if there were more out there and she was the distraction?* Chris's mind was in top gear, searching for solutions to any and all imaginary situations. He identified his escape route and what he would do if things went south. He began weighing his options and cursed to himself that there were too many people—too many women, children, and strollers. This was exactly what he was looking to avoid. This was definitely not the way he liked to do business.

Anna made eye contact with Cindy and hesitated for a moment; she wasn't sure if this was the person she was supposed to meet. They had never met before and only talked briefly over the phone a few times. Cindy's eyes remained locked on Anna, but a keen observer could have easily recognized the tension and nervousness in the young woman. Cindy was still shaking when she placed the brown envelope that she was holding on the table in front of her. It was Anna's signal to sit down.

No, no, not there! Chris's internal voice screamed. It was in the very center of the seating area, surrounded by a whole host of kids, parents, and grandparents. It was a Saturday, and the place was packed. He found a seat on a nearby table, but was extremely uncomfortable with the fact that he could not put his back to a wall and he could not scan the area like a lighthouse without drawing too much attention to himself. *Shit, shit, shit— how the hell did I get myself wrapped up in this? This could easily go to rat shit if I'm not careful. Stay focused. Be cool.* On the inside, Chris's mind was scrambling for rationality and clarity, but on the outside … he was Steve McQueen.

Anna cracked the ice. "Thank you for coming," she greeted Cindy.

Cindy remained silent as she watched a young, fit, confident-looking man sit at a nearby table. He gave her the most direct and piercing look from a man that she ever had experienced. She shifted in her seat and tried to remain focused on why she was here. Nervously she spoke, her voice almost cracking, "Did you bring the money?"

"I have something for you," Anna replied, "but please tell me where did you get this information from, and who are you?" She had decided to be direct.

"Show me the money first; then we can talk," Cindy said, feeling a little guilty. She really wanted to say, *"I'm not a bad person—I really liked your husband, and I want to help you find those responsible. I've never done this before, but I need money to get me out of this mess. I need to disappear. Just help me, and I will give you everything I have."* But she had to stay strong; she needed to be in control. And she needed *money*—it was the only way she knew how to help herself.

Chris was already up to Tango 6 and trying his best not to listen to the conversation; it wasn't his business.

"If you have information on my husband's death, then I want to know about it right now!" Anna said forcefully. "I'll give you your money, but I need to have something in return, let's say, something in good faith. I need to know that I'm not wasting my time."

"You're not wasting your time, Mrs. Heymann," came the reply. Anna was surprised by the formality. The woman continued, "The information that I have will have repercussions throughout Washington, DC, and further. I want to make sure that none of this will come back and get me in trouble. You're a lawyer, Mrs. Heymann; you know how these things work. I need to be sure there will be no charges against me. I just want my money, and that is all."

Anna hesitated and looked deeply into the woman's eyes. She was still distraught over her husband's death, but she knew she had a mission to complete. All she wanted was justice, but justice sooner rather than later. She, if anyone, knew how the criminal justice system worked in this country: it was slow, methodical, bureaucratic, and above all, unnecessarily technical.

That is what she always worried about the most in a court proceeding—a technicality. There had been so many court cases that she tried as a young criminal prosecutor that were thrown out on technical problems, so many that that she walked away from the system in disgust. She believed in justice for all, but she wasn't sure at what price.

Anna had then gone into international law with the offices of Lauren, Rees, and Associates. She became a partner after five years of solid work overseas as the company's international expert. It was a perfect setup with her language skills and her willingness to travel throughout Europe.

Anna Heymann looked again at the woman in front of her, grudgingly reached into her pocket, and pulled out a bulky letter-sized envelope. "Here is fifteen thousand dollars—this is all I could get on such short notice."

Cindy's eyes lit up like candles on a birthday cake; her plan was working. In return she pulled out a large black and white photo and laid it on the table in front of her.

The silent pan-tilt-zoom camera strained to focus on the image on the table from thirty feet above the food court. Chris had noted that a number of CCTV cameras were strategically placed throughout the mall, but for the most part he couldn't tell which way they were focused. Clearly not all the cameras were fixed in positions, though—a number of them were of the PTZ variation and had the capability of viewing 360 degrees with relatively good color and sharpness.

The agent stood over the shoulder of the operator who controlled the joystick for the camera pointed at the table with the photograph. The image was difficult to see, though the agent could make out the shape of two people—and it was quite possible that one of them was wearing a uniform. The agent looked up at the VCR to see if it was still recording; it was. He returned his focus to the screen, but to his dismay, the photo had been put away.

The agent watched for a few moments more, trying his very best to lip-read one half of the conversation. He knew that it was Anna Heymann sitting with her back to the camera, but his attention was focused on the woman sitting opposite her. As much as he concentrated, he couldn't figure out what she was saying, so instead he focused on her body language and the clothes she was wearing; maybe they would provide a clue. He needed to find out who this woman was—and why she was passing photos over to Anna Heymann.

He eventually gave up, walked over to the VCR, ejected the tape, and began to walk out the door. "Hey, you can't take that," the security-camera operator protested.

"The fuck I can't," came the agent's gruff, pissed-off reply.

———

It wasn't Chris's fault that he had been followed from DC. Although he had driven the Heymanns' private car and practiced all his counter-surveillance tactics, he was still in unfamiliar territory, and there was a lot of ground to cover. It was also unfair that the agent had called in extra resources from the FBI to perform the surveillance on Anna.

These guys were the experts on surveillance since their job was nearly exclusively to tail and watch foreign diplomats. So this basic exercise was exactly that: simple. The agent legitimized his request for a team by stating that Anna was in danger and she needed covert protection. So a small team was set up to support the agent to shadow and observe Anna Heymann's activities. As soon as the agent left the mall's security control room, he instructed his team to follow Heymann back to DC and then observe her until further notice. The agent had other business that he needed to focus on.

———

"Before we go any further, Mrs. Heymann, I want your written guarantee that nothing will happen to me," Cindy stated. "If it means you sign me as one of your clients so that I'm protected by client/lawyer confidentiality, then so be it. I want a guarantee that I won't be charged with anything in a court of law. Do you understand?"

Anna did not want to commit so early on, so she fished for more information. "I understand your situation, but in order for me to protect you I must have your name, address, and such—there are formalities to follow if you're to be my client." She paused, then asked, "Who is this man in the photograph?"

Cindy held her ground. "It's nice of you to try to change the subject, but as I said before, if this relationship is to proceed, I want guarantees. Give me your word now that I won't face prosecution, and when we meet again, I want the rest of my money and a written letter from you and your company stating that I'm your client. If you don't, then I'll simply go to other people who I'm sure are interested in keeping this type of thing out of the public eye."

Chris was still working the mall, looking for potential problems and trying his best to look causal. He already cancelled out the woman talking to Anna as a threat, but nonetheless, he kept a keen eye on the body language of both women. He picked up a few words from the nearby table, but didn't listen intently to the conversation. The only thing he did for certain pick up on was the fact that the attractive woman opposite Anna was looking in his direction a little too often.

Anna Heymann leaned across the table towards Cindy and again looked deeply into her eyes. "I don't know who you are or what your reason is for doing this, but I won't be threatened by you or anyone. I have just lost my husband, and nothing will stop me from getting those responsible to pay for what they did. I can do that with or without you, but let me make myself clear," she said as she reached over and grabbed Cindy's wrist, "don't get on the wrong side of me."

Chris's head snapped around as soon as he caught the sharp movement from the table. He stood up and made his way over to stand directly between the two women. Anna paused and composed herself for a few seconds but noticed that Chris was standing nearby. "I'm going to need a little time to look into this before you get any type of guarantees from me," she finished and then released her firm grip on Cindy.

Chris felt awkward; he was there to look after Anna—and he was not expecting her to go on the offensive. "Mrs. Heymann, is everything okay?" he asked.

Cindy looked up at the man standing at their table, staring down at her. She was surprised to hear a British accent.

"Thanks, Chris," Anna interjected. "I'm about done here."

Cindy squirmed in her seat. Although she felt intimidated by Chris and his physical presence, she felt something that she had not experienced in a number of years. She suppressed a huge urge to smile; she was smitten. She tried to focus on the turn the discussion with Anna had taken, but she couldn't concentrate on the words.

"Are you listening to me? What is your name?" Anna pressed one more time.

Cindy regained her composure and stared back coldly. "You may call me Sarah for the moment, Mrs. Heymann. The next time we meet, you had better have the rest of the money and a letter with you, or our deal is off."

Now Anna was fuming. "Don't be so melodramatic, you silly cow! I can't give you a letter to protect you if I don't know your name. It's impossible!"

Chris stood solid as a stone, but he could have crushed a walnut in his bare hands; this was turning into a mess.

"There's no need for name-calling, Mrs. Heymann. I'm here to help you. All I want in return is the rest of the money and a letter. Those are my terms, whether you like it or not—that is my final word. I'll be in touch soon." As Cindy got up to leave, Anna reached over and grabbed her by her sleeve. "I'm sorry, it's just that … I am not sure you understand the loss of someone so close, my husband was—"

"Don't talk to me of pain, Mrs. Heymann," Cindy hissed. "When you have lost your own flesh and blood, let's talk. Until then, get me my fucking letter." Then she stormed off.

Chris felt like an idiot. He stood still next to the table, not sure what to do next. This was definitely something they did not teach you in Executive Protection 101. He tried to remain focused and scan for trouble, but when he looked down at Anna, who was beginning to cry, his attitude changed completely. Chris pulled up a nearby chair and sat as close as he thought appropriate. He wasn't sure if he was about to cross a line, but he took her hands anyway and looked compassionately into her eyes. "Let it go, Mrs. Heymann; let it go. There's no rush, we can stay here a while longer."

⸙

Cindy took one last look back before she left the food court, in time to see Chris pull up a chair and make just a little more eye contact. Although she was angry at the way things went, she realized that she had made a huge step in her plan to get out of her miserable life. She now had $15,000 in her purse, and the prospect of more to come fueled her drive to complete her task. The only thing she worried about was the inevitable return of her husband.

She had already repaired the damage to the bathroom floor in case he returned unexpectedly, and she placed the box as it was found. Copies of the contents, however, were safely stored in a safety deposit box at a local branch of the Bank of America.

The problem now was that it had become a race, and her mind was tortured by numerous worries: *Would she get the rest of the money and be able to escape before her husband came back? Did she make the right decision by withholding her name? Should she have been more forward and open with Mrs. Heymann?*

As she got back into her car, she tilted the rearview mirror and checked her look. She was surprised with what she saw. She looked like her old, confident self—full of energy and drive. She smiled to herself and turned on the ignition. *Oh, and that Chris, he can protect me anytime,* she thought as she drove away.

If Cindy had remembered to correct the rearview mirror after checking her look, then she might have noticed the blue Ford Taurus that left the parking lot at the same time. She did not.

CHAPTER
TEN

GEORGETOWN, WASHINGTON, DC

CHRIS WAS SUPREMELY FRUSTRATED, BUT TO LOOK AT HIM, ONE WOULDN'T KNOW. In another life, another time, he might have been a great actor.

In retrospect, the first mission to chaperone Anna Heymann wasn't as bad, since she at least informed Chris of their destination, although not the purpose of the trip. This time, she told him of the purpose of the trip, but not the real destination. Yes, that was worse.

All she said was that she was going to see a friend in Georgetown. Chris was again getting out of his comfort zone—he felt like a one-legged man in an ass-kicking contest. But, as a true soldier, he sucked it up and focused on trying to do the best he could with what little he had: no weapon, no backup, no route planned, and no idea if he was headed to another confrontation. And to add salt to his wounds, he had to ask his passenger for directions. On paper, it could turn out to be a great recipe for disaster.

Anna Heymann didn't say much on the way over to Georgetown from her offices in Alexandria. Chris thought that the events of her husband's death were finally catching up with her, as she looked exhausted, so he didn't open up any discussions, playing the role of executive chauffeur to a T.

They arrived at the small, squat Mortara Building on the eastern edge of the Georgetown Universitxy campus in mid-afternoon. Parking was difficult, but Anna seemed to be in no rush. After they found a suitable spot, Chris was surprised to learn that Mrs. Heymann had no objections to being escorted. He'd already rehearsed a line or two in case she protested, but there was no need. She led the way into the building as if she had been there before, and since Chris was better able to judge her demeanor after the events of the day before, he didn't think he was walking into a hostile environment. The building, although minute in its real estate in comparison to the other facilities, libraries, and dorms of the university, housed the prestigious Center for International Studies.

They moved quickly through the maze of offices and cubicles, making their way up to a corner office on the second floor. Anna politely asked Chris to wait outside, and being the consummate professional, he simply nodded and began scanning the environment for threats and escape routes. He found some comfort in the fact that it was a corner office near a fire escape, and that most people around were too busy in their own worlds to pay attention to him. So he began to relax a little, making his way to a comfy-looking sofa, in direct line of sight of the office and with good views of each end of the corridor. Chris looked at the nameplate on the office door and assumed that this couch was used by many a student when visiting Prof. Robert A. Crauford, Gen., US Army (ret).

"Anna, it's so good to see you. How have you been?" Bob Crauford gave his friend a warm hug. She sat and took off her coat.

"It's slowly catching up with me, Bob—it's sinking in that he's gone, but I'll be okay. Thanks for taking the time to see me."

"No thanks needed, really. I meant it when I said if I can help in any way, I will. You know that I'm here for you. Many of us around here respected and admired what Winston did for this country; he will be missed. And I'm sure that I would not be the first to stand in line to help ... Do you need a coffee or something?"

"No, I'm fine, thanks."

Crauford reluctantly got into business "It sounded urgent yesterday, and you said that you have something that may help in the investigation?"

"I do, but, Bob, I need to trust you. I haven't been to the FBI with this information yet, and if you feel uncomfortable with that fact, then I need to know, but I have my reasons ... I have some suspicions, but I can't go into everything right now. I need to be sure first."

"Anna, we have known each other for too long; you know that you can count on my discretion. Winston and I had a special relationship, you know that. I was his commanding officer, and he was my friend. Anything you say or ask me to do will be in the strictest confidence."

"Thanks, Bob. I wasn't sure who I could take this to," she said as she passed him the photograph she was given by Cindy Whittaker.

"I need to find out who this man is—if he is in the army, Marines, or whatever."

Crauford expertly reviewed the image and quickly made some general assumptions aloud. "Well, I would say that he could be Special Forces. The weapon he is holding is not standard US Army weaponry—it's a Russian sniper rifle. I'm guessing that the other guy is not from our military forces. The uniform is probably eastern European or even Russian; it's hard to tell these days without going into more research. On reflection, I would say that this guy was on some kind of training mission with another allied force. The Green Berets do that kind of thing all the time."

"So where do I find him, Bob?"

Chris sat patiently outside the professor's room; he'd already done his security scan, and there wasn't much action to monitor. Thus he was challenged with keeping his mind focused. But this time he let his mind wander a little as he realized he was in a safe location. He began to contemplate his long-term future. The prospect of dealing with a new chief of station in Germany did not sit well with Chris. Richard Nash was due to rotate out of Berlin within the next eighteen months, and so far, no successor had been named. It wasn't as if Chris could go with Nash on a new assignment to places like Korea or Botswana—he was just another driver at another embassy, not Nash's private chauffeur. He would not be given special privileges to work as Nash's driver wherever the chief went—it didn't work like that.

What bothered Chris most was the mystery and suspense of meeting a new chief. He had been hired by the US Embassy Berlin, and it meant if the new CIA chief turned out to be like Elmer Fudd, then Chris would have to deal with that or go elsewhere to work—there were plenty of other eager drivers to take his place.

Chris's latest thought-provoking scenario involved the potential of not having a boss as concerned with his own personal safety as Nash was. Most diplomats posted overseas viewed security as a hindrance rather than a need. Once too often, Chris had come across Americans at the embassy whose attitude was, *Nothing is going to happen to me. I can drive myself. I need a driver just to help me with the shopping and parking.*

Chris immediately went on alert when he heard a door opening and the sound of voices down the corridor, some thirty feet away. He couldn't make out what was being said, but he did see and hear a sudden crash of books that preceded a young woman exiting the door. She was tall, athletic-looking and somewhat attractive.

Chris checked his surroundings quickly, assessed the situation, and moved to assist in picking up the confetti of books and notes on the ground. Always aware of his surroundings, he placed himself between the girl and the professor's study.

Then Chris bent over, collecting some books. "It's not every day my good looks get a woman to drop everything," he said with a smile.

Taken aback, the girl looked at him, paused, and then concentrated on the mess in front of her—but she did smile. "It was the shock and horror from seeing your ugly face that did it," she cracked.

Chris picked up a leather-bound notebook with the letters PWC embossed in gold on the cover. "Yeah, well, I got like this for not helping a pretty lady the last time this happened, so I'm not going to make the same mistake twice."

"Well, on behalf of all ladies out there, pretty or not, thank you," the girl said with another smile. Their eyes met for the first time, and Chris's blood pressure jumped a few notches higher than he was used to. Before he blurted out something stupid, he was saved by a door opening behind him and Anna's voice.

He looked over his shoulder to confirm that she was on the move, and as he turned to look at PWC, she was already walking down the corridor away from him. Chris got back on the job and made his way to his principal.

What he did not see was the pretty girl looking back over her shoulder, watching him for a second longer than she would normally have done.

——— ⚬⚬⚬ ———

"Bob, may I introduce Chris Morehouse, US Embassy Berlin."

The general offered his hand. "It's a pleasure to meet you, Chris, and may I say how much I and a number of people in this town really appreciate what you did in Bonn for Ambassador Heymann."

Chris offered a timid "thank you, sir" in return.

"Anna tells me that you're ex-military. Which regiment, SAS?"

"The Royal Green Jackets, sir, infantry. I had a brief attempt at the SAS, but circumstances were not in my favor."

"Knees or back?" the general offered.

Chris realized that he was talking to someone who knew the injury issues of Special Forces. "Both, sir. The Brecon Beacons in Wales proved my end."

The general tapped his right leg. "Panama. Fell out of a helicopter going in with some of the boys. Highly embarrassing."

"Happens to the best of us, sir," Chris replied.

"Yes, well, luckily for us you didn't make it into the SAS. Listen, when you're next in town, why not stop by for a chat, have some lunch or something?"

Uncomfortable, Chris responded with a white lie. "Thank you, sir. I would like that."

Anna and the general said their goodbyes and gave each other a warm hug. To Chris, she seemed a little more relaxed as they both headed down the corridor towards the exit.

Chris, two steps behind his principal, was getting his mind back on track after quite an interesting afternoon. He quickly began his usual "prepare for everything" drills.

As they left the building, he stepped it up a notch, imagining himself a sort of robotic Terminator-like creature with his own heads-up display—scanning immediate, middle, and far distance; breaking areas down into quadrants, sectors, and mini-sectors; identifying things as threat, no-threat, watch list, and possible Tangos.

He spotted a man on a nearby park bench with crutches: no threat. He noticed the usual little groups of students immersed in discussion sitting on the grass lawn, under trees, or on picnic tables: no threat. He observed parked cars and people riding bicycles: no threat. He watched … PWC being followed by a white Ford Crown Victoria.

PWC's safety wasn't his problem. He already had a principal to take care of, and he didn't need a distraction. But he struggled to keep his concentration on his robot-like analysis of the area because he sensed that PWC was in trouble. He quickly assigned the problem to his "watch list" and checked the area for other correlating attack identifiers. There were none.

As Chris and Anna began moving away from the general campus area to the faculty block, he noticed that the Crown Vic had slowed down and had a window open. The driver seemed to be having a one-way conversation with PWC. Judging from her body language, Chris thought she wasn't comfortable with the situation, as she kept on walking. Although Chris and his principal were heading in the other direction, they both could hear a voice in the car shouting at PWC. Chris labeled this as a potential domestic issue: no threat. He needed to walk on and focus on getting out of there before he and his principal got caught up in a boyfriend/ girlfriend, husband/wife confrontation. It wasn't his problem.

On reaching the car, Anna said, "It's so sad that people have to shout at each other on the street to resolve their problems, Chris."

Chris just gave a nod and thought about his problem-solving tactics in the hotel bar in Cyprus with Dirk. He was not impressed with himself. "I just hope it wasn't anything serious," he said, and he meant it.

As they headed away from the university, Chris spotted the white Crown Vic parked on the side of the road with two people inside. As they passed, he glanced over to see PWC in what looked like a heated argument with the driver. Chris couldn't make out the features of the man, as he had his back to the driver's side window and was obviously facing PWC.

He returned his focus back to the road but then noticed the man on crutches again, this time with a professional-looking camera in his hands, pointing it directly at the white Crown Vic with PWC inside. Chris instinctively dropped his sun visor, as he did not need his photo taken by someone he thought might be some private investigator on a cheating husband/wife case. He drove on, putting the bizarre scene behind him, but when he checked his rearview mirror to monitor the activities again, he noticed the driver of the Crown Victoria also had his sun visor down. *Well, I see that someone else is taking precautions, Wonder what the hell is going on there,* he thought.

There was no time to dwell; he needed to get his charge home. Anna already had her eyes closed. She was not asleep, but he could tell she was exhausted and there was no need to engage in small talk to keep her company. He needed to find his way back to her house without disturbing her. He was up for a challenge as the car clock changed from 5:00 to 5:01, rush hour in Washington, DC. He smiled and thought, *Outstanding. I wonder what's worse, being stuck on the DC Beltway in snail's pace traffic or having a chihuahua hump your leg for an hour.* He didn't have an answer; he slipped the car into gear, suppressed a sigh, and moved forward, slowly.

DAY 20
AUTOBAHN A63 RAMSTEIN, FRANKFURT, GERMANY

Whittaker was wide awake watching the speeding traffic, but Preacher was sleeping with his head resting on the window of the car. They had parted ways with the Protector eight days before at the small commercial

Turkish airport in Adana where they had dumped the stolen car and said their goodbyes. Whittaker and Preacher waited until the Protector was out of the way before they found a taxi, which took them to the US Air Base at Incirlik which was on the opposite side of the city. They could have easily stopped at the air base first on the way to the civilian airport, but Whittaker did not want his newfound friend to know of his connection to the military so he was hoping the Arab would go his way and they would go theirs.

On reaching the Incirlik base, Whittaker called on one of his old air force contacts and drinking buddy who tried to wangle two spots on a military flight to Ramstein Air Base in Germany. However, the request was not that simple as flights to Germany were less frequent than Whittaker thought and were booked way in advance with two spare seats being virtually non-existent. While they were waiting for the flight, they managed to get cleaned up and were able to get a set of clean clothes from the base PX, which made them look presentable even though they looked like typical American tourists in Europe. On their eventual arrival at Ramstein, Whittaker pulled some more strings and was able to source an air force driver and vehicle to take them to Frankfurt International Airport. Whittaker's plan was to get both of them on a flight from Frankfurt to Berlin, hook up with the agent, and lie low for a few days, recoup, and form a plan. All that was left to do on the drive was to make sure the young driver stayed focused with getting them there safely and getting Preacher to stop snoring.

DAY 22
ARLINGTON NATIONAL CEMETERY, VIRGINIA

The weather of the day set the mood of the service. It didn't pour down, but it drizzled—which made the mourners uncomfortable no matter which way they looked at things. Attendance was high, as one would expect in Washington when a much-loved and respected official was put to rest. Dozens of sitting ambassadors from multiple countries, dozens of bureaucrats from State, the DOD, the CIA, the FBI, former executive-branch members, congressmen, senators, family, and friends were all in attendance.

The eulogy was to be given by the current secretary of state, Charles Maxwell. Aside from the heady list of diplomats and government officials, there was also a smattering of staff who had served the ambassador over the years—the cooks, cleaners, groundskeepers, drivers, and security personnel, who all appreciated and respected the Heymanns.

Although Chris was comfortable in the midst of this latter category of mourners, he still felt uncomfortable with the rest of his surroundings, as if he didn't belong, even though he was off duty and a guest at the ceremony. There were so many important people here that he didn't know and, for that matter, didn't want to know.

Although he had played a huge part in the ambassador's life over the last few weeks, he still wished he could have done more to protect and serve the man who was now being laid to rest.

As the crowd jostled for position, Chris felt uneasiness, and he slowly began extracting himself from those who he thought deserved to be at the graveside. As he looked around for his escape route, he spotted the virtual parking lot of official cars that lined the driveways around the cemetery. He noticed the drivers, the on-duty security details, and the police. That was his crowd—that was where he belonged, not up front and center with principals and family. Chris inched his way backward, he came to a halt when a firm hand was placed at the small of his back.

"Stand easy soldier," came a hushed order from behind. Chris recognized the authoritative command of General Crauford, and he froze in place. The general whispered into his ear, "Mrs. Heymann really appreciates your assistance and support over the last few days. I'm sure she would miss you if you took off now. If you get a chance, make eye contact with her to acknowledge your presence, and then slowly back away if you still want to go. I know you're not comfortable here, but stick with it for a short while, okay?" An embarrassed Chris knew when to keep his mouth shut, especially when receiving an order from a general. He offered a simple "yes, sir" in reply but was glad someone at least understood his plight.

Events took another uncomfortable twist when the honor guard showed up. This time, Chris began to remember the military funerals that he had attended during his time in the service of his country. Northern Ireland was truly a misery maker.

As he watched the servicemen go through their rituals and drills, Chris could not help but be impressed with their seriousness and dedication to their jobs. Some thought of this as a spectacle or glorious pomp and circumstance, but these soldiers, airmen, sailors, and marines showed perfect synchronization, poise, and most of all, respect for a fallen comrade.

As Charles Maxwell stood to give the eulogy, Anna Heymann and Chris made eye contact. The general had moved on, and Chris, remembering his orders, stayed a few more minutes and then began his slow retreat.

One of Chris's faults—one of many—was that when he was in a certain mode of discomfort he made himself vulnerable. The general sneaking up behind him was bad enough, but what he experienced next was much more of a shock to his system.

"Hello. Nice to see you again," he heard as Cindy Whittaker sidled up to him. Chris almost jumped twenty feet in the air but regained his composure and simply replied, "Hello."

If Chris's bad traits were the zoning of his personal feelings, then his recovery back into job mode was his strong suit. He suddenly went from being borderline depressed to switched-on and focused. Chris ran the events at the mall through his mind and wondered, *Is she a threat?*

"Are you a relative of the deceased?" she asked in a hushed tone.

"No," came the blunt reply.

"A friend of the family, colleague, or something like that?"

"Something like that."

"Well, you're the talkative one, aren't you?"

"This is not the time or place," he whispered back. There followed a pause in the conversation as Charles Maxwell doled out praises for his friend Winston Heymann.

"Can we go somewhere to talk?" Cindy asked.

"About what?"

"The information that I have for Mrs. Heymann."

Chris became immediately intrigued. Theoretically, he was not supposed to get involved in the case. Nash told him to stay close to Anna, but how close was too close?

Sensing Chris's hesitation, Cindy added, "Something that may help the investigation."

Chris almost went back down into shutdown mode. *Goddamn it, why me?* He thought. *I should have planted myself with the other drivers sooner, and this shit would not have happened.*

Nevertheless, he felt the urge to close some loops; there was still so much to figure out, so many unanswered questions. He relented. "Okay, but this is not the right place. Did you drive?"

"Yes, my car is over there," she said as she pointed in the general direction of some civilian cars parked in the area. It was close to where he was parked.

"Okay," he said. "There's a Starbucks across the street from the Whole Foods Market on Clarendon, here in Arlington. It's probably a ten-minute drive."

Her face wore a beaming smile. "Okay, see you there soon?"

"Yeah, sure ten to twenty minutes," he replied and watched her leave.

As Chris turned to head back to his car, his instincts told him that he was being watched. Now that he was back in the game, his senses were ultra-aware. When he thought that something was wrong, he was usually right. It was hard to tell exactly who was who in the crowd of mourners. It was like walking into a rock concert—just a sea of faces, hundreds of them. As he made his way to his rental car, he could not help but feel that something was out of place. It wasn't the woman he had just met; he still didn't know her name—but it was something that he could not put his finger on.

Neither the security details, police, nor drivers paid attention to Chris's leaving, but others did. They were called the Special Surveillance Group, or SSG. The SSG worked mainly for the FBI, but were also used by other agencies in DC.

These people were civil servants, not FBI agents. They were trained in surveillance, photography, communications, and electronics, but all the SSG did was observe and report. They were also specialists at blending in because they were a set of normal-looking people with normal everyday skills, but with certain extra skills that were in very, very high demand in Washington, DC. These people could look like your average fifty-five-year-old overweight female mall walker, with hand weights and tennis shoes to match. They were also Asian postal workers, garbage collectors, skateboarders, and unionized construction workers with tattoos and attitudes to match. They came from all walks of life, and there were many of them.

These people were not sworn law-enforcement officers; they did not kick in doors, guns blazing. They had the same arrest powers as regular citizens. These were your moms and dads, aunts and uncles—but these were people who could really, really observe. Chris would be in awe if he knew the depth of their surveillance skills, their technical expertise, and their seamless teamwork.

Two small SSG teams were on duty that day. Chris had a hunch that something was going on around him, but he attributed it to the need for securing a whole host of VIPs at the ceremony. If he could have heard the initial conversations of the SSG over the FBI radio channels, he would have stopped in his tracks and continued to grieve with the rest of the mourners.

"This is Baker 1. Subject Alpha on site," a groundskeeper spoke over the radio at the cemetery.

On hearing this over his earpiece, the agent stepped away from the crowds and began scanning for Cindy Whittaker. The agent knew this could happen and was not surprised. Her potential presence was the reason for the deployment of two SSG teams that day. The agent had rationalized that while Whittaker was not invited, she would be just the type to gate-crash such an event.

Subject Alpha was under twenty-four-hour surveillance as directed by the agent, although it wasn't officially sanctioned by the upper echelons of the FBI. A few minutes had passed after the initial sighting, but the agent still didn't have a visual on the subject. He didn't worry; that was what SSG were for.

"Baker 3. Alpha talking with unknown," came the call from a limo driver who turned up to the cemetery without bringing a passenger. "Baker 3. Team Lead, description of unknown," came next.

The limo driver began his report, and the agent shook his head in disbelief. He blurted out a profanity, much to the disgust of the nearby ambassador from the United Kingdom. Before the diplomat could address the foul-mouthed man, the agent rushed away from the funeral to get a visual on the unknown, although he knew who it was.

"Baker 3. Looks like Alpha is getting directions from unknown."

"All call signs, all call signs, this is Team Lead. Designate unknown as subject Bravo. Baker 3, give me RC on Bravo."

The limo driver began a running commentary of the events taking place, detail for detail, leaving nothing out. Baker 1 and 2 moved into position for additional coverage.

"Baker 3. Alpha in vehicle heading out of area of operations. Subject Bravo heading in same direction. Request instructions."

The agent cursed again. He needed to slow Chris down.

"Rembrandt, Rembrandt, this is Team Lead. Action delay on Bravo. Repeat, action delay on Bravo."

As Chris took off, he tried to read the Virginia license plate he was about to follow. She had gotten a little ahead of him, but it was enough for him to decipher it. The problem was that he was not in his regular vehicle with his notepad and voice recorder handy. He began searching for something to write on and wasn't paying attention to his surroundings as well as he should. His rationale was that he was on his own, he had no principal with him, so he was technically off duty. He was for all intents and purposes just a visitor to the cemetery.

The landscaper's truck hit him on the passenger's side door at 15 mph. Although it was a relatively low speed, the impact was substantial enough to jolt Chris, who smacked his head on the driver's side window. The force from the truck was also enough to ram Chris's car into a high curb, forcing the vehicle to be wedged between it and the truck. Although dazed, he opened his door quickly and rolled out of the car, looking for immediate cover. His right hand went instinctively to his right hip, but it found nothing to grasp. *Naked again!* He inwardly cursed. Crouching, he made his way to some nearby bushes and trees and then looked back at the scene.

The agent also stopped at a covert distance, the running commentary still rattling over his earpiece. A nearby motorcycle cop was quick to get to the incident, but instead of worrying about clearing the wreckage, he did what he thought he was supposed to do—he called it in and got out his booking sheet.

Chris regained his composure and realized that he had only been involved in a regular traffic accident. Two Mexicans were standing by the cop, explaining what had happened. The younger of the two Mexicans became animated with his version of the crash, but his older partner was quiet and obviously irate: His cover had just been blown. All SSG team members were trained in various forms of delay actions, but none ever wanted to perform them. It meant that, although the FBI always covered them from any charges of neglect or responsibility, until the dust settled, they would be off SSG surveillance duties for at least a month.

The cop made the mistake of standing there in the middle of the road too long though, writing his notes from both Chris and the Mexicans instead of clearing the road. The cop didn't think it important enough to clear the site expeditiously, as they were in a cemetery and not in some busy downtown intersection. The cop was not trained on VIP delegations, however, and didn't realize the importance of keeping the area clear of such mishaps, especially on days with state funerals. Chris was about to say something to him when two members of the Secret Service from Maxwell's security detail came running down the road, hands on holsters ready for action.

"Move the truck! Move the truck!" one of the Secret Service agents blared. Chris and the cop then realized the service was over and the convoy of vehicles was trying to leave the cemetery.

For a protective agent, gridlock of any sort was their worst nightmare. Nothing could be worse than being stuck with your principal without being able to move any which way. Chris's inexperience had showed through again. It was not his place to follow up on leads, take matters into his own hands, or make significant decisions. He had to realize that he was just a driver. *Why do I keep forgetting that?* He thought, berating himself.

He had caused an accident, the worst embarrassment for any professional driver, and he had caused delay and frustration for the head of state and countless other diplomats and officials. He truly felt like an idiot. If he wanted to get more eye contact with Mrs. Heymann, he was surely going to get it, standing at the scene of an accident blocking her exit from her husband's funeral.

For Cindy's part, she had already made it to the Starbucks. She didn't waste any time getting there, but when she arrived, she did take some time to check her look in the mirror and add a little lip gloss to finish it off. She was excited. She ordered a double-tall extra-hot latte and perched herself near the window so she could get a better view of Chris when he arrived. She was lost in her thoughts and didn't pay much attention to the sirens and lights of a police car followed by a tow truck, heading back in the direction from where she just came. She picked up a used copy of the *Washington Post* and patiently waited for Chris to show up.

CHAPTER
ELEVEN

DAY 22

FREDERICK, MARYLAND

WHEN IT CAME TIME TO EXPLAIN TO NASH ABOUT THE CRASH earlier that day, there wasn't too much to say.

"So what's happened to the car, Chris?" his boss began.

"I managed to swap it out. It's pretty much a wreck, but nothing that can't be fixed. It has a broken door and window, scratches along one side. The front bumper came off and the front left tire blew out as well."

"But you're okay. You didn't get hurt, did you?"

"No, sir, I'm fine, just an embarrassing situation, that's all. I should have never agreed to go and meet that woman. I don't know what I was thinking."

"But you have a sore head, don't you?"

"It's not so bad; the impact did throw me up against the side window. I saw stars for a while, but nothing permanent that an aspirin couldn't fix." Chris paused for a second.

Nash prompted his hesitation, "What? Is there something else?"

"Another place, another time, Mr. Nash, that would have been a pretty good take-out maneuver. The truck T-boned me pretty good. The car wasn't going anywhere. I'm glad you weren't in the car with me."

Nash pondered that statement for another moment. "Be that as it may, Chris, I don't think you were exercising good judgment at that point. I also heard you got your hands dirty at the tow-truck shop. What did you get up to there?"

Jesus, this guy doesn't miss a thing, Chris thought. "It's nothing, Mr. Nash."

"Well, it's obviously something. What were you up to?"

Chris felt uneasy with the line of questioning. Surely a man of Nash's stature had better things to worry about than broken rental cars. "I may have taken a hammer to beat out a panel or two, which kind of made things worse in the long run. Sorry, Mr. Nash."

"So you spent some time and money on trying to fix things?" his boss inquired.

Chris nodded.

Nash already knew how much Chris had spent. Gene Brooks, the instructor from the Farm, was training a team of CIA counter-surveillance operators in the area, and Chris was chosen as a target for a short while. Apparently more than one of the trainees was tempted to help Chris repair the front bumper of the car in the pouring rain at the tow-truck company yard.

"Where's the police report, Chris?"

"Right here, Mr. Nash," he said, handing it over. As Nash was scanning through the document, Chris added, "Mr. Nash, I'm not sure how things work here, but I guess this means a fine in court or something for the truck driver, but would I need to go to court? I wasn't the one who hit somebody."

"No, I don't think so, but let me pass this by our Office of Security, see what they think. I know that this wasn't your fault, but if this is a bunch of Mexican landscapers, chances are they're illegal, and they probably won't show up at court. But if they're legal and one of them has whiplash or some such bullshit, then we'll have to deal with it, but whatever it is I don't like it."

Chris could tell that something had caught Nash's eye; something was up.

"You should have let the rental company take care of the car, Chris," he said.

Chris tried to rationalize his decision but knew he should have just kept his mouth shut. "I know," he replied. He was so embarrassed by the incident he thought that he could win favor by fixing things himself. It was his way. "But the less paperwork, the less hassle, Mr. Nash. As you say, if these Mexicans start a claim, then it could turn nasty with the insurance companies ..."

"That's more the reason to report it, Chris," Nash snapped back. "Now you're out of pocket; that was a dumb move."

Chris flushed red, and Nash could tell he had gotten to him. He let his silence and long stare be the learning lesson. He eventually sighed. "Okay, let's leave if there for the moment. I'll make a copy and send it down to security, let them do some digging."

Nash shuffled the paperwork around and then continued. "Right, now on to other things. We need to start thinking about heading back to Germany, but I don't want you to go just yet. I may go ahead of you. If you need to sort this out with the authorities, you need to be here. Gene will be around; I'll make sure he gives you a hand.

"In the meantime, your training is off, but before you go home, some people down in Fort Bragg would like to have a chat with you. Gene has the details; he's going with you. You fly down later this afternoon. Let him drive when you get there; he knows his way around. By the time you get back, we'll have answers for you on the accident, and I'll be back in Berlin, okay?"

Chris had no idea why he was going to Fort Bragg but reluctantly replied, "Yes Mr. Nash. Should I arrange for someone to pick you up at the airport?"

"No, I can take care of that, Chris," Nash said. "Go find Gene and make your arrangements for your trip. I'll see you later."

Chris felt dejected. He had thought by trying to take care of the car himself his carelessness in being involved in an avoidable accident and his naïve curiosity of the woman at the cemetery could be overlooked. But now it felt as if he was being punished, and Gene was going to be his chaperone for the remainder of his time in the United States. Worse still, he felt the ultimate slap in the face for a professional driver—having a chauffeur take him everywhere.

DAY 22
DILBECK, VIRGINIA

Corbin called it Stonewall Retreat, but locals called it Jessup Hill Ranch, known for its former owners Ray and Martha Jessup, who resided there for almost forty-one years before their passing. Corbin's name was not on any court document listing him as the owner; instead, his cousin Billy Palmer was. They retained the old Jessup ranch sign at the end of the trail leading up to the five-hundred-acre ranch just so nobody got too nosy. Corbin always said to his family that he would take the sign down when he found a good name, and although there were a dozen suggestions, he never did. And besides, those who came out there more often than his family couldn't have cared less if it was called the Taj Mahal or the Liverpool dockyards.

When Corbin first bought the place, he knew he didn't want just anyone taking care of it. He couldn't spend all his time out there—it was just too far from the action in DC. That's when he proposed to Billy that he could be the owner on paper and could live rent free as long as he turned a blind eye to the goings-on from time to time.

Billy didn't have a problem with this arrangement: There were no crops to harvest, no cattle to speak of, and only a few of Corbin's horses to tend to. When he needed some maintenance done, Billy just hired some local kids for a few days.

Billy loved the place; he loved the image he portrayed of the crusty old rancher with stubble rough enough to sand down a rusty tractor. He also took pride in a pot belly that defied the laws of gravity and looked as though it needed parts of the Golden Gate Bridge to suspend the twenty-year-old, permanently dirty jeans he favored. He often carried a sidearm and raced around the property with a shotgun in the back of his pickup truck to deter hikers and mountain-bike enthusiasts from coming too near. As confident as he felt with his authority on the ranch, though, it was made perfectly clear to him from the get-go that he was the guard dog and Corbin was his master.

Corbin had the dirt on Billy from years past, and it was inevitable that Corbin would always end up being the organ grinder while Billy played his monkey. When they were young, Billy was always getting in trouble for fighting, breaking windows at the school, and even petty theft, but no charges of illegal behavior ever stuck; Corbin always had an excuse or alibi that fitted both of them when the police came calling.

It seemed that even at a young age, Corbin, the mischievous planner, was destined for a career in politics. He could scheme, plan, and basically waffle his way out of anything and everything—and he always, always got his way and people's attention. That was how Corbin made his way through life, and nothing ever changed; he was considered a lying bastard by friend and foe, both inside and outside Washington, DC, and even by some of the most senior politicians on both sides of the House.

Corbin's other forte was manipulation. He did it all the time, never letting up on an opportunity to take advantage of people young or old, innocent or guilty, male or female—he simply didn't care. He was brash, ruthless, and downright rude. He had built up his empire on the weaknesses of others, and his mission in life was to be on top, to make others accede to his rule, to make everyone succumb to his wishes. And somehow, he managed to stay in politics.

One individual that eventually got sucked into Corbin's web of deceit and manipulation was a young police officer who was assigned to the protection detail of the then-governor of Michigan, Robert J. Corbin.

Michigan State Trooper John Bowman was, at twenty-three, a fresh-faced rookie just graduated from the Michigan State Patrol training academy in Lansing. Corbin, ever the manipulator, picked his security personnel carefully, needing as much discretion from his protectors as possible. After reading the results of Bowman's average grade report from the academy, his average educational file, and average personnel file, the governor realized this guy could be developed into a shape for Corbin's future endeavors. Corbin just needed the hook to get his catch to go for some bait.

It came unexpectedly one night after the usual four-man security team was dismissed from the governor's mansion following a particularly long day on the job. As the rookie on the team, Bowman got the stay-on-site, residential, overnight detail to add to his already long day. Some considered this a perk; others just saw it as a balls ache.

Staying overnight at the governor's pad meant they had to be on their toes all the time. There was no relaxing, no kicking back to watch the game or funny home videos. Sleep was allowed, but there still were regular ground patrols to make—and as long as the governor was awake, so was the duty officer.

The trap was set just after midnight when Corbin came down to the watch room and handed Bowman a beer, thanking him for all his good work over the past few weeks. Bowman was reluctant to take the offer, but Corbin insisted, and the young officer thought if the governor was getting relaxed and wanted to socialize, who was he to argue?

After the fourth beer, Corbin took his leave and left the glassy-eyed rookie to his own devices. There were still two beers left on the table as Corbin climbed the staircase to his bedroom with a smile on his face. He knew that the bottles would more than likely be empty by morning.

At 3:35 a.m., John Bowman was rudely awakened by the screeching tone of the fence detection alarm system going off in the watch room. He had fallen asleep exactly where Corbin had left him, beer in hand. His heart pounded at a thousand miles an hour as he tried to take stock of the situation. He cleared leather, grabbed his service revolver in his right hand, and scrambled to cancel the loud noise by hitting every button on the alarm panel. He tried to look at the security camera system, but he couldn't make out anything from the poor black-and-white images in front of him. To make matters worse, it was snowing.

He immediately sprinted outside to the gravel driveway to establish what the hell was happening when he spotted two car headlights in a place where they shouldn't have been: in the small pond on the wrong side of the fence line—his side of the fence line.

As he ran over to the car, his mind raced with all sorts of possibilities. His gun was in the up-and-ready position, his finger on the trigger; he was primed to go.

When he reached the wrecked car, he managed to make out the lifeless body of a passenger, crunched up between the dashboard and the windshield. Blood covered the inside of the car, and he could not tell if the victim was male or female. The driver was alive, but incoherent. Bowman approached the driver cautiously and let his training take over. He shouted his standard police warnings to get the driver to show his hands, but the driver was not complying.

Visibility was poor, the snow was falling heavily, he did not have a flashlight, and his sight was slightly blurred. He kept shouting his warnings, to no avail. The driver let out a gut-wrenching scream as he reached down to remove the Club anti-theft device out of his ribs. As he was pulling it out of the left side of his body, he drew it in the direction of Bowman. Bowman didn't hesitate and shot the man through the driver's side window four times—twice in the chest and twice in the head.

Bowman didn't hear Corbin come up behind him. As soon as the alarm went off, the governor was out of bed. With weapon in hand, he went to investigate. He arrived outside just as Bowman fired on the crashed car in his pond. He had expected the rookie to fuck up, but he hadn't expected dead bodies on his premises.

Corbin managed to coax the weapon out of the rookie's death grip and began to take stock of the scene. He looked into the carnage of the car and saw the dead bodies of two young teenagers. He saw the bloodied Club and smelled the unmistakable aroma of marijuana emanating from the car. Corbin opened the driver's door gingerly, and as he did, two beer cans fell onto the silent, snow-covered lawn.

Sharp as a razor, Corbin took action. He eased himself into the rear of the crashed car behind the driver's seat and then reached over to grab the driver's right hand. He inserted his own semi-automatic pistol into the dead hand and positioned the fingers around the pistol grip and trigger. Bowman came in for a closer look. As he did so Corbin pulled the dead finger on the trigger and shot the police officer in his left shoulder. For good measure, Corbin let off three more rounds in the general area near Bowman's now-prone position. Corbin let the dead man's hand fall, and with it the pistol. He always had weapons in the house for just this sort of occasion—rifles, shotguns, and pistols—all without serial numbers. He knew this day would come.

"Jesus Christ, you shot me! You fucking shot me!" Bowman screamed.

"No, you idiot, the drunk teenager did; I just saved your life." Game, set, and match, Corbin.

Corbin spotted the blue Ford Taurus more than a mile away as it spewed up dust behind it like a horizontal tornado. He shook his head in disgust as he thought of the sheer number of times he told his special visitors to the retreat not to cause a stir or piss off the locals by throwing a ton of earth into the air every time they drove in. He kicked back in his rocking chair, continued to sip his single malt, and waited patiently for Bowman. He spotted Billy sitting quietly out of sight of the road on a large stone under a tree near the driveway, shotgun resting across his lap, hoping for trouble.

It was the drill they always practiced, unless family were coming to visit—then Billy would hide the shotgun and pretend to fix a fence or dig a hole. It was just for show, except when it came to business, which it was more often than not.

When Corbin bought the ranch, his immediate and extended family were all over the place. Every weekend someone was out hiking, mountain biking, riding horses, or visiting the nearby Massanutten Resort for golfing, the spa, or skiing in the winter. It was a great retreat, just hours away from the hustle and bustle of the Capitol. Corbin even set up a small outdoor shooting range just for the family, to teach the kids a skill he thought was priceless. Everyone loved the place. Even outcast Billy became an accepted member of the Stonewall family. Life was good.

The spread was sandwiched in a valley between the Blue Ridge Mountains and the Shenandoah Mountain Range. Located at the north end of the cigar-shaped valley, the place was designed by Corbin for business, though he never let on his intentions. It was true that he needed an escape from DC, and he needed to offer his family an option from the harsh winters of Michigan. So early on, as intended, they came and stayed and carried on in the normal family way.

If he didn't want anyone out there, he simply said he needed the place for the weekend or a few days to discuss matters of state, which everyone took to meaning politics, so no one bothered him. If any of his political friends asked him what he was up to on his time off, he would simply say that he was heading to the Massanutten Resort for golf or to kick back at the spa. Which to some extent was true—but if he wasn't conducting business for the good of the government at his ranch, he was up to no good. He'd often taken a mistress to the place for a few days when he knew no one would be there to disturb him. He even started taking people like Whittaker and Bowman there for briefings, and sometimes even hunting. Billy always turned a blind eye to all the nefarious activities—that's what he was paid for along with the free rent, and he really didn't care.

Corbin's family continued to visit the place on regular occasions, but later they were allowed in only by appointment, and Billy was the gatekeeper.

Things were great for a while; the ranch became a home away from home. Everyone had settled into a routine of going out there on special occasions and enjoying it as a family. It was a bit of a pain always checking in with Billy to see when they could use it, but they understood that Corbin, the heavy-hitting politician needed his privacy from time to time.

His wife, Jean, knew about his flings with other women, and she correctly surmised that the ranch was used for his extramarital affairs, but she also turned a blind eye. She had long stopped loving Corbin for the man that she had married thirty-two years before—a young and inspiring leader with crazy ambitions and plans to rule the world. Her role was destined to be the perfect cocktail-party hostess, a quiet but supportive spouse that could be shooed out of a room when men discussed politics. It was what her mother did when she was married to a politician, and she assumed that that was also the role for her daughter when her time would come. Jean Clement-Corbin never had a want for anything. Both she and her husband knew that in order to maintain a certain lifestyle, sacrifices were needed to keep up the public side of their life, but when it came to the private side and matters of the heart, "don't ask, don't tell" was the rule. To that end, if she was to put up with his womanizing, then she would also find time to be entertained by other gentlemen friends.

Billy also knew of the private agreement between Jean and his cousin. She had actually called him one night to establish the availability of the ranch for a weekend, and when he wanted to check with the boss, she quickly changed her mind and hung up the phone. Billy knew she was also playing the field. Eventually, though, his bad judgment and half a bottle of Jack Daniels ensured that he and Corbin would be able to maintain the retreat for themselves and keep his snooty wife out of the picture forever.

It was a typical late summer's night at the ranch with the family. Everyone was about to turn in for the night, but Jean wanted to check on the horses before heading to bed. Billy, who watched everything from the shadows, rocked on his heels underneath a nearby tree as he took another swig of Jack's finest. He scanned the area for the rest of the party, but nobody seemed to want to help poor Jean in the barn. He emerged from the tree line and followed her in. Jean heard him scuffing his feet behind her. She glanced over her shoulder to see Billy approaching with a bottle in his hand.

"You come to help me, Billy?" she asked politely.

"Nope."

"Anything wrong?"

"Nope."

She sensed that something was indeed wrong, and she moved into one of the stalls, hoping he would go away. He followed her in and blocked her way out. She was scared; she didn't like Billy, but she tolerated him for her family's sake.

"I need to get back to the house. Excuse me," she said and tried to brush past him. He grabbed her waist and leaned over as if to kiss her. "How 'bout it, little lady? You an' me, nobody need know, just me an' you?"

His breath repulsed her, and she struggled to get away.

He dropped his bottle and grabbed her ass with his other hand. "C'mon, bitch, I know you put out. What about poor little ol' me?" He squeezed her harder, and she wanted to scream, but his physical presence was too much; it was getting hard to breathe.

She never said a word but smiled and nodded her submission. He began to release a little and smiled. "That's right, honey, you an' me." She finally was able to create a little gap between them, and she made her move, sliding her right hand down into his pants and struggling to find his tool. Billy thought that he was going to get lucky.

When she found his dick, she grabbed it with all her strength and yanked it down and away from him. He backed off in shock and fell to the ground, reeling in pain. She had never used foul language in her life, but this time Jean thought it was appropriate. She calmly spoke to him as he was rolling around in the hay. "That's the smallest prick I have ever felt! You touch me again, and I'll cut the fucking thing off and feed it to my horse." He made a move toward her, hissing, "You fucking whore," but she stepped back from his grasp and kicked him in the nuts. As he grabbed his privates again, she reached over to the whiskey bottle that was lying in the corner, picked it up, and threw it at him for good measure. It connected with his head and almost knocked him out.

She made it back to the house and managed to get into the shower before anyone suspected something was wrong. Later she explained everything to her husband, who she expected to take action. She wanted Billy fired, even charged with assault, but Corbin defended him saying he would take care of it. When Corbin went in search for his cousin that night, he couldn't be found.

Corbin knew what action he would take. Whittaker was going to be out a few days later, so he could wait. He'd get one of Whittaker's boys to shove a gun in Billy's face to send the message: Don't fuck around with the boss's wife. Family or not, there were still limits to respect, and Billy would have to learn them. But Jean couldn't wait. The next day she left, and she never set foot on the property again—and that suited the politician just fine.

The blue Taurus finally pulled into the drive, spewing a cloud of fine brown dust into the air. Corbin placed his hand over his whiskey glass and stared with contempt at Bowman, who exited the car. The senator let his temper cool before berating the man in front of his guest but knew he would lay into him later for causing such a stir. He also would have a word with Billy, as he even broke from protocol to leave his guard position to come and stick in his nose to see who the guests were. Normally Billy didn't care, but this time something sparked his interest.

Cindy Whittaker exited the passenger side of the car and began taking in her surroundings. It was not an unfamiliar scene to her, being a country girl herself, but what was strange to her was that she was brought to this place by an official of the FBI. She was told by the very *unfriendly* agent that her husband was in Virginia working on a government program and he wanted to see her. She insisted that she could wait for him to come home, but the agent expressed his concern that her husband had been sick and was convalescing in a government-sponsored retreat and he would not be home for some time. She knew that he had had bouts with malaria from some of his overseas trips, and she was genuinely concerned. She hated and wanted to be free of him, but she still cared for him in some obscure way. Maybe because she remembered the good times when they met, and she knew that after she left him, she'd never see him again.

As Bowman retrieved Cindy's overnight bag from the trunk, Corbin introduced himself with his cheesy used-car salesman smile.

"Mrs. Whittaker, so good of you to join us. Robert J. Corbin at your service."

"I know who you are, Senator. Nice to meet you. I've heard so much about you," she said nervously.

Inwardly she was panicking; she had seen his name plastered all over her husband's hidden documents. She didn't know what was going on but tried to remain calm. With any luck it was possible that Corbin didn't know about her husband's information. When she left her home with the agent, the floorboards in the bathroom were intact, and nothing was out in the open, so there was no way of him knowing about the stack of paperwork her husband had amassed. She had to think this through, though. Why was she here?

"Is my husband here?" she asked.

"Not at the moment. He will be joining us shortly, though," Corbin said as he turned his attention to Billy. "Billy, why don't you take Mrs. Whittaker up to one of the guest cabins so she can freshen up?"

Billy's face lit up like a Christmas tree. He grabbed her bag from Bowman and, with a shit-eating grin, turned to Cindy, saying, "This way, please."

"So where is he?" she pressed. "I thought he was sick. I thought he couldn't travel."

"He's fine. We have a military hospital nearby, and he will be transferred over here later," Corbin lied. "Billy will show you the way. We can catch up in a little while," he said, again flashing the pearly white smile.

"You'll call me the minute he gets here, won't you?" she asked.

"Absolutely, don't worry about a thing. Just go and freshen up, take a rest for a short while. You'll find everything you need, and if you're lucky, Billy will make you a pot of coffee."

Cindy took one look at the creepy caretaker and slumped her shoulders, feeling dejected. "Okay, thank you, but please come and get me when he comes."

As both she and Billy sauntered off towards the log cabins, Corbin shook his head and commented to Bowman, "Billy looks like a horny dog just waiting to hump a leg—but he may get his wish with that one."

He then turned to look at Bowman, and his mood swung in a different direction.

"How many times have I told you to drive like a *grandfather* when you come up here? I spotted you miles away—take it easy for Christ's sake. Do I really need to tell you to stop drawing attention to this place?"

He paused for a second and then went back on the offensive. "I'm getting seriously pissed off, throwing away good whiskey every time you yahoos come up here. And explain to me why you had to bring that damn car. It has "fed" written all over it. Couldn't you have brought something more appropriate?"

Bowman defended himself. "I thought this would be the only way she would come." Then he changed the subject. "Have you heard from Whittaker?"

"That is something you should be telling me, not asking me," his boss said curtly. "Did you bring the paperwork?"

"No, Far Sight is working on that," he said, changing to using call signs as Billy approached. Billy knew a lot of things that went on at the retreat, but he didn't know, or need to know, everything.

"Okay, when is he going to get me that?" Corbin pushed. "Billy take a hike!"

"He'll be coming out tonight. Don't worry. I'll tell him to tone down the federal look." *And bring an ice cream truck if that makes you happy, asshole,* Bowman thought.

"Okay, you need to get back to Berlin. You've got work to do, and Whittaker may show up there for all we know."

Orders were given, so not much more was needed to be said. Bowman went for a leak and a Coke and hit the road, glad to see the back of the ranch. Corbin went off to the shooting range, which was being used by one of Whittaker's teams. He had a job for one or two of the boys.

CHAPTER
TWELVE

CALL SIGN FAR SIGHT WAS THOROUGHLY ENGROSSED in the material he found under the bathroom floorboards at the Whittakers' home. There was so much information that he relocated to the living room couch, kicked off his shoes, and began to read. He knew he was getting behind schedule and needed to get on the road out to Dilbeck, but his instinct for gathering and retaining information compelled him to read, digest, and begin weaving plots and subplots in his mind. Far Sight knew he was playing a dangerous game with Corbin, but the more information or ammunition he had to defend himself, if and when the time came, the better.

After spending close to three hours of furious reading and note taking, he left the Whittakers' in search of a Kinko's copy store. He knew he couldn't reproduce everything he wanted, but he made sure to capture the most interesting pieces: references to Munich 1972. He'd have to dig further in the stash to find out what that data meant, but for now, he had to copy what he could and then get on the road.

Far Sight begrudgingly dished out seventy-nine dollars in copy fees and took his newfound cache to a storage unit in Falls Church. He knew it would be safe for the short term, and on his drive out to Dilbeck, he could figure out a more secure location for this goldmine of information.

DAY 22
VIENNA, VIRGINIA

Although Chris had been in the area numerous times, it was still a frustrating area around which to drive. His target was the Tyson's Corner Shopping Mall where he was intending to buy some clothes for his trip to Fort Bragg.

Chris's expedition to the States, meant to last only ten days including his training, was now into its eighth day with no end in sight, and he soon became frustrated navigating around the side streets and boulevards of the Lego-like city that made up the mall.

Chris was always frustrated and just plain pissed off when it came to one of three basic elements in life: shopping, eating, or finding somewhere to sleep. He couldn't count the number of times he went out to shop for a new shirt or sweater and came back with either a sweater or a watch that he didn't need while neglecting to purchase the items he really needed. He could never find the basics he sought, even after hours of perusing endless stores and clothing racks. And he absolutely hated the idea of having a perky salesperson try to help. When it came to eating, he knew where some good restaurants were in places like Tyson's Corner, but he always felt like a castaway sitting alone looking up at the ceiling with nothing to do but wait for his meal, so he usually ended up at a roadside diner or a McDonald's. If he was traveling alone and needed somewhere to sleep, he'd always end up in a cheap motel on the side of a freeway, not because he was cheap; it was just quicker and simpler.

On this occasion, it was no different. It was getting late, and Chris was happy that nobody was with him in the car, as his language was becoming more colorful by the minute. He had just made it back to Vienna after doing something he actually wanted to do: checking out the White House. He wanted to see first-hand how the Secret Service recently blocked off Pennsylvania Avenue in response to the Oklahoma City bombing earlier in the year.

As he drove, he could plainly see the bright lights of JC Penney and Macy's, but he was too slow in getting across the three lanes on Chain Bridge Road that would allow him to take a right turn into the mall. He decided to take a left turn onto Tyson's Boulevard to find a good turnaround but ended up at the rear of Tyson's Galleria—yet another Legoland-shaped mall, albeit much more upscale than the Corner Mall.

He finally made it to the nearby Ritz Carlton Hotel, where he found an opportunity to do a *U*-turn.

Chris waited for traffic to subside before pulling back onto the street, and he caught a glimpse of the office buildings around him. His Terminator-like analytics kicked in as he began reading a neon sign on the side of Tyson's Boulevard number 1800. *PricewaterhouseCoopers, where have I seen that before?* he asked himself. He eventually pulled away from the hotel driveway and mulled over the brightly lit name on the sign. He knew the firm was some sort of international accounting and risk-management company, but he couldn't figure out why he was so fixated on its words.

He finally made it into the parking lot at JC Penny's and tried to concentrate on finding some new shoes, underwear, and socks. He thought he'd be smart with his shopping tactics, and this time, he headed straight for the socks. On finding a couple of nice ties, he decided to bag it for the day; he was hungry and getting tired. As he was cashing out it came to him: *Price, Waterhouse, Coopers—PWC. That makes sense,* he thought, remembering that was the moniker he'd attached to the cute girl at Georgetown. He had been thinking of her more than he'd realized. He wondered now what she might have been doing at the university that day. *She was probably some intern or graduate student studying part-time at Georgetown. That was why she was in the Center for International Studies* … But he had no more information over which to dwell. His stomach began to rumble, forcing him to move on. *Ah well, that solves that little mystery,* he thought. *Hmmm, where's the nearest Burger King?*

DAY 22
DILBECK, VIRGINIA

Far Sight eventually made it to Stonewall late that evening. Rain was falling lightly, and a few lights burned from the cabins nestled in the dark of the forest.

"The boss has been waiting for you," came a raspy voice from the shadows near the main driveway. Billy, standing with his trademark shotgun, was less than ten feet away. He spoke to the visitor with typical loathing. "He's pissed, so you better get up to the main house."

Although startled, Far Sight pretended to be in control—even as a shot of adrenalin sped through his veins. He thought he was tough and switched on, but sometimes his situational awareness just sucked. *How did he miss this guy back there?*

"Give me a hand with this stuff," he replied, trying to avoid eye contact with the watchman.

"What's in the box, pencil neck?" Billy, insubordinate, shot back.

Far Sight tried to brush him off. "Nothing that concerns you. Just grab a box."

"Carry your own shit, pansy," spat Billy. He shrank back to the shadows and into his own little world, fantasizing about shooting one of Corbin's arrogant minions.

Corbin appeared and immediately barked at Far Sight, "Where have you been? You were expected hours ago."

The visitor defended himself. "I can't just drop everything. I've still got a job to maintain, and I can't always be your errand boy—so cut me some slack!"

"You watch your tongue, asshole. Don't forget whom you're talking to," Corbin warned.

"Sorry, it's that creep Billy that got me going. He spooks the shit out of me sometimes."

"Seriously? Remind me of who you work for again? On second thought, forget it. Let's get this in the house. Have you looked at this stuff?" Corbin was eager to know what exactly the agent had found at Whittaker's house.

"No. Why should I? Is it something worth reading?"

"I don't know yet. It seems that Whittaker has been creating some kind of insurance policy for himself. I've got his wife as collateral if he decides to play hardball."

"Where is he?"

"If either of you two numbskulls asks me that again, I'll shove Billy's shotgun up your ass so far that smoke will come out your mouth after I've pulled the trigger. *I don't know* where Whittaker is. I pay you and Bowman to get me that sort of information—and right now, I feel as if I deserve a rebate. Jesus … Help me up to the house with this shit. Then you can either get back on the road or sleep in one of the cabins and leave early in the morning. Just make sure you're gone before the Whittaker woman wakes up. On second thought, get lost ASAP. I don't want any possibility of her seeing you, period. She's already spent too much time with Bowman. Go grab a coffee or something and get back on the road. When you get back to town, find Bowman; he'll tell you what to do next."

It was already too late. The car door slamming and the clear, loud voices had pierced the silence of the woods. Cindy stood in the darkness on the wraparound deck of her cabin, peering across to the main driveway. She saw Corbin and a younger man moving boxes into the house and made out just enough words to put her mind into a tailspin. *Whittaker … insurance package … I don't know where Whittaker is.* That was all she needed to hear.

On meeting Corbin earlier that night, Cindy sensed something was wrong. Why would a slime bucket like that spend time with her, playing happy campers in the woods? She was racking her brains when she thought she heard some movement in the trees and bushes nearby. She put it down to nerves and withdrew back into the cabin, trying to think of what to do next.

Billy stood at the edge of the tree line, also contemplating what he had just seen and heard. He hated Whittaker. The man often came along when the teams were training at Stonewall. The soldier constantly shouted orders to all within earshot—including Billy. But Billy didn't play. Billy saw Whittaker for what he was: a condescending, arrogant, and stubborn jerk who was used to having his way with his toy soldiers. The mere mention of him being in some kind of trouble put a smile on Billy's face. In his opinion, *what goes around comes around, motherfucker.*

But Billy could never get Whittaker back on his own; the soldier was too smart for Billy, and besides, Whittaker never went more than ten paces without one of his pack sniffing at his heels for orders. Now faced with the prospect of Whittaker's wife being held at Stonewall made the watchman lick his lips—and he began fantasizing of the many ways he could hurt the woman.

He debated whether to first head off to the bathroom or see Corbin. He rationalized that Corbin was going to be busy for a while, so he might as well go and relieve himself first. As he started for his own cabin, the door to Cindy's slowly creaked open. Billy halted, then took two paces back into the shadows, and watched with some nasty images on his mind.

It didn't take Cindy long to make up her mind. She knew she had to get away from the ranch. She gathered what she could of her belongings and made for the safety and the darkness of the woods, even though she had no idea where she was going or how she was going to get there. On the drive into Stonewall, she had tried to remember the way she came, but since she didn't think she was in any danger then, she didn't pay enough attention to the route they were taking or what houses and farm lands they were passing through. Each time she asked Bowman where they were going, she was met with the same reply: a military retreat in the foothills of the Shenandoah. She accepted the response and relaxed, eventually falling asleep on the journey. It wouldn't have mattered anyway; Bowman took forever to get there, by design, even doubling back a few times without her realizing it.

Cindy made a decision to head through the woods and away from the roads and surrounding farmlands; she didn't want to take the risk of finding a Corbin sympathizer this close to Stonewall. She had seen some trails earlier when it was still light, and she surmised they must lead to somewhere. Back in her native Montana, she was no stranger to the outdoors—she grew up hiking, camping, and fishing. The only thing that she was afraid of outdoors was bears; she hoped they didn't exist in this part of the country. She took a cautious step into the quiet unknown and stealthily crept away.

The only real thing of value that Billy had ever gotten from Whittaker was a pair of military spec night-vision goggles, which he proudly carried every night as he made his patrols around Stonewall. When Corbin wasn't around, Billy also used them as he ventured into the small towns and villages in the area late at night, spying on others with his all-seeing goggles. For the most part, he didn't get to see too much, but now and again, he managed to find a ground floor bedroom with open curtains and watch as couples made love deep into the night, or, if he was really lucky, young girls stripping down, getting ready for bed. On more than one occasion, he took his hand-held recorder for future viewing pleasure.

He now watched and tracked Cindy's every move. It took her a while to gain her own, unaided, night vision and more than once made the mistake of looking back from the woods to the glowing lights of Stonewall. She stumbled a few times and tried her best not to let out a scream or moan from tripping over an object. Billy just smiled and watched with anticipation. She wasn't going to get too far; he wanted to play this one out just a little longer. He followed her deeper into the woods, never more than fifty feet away. Billy was in stealth mode; every time she stopped, he stopped. Every turn was the same, every step was in the same place. He was her shadow.

The pitch blackness of the woods soon began to overwhelm Cindy, and she became paranoid as she thought she'd heard on more than one occasion nearby small twigs or branches snapping. She began to question her decision. It was one thing to be traipsing around the woods with family or friends, with flashlights and routes planned, making jokes as you go—but to actually be on the run without light or direction was a daunting task for anyone, let alone a former dental assistant from Montana. She willed herself not to cry, but it was of no use.

As Cindy began to sob, Billy's smile grew broader. He liked the thought of a woman in submission—but on the other hand, he knew that a panicked woman made some rash and unpredictable moves. He was speaking from experience; he still had a scar on his neck from the first rape he had committed. He didn't want to make the same mistake twice. He understood correctly that he was not in complete control of the situation just yet. He didn't want to frighten her more; she might run and trip, break a bone, or cut herself. He needed her whole, needed her healthy. He had long-term plans for this one.

Cindy was by now trying to feel her way through the forest, to no avail. Thousands of acres of trees lay before her. She stopped again to listen for sounds, heard the snapping of branches again, and was sure that something was out there tracking her. This was not some teenage camping version of *Fright Night*—this was real; some beast was hunting her.

Her fear created an immediate need to relieve herself. But she held off, as the snapping of branches continued. She spun around to find the source, but now it was coming from more than one direction. She stopped in her tracks and swiveled her head from left to right and then turned her body around and around until she was almost spinning in one spot.

She stopped herself to concentrate on the sounds around her and spotted a weird set of green lights in the distance. As she tried to focus on the lights, she saw the shape of a human head. Terrified, she let out the loudest scream that she had ever made and spun away in the opposite direction, only to come face to face with another set of green lights. She screamed again and turned to run when a set of firm hands grabbed her. As she began to struggle, she saw more green lights, now surrounding her in the darkness of the woods.

"We've got trouble!" Far Sight shouted to Corbin through the door in the main house.

Corbin dropped some of the papers he was reading. "What's going on?"

"I just heard screams from the woods," the agent told him.

"I'll take care of this. You get moving—go back to DC. If you see Billy on your way out, tell him I need him, *now.*"

Far Sight jumped into his rented Ford Explorer and powered out of Stonewall, a huge cloud of red dust behind him. He was all too happy to get out of that place.

Corbin, walking along the drive, coughed as he sucked in portions of the cloud. He stormed towards Cindy's cabin, shouting at no one in particular, "I'm going to shoot one of those two idiots any day now, I shit you not!" He made his way through the unit and onto the rear deck just in time to see Billy emerge from the woods. "Billy, I hope you haven't done what I think you have done," he warned.

"Not me. I was tracking her after she heard your conversation with pretty boy—she tried to do a runner." He paused as he turned around to see the first of a five-man patrol returning with the now bound and gagged woman in tow. "I saw the boys moving in, so I let them take over. I guess she screamed when she saw them."

Corbin, skeptical of Billy as ever, called out to his patrol unit. "Sanchez, is that right?"

"Not quite, sir," Sanchez replied. "Billy did take his time before he made his presence known."

Corbin sighed and turned back to his cousin. "Billy, are you playing games again?"

Billy smiled. "Now why would I want to do that?"

Corbin decided not to pursue it. He had more important things to do. "Sanchez, take our guest to the training room. I'll be there shortly. Billy, come with me."

As the patrol made their way to the training room, Corbin led Billy to the main house. Once inside he got down to business. "Tell me what happened—what she saw, what she heard, what you saw, what you heard. And then tell me why you were near her in the first place."

Cindy was placed in a room that was similar to a student classroom, but without windows or the cheery trimmings of a place of learning. There were plenty of desks and chairs and numerous whiteboards and easels with black covers draped over them to protect their contents. Still bound and gagged, she was left in the room with two of her captors—the one they called Sanchez and the other who had restrained her in the woods. Both men stared at her and said nothing.

Cindy was used to uniforms and military insignia, but her jailers bore no rank, emblem, or unit designations on their camouflage fatigues. Their faces were painted in green, black, and brown; their hands were gloved;

their boots were muddy. But their weapons were in pristine condition. They looked military, they took orders like the military, and they moved and behaved as only the military could. But this was no military Cindy was familiar with.

Her bonds were tight, and her gag, which smelled and tasted of camouflage paint, made her want to vomit. Her eyes stung from a mixture of dirt, sweat, and tears; her nose was filled with the stench of the unwashed bodies of soldiers who had spent too much time out in the woods. Cindy had a very keen sense of smell, and so she also picked up the smell of gun oil. As she looked around the room she caught sight of a workbench and what looked like gun-cleaning equipment, set up nice and orderly, on top. Next to that were a few paper targets, which meant to her that there must be a gun range nearby.

After what seemed forever to Cindy, Corbin marched into the training room. The two soldiers immediately stood up. Billy bounced in from behind, following his master like an eager puppy. Corbin glanced at Cindy, but then turned to Sanchez and his colleague Montoya. "I think you two need some target practice—let's go." He headed to an adjoining door.

Sanchez grabbed the woman and followed Corbin into the indoor range. Corbin again turned to Sanchez. "Grab a chair and take her down range—and make sure she can't get out of it." Both of Corbin's men dragged Cindy down range and bound her to a metal chair. Corbin joined them, stood behind Cindy, and placed his hands on her shoulders.

"Boys, go back fifty feet," he said and then leaned over to Cindy's left ear. "Now young lady, I have complete confidence in my boys' accuracy. Have you ever been shot at?"

She shook her head violently and tried to muffle a response. Corbin ignored her. "Sanchez, give me one round, ten feet to my right. Montoya, one to my left. Go!" The two henchmen did so with lighting speed and accuracy, made possible not only with their skills but also by the precise actions of their Heckler & Koch MP5s. The two shots rang out and whizzed harmlessly by into the sand bunker at the end of the range.

Corbin was smiling. "Sanchez, give me one round into the beam above my head, come closer if you need to. Go!" *Crack, thump*, the shot hit the wooden beam and sent some splinters down onto the petrified woman.

"Whoa, that was a good one," Corbin laughed. He leaned back over to Cindy's ear. "This guy is good, don't you think? But hang on. I have another idea. This is going to be fun."

Corbin moved to the opposite end of the range and killed the lights. As he did so, both soldiers went to their night-vision goggles and depressed their laser sites, fixed to their weapons. Corbin joined Sanchez and Montoya, whispering, "I want to scare the shit out of her. Don't hurt her, but get close enough to worry her permanently."

As he stepped back, Sanchez opened fire with a single shot to Cindy's right, just to get her attention, and then two to her left. He then went to three-round bursts to her far right and then full auto to her far left. He changed magazines while moving forward. Two more shots to the left, two to the right; one over the top, three more to the right. Cindy could see the bursts of bright bullet flashes in the dark, which completely killed what-ever night vision she had gained while sitting in the darkness. The flash did highlight the face of the camouflaged soldier as he moved closer, inch by inch. Finally the shooting stopped, and there was complete silence. Cindy had temporarily lost her hearing anyway. It seemed like an eternity before anything else happened. Then, "Billy, … lights," Corbin ordered.

As Cindy blinked to adjust her eyes to the artificial light, she became aware of Sanchez standing three feet in front of her, his gun aimed direct-ly at her head. What she didn't see, but felt, was the sharp edge of a blade at her throat. Montoya had crept up behind her and grabbed her hair. He spoke softly, "Don't move if you want to live." As she concentrated on trying not to breathe, she became aware of a warm sensation beneath her crotch. Earlier she'd needed to urinate; not anymore. It felt disgusting, but it didn't matter—she wasn't even considering moving.

Corbin stepped closer. "Now then, madam, as you can tell, my boys have some very specialized skills. You should really see what they can do if I want someone killed or cut up. It's quite interesting the number of ways a human can kill another human. But these boys, well, they are artists; they have, I would say, some *panache*, some flair for what they do."

He let his comments sink in for a few seconds and then with utter se-riousness told her: "You are alive only because I choose to have you alive. I could have had you killed in the most painful manner the moment you set foot in this place. But the next time you decide to leave my humble abode, Sanchez and Montoya will come looking for you, and they'll find you. If they do bring you back in one piece, I'll turn you over to Billy— who has a different appetite towards pretty young women like yourself."

He was pleased; he could tell she was petrified. "Once he has finished playing with you," he went on, "after a few days, weeks, whatever, you're going to wish that my boys had killed you. After Billy's done, I may even take pity on you myself and put a bullet in your head, just to put you out of your misery." He paused again. "Are we understanding each other?"

She nodded as quickly as she could.

"Good, so I think it's in your best interest that you do as I say from here on out, don't you?"

Again she nodded her fast agreement. "Now I may have a change of mind by the time I get back to my cabin, so I'm going to leave you here just in case I do. I may not need you after all."

The group marched out, hit the lights, and slammed the door behind them. Cindy was left in the darkness alone and scared. She wanted to scream as if there was no tomorrow, but she couldn't. She cried until her head throbbed and she thought she would pass out. But then she thought of her husband. *That bastard, that fucking bastard, he got me into this mess. He's ruined my life! If I ever see him again, I'm going to kill him. I hate him! I hate him! Where is he, that sonofabitch.* And she continued to cry.

CHAPTER
THIRTEEN

DAY 23

FAYETTEVILLE, NORTH CAROLINA

CHRIS BEGAN THE MORNING WITH A COUGH AND A SNEEZE. He thought maybe he was getting a cold, so he decided to bag his morning routine of going for a run. Besides, he was unfamiliar with his new surroundings; he and Gene had arrived in the military town long after the sunset the night before. Gene had explained they would be there for only a few days, but if Chris really wanted to go for a jog, Gene could put Chris in touch with some army buddies, who could easily take him through his paces on Fort Bragg—if that's what he really wanted, of course. Chris felt intrigued and agreed to meet some of Gene's army buddies—it would be nice to get a tour of the base, anyway.

Chris was genuinely interested in seeing the base. He'd heard that Fort Bragg was home to the famous 82nd Airborne Division, and he wanted to see what type of environment they trained in. Most British Army military bases were probably not even a tenth of the size of Bragg, so he was excited to see how the other half lived and trained.

Chris didn't know it, but he was one step closer to finding himself at the door of the most secret and highly trained unit of the United States Army—the Delta Force. He'd been peddling his story about Bonn for some time now, and he still couldn't believe how many military people were still trying to get information from him about the attack.

Delta was no different. Like all major Special Forces units around the world, one of their specialties was executive protection. There were two reasons for having this expertise: the first was to protect the highest of endangered personnel; the second, how to *overcome* executive protection and get to the highest of endangered personnel.

The only way they could get this tactical information was to train, train, and train again on the hundreds of potential what-if scenarios. So when Delta heard about the attack in Bonn and found out that it was a CIA driver who survived and rescued a US ambassador, they knew that they had to pick his brain.

Chris wasn't aware that it was Delta that wanted to chat with him; he just thought that his curious audience had never been in those situations before and were interested to hear all about it. It did matter to him, though, that he wouldn't be speaking casually about it in a pub or over dinner, but in a more formal, training-like setting. He enjoyed talking shop with peers, or at least those in the same general line of business.

Realistically though, talking in depth about the attack became therapeutic for him. It wasn't easy to kill someone, no matter how simple Hollywood made it seem. Countless numbers of hard, skilled, well-seasoned men suffered from post-traumatic stress disorder from being in combat-like situations. Some made it through; others made it to the bottle. There was no rhyme or reason to it; it just was.

Lucky for Chris, he was coping well mentally with his acts. He was able to justify killing terrorists in Bonn and Northern Ireland, so in his mind, he was still healthy. How long this would last, he didn't know, but talking about it to like-professionals seemed to ease the burden. Physically though, the strain of the past few weeks was beginning to show. Along with the coughs and sputters, his engine just didn't feel as if it was running on all cylinders. His bruises weren't healing as fast as usual, and some were more than a little tender. Some of his cuts needed daily care, and his typically high level of stamina began to drop. He was tired.

He lay in bed a few extra minutes before deciding to get up, but just as he started to rise, a wave of nausea and chill ran through his body. He thought perhaps was getting the flu. He managed to drag himself groggily out of bed and head for a cold shower. On the way in he glanced at the image he saw in the bathroom mirror. He didn't recognize the man standing there. He looked as white as a ghost. If it were not for the bruises on his body, he would look like a corpse. He shook his head and got into the shower thinking that he needed a long break. Cyprus wasn't at all a holiday, the trip to the US was full of drama, and losing Astrid had left him sad and very lonely.

He was hoping that the cold shower would make him feel better, and after getting out, he did. Naked, he began to dry himself off. He made it down to his toes, but when he tried to straighten up he couldn't.

The nausea hit him again, but this time it was accompanied by a sharp needle-like pain in his lower back. As he tried again to stand straight, a more powerful pain hit his side. He reached back for the dagger that must surely have been there but found nothing. Still bent over, he managed to get to the toilet seat and slumped there in a sitting position. As he sat, his breathing became more labored, so he felt his way to the pulse in his neck. It was racing. Sweat from his body began dripping to the bathroom floor. He didn't know what was going on but felt like shit, and he didn't think he was going to be able to get off the seat. Each time he tried to straighten his posture, the now Bowie knife-size pain shot through his lower back and side. He was in shit state; he needed help.

His clothes were hanging on the bathroom door hook. He made it there by crawling on all fours. From the floor, he was able to pull his sweat pants off the hook, but his T-shirt wouldn't budge. He gave it a forceful yank, ripping the shirt and sending the door hook flying. *Great,* he thought, *anything else? Anybody else want to give me some shit? I've got enough room for a little more.*

It took him a while to get his clothes on while sitting on the bathroom floor with his back to the door. Once he did so, he turned back over onto his knees, and then on all fours. He next tried to open the door but only got it halfway. It was stuck on something, some kind of wedge. Frustrated and sick as a dog, he yelled out loud, "Is someone taking the piss or what?!" He looked around the base of the door and spotted the door hook wedged solidly under it.

Exasperated, he bitched again. "I don't fucking believe this." Sweat was still pouring from his body and his clothes were soon soaked. He tugged as hard as he could, making matters worse. *I'm going to die in a fucking bathroom in some redneck city by myself in my favorite, now fucking ripped, T-shirt. Outstanding!* He thought.

His choices were becoming limited. He knew he had to get out of the bathroom to the phone next to the bed, but his strength was leaving him. He *had* to squeeze through the door and get to that phone. He tried again to stand, but his efforts were in vain; the pain was becoming unbearable. He stayed on the floor and did his best impression of a caterpillar, slowly squeezing through, cursing, and almost crying as he went.

He made it out and crawled to the bed to reach for the phone. He didn't make it, and the effort almost made him pass out. He was now lying flat on the floor next to his bed, trying not to think of what the carpet had seen or experienced in its fifty years there. He moved his head around to see if he could grab something to support his weight so he could lift himself up. As he looked under the bed, he spotted the telephone cable, lying loosely near the base of the headboard. He managed to grab ahold of and drag the wire to him until the phone followed suit. He winced on seeing and hearing the phone crash to the floor, and hoped that he hadn't screwed up again by breaking the apparatus.

He dialed Gene's room. The man answered on the third ring. "Hello?"

"Gene, it's Chris. I'm in shit state. I need your help."

"What's wrong?"

"I don't know. I need a doctor or an ambulance."

"I'll be right there," Gene replied and hung up the phone.

Chris dropped the phone and stared off under the bed, looking for answers.

Either his mind started playing tricks on him or his training started to kick in as the usual what-if scenarios came pouring into his mind. *Has someone drugged me? Is this some whacky CIA training selection technique that's gone bad? What did I eat last night? What did I drink? Did Gene put something in my food?* His mind kept spinning until he heard a shout at the door.

"Chris, Chris!" Gene called out.

Chris tried to shout, but to Gene on the other side of the door, it was almost a whisper: "I can't get to the door. I can't get up. Go and get a key."

"Okay, I'll be back. Hang on!" came the reply.

Although it took a few minutes for Gene to return, to Chris it seemed like an hour. During that time, he managed to get himself out of a fetal position to lying flat on his back. Then he just lay there waiting. A sense of shame washed over him knowing, for one of the very few times in his life, he needed real help. He never liked to rely on others; he was the one that people looked to for aid. But not him, not Chris Morehouse, he never asked. He was too proud, too independent to seek anyone's assistance.

He finally heard the door open. As he tried to raise his head to see who was there, another wild scene went through his mind: *This is it. The IRA bastards have tracked me down. It's over."*

Then Gene came into focus. "Chris, what the hell's going on?" he asked as he kneeled down to help.

"I don't know. I have pain in my side and lower back. I don't know what it is. I can't get up."

Gene grabbed Chris's wrist, feeling for his pulse. "Shit, it's racing. You're sweating like a pig; you're as white as a sheet; you look like death warmed up, son."

"It's nice to see you too, Gene," replied Chris, finding the humor in his sad state. "You look marvelous by the way."

Gene sniggered. But then he was serious. "You don't look good, my friend," he said and then turned to the hotel clerk who had allowed him access to the room. "Nine-one-one, now. Make the call—male, late twenties, back pain, immobile, high fever, high pulse. Repeat what I just said." The clerk grabbed the phone off the floor and repeated Gene's words dutifully.

Gene grabbed Chris's hand. "This doesn't mean we're going to ride off into the sunset and swap spit, Chris. Hang on. Help is on the way." He then turned to the clerk, "Go back downstairs to the lobby and meet the paramedics—go now!" Gene didn't shout or bark, but he was obviously used to giving out serious orders. The clerk scurried away.

Chris finally perked some. "Thanks, Gene. By the way, your hands need some moisturizer; they're pretty dry. We don't want your skin to crack, now do we?"

Gene appreciated the gallows humor from a man who was obviously in severe pain. He looked at Chris with a faint smile, mouthing the word, "asshole."

DAY 23
GEORGETOWN UNIVERSITY, WASHINGTON, DC

The man on the crutches was once again sitting on a park bench just across from the Georgetown University international building. He'd been coming to the same spot off and on for about two weeks with the confidence that no one would take too much notice of him. His appearance was altered somewhat to make himself look worse off than he really was. He dressed like a bum but was mindful of not acting like a complete scourge by begging for food or money from the countless number of rich students that passed by. The crutches were an added bonus to his superficial disguise. They were in fact needed, though, as supports for the injury sustained when the senator's henchman had shot him in the legs weeks earlier. The wounds had not healed completely, and he was still in considerable pain.

Mazzim waited patiently for his target to appear. He had his timing down well, neither showing up too early nor too late and never leaving too soon. He thought he practiced a fairly good form of surveillance, but to the trained professional, his activities should have set off alarm bells. He had confidence that his target was not protected by law enforcement agencies so he felt relatively safe, and he never pushed the limits of overstaying his welcome. He knew the University Campus Police were patrolling the area, but from his park bench beneath the trees, he was still slightly off the beaten path.

At first, he showed up every morning to catch a glimpse of his target, but he could never establish a pattern. He later switched to afternoons for ten days straight, and only then was he able to identify the regular comings and goings of students, teachers, janitors, delivery couriers, and the like. After weeks of patience, he finally made up his mind. The schedule was clear: Every Monday, Wednesday, and Friday, the target would finish class at 2 p.m., take ten to fifteen minutes to get out of the building, and then take a few more minutes to unlock the bicycle that was parked in the same spot every day. The target took thirty seconds to don the bike helmet, reflective jacket, and backpack and then, after checking traffic, would head southbound out of the sprawling campus. The bicycle would be the key.

Others on his team had given up on establishing a pattern around the target's residence; the movements were too unpredictable. The subject didn't always get home at the same time, often came home with other students or friends, and sometimes came home for only a few minutes before heading out again for the night. The morning schedule was not much better. Some mornings the target worked out, sometimes worked at a local bookstore, sometimes jogged, and sometimes stayed at home. But for some reason, the afternoon class schedule forced the target to leave the Georgetown University International Building at almost the same time, each of the three days of the week. The watcher had made a decision to hit the target on one of the three class days. He needed to set some other things in motion before he made his move, but it was going to happen and happen soon.

One of his concerns was that his team could be at the attack scene for only ten to fifteen minutes before people started to take notice of strangers sitting in parked cars. The group could also not simply turn up, conduct the act, and move on. Practice was needed, escape routes needed to be chosen, vehicles and drivers selected, and a multitude of other minute details attended to that could either sink the mission or drive it to success.

Planning and logistics were some of the fundamentals of terrorist acts. Other elements included intelligence gathering, planning the attack, providing the necessary tools, practicing the attack, carrying out the attack, and most important of all—practicing the escape from the scene.

Mazzim had gathered his intelligence; he had his target; he had a plan. Now the implementation phase just needed to be carried out.

DAY 23
FAYETTEVILLE, NORTH CAROLINA

"Kidney stones," the young doctor in the emergency room said.

"Okay, what the hell does that mean?" Chris answered back.

"It means you have dehydrated your kidneys. Calcium has formed around them from drinking sugar-based drinks—or even too much alcohol in some circumstances—and has now formed like crystals around your kidneys. The discomfort you feel are the stones trying to break free or rubbing up against some of your other organs. It's quite painful."

"No shit, doc, thanks for stating the obvious." Chris was feeling surly.

"You have a couple of options here. One, we could wait for a bed at the hospital and have you here for a few days while we zap the crystals into smaller, more manageable pieces; or two, we could wait until you pass them naturally, then analyze them to see what we're dealing with, in case you need long-term care."

Chris was confused. "Okay, I know this is going to sound strange, but how do you pass kidney stones naturally?"

"You drink at least a gallon of water a day until you do. When you urinate, you'll have to filter it—hopefully you'll catch a stone or two."

"How big are these stones?"

"Hard to say. Some are quite small and difficult to see; others can be larger, the size of a pearl or a pea. I'm not going to sugar coat it. It's going to be uncomfortable for you for a while."

Why do doctors always say that it will be uncomfortable for you? Chris thought. *Why not just say it will be as painful as getting your balls sawed off with a rusty lid from a can of tuna?* Instead he said, "So how much time do I have before all this happens?"

"Well a bed probably won't be available for a few days, maybe even a week. As for passing the stone, could be today, tomorrow, next week—hard to tell. But no matter what, you have to increase your fluid intake substantially. Keep drinking water, a gallon a day right now, stay off the booze for a while, take a few days off, get some rest. Stay away from stress. I see that you have some other wounds that need to heal as well; it looks as if you've had a hard time of things lately."

No stress! Chris thought. *Try telling that to all the people who have involved me in all their shit lately. No stress, my arse!* But he kept his mouth shut.

DAY 23

BERLIN TEGEL INTERNATIONAL AIRPORT

Nash finally touched down at Berlin Tegel Airport after the long flight from Frankfurt and Washington, DC. He'd been out of the loop for some time and hadn't seen any of the latest news—or even picked up a local newspaper. As a typical intelligence officer, he felt naked without information. He trusted few with driving if Chris wasn't around, so instead of scheduling an embassy driver for a pickup, he opted for a taxi ride. As he jumped in the back of the cream-colored Mercedes, he shuffled some newspapers out of his way and got comfortable. As much as he wanted to focus on his own personal safety and keep an eye on the taxi driver while he loaded Nash's luggage, Nash's urge to pick up the newspaper was greater.

He flipped through the pile and came across Germany's best-selling tabloid the *Bild-Zeitung*. His German was passable, so he could easily pick up the headlines of the newspaper, fully expecting to see a political sex scandal or gossip from wannabe stars and starlets.

On seeing the headline "CIA Hört Terrorangriff auf" (CIA Stops Terror Attack), Nash starting boiling inside, but ever the professional, he remained poker faced and still as a rock in front of the taxi driver. He put the paper down, not needing to read more. He was sure a report would be waiting for him at home and the office; if not, there would be hell to pay. He wasn't simply mad; he was livid.

The attack in Bonn drew the media around the US embassy like flies around shit. Things had died off for a while, but now a leak of significant proportions had surfaced, and Nash would be in the thick of things again, trying to stifle the discontent. Public perception of the CIA in the United States was borderline acceptable at best, but the people of the European nations took a different view of spies from other countries operating under their noses. Calls for explanations from the German political opposition would surely be winding their way to the embattled German chancellor, and the Berlin Reichstag would be in uproar as voices would be raised and fingers would be wagged.

As the taxi driver drove away from the stand, he asked his passenger for a destination. US *Botschaft, bitte*, Nash replied. His wife would have to wait, she would understand.

———✦———

Two hours later, the KLM flight from Amsterdam touched down at Berlin Tegel Airport, and a grumpy FBI agent made his way through the throng of travelers to the arrival gate. Bowman spotted his partner way before Nick Seymour spotted him. The older agent wasn't quite ready for a chat with his young counterpart, so he decided to make him wait and went in search of a coffee.

After a few minutes, coffee in one hand, luggage in the other, Bowman walked straight up behind his colleague and whispered, "I really do hope you're not carrying."

Seymour spun around. "Why wouldn't I be?"

"You dick, you stand here in the middle of the airport where you know some of the best pickpockets in Berlin operate, and all you can concentrate on is the Lufthansa ticket agent. Can you stand out any more than you do? Forget I asked. You probably could. Where's the car?"

DAY 23
WEST ALBURG, VERMONT

The Protector stamped his muddy feet on the hard concrete at the junction of Line and Bay Roads in West Alburg, Vermont. He spat on the US soil and looked to the heavens thinking to himself, *I am here for you Gadwa, only you. I spit on the devil's lair for you, and I will have my vengeance, as Allah is my witness.*

He'd been walking through the fields for over two hours after being dropped off sixty miles south of Montreal by another Islamic sympathizer who gave him a map and compass and told him to head due south for the unmanned US/Canadian border crossing. It was almost midnight, and he had another three miles to go before he could be met by yet another friend, who would insert him into the underground world that took illegal immigrants along multiple routes to New York City or destinations beyond. The Protector was well briefed and fully prepared physically and mentally for the long journey ahead, and his motivation to reach Washington, DC, overruled simple discomforts such as muddy boots or being soaked to the skin.

CHAPTER
FOURTEEN

DAY 23

GRUNEWALD, BERLIN

IT WAS AN UNENVIABLE TASK, BUT ANNA HEYMANN KNEW SHE HAD TO DO IT. She could have easily called on a member of Winston's staff or her relatives to scour through his belongings but she was the only one who really knew what he would have wanted done with all his clothes, books, notes, photographs, gifts, trinkets, and other accoutrements that made up a diplomat's traveling life.

She decided to begin with the paperwork first, as a lot of his own personal papers were needed by the embassy for follow up, archiving, or destruction. He often worked from home on weekends or evenings, so the pile of papers in his home office was quite substantial.

She set about the task in typical legal fashion. Her intent was to treat any papers in the mountain of information that bore official logos or letterheads as superfluous to her, and as such she boxed them for pickup by the embassy. Unfortunately, any handwritten notes required a brief read before being put into another stack for future attention. At first she was able to detach herself from the personal side of the paperwork by concentrating on the official documentation.

It was easy for her to set aside some of the boring State Department literature. Now and again, she would find documents relating to his past life as an intelligence officer, and she decided to ask her friend and his former boss, General Crauford, for advice on their disposal. She assumed that her husband wasn't naïve enough to keep classified documents at home; nevertheless, it was another pile of stuff that she had to go through. She also found correspondence to and from a number of other foreign ambassadors, and she realized she was going to have to reach out personally to a number of people over the next few weeks and months and thank them for their letters of sympathy and support.

She started to feel sad when she created yet another stack, which she called the reply-to pile. It quickly became much greater in volume than the other stacks. *He touched so many people,* she said to herself. Since her husband's death, she had managed to hold back most of her tears by keeping herself busy with a whole host of things both at work and for the funeral. She hadn't sat around long enough to think about how life would be without her husband. She knew it would catch up with her soon, but for now, she had to stay focused on her immediate task.

It was almost dinner time when she finally turned her attention to the safe. There she found the usual everyday documents that families like to keep secure—tax documents, emergency cash, birth certificates, passports, and copies of this, that, and the other. On one of the hanging file folders, she pulled out a thick manila folder that she didn't recognize. As she opened the front cover, a number of photographs fell to the floor. As she picked them up, she realized they were photos of the embassy in Berlin and the ambassador's residence. She thought it strange she had not seen these photographs before, besides which, they were not of the best quality. As she picked her way through more photos, she saw the faces of men she didn't recognize: first shots of them close up and then from further back, which showed where they were standing. More photos showed the men from different angles, each one grainier than the next; it was as almost as if someone had taken the photographs while in a moving vehicle.

She eventually surmised that the images were taken by someone who was surveying the embassy. She wasn't sure what to do with them but thought her husband must have been given them to inform him that the embassy and the residence was at some stage under surveillance, not that unusual for foreign missions overseas, especially buildings officially tied to the United States. *Yet another set of documents to go along with the general's pile,* she thought.

As she dug further into the folder, her thoughts were confirmed when she found correspondence from the German BKA stating that these subjects were seen acting suspiciously around the area, although no criminal activity was reported. She pondered this information for a short while and wondered if these individuals had anything to do with the attack in Bonn. *But surely the BKA must have followed up with this type of information,* she thought. She decided she would make a call the following Monday to some of her legal colleagues in Berlin.

As she flipped through some more of the folder, she came across yet another BKA photo, but this time it was a picture of a man she had seen before—and not that long ago. It was the same man in the photo she was shown weeks ago in the Potomac Mills shopping mall. Her heart froze. The same type of heads-up report from the BKA was attached to the picture. She asked herself, *Could this be one of my husband's killers?* She racked her brain. *Who was this guy? Where did he fit into all of this? What happened to that silly woman, and how are they connected?*

She was about to pick up the phone to ring the general but then looked at the clock and decided it was probably still too early to call. As she put down some of the documentation, another pile caught her attention. It looked like US Military Intelligence papers that she thought were still classified, or at least copies of classified material. She wondered why her husband had such reports at home. She could not fathom the reason, the same way she wondered why her husband kept the folder and surveillance photographs in his personal safe at home—not the embassy.

She kept reading despite the late hour. She was tired and knew she needed rest, but she was intrigued, excited, persistent, and perplexed all at the same time. She eventually came to some information written in German from construction companies in and around the Munich area with dates of 1970, 1971, and 1972. There were also detailed construction specifications for the building of the Olympic Village in Munich. She even found copies of blueprints of athletes' dormitories, at which she took a sharp breath.

She cast her mind back to that fateful time when eleven Jewish Olympic athletes were brutally murdered by Palestinian Black September terrorists. She vividly remembered the outcry for revenge from the Israeli people after the attacks. It did not take the office for the residing prime minister of Israel, Golda Meir, long to form a violent and justified response. The prime minister turned to the Israeli intelligence agency Mossad and instructed them to find and kill those responsible for the attack. Mossad created a clandestine team known as the "Wrath of God," whose boundaries were none.

For German Jews like Anna, it was difficult growing up and feeling safe in East Germany, especially since later investigations into the Munich massacre pointed to the East German government's involvement in the attacks. Evidence of Stasi dealings with terrorist groups was suspected for many years before the fall of the Berlin Wall; subsequent findings of intelligence documents at Stasi headquarters confirmed any doubts. Even the Soviet KGB came under scrutiny for training and harboring known terrorist leaders and groups.

As the Wrath of God left a trail of blood through European capitals and the Middle East to the content of most Jewish people, Jews in the Eastern European countries were afraid of the potential persecution from the various secret services of the Communist Bloc. This fear drove hundreds into the arms of the West—including Anna Heymann.

Anna contemplated what she held in her hands; she knew she had to find out more. *Why was her husband collecting this type of information? Where was it leading?* she asked herself. It was quite possible that her husband had found some information that was relevant at the time but was never made public. Perhaps these documents were copies that her husband held for research into the book he promised to write on his retirement. Or it really was something of value that had yet to see the light of day.

Looking further at the German documents, Anna sensed that her husband was creating a list of people involved with the construction of the Munich Olympic Village. She found the general contractor, architects, project-management companies, financiers, and various agencies of the West German government. She found a half-dozen pages of names and companies, mostly German, who had some kind of dealings with the games of '72, but now and again, some French or Spanish company names would appear along with British, Swedish, Japanese, Danish, and American.

This was not unusual for the scale of a project like an Olympic Games, and to Anna, its relevance was unknown. Perhaps her husband knew of or found some kind of link to the terrorist attack. But what really caught her eye were the names circled in red ink—all names of US citizens from US companies who were involved with the games. There were at least a hundred to peruse.

She decided to take a break and make some coffee. She put the ground coffee in the pot and hit the on switch and then headed back to the safe to pick up where she left off. She was so engrossed in finding information about her husband's death—she knew instinctively there was a link with Munich—she simply forgot about her surroundings and the basic necessities, like plugging in the coffee machine. She was sure her husband had stumbled onto something about the Olympics' terror attack, but she still had to figure it out and prove it.

———∞———

The very next morning less than a few miles from the US ambassador's residence where Anna Heymann was still sifting through sheaves of information, Whittaker and Preacher sat patiently sipping the "not-too-hot" coffee at McDonald's on Clay Allee in Southwest Berlin. Whittaker eventually got a hold of Bowman and agreed to wait at the McDonald's until the agent could get away. They needed to meet to bring each other up to speed. But first Bowman needed time to extract himself from the office and find an excuse not to bring his puppy dog Seymour along for the ride.

Bowman was already taking a risk. He had been told he needed to be available to the deputy chief of mission at the embassy, as the heat from the media was once again rising about the incident in Bonn. Right now, there was an all-hands-on-deck effort to protect the US diplomatic mission in Germany from the hounds in the press and the constant cackling of the political crows in the German government and opposition parties.

Although the German chancellor sympathized with the death of the US ambassador, the chancellor knew the exact details of the kidnapping in Bonn and who had actually saved Heymann. Behind closed doors, he expressed his gratitude—but his political well-being told him his coalition government was unhappy, the security apparatus of the German federal government were seething, and the citizens were incensed by the idea of trigger-happy foreign agents roaming the streets. The German/Turkish community even came out and said that the CIA targeted and assassinated innocent members of their population without reasonable cause, and so they also called for demonstrations against the United States.

The US embassy's regional security officer was pumped up and ready for war. He cleaned his shotgun in the office almost daily, as if expecting someone to jump the embassy wall, but he and a few hard-ass Marines were ready and would send them back over with lead poisoning if they had to. All the local intelligence pointed to violent demonstrations and attacks on US embassy personnel. The RSO conveyed his concerns to the mission deputy, who in turn looked to the FBI to convey a request of German police support. This dictated the all-hands-on-deck approach for dealing with a potential attack.

Bowman finally pulled into the McDonald's parking lot at midday so he would at least blend in a little with the lunch crowd. He ordered a Quarter Pounder with cheese and coffee to go. After picking up his order, he headed for the door, with Whittaker and Preacher following innocently behind. Nothing was said between the trio until they all were safely inside Bowman's car and on their way to the nearby sprawling Grunewald Park, just north of the US consulate.

Bowman let Whittaker to do all the talking while he ate his burger, nodding and grunting and sometimes pausing here or there to make a comment or two. Preacher remained quiet throughout the debriefing but kept a watchful eye on their surroundings. Bowman noticed this and wished he could swap his lapdog for Whittaker's bulldog—but that was not to be.

After thirty minutes, Whittaker had brought the agent up to speed. Bowman didn't have much to give back in return, or rather, he didn't want to give anything back of value—especially the situation at Stonewall. Instead, he focused his information on the media flap over Bonn and the activities around the Berlin embassy. He urged the duo to keep a low profile over the next few days, as any Americans could be targets. The last thing any of them needed was to have their faces plastered over the news for being beaten up or killed by some overzealous Turkish mob.

Bowman wasn't prepared for taking care of his co-conspirators, and when Whittaker asked him to find somewhere off the grid for them to stay, Bowman knew he had to get back to the office for the keys to the rental apartment that he kept for Corbin's visits. He left the pair at the park, telling them he'd be back within the hour with the keys to the apartment from where they could plan their next move.

Bowman made it back to the embassy just in time to find Seymour sticking his head in every office or room in the complex, obviously looking for his partner.

"What's up?" he asked the young agent.

"I've been looking for you everywhere. The RSO is having a security meeting in fifteen minutes—he wants you there!"

Bowman could always find something negative to bitch about in every situation. "So you've been to every office in the building looking for me?" he said, accusatorily.

"Yes, so?"

"So now everyone in the building knows I haven't been around?"

"Yes, I guess so."

"You're a fucking dumbass! Why didn't you page me?"

"Here's your pager, dumbass. You left it on your desk!" Seymour slapped the device in Bowman's hand. He was about to walk away when Bowman offered a rare apology.

"Nick, I'm sorry. I'm a little frustrated right now about this whole thing. The deputy ripped my head off this morning, and after that, Washington decided to pour more shit down my neck. Things are going sideways, and I don't need to go to another meeting at the sandbags with an alcoholic RSO who can't keep his shit together. I shouldn't take it out on you, sorry."

"Okay, okay, I get it," Nick replied, "but just let me know where you're going next time so I can cover for you. Where were you anyway?"

"I just went for some lunch."

"I guess you figured I didn't need anything, thanks," Seymour said, offended.

"Sorry, I just needed to get away for a while. Listen, I do need you to cover for me though. This RSO thing, can you take it?"

"Seriously?"

"Yeah, why not?"

"Because they expressly asked for you," Seymour said, incredulous. "The BKA and the local chief of police are going to be there. So man up and get your ass over there—and do yourself a favor and get there early for a change."

Nick turned once more to walk away, and Bowman grabbed Nick's wrist before he got too far. "Okay, okay, Nick." Bowman swallowed his bile. He didn't want to do this but he couldn't leave Whittaker hanging out there any longer.

"You have to take care of something for me," he said and began to explain an on-the-fly cover story for Seymour to meet with Whittaker and Preacher and give them the apartment keys. Bowman knew it was a risk, but he had no choice. He hoped that Whittaker was smart enough not to answer any questions the young agent might have, and he hoped and prayed that Junior wouldn't ask too much either. He needed to act quickly, as German police patrols were increasing in the area of the consulate—and that included trolling for potential gathering spots at the Grunewald Park. The last thing he needed was for Whittaker and Preacher to get picked up for loitering or acting suspiciously. He needed to get them off the streets.

DAY 24
GRUNEWALD PARK, BERLIN

"What the hell are you doing here?"

Seymour spun around to see a gruff-looking man staring at him as if he'd just trespassed onto private property. The young agent had been walking around the Paulsborn Gasthaus and parking lot for almost ten minutes looking for two Americans. Bowman did not give much more to go on as he was in a rush. He just told Seymour they would see him before he saw them. Seymour thought it a very vague and puzzling situation. It reminded him of some of the training exercises that were run out of the FBI training facility in Quantico.

"Excuse me?" came his confused reply.

"What are you doing here? You're supposed to be in DC!"

Seymour, now thoroughly confused, took in his surroundings. He spotted another American loitering near the tree line. Bowman had sent him out to meet two security experts who were helping out with the current embassy crisis; he was not expecting a confrontation. The surly man approached quickly. He had been standing over fifty feet away when he made his challenge.

"Do I know you?" Seymour began.

Whittaker stopped in his tracks, realizing his mistake. The man in front of him was different, but so like the Seymour he knew. *This must be his brother,* he thought, *but why didn't Bowman tell him about this?* The likeness was uncanny. He tried to recover. "No, I'm sorry, I thought you were someone else; you look like someone I know."

"You must be talking about my brother Paul. It happens a lot," he said as he extended his hand. Whittaker drew nearer, and Seymour introduced himself. "My name is Nick. Bowman sent me."

They shook hands, but Whittaker seemed standoffish and didn't speak. Nick pushed, "So you know Paul. Where from, NSA?"

"Um, yeah sure," replied Whittaker. "We met once or twice in Mead."

It wasn't unusual for siblings who were born and raised in the Maryland or Virginia suburbs surrounding Washington, DC, to go into government service. It usually happened when the father or mother—or both—were working in one of a hundred government agencies, raising sons and daughters to follow in their footsteps. For law enforcement or intelligence organizations, it made life much simpler when the children of respected career intelligence officers or diplomats needed clearances to get jobs at places like the CIA, FBI, or DEA. So to have one brother working in the FBI and the other in the NSA at Fort Meade was not uncommon.

"So you guys NSA?" Nick asked as Preacher approached.

"Not quite," Whittaker replied, but did not offer any more.

Preacher closed in and gave him a questioning look but didn't say anything.

"Okay, got it. Sorry, shouldn't have asked." Seymour was starting to realize he shouldn't pry. He got a bad vibe from the two agents in front of him and decided not to pursue any further work chit-chat.

He did want to know who they were, though, so he tried one more time. "Sorry, didn't catch a name," Seymour said, trying to be casual.

"That's right," Whittaker replied blankly.

Seymour, not ready to give up, tried again. "Ok then, this will be a merry little trip, but let me get this straight—you need my help, right?"

Whittaker began to realize this wasn't going to be a breeze. "Where's Bowman?" he asked.

"He got tied up at the consulate and asked me to babysit, sorry, I mean … *accompany* two security consultants who were helping us out with the embassy crisis and were in need of assistance."

"What cri—" Whittaker almost slipped up. "Did Bowman give you instructions?"

The comment was not lost on Seymour, but he held his question back. "Yes, I'm taking you to an apartment near here," he simply said.

"Okay, then I suggest we keep the bullshit to a minimum, and you get us over there PDQ. We've been on the street for too long, and if we're going to assist in the embassy crisis, we need to freshen up and get back to work. Can we get moving?"

"Sure, whatever, let's go."

DAY 24
FAYETTEVILLE, NORTH CAROLINA

Chris was supposed to be on bed rest, so his visit to Fort Bragg was not going to happen. He was disappointed, but he understood. The last thing he wanted was to be a hindrance to anyone and the thought of him being treated as an invalid by the Special Forces community was not the way he wanted to be remembered, so he was happy to rest up and hope that his stones would pass quickly.

Gene had already taken him back to the emergency room for another bout of pain and suffering and cursing. This time, the doctor gave him some heavy-duty painkillers and pushed him back out the door. He was basically told to suck it up until the stones passed. So there he sat in the hotel room, watching Jerry Springer until he could laugh and pee no more.

But Delta Force had not given up on him entirely; Gene brought two visitors to chat with Chris early one morning. They brought some kind of wonder doughnuts called Krispy Kremes, which definitely helped Chris's pain. Later two more visitors showed up. As the morning progressed, his room filled up; at one point, there were twelve operatives listening to his story. One member of the team brought a small whiteboard and began sketching the attack scene as Chris gave his play-by-play. They asked some very detailed questions, and it was plain for Chris to see that these guys were not just thinking about how Chris had slotted a few bad guys but also considering how to reconstruct the attack.

The briefing took a few hours, and at one point, a couple of guys left for lunch and came back with enough take-out Chinese to feed an entire battalion of soldiers. The crew wolfed it down without leaving as much as a grease stain to reveal the meal's presence. As the afternoon wore on, the soldiers left as they came—one, two, three at a time. Those remaining of the group were the original visitors, and the only ones that offered their names. Chris didn't need to know this, and was honored that he had established enough trust with them that they would do so.

Before the last two left, they mentioned they were going to reconstruct the attack scene at the base, and they wanted Chris to come over and check things out. Chris was on the edge of his seat with excitement, but Gene burst the bubble. "Sorry, guys," he said, "Chris has to get back to Germany. We're heading for DC tomorrow, but I'm sure we will be back. We'll be in touch. Thanks for coming over."

CHAPTER
FIFTEEN

SELDEN, LONG ISLAND, NEW YORK

THE PROTECTOR WAS DROPPED OFF IN THE PARKING LOT OF THE HOME DEPOT, just across the street from the Islamic Association of Long Island in Selden, almost fifteen hours after he crossed the US/Canadian border earlier that day. The trip, which would normally take just over eight hours, lasted almost twice as long as the driver stopped and doubled back on routes for their own security.

They often took breaks along the way and traveled down roads that led them down the less beaten paths. The driver had obviously done this before, and his sole task was to get his passenger to his destination intact. There wasn't much said between the two during the ride, just simple instructions from the driver on how to act, what to do if they saw the police, what to do if they got stopped by the police, and above all the golden rule: play dumb but be courteous with the police.

At the parking lot, the driver instructed the Protector to get out of the car and walk two blocks north to a house on Carston Street, where he would be met. As far as the driver was concerned, he was done. He didn't care who this person was or if he was going to stay in the country illegally. He just knew by instinct that the man in his car for over fifteen hours was not a Bob Hope or Gandhi—he was just plain scary, and the driver was glad to see the back of him.

The Protector did as he was told and made his way to the house for a meeting with those who knew of his reputation but were not told of his mission in the United States. When he arrived, he was patted down, which at first he was offended by, but then he respected the security procedure as a necessary means of survival for his brothers in America. He was offered tea and a place on the floor in the center of the square carpet of the living room. In obvious positions of rank, three men sat before him on cushions, which gave the appearance of subordinate and master. And it also sent the message: Whatever the Protector wanted, he would have to show some respect if he was going to get it.

In normal circumstances, the conversations would begin around the family, travel, weather, and any other general chit-chat that would engender trust and understanding with a fellow traveler. As was the custom in the Islamic world, trust is everything; respect is another; and following tradition, the cornerstone of their beliefs. This gathering was different. By inviting this traveler into a home to share tea and exchange news of like interests was the minimum expected of good Muslim hospitality. However, after the hot beverage was poured, the conversation of business began, and the pleasantries of life were ignored.

"We are led to believe you are on a mission that has not been sanctioned by your commanders." It was the youngest of the three men sitting before him who opened up the dialogue.

"I am here thankfully by the grace of God, who has led me to this house for help in a personal mission to avenge my family's loss."

"Praise be to God, my friend. May Allah be with you," the young man said, and then in unison, all three chanted, "Allahu Akbar, Allahu Akbar."

"We have heard of your pain, brother, but what is it that you want from us? Do you understand that we are lucky to be here, you are lucky to be here, and your request for help may jeopardize our safety in this country?" There was a momentary pause in the conversation. "We all have one mission in our lives, friend, but we must all pay penance and provide a service to God. If this is truly God's mission for you and we can help you on your journey, please tell us what you wish of us."

"I need intelligence, I need a weapon, and I need someone who knows his way around Washington, DC."

The oldest of the group, who was obviously the leader, chimed in. "My friend, out of respect, you may state your wishes but not your needs. We will decide what you need and what you will get. This is our operational environment; you are not in Lebanon now."

The Protector, although seething inside, was deeply apologetic; he knew he was going out on a limb coming to America, and he desperately needed the help. He placed his right hand on his chest and bowed his head slightly.

"My sincere apologies to you and to all in this house. I bring no disrespect, only shame on myself for not appreciating your surroundings. Please forgive me."

The older man bowed his head in acceptance and said no more. The look was enough for the Protector, and he thought he needed to be careful, very careful, as nobody would miss him here; nobody knew he was in the United States. The younger man broke the silence. "Tell us why you seek our help. What is it you hope to achieve?"

"The politician in Washington, Corbin, has brought a painful shadow across my family. He killed my daughter, and it is my mission to punish this infidel and claim retribution. It is God's will that he must die. It is the only justice that is right. It is my mission and the penance I must pay to Allah for my sins and mistakes that I have made throughout my life."

If the three men before him were surprised by this statement, then they did not show it; there was no emotion. They knew what he was trying to say. If he was going to carry out an attack on Corbin, then he would pay the ultimate price and become a true martyr to accomplish his mission.

DAY 25
BUDDY ATTICK LAKE PARK, GREENBELT, MARYLAND

They had met at Greenbelt Lake more than once before. Paul Seymour, call sign Far Sight, showed up in his standard fleet car, a white Ford Crown Victoria; Corbin drove his personal Cadillac after dismissing his driver for the day. The location was perfect for Paul; the popular lake was located between Washington, DC and the NSA at Fort Meade, which gave him enough time for an extended but not exaggerated lunch. As for Corbin's lunch schedule, well, nobody cared.

It wasn't a large lake, but it was situated within the Buddy Attick Lake Park, named after one of Greenbelt's former city planners in 1935. The lake was long enough for casual joggers to get around comfortably but too short for serious runners, unless they did ten or more laps.

There were enough quiet spots for birdwatchers, nature lovers, picnickers, and the like, and during lunchtimes, it was wasn't uncommon to see a few business suits and well-dressed ladies taking a brown-bag lunch from the district courts or nearby law offices. Corbin believed in hiding in plain sight and wasn't worried about the proximity of the government offices. Still, he chose a park bench just far enough away from the parking lot, out of earshot from the walkers or joggers yet with all-around visibility, so they could manage their conversation if needed. Seymour brought sandwiches and drinks, and to all who passed by and did not recognize the senator, it looked like two businessmen on a lunch break.

Paul Seymour produced a color photograph.

"What's this?" asked Corbin.

"It's the *Juno* on fire in Iskenderun, a port in southeastern Turkey," Seymour replied.

The photo was dramatic, even to the jaded Corbin. "Jesus Christ, what the hell happened?"

"I'm not sure. We were tracking it ever since it left Cyprus, which, by the way, is getting a little risky ..." Seymour paused, as he could tell that Corbin was engrossed by the picture. "There was a massive storm in the area, which totally blanketed our satellite coverage," Seymour continued. "Next thing I know, everyone in the office is shouting and screaming as reports of an explosion in the port came in. I don't think anyone has put two and two together yet, but when they do, the shit is going to hit the fan."

"Well, you had better make sure it doesn't then," Corbin replied.

"I'm afraid that's beyond my control. When the Turkish authorities get onto what's left of that boat, who knows what they'll find. I only hope enough blew up or sunk beyond salvage so no connections are made—and I'm praying that the ship's log can't be found." Seymour paused once again and then asked cautiously, "There is no paper trail, right? I mean, there's nothing on the boat that will point back to us?"

"Of course not. Do you think I'm that much of an idiot?" Corbin said, insulted.

Corbin needed to gauge the body language of the man sitting before him and figure out where he was coming from. Did Paul Seymour know more than he was letting on?

It was as if they were starting some sort of chess game, with Seymour thinking the same things about Corbin—and he wanted to see how much the senator was willing to give up. Were they really partners, or was Seymour just being used for information? He knew already his own name was nowhere to be found in the Whittaker files, but he wanted to be sure he was being protected by Corbin; else he would have to protect himself. And so the chess game began.

"Don't worry, Paul," Corbin assured. "I've got all this covered. If anyone's fingerprints are on this, it will be that Cypriot Customs guy—what's his name again?" Corbin knew Paul should not know; it was Corbin's first move.

Seymour was sharp enough to spot the trap. "How should I know? Isn't Whittaker running that side of things?"

Corbin nodded. "I guess so."

The cogs were turning in the older man's head. Although he was fencing ever so slightly with Seymour, he was also thinking about the bigger picture. His organization did not anticipate this kind of situation. Preparing for Customs inspections was one thing—influencing and bribing corrupt officials in places like Cyprus and Turkey was his forte—but outside forces like storms and explosions were something that he didn't contemplate. Although he didn't show it, he was thinking about how much of a disaster this really was.

Seymour interrupted his thoughts. "So what are you going to do with the Whittaker woman?"

"Why do you ask?" came the sharp and quick response. Corbin started to think that Seymour was building his defenses. First the paper trail question; now Whittaker's wife.

Paul Seymour continued to push. "Well, have you thought that Whittaker could have been on that boat? What if his body is still on there? What if a positive ID is made on him?"

Corbin stalled for time. "Wow, you've got a thousand questions today. What's gotten into you? Are you getting a little sweaty? What's the matter?"

Seymour began getting worked up. He couldn't understand why Corbin was so cool with all the bad news. "What's the *matter*?" he replied incredulously. "Whittaker is missing—he could be dead in that boat; you have lost an entire shipment; there may be a paper trail on the boat; and you have his wife as prisoner!" He let his statement hang for several moments, waiting for a response, but nothing came. He then added, "That's what's wrong. Eyes may be on us sooner than you think, maybe even now for all I know."

Corbin stared directly into Seymour's eyes, leaning forward to make his point. "And I thought your brother was the one without balls, you fucking wimp."

"Hey!" Paul interjected. "Don't bring my brother into this. He has nothing to do with this whole thing, he's off limits—"

"Yes, yes, sorry, I forgot that we need to tread carefully with him," Corbin said, thinking, *What a pair of tits these two are.* He continued, "This is a small setback in the grand scheme of things. You seriously don't think I have only one ship sailing the oceans, one customs official, and one corrupt politician? I didn't get where I am today by putting all my money on one horse. When the time is right, I'll give you the names of a few more in our fleet that need tracking."

Ultimately, that was Seymour's job, to track the illegal shipments and redirect the *Juno* away from the prying eyes of the world navies. Paul Seymour was a maritime analyst with the NSA and a fantastic asset. His whole function was to monitor and track foreign national fleets by satellite as they crisscrossed the vast expanses of the world's oceans. Seymour used his teams to track them for the government, and for Corbin. His senior position as director of the division allowed him access to classified material that was deemed as "eyes only." He was the last stop of secret or ultra-secret information before it went to the director of National Security and the president of the United States.

"Don't worry about the Whittaker woman," Corbin continued. "When her husband resurfaces, he'll deal with her. And by the way, she is not a prisoner—she is a guest. She can come and go as she pleases."

Seymour was shocked. *More ships, what the hell is he talking about?* he wondered. *There's nothing in the files to indicate there were more ships; he's got to be bluffing.* He decided he needed to follow up with that one. "It seems to me you need to scale back operations, not increase," he said. "If the NSA finds out about the antenna..."

Corbin didn't hear anything else that was said—that was the trigger he was waiting for. He knew that Seymour was bluffing. Out of all the documents that Whittaker had hidden under his floorboards, there was only one brief mention, *one single word, in one single sentence* that ever discussed an antenna. Whittaker didn't know about it but had always speculated there was some sort of secure communications link to the *Juno*. The antenna was so well hidden in the backwoods of Michigan that Corbin never told anyone about it. Only he and his half-brother Chuck Dunbar were aware of its existence and its ship-to-shore capabilities.

Corbin now knew Far Sight had lied about not looking at the documents and must have poured over them for hours if he had found that one small piece of information—the one thing that could jeopardize his entire operation. Corbin's thoughts kept chugging away as Seymour rambled on.

Corbin had a talent that most politicians had; they could look you in the eye while you talked about the most important life-changing event in your existence, all the while thinking about how to get a vote or how to get on to a more important topic, such as re-election. Or perhaps revenge and murder.

As Corbin watched Paul speak, he was deliberating how to deal with him. *He's different from the rest,* he thought. *He's not motivated by money or power, its lust—and that's not something that can easily be overcome. If I have to lose someone in this enterprise it can't be him. Whittaker, Preacher, and their toy soldiers could always be replaced. But people with restricted access to sensitive information like Bowman and Paul Seymour are hard to come by. This is a setback for sure. No, hang on, it's a fucking disaster.*

Corbin was distracted from his thoughts for a moment as he followed Seymour's gaze toward two young girls lying on the grass nearby, bodies entwined, lips locked. If there were ever a scene to break a man's concentration, that was it.

DAY 25
ISRAELI EMBASSY, BERLIN

"Anna, how good it is to see you. Please accept my deepest condolences. Your husband was not only a friend to me but also a true friend to Israel. I am very sorry for your loss."

"Thank you, Ari, I know Winston valued your friendship."

"Please come, sit down. How are you?" asked the Israeli ambassador to Germany.

"I'm fine, thank you," she replied. "It's been tough. I won't deny that, but one step at a time."

"You will let me know if I can do anything for you, Anna? Both Leah and I want to help; you know that."

"Yes I do, Ari, thank you, and please thank Leah for me." She paused and waited for a moment. The Israeli ambassador knew there was something else but waited a few seconds more.

"In fact, Ari, that's why I'm here. I do need your help with something," Anna finally said.

"Tell me. What can I do? What's on your mind?"

She began asking for his complete confidence, which she knew was never in question. On receiving his assurance, she went on to describe the information and pictures she found in her husband's safe. They then both looked at the photos of the men surveying the embassy and of the one of the man in uniform—the one that she had seen weeks before at the shopping mall in Virginia.

She had contacted Crauford once again to see if he had made any progress on the picture, to no avail. In fact the retired general had tried to persuade her to give up the search for the mysterious man. She had lied to him and said she would, but here she was, stubborn as ever, reaching out to the Israelis for help.

At first Ari Bachmann paid only lip service to the request, but as Anna presented documentation about the Olympic Village in Munich, his demeanor changed completely. He became very studious and attentive. Although the massacre by the Palestinians there was a sad part of Israel's short history and the Wrath of God team was now defunct, the memories of those involved in those fateful days never faded. There were still members of the government and academics who were trying to piece together every minute detail of the entire episode.

The Mossad, in particular, did not leave a single stone unturned in seeking out those responsible for the attack, but just as with the Holocaust evidence or facts, new information would open old wounds and cause the Israelis to question once again: Did we get everyone? Has everyone been held to account?

With the Holocaust, the answer would almost always be no. For Munich, there were still things unanswered, but revenge had been meted out; it was a closed chapter for most.

But Ari Bachmann was now looking at potentially new information that could close a gap or two about what had happened at the Olympics. Even if this were not Anna asking for help, this information involved his nation's history, maybe even his nation's security. There was no doubt in his mind he would utilize all resources to dig into the documents, and while he did so, he would identify the man in the picture for Anna.

DAY 25
FBI HEADQUARTERS, WASHINGTON, DC

Junior Agent Patrick Harvey sat at his desk in the basement of the Hoover Building, going through the files for all his European field agents.

Harvey had the unenviable task of sifting through the mundane and tedious day-to-day administration of field agent expense reports, general logistics, travel, lodging, and all manner of upkeep for agents in the field. He was never engaged with actual FBI field operations so he did not have information on projects or activities that were currently underway, but he was an integral part of the FBI bureaucracy nonetheless.

For each agent, he had a hard-copy file for each request, approval or denial of requests, as well as a file for everything non-operational. He had a mountain of information at his fingertips. Most of the documents that he received were copies that came from other divisions in the organization, and most of the time, operational managers never saw the complete dossier of an agent's requests. Thus they never saw what was happening from a budget perspective, unless people like Harvey flagged an issue.

For the most part, agents played by the rules and filed their requests appropriately, but now and again, he saw some extroverted desire for a helicopter or plane, which ended up pretty close to a popular tourist destination. The other junior agents in his department had an ongoing bet to see which agent under their control could come up with the most exorbitant request, but usually everything was just plain boring—and the life of the junior bureaucrat equally so.

Harvey eventually reached for the Bowman file and noticed it was one of the thickest in his collection. As he opened the file, he realized Bowman had forgotten to process a copy of travel expenses for a trip to Cyprus by agents Bowman and Seymour, a sojourn which had racked up thousands of dollars in expenditure and was almost at the ceiling of allowable costs for travel and lodging.

What concerned him more, though, was a repair bill from the FBI motor pool for damages incurred to one of their surveillance vehicles recently at the Arlington Cemetery. Harvey thought it strange that the motor pool had Bowman's name as the operational agent in charge on the request form because Bowman was not an active DC agent.

Instead of filing the paper away, he began to rummage through the folder to see if anything else was out of the ordinary when he came across another document that piqued his interest. Rent for an apartment in Berlin. How he did not see this before? It was surprising to him, but when managing hundreds of field agents' requests, some things did fall through the cracks. He closed the folder and took the elevator up to the fourth floor to where the section chiefs worked.

Harvey found the office of European Special Agent in Charge Jim Duran and knocked on his open door. Duran looked up.

"Jim, sorry to bother you. Do you have a minute?" Harvey asked.

Duran closed the folder on his desk. "Sure, Pat, I've got a few, but I need to make an overseas call in a bit. What can I do for you?"

"I'll try and be brief. It's just that I thought I had better bring something to your attention in regards to John Bowman in Berlin."

Duran wasn't really interested in what the pencil pusher had to say, but on hearing Bowman's name, he leaned forward and placed his elbows on his desk. "What's he done?"

"Well I saw this expense report that is a recurring cost, and I saw this repair bill from the motor pool, which I think are kind of unusual." Harvey handed both documents over to his senior, who took great interest in the paperwork.

As Duran read and reread the information, he not only got pissed about the costs, but he also was getting more and more curious about the dates on the forms, which indicated that Bowman was in Cyprus—and shortly thereafter was running an operation in DC.

Harvey could tell he had sparked some interest. "I wasn't sure if these were normal costs," he said, "but if you combine them, they'll definitely affect the bottom line for his operational budget. I just wanted to make you aware, that's all."

"Is that his file that you're holding?" Duran asked.

"Yes, this is for 1995. I can dig up '94, '93 if you want. How far do you want me to go back?"

"Ninety-five is fine for now, Pat. I'll give you a call if I need more. Thanks for bringing this up. I'll get it back to you as soon as I can."

"Anything to help, Jim. If I can get you to sign for the folder, just sign here ... initial there, and one more signature there ... great, thanks."

"Thanks, Pat. Could you close the door on the way out?"

As soon as Harvey left, Duran reopened the other file on his desk and pulled out two more documents. Both were letters of complaint. The first was a cable from the US deputy chief of mission Berlin, detailing Bowman's lack of support, the frequency of his absence at meetings, and Bowman's not being at the embassy at a time when significant security incidents were taking place in Berlin. The DCM wanted to know if Bowman was working on an operation that was related to the current situation in Berlin. If he was, then he wanted to know about it.

The second document was another complaint, which he had not seen until now, and this time it was from the manager of the Potomac Mills Shopping Mall who understood the need and was willing to cooperate with law enforcement but was disappointed by the attitude of an FBI agent who removed a surveillance tape from the mall security office without consent. The letter stated the agent did not provide a name and only briefly showed his FBI ID card, but a photo of the agent was embedded in the document, and the manager requested that FBI managers be engaged to retrieve the missing tape. Duran studied the picture, which was taken from another CCTV camera in the mall, and he was easily convinced it was Bowman.

Duran looked at the clock on the wall, made a quick time conversion in his head, and picked up the phone to dial Bowman's desk in Berlin. After three rings it was picked up. "LEGAT Office, how may I help?"

"Nick, Jim Duran. Why didn't Bowman answer the phone?"

"He's out of the office, Jim, been gone a while," agent Nick Seymour replied.

"What's he working on?"

"I'm not sure," came an uneasy answer. "What do you mean you're not sure?" Duran was becoming irritated.

"Sometimes he doesn't tell me where he's going, that's all," Bowman's partner said.

Nick considered covering for his boss, but that thought only lasted a second in light of the way he had been treated lately. There was a pause on the other end of the line so he added, "He could have gone out to meet those contractors that are in town."

"And who the hell is *that*, Nick? What contractors?"

"I don't know … two military types."

Duran was trying not to let his emotions get the better of him. He was in the dark on operational matters, and he didn't like it one bit. It's not as if he needed to know every move or decision made out in the field, but he did need to know if it involved money and personnel.

He decided to play things cool. There was no point taking it out on the young agent, but he pushed for more information to find out what Seymour really knew. "Do you think he's over at the apartment?"

"Could be. That's where the two contractors were heading. I gave them the keys to the place."

Duran stewed on that a little more. So the apartment did exist, but it wasn't sanctioned by the FBI. He knew that if it was a State Department rental he would have received a monthly bill. Again he wasn't sure of the reputedly naïve Seymour's involvement so he changed the subject. "How are things at the consulate, Nick?" As Seymour began his report, Duran covered the phone and called for his secretary. When she arrived, he scribbled on his notepad and held it up for her to read: Next flight to Berlin!

CHAPTER
SIXTEEN

DAY 26

GEORGETOWN UNIVERSITY, WASHINGTON, DC

CHRIS FOLLOWED TYPICAL BRITISH ARMY STANDARD PROCEDURE and arrived five minutes before required at the general's office. He had hoped the general had forgotten about their lunch date, but somehow he had found out Chris was back in town and left a message at the Embassy Suites to call for a luncheon.

Although Chris didn't feel 100 percent, he didn't want to get stuck in another hotel watching soap operas or reruns of *The Golden Girls*. He'd attempted to go to a movie to watch the latest Tom Hanks movie, *Apollo 13*, but was beaten back by the line of kids trying to get into *Toy Story*, and since he hated crowds, he gave up on the idea. He also thought it might be nice to get out and about and have a decent meal for a change.

But Chris wasn't comfortable; he didn't like what he was getting into. Again he kept thinking to himself that he was just a driver, an underling only meant to serve and not partake. Having lunch with a retired general, even if a civilian far removed from the military, was above Chris's station. This type of harmless activity would be unheard of in the United Kingdom; it just would never happen. It would not be appropriate behavior for a soldier of Chris's rank to socialize with a man of such stature as Crauford.

Chris's beliefs spilled over from his days within the British Army's autocratic machine where he was indoctrinated into believing that the upper class of the establishment—the officers—were the all-seeing, all-knowing, unapproachable nobility of the Crown. Although his duty was to serve at Her Majesty's pleasure, it actually meant he was to serve at the whims of the privileged English gentry—the few, the rich, the powerful.

This put Chris in an awkward situation with the Americans, as they did not understand how powerful the pressure was on the lower classes in the UK. Americans always thought everyone was on an equal status and positions of power and influence were earned, not inherited. The people that Chris worked for sometimes thought he was cold and standoffish, but he wasn't. It just wasn't his place to dine with educated and influential people. Chris would rather be driving the general to lunch in his limo and dropping him off, not sweating over which fork to use or talking with his mouth full.

They didn't stay in the office long; instead they headed straight out for the meal. The general suggested they walk, if Chris was up for it, to the Au Pied de Cochon restaurant, about six short blocks from the office. Chris was all over it. He even went on to explain to Crauford the recent history of the place involving a Russian KGB agent, Vitaly Yurchenko, who defected to the United States in 1985, only to defect back to Russia after eating a meal at the same restaurant. Chris joked that he hoped it wasn't the food that pushed him back over the wall.

During their walk and meal, most of Crauford's questions were centered on the attack in Bonn and the later attack at the airport that finally took his friend's life. It was plain to Chris that the men were very close, and he actually thought he caught a glimpse of a tear from the old soldier when he talked about Heymann and the days when they served together in Germany. They also talked about the differences between the British and US Armies. Crauford surprised Chris with his knowledge of military history, modern-day warfare, and the worldwide problem of terrorism, but then Chris mentally kicked himself, remembering this was an academic he was talking to, after all.

As they headed back to the campus, the General's pace became a little slower, and he explained that the leg injury he had received in Panama still plagued him. Chris sympathized, and they jokingly compared war wounds as they hobbled down the street. Chris explained his disappointment in himself for not completing his SAS selection course because of back, knee, and shin injuries. Crauford genuinely sympathized and added that Chris had come a long way since he was humping rucksacks over the Brecon Beacons in Wales, that his future was bright, and that he need not worry—he had a lot of friends in town that would bend over backwards to help if he needed it.

As they finally approached the Mortara building, Chris's what-if instinct kicked in again. Just before entering the building, he noticed a number of parked cars in the area that were not there before lunch, but other than that, not much more had changed in the time that they were away.

What piqued his interest, though, was the parked panel van sitting too close to the fire hydrant, and a nearby silver Oldsmobile with two occupants inside who looked as if they did not belong—they weren't typical students or teachers. Chris tried to scrub it from his mind, but sometimes he could not simply switch off. He saw something he didn't like and started running scenarios in his head, all the while still engaging the general in a conversation about Chris's educational goals.

Chris eventually rationalized that if something was happening—and he could not be sure there was as this wasn't his turf—then he had nothing to do with it. Perhaps he was just having a little healthy dose of paranoia. Just before they entered through the main door, Chris scanned the area for more potentially harmful things, but came up empty-handed. But as he held the door open for the general, he saw a movement out of the corner of his eye and spotted a man on crutches. His brain's filing system then went into overdrive.

Alarm bells were going off in Chris's head. *Wasn't anyone else seeing this?* He asked himself. *No, chill out, there's nothing here*, he added. *Switch off, dammit!*

Crauford suddenly turned to his lunch mate. "Everything okay, Chris? You look a little jumpy."

"Sure, it's all good. I just get a little paranoid from time to time. I see things and have suspicions about everything and everyone; occupational hazard, I guess you would call it."

"Don't worry about anything here," joked Crauford. "There are no ambassadors or other worthy targets to worry about. Relax."

"Whatever you say, sir," Chris relented.

"And do me a favor. Call me Bob. Drop the sir."

"It's out of respect, sir."

"I know, and I appreciate that, but it's okay, really." Chris was impressed, and he began to like the man more for it. He heard that a lot of retired generals got off on being called "sir" for the rest of their lives, as if they expected it.

They headed to Crauford's office and chatted some more about education. Chris was surprised when, at the end of the conversation, the old soldier offered Chris a place in his program at the university.

As sharp as Chris was on the outside dealing with bad guys with guns and sticks and stones, he didn't realize he had just been through a scholarship interview and had passed with flying colors.

Chris was elated beyond words; he actually became speechless and motionless, totally taken aback by the general's offer. He didn't know where to begin to thank him.

He didn't need to. The phone rang, and the general looked at his watch. "Chris, I've got to get this. Let's stay in touch. Get well. Speak to you soon." With that, he shut the door in Chris's still-agape mouth.

Chris stood there for a few seconds more, taking everything in. As he turned to head back down the corridor, a door opened midway along it, and out stepped PWC. She didn't see him as she was busy affixing her rucksack to her back and tightening the straps. She was also carrying a bicycle helmet. Chris followed a few discreet steps behind her and didn't say anything. He thought the chances of her remembering him were slim, so why bother? Perhaps outside he would try to make eye contact.

She got to the main door before he did and opened it to the bright sunlight just as Chris felt a nasty twinge in his back. He stopped where he was and bent slightly over, taking in a few deep breaths. He wouldn't make eye contact today. That's when he heard the unmistakable squeal of tires screeching away from being in a parked position.

DAY 26
US CONSULATE, CLAY ALLEE, ZEHLENDORF, BERLIN

The majority of German government buildings in Berlin are protected by the German police. Although dozens of federal and local government buildings require police presence, the service also extends itself to protecting some foreign embassies, foreign trade missions, religious institutions, and areas of cultural and historical significance. To employ a full-time resource to these objectives, however, would be a mammoth and costly expense. As a result, the German government typically drafts in police officers who are officially retired from the force but are willing to act as federal protection officers for those facilities. They are, in essence, armed security guards with special powers of arrest, and their tasks are limited to patrolling and standing guard at the multitude of facilities around the capital. They are engaged not with crime fighting but in basic crime prevention at sensitive locations in and around the German capital.

Most of these officers were the old "crusties" of the force who were fifty-five years and older and who could not, or would not, adapt to a normal job outside the protective blanket that law enforcement gave them. Most of them worked until their late sixties with the reward of sizeable pensions and equally good retirement benefits. It would not be unusual to find a sixty-year-old vet standing outside the gates to the Russian embassy or manning the security gate at the Reichstag. In all weathers and at all hours, they were always there and always dependable.

The US consulate on Clay Allee was no exception to the police protective service. Although the interior grounds there were secured by local security companies who hired foreign service nationals, in the interior spaces of US government facilities overseas, protection duties fell to the US Marine Corps. As such, the US consulate at Clay Allee had three protective layers: the outer ring, protected by the police protective service; the inner circle, inside the fence, by FSN security companies; and the inner sanctum, the buildings themselves, by the US Marine Corps.

One of the main reasons for having a protective police officer at the outer layer of the consulate was to prevent or deter attacks from occurring at the building perimeter. In many countries around the world, more than one US government facility has been the target of rocket, grenade, or shooting attack in some form or another.

———

Chris had been employed at the embassy only six months when he realized how much of a target America really was. It was Valentine's Day 1991 when the German Red Army Faction terrorist group fired a machine gun from across the River Rhine into the embassy building, which caused minor damage but incurred no injuries. It was this incident that pushed Chris Morehouse to pursue a career in executive protection and counterterrorism, as he was just entering the embassy grounds when the first shots were fired. He wisely stayed in his armored limousine until the fireworks had finished before rushing into the safety of the building itself.

———

The main reason for having a police presence at the US consulate was to ensure that visitors who were trying to obtain US visas did not park on the sidewalk of Clay Allee, causing traffic problems. During the mornings when the consulate was open for visa applicants, the protective officer was busy moving traffic along or calling in tow trucks to remove violators. Afternoons, when the visa section was closed, things slowed down considerably. And at night-time, there was just plain nothing for the officers to do.

Following the incident at the Iskenderun fish plant, the leadership council of the PKK acted out a measure of retribution against America when three motorcycles stopped near the consulate parking lot on a slow Friday afternoon. The on-duty police officer made his way to investigate and move the bikers along, but before he could get close, he was knocked off his feet by a speeding cyclist.

The old cop began to curse and was so busy searching for his cap that he did not hear or see a second cyclist come up behind him. All he felt was a sharp thud and then blackness. The second cyclist caught up with the first, dropped the club he was carrying, and both sped away.

Each of the three remaining motorcycles' riders carried a passenger. On seeing the cop was down for the count, the passengers jumped off the bikes and opened up the satchels they were carrying. Each pulled out a grenade and threw it over the high fence and into the parking lot.

The fence line was made up of a three-foot-high wall with an ornamental fence attached, making the total height ten feet. The short masonry wall provided enough cover for the attackers from the blasts of the grenades, which they each repeated three times more before getting back on the motorcycles and speeding away.

The results were impressive. Some grenades were thrown accurately enough to cause windows in the facility to blow inwards, sending glass and debris into the rooms and destroying everything and anyone in their path. Other grenades rolled underneath consulate cars, exploding underneath fuel tanks or causing other cars to catch fire and eventually explode. The security guard booth at the parking lot entry was almost leveled, and the contract security guard was crushed when the wooden structure collapsed on top of him. The explosions continued, and at one point, it was hard to make out how many cars were left to go up in flames as the black smoke spiraled out of control and up into the air.

DAY 26
ISRAELI EMBASSY, BERLIN

As the attack on the consulate was taking place, Anna Heymann was unexpectedly back at the Israeli ambassador's office. After pleasantries were exchanged, the ambassador got to the news.

"We have identified the man you were concerned about, Anna," he said and then paused to see if the interest was still there.

Anna's face lit up. "Tell me, Ari."

The ambassador handed Anna's original picture back to her. "The picture was taken in the Negev Desert. The man on the right is an Israeli sniper; I'm sure you don't need his details. The man on the left was a major, but is now a colonel. His name is James Whittaker. He is, or was, in the Special Forces, the Green Berets, and the picture was taken during one of our joint military exercises in 1988. Does that name mean anything to you?"

"No, not really, but Special Forces, what does that mean? Why would my husband have a photo of this man?"

"I don't know, but there's more," the ambassador said. He paused for a few seconds—a few seconds too long.

"What is it, Ari? I don't care how bad this is. I need to know. If this Whittaker has something to do with my husband, for good or bad, I need to know."

"I know, Anna. If I were in the same position, I'm sure I would feel the same but—"

Anna interjected forcefully, "There're no buts, Ari—tell me!"

"Do you promise me you won't take matters into your own hands, no matter what I tell you? We want to help, Anna. Do you understand? We have people for such things."

Anna was perplexed. What the hell was he saying? After a brief pause, she said, "Tell me what you have in mind, and I'll make my decision—but don't bullshit me, Ari. I don't have time to waste, understand?"

The tension was thick. The ambassador was crossing a dangerous line, and he knew it, but he had made a promise to help, and here he was.

"This is the latest picture of Whittaker," he said and offered it to her, adding, "He's looking older, a bit greyer and heavier, but it's him."

"Where was this taken?

"A few weeks ago."

"I didn't ask when, Ari; I said where."

The ambassador dropped the bombshell. "In Bonn near our old embassy, the day of the attack on your husband." Anna dropped the photo and both hands shot to her mouth. Her eyes began to well up. After she took a moment to compose herself she responded, "How, I mean … how did you get this?"

"When we used to own the Israeli embassy in Bonn, we had a full-time maintenance guy, Jakob Rosenheim. He's retired now, and he decided not to move with us to Berlin. He wanted to stay on in at an apartment in Bonn, which was just around the corner from the old embassy building. We've asked him to keep an eye on the old place for us, just out of curiosity. So now and again, he sends us some pictures of the demolition and the new construction, nothing serious, just nice to know stuff, you know what I mean."

He paused to take a sip of coffee and clear his throat. "Well he was there on the day of the attack with his camera. Here are some more," he said, handing over a few more color photos.

Anna looked on incredulously. There were pictures of Chris, pictures of her husband, the car wreckage, the dead terrorist, the whole attack site.

"Now I must warn you, Anna, neither the Germans nor the FBI have seen these. I received these only in the last few days. I can't let you have a copy, you understand of course." She nodded silently. "We can't let this get out," he continued, "but we need to find a way to … how can I put this … to attend to the situation ourselves."

Anna looked up from the photos with what must have been a huge question mark on her face, but she waited.

The ambassador continued. "Whittaker is working on a special military project, which identifies potential security weaknesses within US military facilities. He contracts out to a team of former Marines or other Special Forces guys who attempt to break into military establishments so they can better their security programs. It's called penetration testing, and it's sometimes very effective in addressing weak security infrastructure. What we don't know for sure is if he is still fully active with the military or on reserve and is just a contractor for the government. But here is something we do know, Anna …" He looked deeply into her eyes to try to gauge how she was feeling but received mixed signals. Ari continued, "One of the sponsors from the government who set up this endeavor is …"

The phone rang on the ambassador's desk before he could finish his sentence. He picked up, saying, "I told you not to disturb me, I am—"

Leaving his sentence unfinished, Ari instead began to listen intently and stood up from behind his desk. Anna became uneasy and was trying to listen into the conversation when there was a knock at the door. Two uninvited Israeli security officers entered the room. The ambassador put down the phone and looked at Anna. "The US consulate has just been attacked. We have to leave—we're evacuating all personnel from this building. It's only procedure. I'm sure we're not in danger. Please come with me."

DAY 26
ISRAELI SAFE HOUSE, BERLIN

"Anna, I'm sorry we were interrupted, but our security personnel like to keep us safe in unusual manners." The ambassador decided the timing was right to carry on the conversation in the relative safety of the protected house in the Berlin suburb of Gatow, but he was referring to the panel van ride from the ambassador's office.

The drive from the Israeli embassy was taken in silence, as the security teams were present and high on concentration. Any false move or comment could send them into warp speed to get their charges to safety.

"But before I begin again, I truly need your assurance that you won't take matters into your own hands. We have an interest in the outcome of what I'm about to tell you. I know you want justice, but so do we—and we have the capability to do something about it without you getting involved."

"I'm sorry; I'm not promising anything, Ari. What is it?"

"We took a long look at the information you gave us on Munich, and it's definitely connected to the Munich massacre. For years we knew the Black September had support from many sources to carry out the attack, and for the most part, we took care of the terrorists in our own way. What's not public knowledge is that a number of low-profile activists were dealt with over the years, but we always knew there remained those who were undetected."

The ambassador paused and then asked, "Can I get you a coffee or something, Anna?"

"No, I'm fine. Please continue."

The Israeli poured himself a cup. "We knew the East German Stasi were part players in organizing some of the logistics for the terrorists. They provided some money, vehicles, weapons, and even some plans of the Olympic Village. But the most damaging was intelligence on how the

West German Security Services would respond tactically to the attack: the Stasi in fact kept the terrorists one step ahead of the West German authorities. Throughout the Cold War, the Stasi ran a very successful operation within the West German government and even had agents placed in positions of authority. When the wall fell, the list of these West German assets was contained in the Rosewood files. The unified German government, on receiving the files, slowly but surely rounded up these agents, and most were imprisoned. During interrogations of these agents, it became apparent that some operatives were used to lay the groundwork for the attack by Black September at the Olympics. But as with all things like this, money was needed to finance these activities."

Anna was becoming impatient; she was getting a history lesson that she didn't need. "And what does this have to do with me, Ari?"

"I'm getting there, Anna. I need to give you the backstory so you can understand the present."

He continued, knowing Anna was about to have a serious emotional episode. "The CIA had identified most of the money trails that the Stasi used in the seventies and eighties. We also found out that money was being funneled through Eastern Bloc countries, such as Hungary and Bulgaria, under the noses of the KGB in the late sixties, so the Stasi had to get creative if they were to finance Black September. The Stasi eventually reached out to an American who at first was reluctant to engage with them, but once an agreement was met for shipping arms into East Germany through Hamburg, the deal was set. As a cover for these financial transactions—"

"An American!" Anna cried in shock. "What are you talking about? An American was involved with the Munich attack?"

"Anna, please let me finish. This American financed part of the construction of the Olympic Village. He provided plans of the Israeli accommodations on Connolly Strasse to the Stasi for use by Black September."

"Oh my God!" she blurted.

"He also rented out a few apartments in Bavaria for what we think were staging areas for the terrorist team. The information that you brought to us was the final piece in the puzzle—the one that we have been waiting for, Anna. We have been waiting, but we haven't forgotten. The West Germans provided huge chunks of the money, but foreign investment was needed for the Olympics and provided by all sorts of people from around the world. It was all legitimate—except for this one American."

"Who was it, Ari?"

"Senator Robert J. Corbin, and we want him."

She didn't say anything for a while, but then she got up from her chair, walked towards the window, and stared out in disbelief. The Israeli left her to her own thoughts, but she broke the silence first. "So help me understand this, Ari. Corbin financed a terrorist operation, and somehow my husband was working on finding a way to prove it?"

"Yes, we think so."

"So Corbin somehow found out, perhaps because he knew of the Rosewood files?"

"Yes, we actually checked on that recently. He was provided a lot of information from the files due to the fact that he sat on the Senate Intelligence Committee. He had full access if he needed it."

Anna looked out the window towards the woods and pondered the information for a second or two. "So he killed my husband to cover his tracks. But how were the Turks involved?"

"We think that Whittaker hired them."

"You think so, or you know so, Ari?"

"We know with a high degree of certainty."

"So now I'm beginning to think the woman who approached me has something to do with Whittaker. Perhaps they're related, maybe even his wife."

"That we don't know."

She began to digest all the information and went into silent mode again.

This time the ambassador interrupted her train of thought. "We've suspected Corbin for some time because of arms coming into the Middle East, and we actually have a file on him. I wouldn't be surprised if the FBI and CIA have something on him as well. We think he provided plans of the Olympic Village to the Stasi in exchange for terrorist contacts in the Middle East so he could start his own arms trade. We also believe he has been selling off explosives, small arms, and ammunition in various quantities to a number of terrorist organizations for years."

What was not known to the Israelis or anyone else was that Corbin, with help from the Stasi, had contacted the Japanese Red Army, a left-wing terrorist group that was causing all sorts of havoc throughout Japan and Southeast Asia. It was Corbin's intention to contract the terrorist group for small operations against large companies in Japan that were competing against US manufacturers in his attempt to slow down the Japanese gains against America. He balked only at the last minute after learning of their communist beliefs and mission for world revolution.

Anna stared off in the distance as the ambassador spoke. She couldn't believe it.

Ari continued on. "For a while, we weren't getting anywhere, but as we continued to dig deeper into the shipments, we were getting information of American weapons turning up in Lebanon. So we went out there to find some hardware for ourselves, and low and behold, we found some that originated out of the Aniston Army Depot in Alabama. But we couldn't prove how the weapons were coming from America—and we've been looking ever since. We needed somehow to close the loop. It's possible that Whittaker is the man who orchestrates all this for Corbin so he doesn't get his hands dirty. I need to show you something that may help us."

The ambassador pulled out a photo from a large brown envelope. "This is the latest photo we have of him, but we didn't need his image. We're concerned with the person who is with him. Do you know who that is?"

Anna looked at the two faces staring directly into the camera. It was as if they were looking at something of intense interest. She looked at Corbin's companion but kept looking back into the steely blue eyes of the politician, and then a tear ran down the side of her cheek. She tried to compose herself and wiped away the tear. "No. I'm sorry. I don't know him, Ari. Where was this taken?"

"Yesterday in a park in Greenbelt, Maryland. We followed the other guy to Fort Meade. We think he works for the NSA."

Anna couldn't hold back any longer. She rushed to the bathroom and threw up. She remained there for some time, sobbing and washing her face to clear the mess, only to start crying again and again. After an hour, she reappeared, calm and in control.

The ambassador was still there, patiently waiting, not wanting to interrupt her grief. He said nothing.

"I want that bastard, Ari."

"As I said, Anna, so do we—and we have a plan."

DAY 26
GEORGETOWN UNIVERSITY, WASHINGTON, DC

Chris was doubled over in pain, his left hand on the door handle and his right grabbing his side, but he couldn't ignore the scream coming from outside. He beat back a wave of nausea, and as his adrenalin took over, he knew that someone outside was in trouble. He gritted his teeth, fought back the bile, and opened the door.

His eyes immediately set on a white panel van, a driver, and two men on the sidewalk—one of which was holding PWC in a bear hug. Both men were struggling to stuff the girl into the van.

He scanned for more targets and spotted a man on crutches—click, a mental picture was saved. He scanned again and saw students looking on in awe—no click. Scanned again, car honking, drivers staring, mouths agape—no click. Scanned the near distance, middle, and far distance, nothing more.

Do something, Chris! he thought. He straightened up, ignoring his pain, and began what he thought was a sprint, but probably looked like a granny dash, the hundred feet or so to the closest target. Both attackers were burly, heavy-set men, and he thought he was going to have his work cut out for him, but he had to do something. He had no weapons, no backup, no tools to work with. This was going to get dirty.

The two men did not see or hear him coming as they were too focused on getting PWC into the van—and she was proving to be more than they had bargained for.

On reaching the group, Chris went for the man who had his back to him, reaching over the man's head and inserting his left hand fingers into the attacker's eyes. As he did so, he also slid his right hand under the man's jaw, grabbing an ounce of flesh at the neck and then finding the throat and squeezing tightly. It had the desired effect; the attacker's hands went straight to his head, leaving his colleague to deal with PWC. Chris pulled his victim backwards and down. He then kicked the man behind the right kneecap, which threw the attacker completely off balance and landed him flat on his fat arse.

The timing could not have been better. On seeing one of her attackers being taken care of, PWC jumped into high gear in an attempt to free herself. She raised her right leg, found the inside leg at the knee of the remaining captor, took the edge of her shoe, and shot her foot down the entire shin, smashing down on top of the man's foot. As the man pulled his foot away in agony, she took his lack of balance as an advantage and stepped forward with her left foot, twisting her shoulder to shrug the man off her. As he fell to the ground, PWC fell on the man's head with both her knees with all the strength she could muster, stunning her attacker. Knowing she probably had only dazed the man, she got up, placed her left foot forward and then kicked the man in the ribs with her right foot. For good measure, she re-aimed and kicked him in the head, breaking his nose.

As PWC looked over to see her rescuer, she saw he had an attacker in a headlock and pinned to the ground, but both men were struggling to wrestle control from one another. Before she could decide what to do next, she saw a third man appear. She assumed he was the van driver, and watched as he kicked the younger man with full force in the stomach. Her would-be rescuer jumped off like a cat on a hot tin roof, releasing the man on the ground.

Her instinct told her to get away from the melee, but she did not. Instead, she ran towards the two thugs who first attacked her, one of whom was lying on the ground after being confronted by the young man, his eyes gushing blood. The driver turned around after kicking the young man on the ground just in time to receive the hardest kick a second-dan, black-belt karate expert's foot could make, which contacted with his chin—knocking the man out in one fell swoop.

Two men down, she spun around to find one of the original attackers—the one whose nose she had broken—backing off and pleading for no more pain. The other two of his colleagues were out of the fight, and he didn't want anything to do with the woman, who was obviously possessed. PWC didn't care—he was a fair target. She went after him again.

She moved toward him as he backed into the side of the van and put up his hands in surrender. This was the open invitation that she dreamt of. She kicked him in the balls and then watched him slither down the side of the van into a crumpled mess. Without remorse, and for good measure, she punched him in the jaw to make him stay down. She then backed up and did a quick 360-degree review of the mess around her, seeing two bad guys writhing around on the ground in pain, another unconscious, and her hero curled up in the fetal position nearby.

As she made her way to him, she noticed blood splatters on his trousers but thought that it was probably from the man who was bleeding from the eyes. She reached over to roll him over and saw that he was holding his privates. His whole groin area was covered in thick red blood. "Somebody call an ambulance!" she screamed. He looked deathly white. "CALL 911, CALL 911!" she shrieked, hoping someone was taking notice.

By now some passersby had started paying attention and came to offer assistance. Someone said an ambulance was on its way, and PWC finally took a breath of relief and tried to comfort the man on the ground.

As her attention remained on the young man in front of her, she forgot to pay attention to the others until someone in the crowd yelled, "He's got a gun!" As screams rang out and the crowd dispersed, she saw through the running bodies a man on crutches holding a pistol—which was pointing directly at her. To PWC it looked like a Glock 19. But when you're staring down the barrel of a gun, the model doesn't really matter; if you're looking at it from the wrong side, you're in the shit.

The man on the crutches said nothing, but the man with the broken nose began helping his comrades into the van.

The man who was knocked out finally came to his senses and began cursing in a language that nobody around could understand. PWC got up from tending to the young man and made ready for another defense. The blabbering attacker made a move to counter PWC but stopped in his tracks, bent over, and threw up.

The man on crutches barked out orders in a Middle Eastern sounding language, evidently suggesting the puker back off. He motioned for him to get into the van, which the attacker, wiping his mouth on his sleeve, obediently did—like a puppy with his tail between his legs.

Things were starting to calm down, and the wails of sirens were sounding closer with each passing second. Crutches began getting anxious and shouted at the men to get moving, which they all tried to do promptly, but were hindered by their injuries. They piled each other into the van and took off before the ambulance and police could arrive.

Chris, being Chris even in his condition managed to catch the license plate of as the van spun away from the curb—click. He tried to watch in which direction it went, but his concentration was focused on squeezing his nuts, and he began wishing he had taken that job as a wedding planner when he had the chance. He was in pain, severe and excruciating pain.

By now faculty and students had poured out of the Mortara Building to see what all the fuss was about. Chris had his eyes tightly shut but felt the presence of a few good Samaritans. Then he heard the familiar voice of Crauford, who was leaning over him, asking, "Chris, Chris, are you okay?" Before Chris could answer he passed out.

He finally came to as he was jolted awake by one of the infamous Washington, DC, potholes. "Fucking roads in this country" was the muffled curse as he opened his eyes.

"Sorry, did you say something?" It was PWC. She was holding his blood-stained hand in the back of the speeding ambulance.

Chris realized he had an air mask on and tried to remove it. "No, keep that on, buddy," came the order from the paramedic. "We're almost there. The doctors are waiting for us. Just be patient, okay?"

There wasn't much to say or could be said with the mask on, but PWC did the talking anyway. She smiled at him, saying, "Hi, Chris. My name is Pam. Nice to meet you," and she squeezed his hand. "Professor Crauford told me you are a friend. He's going to contact your office and let your boss know what's going on. We're almost at the hospital. Don't worry; you're in good hands."

Chris felt the warmth of her hand and took the words literally, but strangely enough he did feel okay. He thought it was some drugs they must have pumped into him to ease the pain, but maybe it was because he was lying down with a pretty girl by his side. But the potholes were pissing him off. Kidney stones or not, potholes pissed off most people in DC.

They finally made it to the Emergency Room of the Sibley Memorial Hospital. As Chris was wheeled in, Pam said, "I'll stick around for a while and come by and check in on you—is that okay?"

Chris nodded his head and pulled the mask off. "Thank you for being here. Sorry for being a bother. I promise it won't happen again," he said and smiled as best as he could.

He was rewarded with an even bigger smile. "Just answer me one thing," Pam said. "Do I need to feel special, or do all your dates start out this way?"

She let his hand go and watched as the medics wheeled him away. PWC turned to search for the waiting room, only to bump into the police officer she had met at the attack scene. "Miss Corbin, do you have time for your statement now?" he asked.

"Sure, let's go and find the waiting room," she said.

CHAPTER
SEVENTEEN

DAY 26

GEORGETOWN, WASHINGTON, DC

NIGHT HAD FALLEN BY THE TIME PAMELA CORBIN LEFT CHRIS at the hospital. She stayed at his bedside as long as she could but kept getting pulled away by the police for more questions about the attack at the university. She wanted to get away, but the police were keeping a close eye on her, so she somehow had to give them the slip. After all her years with police protection on account of her father, the last thing she wanted was to have cops tailing her everywhere.

She chatted with Chris for some time. At first, it was all about the attack, and neither of them could pin down exactly why it had all happened. Their conversations went from the specific to the get-to-know-you type of chat. He told her some of his background, minus his CIA connections, and she spoke of her graduate studies in international business that were soon coming to an end. They laughed as they remembered their first meeting with the books in the hallway. They also talked of families, travels, and plans for the future.

They were bonding quite well until the pain meds kicked in and Chris fell asleep midsentence. She wanted to stay a little longer with him, but she was relieved he was not in any pain and happy to hear that the bleeding came from the kidney stones he had so violently passed—and that he was going to be fine. He looked quite content sleeping and snoring a little, and strangely enough, she would have liked to stay there with him just to watch over him. But she was tired and needed to get out and away from all the fuss; she needed to find her parents to tell them that she was okay before the cops made too big of a deal about it, or worse still, some jackass sensationalist journalist blew everything out of proportion.

"We've tried to reach your father, Miss Corbin, but we haven't located him yet. Do you have any idea of how to get hold of him?" It was the young police officer who had questioned her before.

"I have no idea. He could be in transit somewhere or in a closed-door session at Congress. It happens from time to time that we can't get hold of him straightaway." Outwardly she was trying to brush off her father's unknown whereabouts, but inside, she was seething. *What a surprise that nobody knows where he is,* she thought. *He's probably out chasing a whore somewhere.* "I'm sure he'll be in touch when he can," she added. "No need to worry about me; I can look after myself."

"Miss Corbin, I'm just waiting for a detective from the precinct to show up. He'll be here soon. He'll escort you home and stay with you until other arrangements can be made."

She looked at his name tag. "That's very kind of you, Officer Taylor, but there's no need for that."

"It's the least we can do," he said. "Sit tight. I am sure he'll be here shortly."

"Okay," she replied. "By the way, is there any way we can check to see what happened to my bike?" Happy for something to do, the officer replied, "Let me make a call. I'll be right back."

She didn't wait. As soon as the cop left, she found a nearby exit and made her way out of the hospital undetected and found a taxi that whisked her home. As soon as she got in the door, she left a message with her mother. She hoped by the time her mother got home she would call Pam back. She knew, although her mother was in Michigan, she would be on the next plane, train, or automobile once she heard the news. But Pam wasn't so sure about her father. She hated to call him for anything but decided to give it a try; it was possible he'd be in a sympathetic mood and might even give a damn for once.

Although she tried to downplay events in her mind, Pam knew that what had almost transpired was very serious. She knew deep down that the attack was somehow tied to her father, but since she didn't care about his business dealings, she never thought she would get drawn in. She couldn't figure out why she was the target, but the only way for her to find out if she was in any further danger would be to talk to her father.

She tried calling his home in Alexandria without any luck. She then tried calling his direct line at his office in the off chance he was working late; also no luck. She started pacing her apartment in a flurry of madness, her mind racing, going over all that had happened just a few hours ago. Now that she was alone and coming down off her emotional high, she was beginning to get flustered, nervous—and scared. Before she let her feelings get the better of her, she realized this was nothing new. Her father was never there for her anyway, so why should she even bother with him now?

Pam paused for one more second with the phone still in her hand and stared at the wall. She thought about calling Paul as he was often with her father, but after another second, she put the phone back on the cradle. If her father was the last person she needed to call, then Paul Seymour was the last person on the planet that she would want help from. But if she did call, and even if he was in Timbuktu, he would hijack an airliner, sail a one-oar dinghy, or even ride an ostrich to come to her rescue. It may have been her father's idea to find a suitor for her and to control her independent ways, but there was no way in hell she would ever consider being with an overbearing creep and wimp like Seymour; the thought disgusted her.

Nevertheless, she was disappointed because she had nobody to talk to. The few words that she had with Chris while he was still lucid were pleasant, and it seemed to her he had been through something like this in the past because he had all the right words to let her know she would be okay. He convinced her that she did a great thing by fighting back, and to put icing on the cake, he said she actually kicked some ass. She managed a smile at that thought.

But she returned to the image of her father, who was not there to comfort her, although he probably wasn't more than twenty miles away. She could have been killed or kidnapped—but how long would it have taken for him to find out and actually drag himself away from a woman or politics, to look after his only child, as any loving father would?

All through her childhood, through high school, and even into college, he never showed up or was interested in what she did. If he came to one of her events, it usually was for his own benefit. Her mother tried to convince her that he was in service to the country and he had an important role to play in its future, but she knew deep down that was the typical plastic politician's wife talking loyally.

The few times her father did arrive for one of Pam's special birthday parties or graduations, it was usually with an entourage of assistants and cops, all willing to do his bidding. And while he generally ignored his own daughter, if there was a crowd around, he never missed an opportunity to press the flesh and get in a photo op or two by buddying up with potential voters and would-be financial supporters. He always took the air out of the room and she hated him for it.

The result of his emotional abandonment and her long-lasting misery with her father led Pam to become fiercely independent and a hardcore tomboy. As she was an only child, she was left to her own devices, often in the company of a nanny or household staff who cared for her only when the paycheck was on time. She took it on herself to learn karate as a teenager and excelled in her age bracket. She often trained with men much larger and experienced than she. She was an above-average cross-country skier and runner, and for a while, everyone thought she would compete at higher levels, but as nobody ever came to see her run, she let her competiveness go and only jogged for fun or to let her frustrations out.

Pam grew up with guns—the only thing that she and her father ever really bonded over—and she became an exceptional shot with all sorts of weaponry. She initially thought that to gain her love her father built the range at Stonewall for them to shoot together. When groups of men began showing up at the range, she learned more about firearms. But as she got to know them, she realized they were all just ex-military guys with a freakish passion for weapons and tactics.

For a while, everything was fine until her mother confided in her one day about Billy and the incident in the barn. Pam's first instinct was to shoot the bastard, but her mother convinced her to let sleeping dogs lie. Pam did, but she secretly vowed one day to act some form of vengeance on him, something that he would not easily recover from.

Pam eventually stopped pacing her apartment and tried to decide what she wanted to do. In the pause, she became fearfully aware of the deafening sound of silence in the building. The loneliness and trauma of the attack were about to hit her hard, but she wouldn't allow it. She headed for her bedroom, went to her bedside cabinet, pulled out her Glock 9mm pistol, which she knew was loaded, grabbed her car keys and a half-eaten bagel from the night before, and headed out to the one place she knew she would be safe—Stonewall Retreat.

DAY 26
FBI MOBILE COMMAND VEHICLE, LANSING, MICHIGAN

"He left Dunbar Haulage about fifteen minutes ago, sir. We think he's either on the way back to DC via the airport or heading to his hotel. He's way out in the boonies, so it'll take some time to establish his route."

Special Agent in Charge Terry Billings was on the conference phone at the command vehicle, talking to FBI Director Brian Ross over the secure telephone link.

"Who do you have there, Terry? Is everyone on board?"

"Yes sir. In the trailer, we have representatives from ATF, DEA, State Police, emergency services, county and local police, and our SWAT team. Governor Baker is here also with the state attorney general. We're all listening in, everyone is briefed, and we have our teams in the field ready to go. Just waiting for a green light, sir."

"Okay, good enough. I don't want Corbin to be picked up tonight. Let's see where he ends up and who he goes to next. Wait until he clears the area. You know the drill Terry … Governor, I'd like to keep the press out of this as long as we can. I hope you understand."

"I certainly do, Director, I'll do my utmost to help where I can—you have my full support on that."

"Thank you, Governor. Terry you have a green light for the raid on Dunbar. I repeat; you have a green light; the mission is a GO!"

"Thank you, sir. Corbin won't be picked up tonight; the mission on Dunbar is a go. Billings out."

Billings ended the call and turned to his number two. "Get the message out, let's get the teams from staging to their start points. As soon as we have everyone in place, we go."

Thirty minutes after the teams started rolling towards the Dunbar compound, a Chevy Suburban pulled over to the side of the road to let a small convoy of police vehicles pass. The driver gave a friendly wave as they drove by, but he received no response. He waited till all the vehicles were out of sight and then did a quick *U*-turn and hit the gas. He knew the area well and found a parallel road that was distant enough that he would not be seen. But it was easy to pick out the convoy of fast-moving lights of the five or so cars that were speeding down the road. He had a gut feeling about where they were going, but he had to be sure.

Not a half-mile outside Dunbar, the Chevy driver spotted a helicopter overhead with its searchlight on, so he pulled over and got out to see what it was doing. Then all hell broke loose. Blue, red, and white lights were flashing around the entire shipping complex. He had seen enough. The shit had just hit the fan.

He jumped back in the Suburban, did not turn on his lights, and started moving slowly out. After five minutes of creeping along, he couldn't take it anymore—he flipped the switch and hit the gas. It took him another twenty minutes to find a gas station and a phone. He dialed the only number he knew from memory for Stonewall. After three rings, the phone was answered by a thoroughly bored male voice.

"Hello?"

"Sanchez, is that you?"

"Yeah, who's that?"

"It's Ricky. Dude everything's gone sideways. The Dunbar compound just got raided by the feds. Badges and guns are all over the damn place. You need to bug out, man. They may be coming for you next."

"Whoa, slow down there, soldier. What the hell you talking about?"

"I ain't shitting you, dude. I was out getting dinner for the troops, and when I headed back, I was passed by a convoy of cops. I followed them for a while to the compound; then I busted out of there. I don't know if any of the guys got out, but you need to get the fuck off the phone and bug out. Now!"

Ricky didn't wait for Sanchez to reply. He slammed the phone down and jumped back in the Suburban. Sanchez sat there staring at the phone for ten seconds, trying to process the news. It didn't take him long to come to a decision. He picked up his radio. "All call signs to ops now," he said calmly but forcefully. "Repeat, all call signs to ops double time."

Within a few minutes, his team was present in front of him, including those off-shift that he woke. There was no preamble—he got straight to business. "The Dunbar compound in Michigan has just been compromised. The feds are all over the place. We're bugging out. I don't know if they're coming here, and we're not waiting to find out. Pack up your shit; what you carry is your problem. We walk to RV1 together as a team, we go out locked and loaded. If the shit hits the fan, we fight as a team and make it to RV2. After that, we go our separate ways. If anyone has a problem with that, tough shit. We leave in ten minutes. Montoya, get to the road observation point, and I'll send you a relief in five. Radio silence now, everyone!"

Nobody said a word and got on with his business. Sanchez already had most of his gear with him so he began the necessary shredding of evidence. He took a look at the map of the minefield and the claymore plan and pinned it to the outer door of the command bunker; he wanted everyone to see it. He was a mercenary, but he did not want the blood of law enforcement on his hands. His remit was to protect the ranch from foreign terrorists and nosy neighbors, but he wasn't sadistic enough to take the life of a cop in that way.

After a few minutes, Montoya rushed in. "Headlights on the road, single vehicle, don't see any other bogies."

Sanchez was standing with the phone in his hand about to dial the last digit for Corbin's home phone number. "Is it Billy?"

"No," said Montoya. "His truck is still here."

Sanchez slammed the phone down. "We're out of here, let's go."

"What about the woman?"

Pam finally pulled into Stonewall after two hours of solid driving from DC. As she swung around the driveway of the main house, her headlights caught some movement in the trees. She tried to concentrate to see what it was, but it was quickly gone, so she put it down to a deer or some other form of wildlife, which was common in the area.

She had half-hoped her father would be there, but his car was nowhere in sight. She did let out a sigh of exasperation when she spotted Billy's pickup near the barn. She turned off the engine and was expecting him to show his face, but the place was dead. She made her way to the main house, but the doors were locked, and the place was dark. So she headed over to the first cabin, where she could hear music and see a dim light on in the bedroom.

As Pam got closer, she thought she could hear the voice of a woman, but it sounded like she was pleading for something. Her first thought was, *If that bastard father of mine has brought one of his whores here …* but as she drew nearer, she could hear Billy telling whoever it was to shut up. *So it's the pervert this time*, she noted.

Pam thought about backing away as it really was none of her business, but then she heard the scream. She pulled out her weapon and cautiously moved into the cabin. As she crept in, she noticed the beer cans and whiskey bottles strewn on the living room floor. She gingerly stepped over them and then placed her hand on the bedroom door handle, listening to what was going on.

"Shut the fuck up, you bitch!" she heard, followed by a slap. She hesitated at the door and heard more. "I'll cut you deep, and I will skin you from your toes to your fingers. Now stop your bitchin, you fucking whore!" This was followed by another slap. Pam turned the handle.

The woman's voice sounded terrified. "Please, please don't kill me. Don't touch me with the knife, I beg you, please ..."

Pam opened the bedroom door but couldn't see much; the room was too dark. "I'll do anything," she heard, "but please don't hurt me anymore."

Pam stepped into the room, gun drawn pointing it at Billy's head. He was standing at the side of the bed, naked, a large butcher's knife in one hand, the other fondling his penis. He was so engrossed in what he was doing he didn't see or hear Pam enter the room.

Pam saw the woman, who was naked, blindfolded, and tied spread-eagled to the bed. The TV was on in the room, and the videotape that was playing was a home video of young girls taking showers and mothers breastfeeding babies. Pam had seen enough and was totally disgusted. Billy was obviously trying to get himself aroused before he took the woman on the bed. Billy swayed above the woman, muttering to himself, "Bitch, whore, slut, you're going to wish you were never born."

In the calmest of voices she could command, Pam said, "Okay, Billy, that's enough. Put the knife down."

Billy snapped to attention and immediately covered his parts with the hand holding the knife. On realizing who it was, he dropped his hands, fully exposing himself. "Well lookie here. If it ain't Miss Perfect herself. You here for some lovin' too, sugar? You want some Billy relish?"

"Drop the knife, Billy, she demanded. "I'm not taking any of your shit."

"No need to be like that now. We can all have a bit of fun, don't you think? I can do this one first if you like; then I'll show you a good time too. How about it, pretty?"

"I'm not telling you again, Billy. Drop the knife and back off!"

Billy started making his way around the bed towards Pam. The other woman was silent, trying desperately to figure out what was happening, but she couldn't see a thing.

"Don't you come near me, Billy. I'm in no mood for your shit. Just drop the knife."

"You're one spoilt bitch, just like your momma. She thought she was too good for me as well, but you ... well, you're going to get some of this whether you like it or not," he said as he grabbed his balls. "Now you drop your gun you stupid cow, or I'll slash this bitch up in front of you and make you taste her blood."

"You go near her with that knife," Pam insisted, "and I'll shoot you in the nuts. Now back off!"

"As if you can order me around. Who the fuck do you think you are?" Billy placed the point of the knife on Cindy's breast and drew a small sliver of blood. He smiled to Pam, saying, "You want to drop the gun now, bitch, or do you want to see some dark red?"

Pam had waited long enough. She took one aimed shot into the corner of the room, safely away from the bed. Billy was startled and made his move, raising the knife to attack Pam.

Pam pulled the trigger again and shot him where she had promised. He dropped the knife and rolled over in agony.

Pam picked up the knife and began cutting the bonds that held the woman to the bed, but she didn't take her eyes off Billy for long. Cindy Whittaker, with her hands freed, pulled the blindfold off her face and began to take in her surroundings. She did not know who the woman was who had saved her, but she saw that Billy was curled up in the corner of the room groaning.

Cindy did not cry. She picked up the bed sheet to cover herself then went over to him and spat blood in his face. She did not say a word but let Pam speak for both of them.

Pam went and stood over him. "Billy, I missed your dick by about a half inch—it was too tiny to get an accurate shot. But I did manage to cut your femoral artery. With any luck, you'll die from blood loss in about fifteen to twenty minutes; longer if I'm lucky. You'll pass out in about five. Shall I leave the TV on for you, you sick bastard? Because that's the last thing you're ever going to see. On second thought …" *Bang.* She shot the TV, saying, "You don't deserve that much, you shit!"

As Pam made her way to the door, Cindy hesitated. The younger woman turned and said, "Come on. Let's get out of here."

"No, the soldiers," Cindy replied.

"What soldiers?" Pam asked.

"They're in the woods. They'll find us. They'll kill us."

Pam thought about what she had seen earlier on the drive into the ranch. "I saw them leave," she said. "If they were here, they would have come running after they heard the shots."

"But … they, they …"

"Let's not worry about them. I can take care of us. Let's get you some clothes, and we can call the police."

"No, we can't wait. They'll be back. They'll find us. They'll shoot us."
"It's all right. Nobody is going to shoot us. I'm going to call the cops."
"No, you don't understand … I have to get away. I can't stay!" Cindy shouted. Her memories of the shooting range came back to haunt her. She reached down, picked up the butcher's knife, and held it feebly in her hands. She began to cry, blood still pouring from her face and from her wounds. Then she turned to Pam and demanded, "Drop the gun!"

"Now, hang on a second!" said a surprised Pam.

"Drop the gun and give me your car keys, NOW!"

Pam was not going to give up her gun. "I'm just trying to help you. Give me a break."

"You can help me by giving me the keys. I'm driving out of here now."

"Okay, okay, I get it. We're leaving. I'm not giving you my gun, but let's get you cleaned up and dressed, and then we can get out of here. You know what I can do when someone threatens me with a knife, so hand it over. I'm not going to hurt you; I've had enough excitement for one day."

Cindy held the knife close. "No, I think I'll keep this for a while longer."

Pam didn't feel like arguing. "Okay, okay, let's go."

DAY 26
228 SOUTH FAIRFAX STREET, ALEXANDRIA, VIRGINIA

Corbin managed to put down his bags just in time to catch the phone before it went to the answering machine. "Hello?"

"Good evening, Senator. This is Anna Heymann."

"Mrs. Heymann, this is a surprise. How are you?"

"I'm fine, Senator. Thank you."

"Please, Anna, may I call you Anna? Call me Robert."

"Okay, Robert, thank you for that. I just hate these formalities we all have to go through sometimes, don't you agree?"

"I couldn't agree with you more, Anna. What can I do for you? I just returned home from a business trip so I am in a bit of a fluster."

"Oh, I'm sorry if I caught you at a bad time, but I was wondering if we could catch up. I'm only in town for a short while and I was hoping to chat with you about some documents that my husband had regarding you."

Corbin was both intrigued and shocked but decided to play it cool. "Oh that sounds interesting. Why don't we have lunch sometime next week?"

"I was really hoping to catch up in the morning. I have another breakfast appointment in Alexandria, so I thought I could come over for coffee, say around 9 a.m.?"

"What a perfect way to start the weekend. Coffee it is. I shall expect you then, my dear."

"I look forward to seeing you in the morning, Robert. Goodnight."

"Good night, Anna."

Both hung up the phone at the same time. Anna almost gagged when he had called her "my dear," but she shook it off.

Corbin stared at the phone in the hallway trying to figure it out. *What the hell does that old bat want?* he thought. He turned to the still-open door behind him and saw a man walk slowly by. He thought nothing of it and closed the door.

The Protector thought to himself, *It is God's will that I have been able to lay eyes on my enemy at last?* Not only had he identified Corbin; he now also knew where Corbin would be at nine o'clock the next morning.

DAY 26
FBI FORWARD OBSERVATION POST, ALEXANDRIA

"Did anyone get that conversation?"

"One, negative."

"Two, negative."

"Three, negative."

Lead agent Charlie Hallarn picked up his log book, entered the incident, and then called his report in back to the operations center at the Hoover building. After he hung up, he thought about the account he had just given. *Great, just great. The guy was loud enough to wake the dead, but three highly trained FBI surveillance specialists sitting in the bushes couldn't hear shit.* He turned to his partner. "How's it coming along with the wiretap?"

"Boss, you been awake too long. Do you know how difficult it is to get a judge to sign off on a wiretap in this town, especially for a senator?"

"Yeah, yeah, I know. The director was trying to pull some strings, but here we are, not knowing if he was ordering a hooker or going frog hunting for the weekend."

"Frog hunting …?"

"You're obviously not from the South are you? Let me tell you about frog hunting …" And so it went, two bored agents on another stakeout, telling each other stupid stories to keep each other awake.

Two minutes later, radio chatter broke their amusement.

"Zero, this is Three. The white van is coming back."

"Roger that. Let's get a plate if we can."

The light on the phone blinked twice. The phone did not have a ringer; instead, the light alerted them that a call was coming in.

"FOP 1, Hallarn."

"Hallarn, this is Billings. I just got your sitrep. So he's just got home I see?"

"Yes sir, looks like he is heading for the sack."

"Okay, no shuteye for you. We're going to bounce this guy in the morning. We're going to go in quietly. This is a political hot potato so we've really got to be careful. Get your boys ramped up. We'll have multiple agents coming to you throughout the night for a briefing. Find them a good staging point nearby. I'll be there as soon as I can, but probably at seven o'clock. Okay?"

"Yes sir, we've got some ideas ready to go. We're pretty close to being prepared."

"Good to hear, Charlie. Let's chat in the morning."

The white Ford van drove until it found a gas station with a phone. The driver got out and made a call. "Mazzim, he is home."

"Are you sure?"

"Yes, I saw the bastard walk into his house. He took a phone call in the hallway of his home. He was carrying his suitcases. I'm sure he will be home for some time."

"Good," said the Turkish wholesaler. "Tomorrow it is then. We will finish him in the morning."

CHAPTER
EIGHTEEN

DAY 27

05:55:06

WASHINGTON HIGHLANDS, WASHINGTON, DC

THE PROTECTOR WOKE BEFORE HIS ALARM WENT OFF, which was set for 6 a.m. He had not slept properly in days, but he didn't feel tired. He knew that today of all days it would not matter how fatigued he was, how hungry, how depressed or overjoyed—he had one task to perform no matter what his personal suffering was.

He began his morning by shaving completely. He shaved his entire body from his nose down to his toes, except for the hair on his head, as he still needed to blend into his surroundings for his mission. He wanted to be pure and cleansed in preparation for his journey to heaven and his ultimate meeting with Allah. After purifying himself, he took no breakfast but prayed for fifteen minutes; he would go hungry to his mission. He sat alone and in deep thought and convinced himself this was the right course of action, the right and only way to meet his daughter again, the right way to avenge her death. He sat alone almost meditating before the driver came and told him it was time.

He was dressed and almost ready to go; the only things left to put on were his jacket and vest. Although he had picked up the vest a dozen times the night before and had practiced walking around with it, this time it felt much heavier. It was as if he held the weight of the world around his torso. The driver helped him with the last part of the preparation; he connected the fuses to the explosives and passed the trigger plunger through the jacket sleeve and down to the Protector's right wrist, where it was taped off.

07:00:01

FBI HEADQUARTERS, WASHINGTON, DC

Special Agent in Charge Terry Billings commenced the meeting promptly at the top of the hour. There were close to fifty agents in the room, including various members of the ATF, CIA, and other federal agencies.

"Good morning, everyone. I realize I'm taking away your precious weekend from you all, but I won't apologize too much. Today is going to be a big day for all of us." He paused for effect. "We're now moving into phase two of Operation Foul Ball. Today I have here in my hand a warrant for the arrest of Senator Robert Corbin and another to search his premises."

He held up his hand with the documents to prove his statement and then continued. "It's taken us almost six months to get to this stage of the investigation, and we definitely have enough information to go ahead with prosecution. Last night's raid in Michigan was a great success. In fact, it was a better haul than we had expected. Your briefing documents will give you the details if you need them." He paused again to let his audience have a brief glimpse of the paperwork.

"I do have some bad news to share, though. One of our assets that was working with us from inside Venture Concepts was found dead in Cyprus. We're not sure at this stage how Corbin or his team was involved, but we have to assume the worst. We have a tight lid on Corbin right now. We're not sure if he's received any information about the raid last night, but we know he likes his guns, so we are going in hot. FBI SWAT will take the lead on entering the premises and secure whoever is there. We'll go in directly behind them. Any questions?"

None were fielded.

"Okay, everyone, let's get down to the nuts and bolts. We have a short window of opportunity before we go, and yes, before anyone asks, 0900 today we go in. Things did not pan out the way we thought last night, as we figured he may run or get in touch with someone else, but that has not transpired. We will not give up any more time. We go in at nine."

07:55:12

BENTON ST, NW WASHINGTON, DC

Chris took a long breath and nervously pressed the doorbell. It was early, he knew, but he was running out of time. She said he could come around anytime, so he rationalized this was "anytime." She said she was an early riser. He waited a few seconds and thought, *Shit. Maybe she has someone over. Shit, shit. Why did I come over? What a dumbass. Maybe she's got some bloke in there.*

He considered turning tail and took a step back just in time for Pam to open the door to her apartment.

"Hi, Chris," she said warmly.

"Hi, Pam. I'm sorry if I'm here too early. I should have called first. I hope I didn't wake you. I just wanted to say goodbye before I left; I'm getting on a plane in a few hours." Chris was rambling. He finally stopped himself, feeling pretty embarrassed. He didn't realize how truly nervous he was.

"It's okay, Chris," Pam said. "Don't worry. It's good to see you on your feet for a change." Seeing two cups in his hands, she asked, "Is that coffee?"

"Yep, thought you'd like a cup. It's black—that okay?"

"Sure, come on in. Um, I have a friend over, but she's asleep."

Chris smiled inwardly. *No mention of a boyfriend. Good.*

"As long as there are no zombies hiding in closets," he joked, "I guess I should be okay, right?"

"Don't worry, Chris," she tossed back. "I'll protect you if they show up."

He smiled and scanned his surroundings as he entered the well-kept apartment.

They ended up in the kitchen where he handed over the cup of coffee. He held one in his hand too and pretended to sip the cup as they chatted, but he hated coffee. They engaged in small talk for a few minutes about his flight, and though he didn't know her that well, his instincts were telling him she was pensive and a little jittery. He wanted to figure it out. He still felt there was something between them. *If only there was more time. Just get her talking,* he thought.

"Were you able to figure out who that was yesterday, the kidnappers I mean?"

"No, I talked to the police for a while, but they only asked questions. Not once did they give me the idea they had a clue, if someone had seen or heard something. Nothing. It's almost as if it never happened."

"Yeah, I know cops can be like that sometimes. Everyone is a suspect in something or other, and they never like to share theories. Didn't they offer you any kind of protection? Are you even safe here?"

Before she could answer, a familiar figure entered the living room just off the kitchen. Chris said nothing but he recognized the woman instantly;

she wasn't aware of him yet. She looked totally disheveled, confused, and obviously in need of more sleep.

Then she entered the kitchen. "I heard some voices," she said. "What's going on? Who the hell are you?" She pulled out the butcher's knife and pointed it at Chris.

"Whoa, slow down there a minute," he said.

She began to refocus, and her head became a little clearer. "Wait a minute. I know you," she said. "You were with that bitch Heymann—some kind of bodyguard or something." As things became clearer, she got more agitated and went on the defensive. "Yes, we've met before. What are you doing here? Have you come for me? You're not taking me anywhere, are you? What's your name?"

"I'm Chris. Now, can you give me the knife? There's no need for it. I'm not here to hurt you or take you anywhere."

Pam interjected, "How the hell do you two know each other?"

"It's a long story, Pam," Chris said.

"Yes, you'd better explain yourself, Chris," Cindy said. "Now I remember. You're that British guy."

"Wait a minute," Pam interrupted and turned to Cindy. "I don't even know *your* name. You had better explain *yourself.* You haven't said a word to me since last night. How did you get mixed up with Billy?"

"That sick bastard works for that slime ball politician. He held me captive there for days."

Pam was confused. "Billy kept you prisoner? I don't get it. Why?"

"Billy was just the jailer; it was that cocksucker politician with his little army that put me there."

"My father owns that ranch. He can't have anything to do with it."

The light bulb went on in Cindy's head. "So you must be his daughter."

"What?"

"Corbin, he's your father; he's the one that held me prisoner because of my husband."

Up until this point, Chris was focused on the knife and was planning a number of potential scenarios to get the weapon away from the woman. He glimpsed at Pam and could tell her world was collapsing around her and then turned his focus back on Cindy. "Can you put the knife down, please? Let's sit and talk about this. We're not going to harm you, I promise. I didn't even know you were here."

They all sat in the living room, but Cindy still would not relinquish the knife. There was an awkward silence as they all looked at each other without saying anything. Chris could tell that Pam was going downhill as she tried to take in what had been said. She finally turned to Cindy and said, "Can we start by you telling me your name?"

"Cindy Whittaker. My husband is in the army, and he also works as a mercenary for your father."

Pam began to cry. "Tell me more."

08:10:23
FOUNDERS PARK, ALEXANDRIA

The driver and the Protector said nothing as they came to a stop at the park on the edge of the Potomac River. The Protector got out and did not look back, walking off in the direction of the water. His heart was racing, but he tried to control himself. The last thing he wanted was for someone to spot him looking nervous and perspiring. He began walking and repeating verses of the Koran to himself. The end was near.

The driver did not wait. The man he dropped off was completely on his own. He had made his own destiny, and only Allah could save him now.

08:13:00
VAN DORN METRO STATION, ALEXANDRIA

They met at the north end of the metro parking lot, arriving in separate vehicles, but all leaving in the same white van that they had used the night before. The broken-nosed Turk was driving; Mazzim, with his crutches, was in the passenger seat; the Turk with sore balls was in the rear.

08:13:07
228 SOUTH FAIRFAX STREET, ALEXANDRIA

The phone would not stop ringing as much as he tried to ignore it. Finally he picked it up. "Jesus Christ, who's this? I'm trying to sleep!" he bitched. "What's so damn important that you have to call me on a Saturday?"

Corbin's attorney, Freddie Laylor, got straight to the point. "Robert, it's Freddie. Get your ass out of bed. Dunbar got raided by the feds last night!"

Corbin did exactly that, putting on his dressing gown with one hand while holding the phone with the other.

"Tell me what's going on and make it fast. Are they going to come for me next?" They spent the next few minutes going over what had happened and began discussing potential scenarios and get-out-of-jail excuses. Corbin told Laylor to get over to his place as soon as he could so they could start strategizing. They made plans to meet in an hour; by that time, Laylor should have a better understanding of the situation from his federal contacts.

In the meantime, Corbin got dressed and headed for the kitchen to make another call.

Although his mind was in turmoil, he waited patiently for the phone to be picked up. After the fourth ring it was answered.

"Hello?"

"Paul, you need to get over right now. We have a problem."

"I'm glad you called, I've been trying to reach you."

"Do you know about the raid?"

Seymour paused. "What raid?"

"We got whacked last night by the FBI and ATF at Dunbar."

"Holy shit. Have you talked to Pam?"

"Why should I be talking to her?"

"Someone tried to kidnap her yesterday. One of my brother's buddies called me up looking for her last night."

"What the fuck? Get over here now. I'll get a hold of her."

08:24:45
BENTON ST, NW WASHINGTON, DC

Pam beat her father to the call. "Dad?"

"Yes, honey, are you okay?"

"Yes, I'm fine, but I need to see you."

"Honey, I can't. Things are getting out of hand here at the moment. I'll come over when I have a chance."

"You can't see me? Why, do you have some whore that you need to get rid of?"

"Pam, there's no need for that, I just have to—"

"Dad, I killed Billy last night. I'm coming over." She crunched the phone back into its cradle, picked up her car keys, and made for the door.

"I'm going with you."

"What? No, Chris you have to catch a flight. You don't have enough time."

"I'll make time. If I have to take another flight, I will. You need someone to watch your back. I'm sure my boss will understand."

"But I can take care of myself, Chris. It's going to feel a little awkward with my father."

"I understand what you're saying, Pam. Believe me; I know you can look after yourself, but after what Cindy just said, I think there are tons of other issues here we don't understand. Besides that, we still don't know who was after you yesterday. I'm really surprised the cops aren't here to protect you."

He paused to gauge her reaction. There was none, but he could tell she was conflicted. "I won't get in the way, Pam. I'll just be watching your back, just paying attention. It's kinda what I do. If it becomes too personal with your father, I'll back off, I promise."

"What about Cindy?" she asked.

"Let's run out now while she's in the shower. Leave her a note that we should be back in a few hours," Chris replied.

Although the shower was still running, Cindy heard the front door thump closed. She tried to peek out through the blinds but didn't want to risk being seen. She considered her position a little while before she moved. She was already dressed in a pair of jeans and clean sweater from Pam. She looked around the apartment to see what else she could appropriate and found herself rifling through the drawers. After a few minutes of searching, she found a few hundred dollars and some loose change. She stuffed what she could in her jeans and headed out the door.

08:30:00
FBI FORWARD OBSERVATION POST, ALEXANDRIA

"Is everyone in place?" Billings asked the senior field agent, who had been up all night conducting a listening watch but was now quarterbacking the onsite operation.

"Not quite. Our teams are minutes away from their start points. Corbin is home. Another fifteen, twenty minutes and we'll all be set."

"Okay, good. I need to call the director. Where's your secure phone?"

08:45:49
228 SOUTH FAIRFAX STREET, ALEXANDRIA

Paul Seymour rapped on the door firmly, and it was opened within seconds. His first question was about his precious Pam. "Did you talk to your daughter yet?"

"Didn't have much choice; as soon as we hung up, she called. She's on the way over. We have another problem to deal with: She said she killed Billy."

"Holy shit. Did she say how, or why?"

"No, I've tried calling Stonewall, but nobody is picking up. We might be compromised everywhere."

They headed to the kitchen towards the back of the house. Seymour stopped in his tracks when he saw the weapons on the kitchen table. The Runner picked up a shotgun and began loading it. He handed Seymour an MP5 submachine gun and told him to do the same.

Seymour protested. "What the hell is this?"

"If Pam was almost kidnapped, it was probably the Turks trying to get to me. They could be coming here anytime, and I want to be ready."

"But what about the feds?"

"Don't worry about that for a minute. I've got Freddie Laylor making some calls for me. He's going to call me in about fifteen minutes to see what his justice department contacts are telling him. As soon as I can get Pam out of here, we'll strategize how we're going to get out of this before the FBI comes down on us. Don't stand there looking like an imbecile. Load the fucking weapon before she comes."

08:52:23
FBI FORWARD OBSERVATION POST, ALEXANDRIA

"Sir, a white van is approaching the target house."

"Leave it play. As soon as it leaves, let's get a plate. It may be something innocent."

08:54:01
228 SOUTH FAIRFAX STREET, ALEXANDRIA

Both Corbin and Seymour were startled by the knock on the door. Corbin motioned Seymour to go to the bay window and check who it was. Corbin stood in the corridor with the shotgun pointed at the door. He knew his daughter had a key and always came in through the back door, so whoever was at the front door was probably not friendly.

He was about to shout out to ask who was there when he realized that Anna Heymann was supposed to come over at nine. He called out to Seymour, "Make yourself scarce. I think I have a visitor I forgot about. I got this."

He stuffed the shotgun behind his raincoat that was hanging on a peg in the corridor and opened the door. To his surprise a young man stood in front of him with a package and a clipboard.

"Mr. Corbin?"

"Yes."

"Please sign here."

"I'm not expecting a package, who is it from?"

The courier checked his notes. "Ah, there is a note to say, 'Compliments of Mrs. Heymann.'"

"Okay." Corbin snatched the package away, slammed the door, and did not sign the clipboard.

The courier shrugged his shoulders and headed back to his white van.

08:55:27

FBI FORWARD OBSERVATION POST, ALEXANDRIA

"Let's roll, everyone, nice and easy. Let's remember where we are."

08:55:59

DUKE STREET, ALEXANDRIA

The Protector timed his walk to get across the junction at the corner of Duke and Lee just before a white van passed behind him. The driver of the van gave him a long stare but the Protector did not care; he was too close to his target. He knew nothing could possibly go wrong now.

08:56:46

ST. MARY'S CATHOLIC CHURCH, ALEXANDRIA

Pam was slightly concerned that there were a number of official-looking vehicles in the area on a Saturday. It was not uncommon, though, in Alexandria to see motorcades, limousines, or motorcycle outriders as this was a favored watering hole and residences of some of the serious movers and shakers of the US government. It was why her father had chosen the area—so he could rub shoulders with the high and mighty.

As she crossed from the parking lot, she headed towards the back of her father's house, located on the corner of Duke and South Fairfax. She noted her father's car was in the parking space behind the house, which meant he was still home.

Chris was reading warning flags as if he was interpreting semaphore communications. He had a list of red flags, some unknown yellow flags, and a whole bunch of the general public going about their business, which he called his green flags. On the drive in, he saw all the cops, the cars, the plainclothes guys with wires sticking in their ears. He heard the radios; he felt the buzz. Something was happening, something big, and he didn't like it. *Here we go again*, he thought. *I've just run out of shit paper, and I ate Indian last night.* His eyes were so wide that he could have won an owl look-alike competition. His brain moved into overdrive as he started looking for options to get Pam out of a potentially bad situation.

08:57:26
SOUTH FAIRFAX STREET, ALEXANDRIA

The white van with the three Turks waited as traffic cleared the junction of Fairfax and Duke before proceeding to Corbin's house. As they waited, Mazzim turned to his compatriot and told him to be ready. The passenger in the back took the blanket off the RPG and raised the rocket launcher to his shoulder. He nodded that he was set.

08:58:14
FBI FORWARD OBSERVATION POST, ALEXANDRIA

"Sir, Pamela Corbin is on site. Repeat, Pamela Corbin is approaching the residence with an unknown subject."

"This is Billings. We take them too, and we don't know her involvement, so take it easy."

08:59:01
228 SOUTH FAIRFAX STREET, ALEXANDRIA

"What's the deal with Anna Heymann?" Seymour asked.

"I don't know. She was supposed to stop by at nine o'clock."

The phone rang, and Corbin picked up, thinking it was his lawyer. "I hope you have good news for me, Freddie."

"I'm sorry Robert. This is Anna."

08:59:38
228 SOUTH FAIRFAX STREET, ALEXANDRIA

The Protector was standing at the front door of Corbin's house, chanting to himself, *Allahu Akbar, Allahu Akbar, Allahu Akbar.* He ripped the trigger plunger away from his right wrist with his left hand and approached his paradise. He was only seconds away. He pressed the doorbell.

08:59:51
228 SOUTH FAIRFAX STREET, ALEXANDRIA

The Turk with the sore testicles exited the van and pointed the rocket at the door to Corbin's house. He paused a second as his line of sight was blocked by a man who was standing in the way of the door.

08:59:53
FBI FORWARD OBSERVATION POST, ALEXANDRIA

"What the hell is going on? We have multiple bogies on the street. I see an RPG, GO! GO! GO!"

08:59:54
BACK DOOR, 228 SOUTH FAIRFAX STREET, ALEXANDRIA

Pam struggled with her purse and looked in vain for her father's backdoor key. It was a minefield in there, with all sorts of obstacles getting in the way of finding what she was looking for. She made it to the back deck and continued to dig away.

Chris was a step and a half away from her and still scanning for danger when he heard a loud radio transmission. He grabbed Pam's wrist, whispering, "Pam wait!"

08:59:55
228 SOUTH FAIRFAX STREET, ALEXANDRIA

The doorbell rang. Corbin motioned Seymour to get it; he was on the phone with Anna Heymann. "Anna, I was expecting you to come over this morning. Where are you?"

"I'm sorry, Robert. I was delayed, but I sent you a package. Did you get it?"

"Yes, I have it in front of me."

"Please open it. There are some things in there you may find interesting." She paused for a second. "I know all about your dealings in Munich, Robert. The information inside the package will validate my statement."

"I have no idea what you're talking about, Anna."

"Please open the package, Robert. It's from my husband. Actually it's from both of us and the state of Israel. Goodbye."

09:00:00
228 SOUTH FAIRFAX STREET, ALEXANDRIA

Three explosions ripped through Corbin's house simultaneously as Anna Heymann replaced the phone back on the cradle in the phone booth and headed toward airport security at Dulles International.

The RPG rocket flew through the open front door, missing the Protector by inches, and exploded in the corridor of the house, engulfing the ground floor in a ball of flames.

To add to the intensity, the suicide vest that the Protector was wearing exploded, decapitating him and killing Paul Seymour as he answered the door.

Corbin died instantaneously when he opened the package bomb on the kitchen table in front of him. The entire ground floor of the house was on fire.

CHAPTER
NINETEEN

DAY 28
GERMAN AIRSPACE, FRANKFURT, BERLIN

CHRIS WAS AWAKE BUT KEPT HIS EYES CLOSED. He was reflecting on the events that had transpired less than twenty-four hours ago in Alexandria. Once again, he ended up being a guest of the local police department, but since everyone who was ever recruited by the FBI since J. Edgar Hoover was in town investigating the death of a senator, matters on the surface, like his, were cleared up relatively quickly. Chris was becoming a known entity within the FBI, and his explanation for being at Corbin's residence was plausible, so they had no reason to question him further. Nevertheless, it took him some time to get away and find Pam in the local hospital emergency room.

"Well, that's one way of sweeping a girl off her feet," she said, referring to the way that he had pulled her off the deck of her father's house seconds before the explosion that rocked the house.

"I knew that something was going on," he said. "But I didn't know how bad it would be. I'm sorry for your loss."

They were holding hands. A tear ran down Pam's cheek. He wiped it off. "I should have moved sooner," he said. "How's your leg?"

"I can't feel much right now. They gave me some kickass meds so the pain has subsided somewhat. Eighteen stitches are going to leave a nice scar, though. Guess I'll have to cancel my Paris modelling gig," she joked.

"And I thought we could go down the catwalk together," Chris played along. "I shaved my chest and was planning a facial and a manicure." The banter continued for a long time until Pam's mother arrived.

The break gave Chris the time he needed to call Nash in Germany and bring him up to speed. Nash told him that Gene was on the way over to pick him up as he needed a full debrief with the CIA's office of security and the FBI. He made his way back to Pam's room and felt a little awkward saying his goodbyes with her mother present. He made it short but promised to be in touch realizing that both mother and daughter needed time to grieve over their loss.

———◦∞◦———

A thump and a rattle brought Chris back to reality. The plane was entering some heavy weather. It was never easy flying from the United States to Berlin; there were no direct flights, and the usual layover was Frankfurt. Chris was happy to be on the final leg of his journey. The passenger next to him was a little startled as Chris sat up straight.

"You ok?"

"Um, yeah, hope my snoring didn't bother you," he replied.

"Not at all," said the passenger.

"How long have I been out?"

"Well, you were asleep when I got on board, so I would say probably about twenty minutes already. Tough week at the office?"

"Not really. Been a little under the weather. Needed to catch up, I guess."

There was a brief pause in the conversation as Chris tried to make himself a little more presentable. He ruffled his hair and rubbed his face, only to realize he had been drooling in his sleep. "Wow, I must look as if I'm ninety and not in control of my bodily functions," he joked. "Hope I didn't pee on myself."

The passenger chuckled. "I'm sure someone on this plane has a diaper if you need one."

"I'll skip that and save you the mental image, but I guess I should go and check it out anyway. Do you mind?" He unbuckled his seatbelt and made his way out of the confines of the cramped cattle-class seat almost at the back of the plane.

He took his time in the bathroom to wash up as best he could. He got back out into the aisle and began some basic stretching exercises just to get his blood flowing, having to dance his way around other passengers trolling the cramped spaces of the plane.

The whole time he was out of his seat, he was digging into his mind's file memory, sifting through faces and trying to match the one that was sitting next to him. He recognized his newfound friend from somewhere but couldn't place him just yet. After another few minutes of general chit-chat with the flight attendants, he made his way back to his seat. As he got there he found the picture, and he found the where: the Hoover Building; the guy was FBI.

"Guess I needed a diaper change after all," Chris laughed.

"We all do someday, buddy, some sooner than others, but good luck with that."

Chris didn't want to be the first to break the ice on the inevitable plane passenger question, "And what do you do for a living?"

For just such conversations, Chris was prepared with stories for dozens of fictional characters—he had been a roofer, a fork-lift driver, a car-parts salesman, and a whole host of other jobs that were completely mundane, and the one he selected depended on the passenger sitting next to him, whom he did not ever want to talk to. If a guy sat next to him with a camouflage hat, then Chris was a network communications specialist. If a geek sat next to him with his laptop out, Chris became a popcorn sales-man. If a schoolteacher, then he picked up road kill for the county.

He was never in law enforcement, the military, medical, or emergency services. He had too much respect for those professions, and he was not trying to be ignorant, arrogant, or rude—most of the time he just didn't want to get into any conversations on a plane, and the more ordinary or off-the-wall job he picked, the quicker the discussions ended. The worst thing he could do was blab about what he did for a living only to find that the person sitting next to him was selling the same bullshit as he was. Be-sides, he was only a driver; he had nothing of interest to pass on, or at least nothing of interest to a schoolteacher or a logger from Oregon.

After getting comfortable again, Chris pulled out a book he'd picked up at the airport. It was one of the Ludlum series, and he knew he could easily get lost in it for the rest of the journey. It was usually the sign he used showing he did not want to be bothered, but he was about to break his own rule.

"I think we've met before," said his fellow traveler.

"Yes, I believe we have," Chris said. "I think I bumped into you in a building in DC where I was giving a briefing to some of your colleagues."

"Yeah, I remember. I couldn't attend for long, but I read some of the briefing materials." He held out his hand. "I'm Jim. Nice to meet you."

Chris recognized that the man was practicing his operational security by not giving his full name away. "Chris. Good to meet you too."

"Heading home at last, I guess?"

"Yes, it's been a long trip. Need to get back into the swing of things. My boss really needs me back there."

"I can imagine."

"You going to be in town long?"

"No, I hope not, but we'll see. Perhaps we can go get a beer when I'm done. Maybe you can show me the sights or something."

"Sure, I think you'll be able to find me. Just let me know where and when. Is there something particular you want to see while you're in Berlin?"

The conversation trailed off to talk of the historic sites and stories of Berlin. As they were chatting, they didn't notice another traveler on the plane who was stretching her legs.

Anna Heymann was about to approach Chris to say hello, but the flight attendant called for passengers to return to their seats, as they were expecting some heavy turbulence. She headed back to first class. She would catch up with him later.

DAY 28
BAGGAGE CLAIM, BERLIN TEGEL INTERNATIONAL AIRPORT

Chris and Jim Duran finally made it to the cramped baggage carousel and waited for their bags to arrive. They were both chatting away and scanning the crowd when Anna Heymann came into Chris's field of view. She gave a happy smile and wave and made her way to him.

"Chris, I saw you on the plane. How are you? I heard you were sick."

"I'm fine. Thank you, Mrs. Heymann; thanks for asking."

Jim Duran felt out of place but remained silent.

"Mrs. Heymann, this is Jim … from the FBI."

Jim held out his hand. "Jim Duran. Mrs. Heymann, nice to meet you."

They exchanged pleasantries for a few minutes more while they waited for their baggage, and Anna offered Chris a ride into town.

"Chris, how are you getting home? I hope to have a driver waiting for me."

Chris felt uncomfortable as he probably knew the motor pool driver who was going to pick her up, and the last thing he wanted was to show his colleagues he was chummy with a late ambassador's wife.

Jim could sense that Chris was getting a little sweaty and jumped in. "Actually, Mrs. Heymann, Chris and I were going to ride together; he was going to show me around a little today."

"Oh, that's great. Your first time in Berlin, I take it?" The conversation carried back to the everyday to kill the pain of waiting for baggage.

DAY 28
BECK'S BAR, BERLIN TEGEL INTERNATIONAL AIRPORT

"Holy shit!" Whittaker blurted, and Preacher and Bowman followed his gaze in the direction of the TV.

The screen at the corner of the bar said it all: The CNN reporter was live from Arlington. "It is now confirmed that a number of people have been killed at the residence of Senator Corbin here in Alexandria. Unconfirmed reports however are telling us that there was a gas explosion, and Senator Corbin was at home. His whereabouts are unknown at this time, but the authorities are assuming the worst." The reporter rattled on for a few more minutes, trading his mandatory two questions with the CNN anchor until they went to a commercial break.

The trio were silent. Preacher looked to Whittaker for guidance but only received a blank stare in return. Bowman took a long drink of his beer. Preacher thought he heard the word "Cheers" as Bowman raised his glass but could not be sure.

Whittaker broke the silence. "Look, we don't know if he was even there, but gas leak, really? That doesn't sound right to me. John, you're going to have to get back to your office and find out what really happened. Find out from Paul what he knows."

Bowman's mind was already made up. Corbin was dead, and that was the end of the game. "You two fuckers need to get on that plane and get out of my face for good. You've caused me a shit storm of problems, so now you need to get lost. You know the drill—head back to Stonewall."

"Don't be a dumbass!" Whittaker replied. "If this is all falling apart and Corbin's dead, the ranch is the last place we want to be. What if someone is using a gas leak as an excuse for a bomb they can't explain yet? Don't you think the bureau will be all over it? We'll be in touch as soon as we get stateside."

"Well, hurry up and fuck off then," Bowman replied.

Whittaker suspected this wasn't Bowman's first beer of the day and wanted to brush off the remark. But Preacher sprang across the table and grabbed Bowman by the throat. He was lightning fast, and neither Whittaker nor Bowman saw it coming.

Preacher was squashing Bowman's windpipe in a vice grip. "Fuck you, asshole!" he shot.

Whittaker tried to intervene. He placed his hand over Preacher's and looked him in the eye. "Virgil, let it go, let it go." The two had become close over the last few weeks, and the bond was pretty tight, so if anyone was going to talk him down it would be the colonel.

Preacher relented and got up to leave, but not before Bowman threw a last comment in. "I ought to take you out back and put a round through your skull, but you're not worth the cost of a bullet. Nobody is going to miss a prick like you."

Preacher ignored the last jibe, although he wanted so badly to beat Bowman's face to a pulp. But discipline took over, and he headed to the check-in desk with Bowman and Whittaker close behind.

Tegel Airport was built in 1960 at the height of the Cold War. The small facility was built in the French sector of West Berlin in the suburb of Reinickendorf, just northwest of the center of Berlin. Its hexagonal design allowed passengers and the public to walk around the facility in less than twenty minutes, and the layout meant you could theoretically get from curb side to plane door in less than a hundred feet.

This layout, while appropriate for the time, proved to be a nightmare for security and passengers alike when checking in or claiming baggage in 1995. Terminal A, the main terminal, had only sixteen check-in desks, and each desk and agent fought for real estate. To check in, you would go to the agent and then enter the waiting lounge to the left of the ticket counter. Those who were disembarking a plane and leaving the terminal would exit to the right of the counter. When two planes arrived at the same time and two planes were checking passengers in, the scene was like a plague of ants climbing its way around a route that followed no logical approach. There were bodies and bags everywhere, and every day for forty-five minutes of every hour at various gates, it was sheer madness.

Anna Heymann led the way out with baggage in hand, followed closely by Chris, taking up his over-watchful position, and then by Duran. Chris was instinctively scanning the sea of faces and seeing what-if scenarios popping up everywhere. He was not on the clock, but his desire to protect others put his mind-set into his preferred mode. On this day, while Anna was in his vicinity, he felt his duty would be to protect her.

Chris spotted Bowman and let out a quiet "Shit" that only Duran heard. Duran was equally perturbed and also quietly commented, "Nick is supposed to be picking me up, not Bowman. Where the hell is he?"

Chris continued to scan the area and noticed a harried-looking Nick running through the concourse towards the party. But both Duran and Chris focused their attention on Bowman, who was equally surprised to see his own boss and Chris exiting the baggage claim.

It was Anna Heymann who broke the tension. "Whittaker!" she shouted as she stopped in her tracks. Chris followed her stare and identified the man immediately. The crowd started thinning, and the ambassador's wife headed over through a gap towards the group.

"It was you. You killed my husband!" Anna pointed a shaky finger at Whittaker.

Duran jumped in. "Excuse me, Mrs. Heymann. What are you talking about?"

"His name is James Whittaker," she said. "He is, or was, a colonel in the US Army, but he is working for Corbin. He orchestrated the attack on my husband."

Whittaker turned to Bowman, not knowing who Duran was. "You'd better get us out of here, John," he said.

Nick Seymour, who now stood next to Duran, moved his hand to his right hip and began to draw his service revolver. "What the hell is going on, John?" he asked.

Everyone saw the movement; Bowman made the same move.

Chris speedily scanned the area for an exit strategy. He found his route out so he took up position to the right of Anna and stepped in front so he could bail her out if things spiraled south. Chris sized up each of the adversaries in front of him.

The group became quiet for a few seconds, and it was as if each was waiting for the other to make the next move. Chris saw Preacher and recognized him from Cyprus. Preacher was smiling back at him. Chris knew that, of the three before him, Preacher would be the dangerous one.

Duran got into the middle of the group and outstretched his arms to keep Bowman and Seymour from drawing their weapons. He looked at Bowman. "John, you'd better start talking, I don't know what's going on, but whatever this is, I need some answers. Keep your guns holstered, both of you. Talk to me, John!"

Bowman remained silent.

The rest of the group remained silent.

Finally Preacher broke the deadlock. "I hope you enjoyed that whiskey. That was some expensive shit." The question was directed at Chris, but he didn't bite. The line just confirmed what he thought, that Preacher was the one that had forced him down the stairs at the parking lot in Cyprus.

Anna broke the silence again and pointed at Whittaker. "Jim, you need to arrest that man," she said to Duran. "He was instrumental in my husband's death."

Seymour heard the word "arrest" and pulled his revolver further out of its holster. Duran caught the movement and instinctively backhanded Seymour's right hand, forcing him to drop the gun.

Chris took the chance to get Anna out of the zone. He began dragging her away but was sideswiped by Preacher, who was sprinting to get away himself. Both Chris and Anna ended up in a heap on the floor.

Duran made a move to Bowman to make sure he didn't draw his weapon; Seymour made a move toward Whittaker hoping to hold him in place. Seymour could not get to the gun that he had dropped, and he didn't want to take his eyes off Whittaker.

Chris thought that Duran and Seymour had things under control and got up to chase down Preacher. As he began sprinting through the airport, he thought to himself, *Why the hell do I always end up in airports chasing idiots? One of these days, I really am going to be just a damn driver.*

The crowd at the airport prevented Preacher from getting too far away, and it didn't take long for Chris to catch up. Preacher fell over some passenger bags and, as he picked himself up, was pounced on by Chris's full weight. The momentum of the run and body slam carried both antagonists into and through some plastic sheeting that was hanging from the ceiling.

They both fell into the area where repairs were being made from the grenade attack during the fighting between the Turks and Lebanese.

Preacher got up quicker than Chris and went to kick him in the head but slipped on the paint knocked over as they fell through the plastic. As Preacher fell backwards, he tripped underneath some scaffolding that was still being constructed, and it fell directly on top of his head. He went down in a heap of paint, wooden trestles, and aluminum scaffold.

Chris picked himself up and made his way over to Preacher. He contemplated digging him out, but there was too much material to move. He realized that Preacher was no longer a threat, as he was either unconscious or dead under the pile of painter's equipment. He decided to head back to Anna and Duran.

As he dusted himself off, he realized he was covered in white paint. *If Astrid could see me now,* he thought, and began jogging back to the group. On the way back, he heard two shots ring out. He went from a jog to a sprint and eventually made it back to the group to find Whittaker lying in a pool of blood, face down on the hard marble. He also saw Duran and Seymour holding Bowman up against the wall.

Then he heard the polizei shout a warning, "*Lass die waffe fallen.*" Two officers were pointing machine guns at Anna Heymann, who had recovered Seymour's gun.

Chris knew she understood the warning, but it was obvious she was not listening and was not about to drop it as instructed. She was on her knees and crying her eyes out, her vision blurred, trying to comprehend what she had just done. The two cops repeated the warning again. She held on to the weapon and pointed it at the floor. Chris wanted to step in but was warned back by the cops.

The struggle between Duran, Seymour, and Bowman continued as they each tried to wrestle a weapon away from the other. During the continued effort, Bowman's revolver dropped to the floor, which caused Anna to point her weapon in the sound of the danger. As she did so, both police officers took this as an act of aggression and shot her twice each. She slumped to the floor, face down into the same pool of blood on the cold marble floor next to the man she had just killed.

The two police officers then focused their weapons on the three Americans struggling with each other. Duran shouted at Chris with one hand on Bowman's collar: "You speak the lingo?"

Chris nodded.

"Tell them what's going on, tell them we're FBI and this man is in our custody." Chris rapidly told the officers exactly what Duran requested. Credentials were shown and the crisis was over.

DAY 28
DAHLEMER WEG, ZEHLENDORF, BERLIN

Chris finally made it to his apartment, tired, hungry, and covered in dried white paint. As he entered the place, he realized it sounded hollow, empty. Sure enough, as he put his bags down in the hallway, he realized Astrid had moved out. He went into the bedroom first and found a mattress on the floor; the closets were mostly empty, save his clothes. He went to the living room where he found his TV on the floor, an ironing board, and an iron. No couch, no table, no decorations.

He made it to the kitchen, which was also bare, but he found a full crate of beer on the floor with a note attached. "Enjoy asshole!" it read. He had no doubt about whom that was from.

Back in the hallway, he saw his answering machine, which was blinking 04. He hit the play button. "Christopher, this is your mother. Where have you been? I've been trying to reach you; your brother is in trouble. Please call me."

He sighed a long breath. *What has he done now?* he thought. He let the machine continue on to the next message. "Good day, Herr Morehouse. Luchterhand here. You have not paid this month's rent. Please call me immediately."

"Sheeet, I don't even know what day or month it is," Chris said to nobody.

The machine continued to roll. "Christopher, this is your mother again. Your brother was arrested by the police. You know what he's like when he's had too much to drink. Give me a call as soon as you can."

"Outstanding," Chris said to the wall. He debated whether or not he should listen to the last message, expecting more crap, but he let it play out.

"Hi, Chris. This is Pam. Just wanted to check to see if you made it home okay. I'd like to hear a friendly voice. Give me a call. I'm home. Okay? … Bye."

CHAPTER
TWENTY

DAY 29

US EMBASSY MOTOR POOL, MITTE, BERLIN

"CHRIS, HAVE YOU SEEN THE LATEST MAINTENANCE SCHEDULE FOR YOUR FLEET?" the motor pool dispatcher, George Geier, asked.

"No, George. I've been out of town for a while."

Chris was responsible for the twelve CIA station fleet vehicles that all needed to be washed, cleaned, fuelled, and maintained. "We've been picking up the slack for you since you've been gone," George said. "We fuelled up some of your cars at our expense, so we'll need to reconcile that pretty soon here. I don't appreciate your office taking advantage of my goodwill when it comes to my resources."

Chris rolled his eyes. He'd been through it all in the last few weeks. He was tired both physically and mentally, and the last thing he wanted was to have some grief from a dispatcher who thought he was God's gift to vehicle logistics.

"I'll get right on it, George."

"And another thing, your cars are disgusting. I suggest you start your day by cleaning them all. I'm not having my mechanics working on your vehicles when they have plenty to do themselves."

Chris knew this was not true. The motor pool mechanic was one of the cushiest and least hectic jobs in the embassy, and the waiting line to be a mechanic was about two miles long. If Chris really pushed himself, he could take a few more classes and get in line as well.

Again, Chris assured the dispatcher. "Sure, George, I'll get right on it."

"Oh, and don't let me forget you need to get down to licensing so you can get those new cars set up—" The phone rang, which distracted George and gave Chris his cue to leave.

He spent the rest of the morning chatting with the other drivers in the waiting lounge. They were all there, some reading newspapers, some playing cards, and others watching TV, patiently wasting the time between driving assignments.

Now and again, the topic of the consulate bombing would come up, which Chris listened into. It was always good to hear gossip about what was said on the ground in addition to reading it in the newspapers. He'd already been out to the consulate to take a look at the damage, and he knew that within a few days he'd be able to formulate his own opinion of what had happened. He felt sad at the loss of the security guard, whom he knew in passing, but rationalized that, when you sign up to guard a target, bad things may happen to you.

Thankfully, nobody asked about what he had been up to, although everyone was aware of the death of the ambassador's wife. Nobody thought to ask if he was at the airport at the time of the attack, and neither did he share.

As the day wore on, he got down to the business of dealing with the fleet and the mundane day-to-day things to do that are the job of the embassy driver. It's not that he had to do George's bidding with the fleet, but he was all about keeping the peace and the motor pool was a valuable resource to the office in case they needed extra cars or drivers. The fleet of CIA vehicles was in high demand for its officers these days.

Midway through the afternoon, he found a quiet corner to rest in, which unfortunately gave him time to reflect on the events from the day before and the last few days and weeks. It had not hit him yet, but he knew that he had failed Anna Heymann.

Although he was not obligated to protect her, it was one of the fundamental tenets of a professional protective agent to safeguard anyone in danger and get him or her out of hazardous situations. It was something he prided himself on, and as he was good at what he did, he always came out on top—but not this time.

He could not have known what was going to happen at the airport, and he really could not read her state of mind. Seeing Whittaker triggered something in her that pushed her in a direction nobody could have anticipated. She was an educated, normally rational woman who everyone thought was taking the death of her husband reasonably well. It came as a huge shock to Chris to see her holding the weapon and Whittaker lying next to her in the pool of blood.

He began running through the events again and again and kept thinking to himself, *If I had only stayed behind, if I had only moved her completely out of there, if I had just stayed as a useless driver and not gotten into this gig in the first place, she would still be alive. I failed. What the fuck am I doing with my life? Maybe I need to get out of this shit. I obviously can't do it. Astrid was right. I am just a driver. Maybe there is something else out there for me. Mrs. Heymann would still be alive if ...*

He fell asleep in one of the comfy lounge chairs and was only awakened when one of the drivers told him his boss was calling to be picked up. It was close to 6:00 p.m.

As Chris entered the driveway of the Nash residence, his boss asked him if he had plans for the evening. Chris hesitated in his response and then lied to him, saying he was going to the gym for a workout, when in reality he was going shopping for some furniture. He didn't want his boss to know that his girlfriend had left with everything.

"Why don't you hang on a while, Chris? I need to have a chat with you. Can you wait for me in the library?"

"Sure, Mr. Nash."

Chris parked the car in the driveway and entered the house through the door left open by Nash. He found himself a leather chair to sit in and waited patiently for his boss to return. The house was quiet, except for the sound of the cook busy in the kitchen. The smell of chicken was wafting through the house, which made his stomach growl with hunger. *That's another thing to take care of tonight,* he thought. *There's no food in the house.*

After a few minutes, Nash returned with two glasses of orange juice. "How are you feeling, young man?"

"I'm fine, thank you. Seems like the kidney thing has finally disappeared."

"Good. Gene filled me in on your trip to Bragg, I feel your pain—I've been there myself. Make sure you keep your fluids up, okay?"

"Absolutely, Mr. Nash. I wouldn't wish that pain on my worst enemy."

"Speaking of which, Chris, you may have made a few in the last couple of weeks."

"You're probably right. It's been a bit of an adventure lately. Who knows what's next with the Turks and Lebanese still bashing each other's heads in."

"Well, that's what I want to talk to you about. You've done some exceptional work recently, and you have made quite an impression with us. Our

Office of Security wants you on board with them permanently as part of the director's security staff—but I don't want you to go there."

Chris sat on the edge of the seat, not wanting to interrupt. He sat and listened intently. He was both honored and surprised that he was being considered for such a position, but internally he felt a twinge as he thought of Anna again.

Nash continued, "I actually think you have some skills that could be used elsewhere. We all know you have a very sharp mind for detail, and you usually don't miss too much. I'll be honest. You have some things you need to work on, and some would argue that you're not mature enough to be fully engaged with us in the capacity I have in mind."

Chris remained silent, sipped his juice, and let his boss continue.

"I don't think of you as an analyst or even a traditional field agent," Nash said. "I see you as an independent thinker who can look after himself with little or no support. We all know how good you are with weapons; even unarmed, you're a handful. You're quick, you're intelligent, you have great presence of mind in all kinds of situations, and you're not easily scared. You can be a leader, but you can also be led, which I like. I think you're way above being just a motor pool driver, or even a bodyguard. Don't get me wrong. I know how much you like doing that, but I see more in you, and I think you have a lot of potential."

Chris didn't know what to say. The best thing he could do was to respond only when a question was directed at him; till then, he would say nothing.

Nash went on. "I want to send you to Virginia for some training that we have for people like you. This is not just any training that you go for a week or two and come back to work. What I'm offering you is a chance to change your life. To walk away from your empty apartment and join the CIA permanently."

If Chris was surprised that Nash knew he had an empty home, he did not show it.

Nash continued, "I won't lie to you, Chris. We have a program that involves sending individuals into some hostile places to retrieve information or conduct covert missions for us. It's not for the faint of heart, but I think you would be perfect in that role." He let things sink in a little while. "I know you're probably wondering about your citizenship and all that. Don't worry. That's not an issue. We have ways of getting around that kind of thing. What do you think, Chris?"

Chris hesitated in his response. He didn't know what to say. Then the phone in the hallway rang; it was as if a bell sounded for "time's up." He took a sip of his juice again, looked down at the floor and contemplated for a few seconds, and then looked up to face Nash. He smiled and was about to give his reply when in walked Jill Nash, Richard's wife.

Chris automatically stood up to attention. "Good evening, Mrs. Nash."

"Hello, Chris. Sorry to interrupt, Richard. The office is calling for you."

Nash got up to take the call but turned to Chris, "Hold that thought, young man."

END